CW00395126

Dr Bullock's

A Revealing and Sometimes Shocking Account of a
Year in the Life of a Young Victorian Doctor

Vernon Coleman

Dedication

To Antoinette: you are, and always will be, the reason my heart beats. You are my world and everything else is just decoration.

Foreword

Everything in 'Dr Bullock's Annals' is historically accurate. By today's antiseptic and rather puritanical standards, the book is a lifetime beyond politically incorrect. And it is, perhaps, worthwhile remembering that the mid-19th century was a time of staggering inequality. While Lord Durham reckoned that £40,000 a year was a moderate income, 'such as a man might jog along with', skilled shirt-makers were lucky to be paid 2s 6d for 70 hours work. Remember, please, that these were rollicking, rude and frequently barbarous times.

Vernon Coleman, Devon 2020

January 1st 1853

Yesterday, on the last day of the Year of Our Lord 1852, I completed the fifth year of my Apprenticeship with Dr Hildebrand Challot, Apothecary, Barber Surgeon and until today the only professional medical man in the village of Muckleberry Peverell.

This morning, at six, I awoke Dr Challot to remind him that my Apprenticeship has been completed. He awakened for just long enough to confirm that I am now a fully licensed practitioner, Surgeon and Apothecary and entitled to call myself Doctor John Bullocks.

I am, in consequence of my having completed my full Apprenticeship in all the healing arts, as dignified under the terms of our agreement, legally entitled to perform all those activities associated with the noble profession of Medicine. I am licensed to dispense medicaments, operate on the sick (or, indeed, the well), remove gangrenous limbs, extract teeth, shave away unwanted hair on the scalp, face or other body parts and facilitate extreme Purgings of the bowel. I am allowed to do all these things without supervision and, most vitally, am entitled to charge a fee for my services as a Surgeon-Barber and for what medicaments I might consider essential. Naturally, the fees I charge have to be accounted for and Dr Challot takes three quarters of my regular earnings.

In a way, my life will not change notably. It is true that I am now officially entitled to practice without supervision but I have been practising without supervision for a good while.

Indeed, I have been running the Practice pretty much by myself since Dr Challot first succumbed to the gout, the dropsy and a deeply troubled liver and prescribed for himself more or less permanent Bed rest with six meals a day, unlimited supplies of porter and mead and the constant attentions of two nurses who are permanently by his bedside or, more often within the bed, warming the cockles of his heart and, no doubt, other parts.

Dr Challot is a short, roundish fellow, no more than five feet four inches in height in his boots. He is as bald as the proverbial coot and wears a thick beard which is, he claims, a leftover from the Crimean War but he was never close to the Crimean War. Indeed, he wasn't alive when it was fought. He wears the beard because he is a constitutional lusk and far too lazy to shave. For as long as I can remember it has been a motto of his to put off until tomorrow anything you cannot be bothered to do today.

After confirming my elevation in professional status, Dr Challot kindly presented me with my own Leech pot containing what he claims are 24 fine river Leeches. He took the pot from the cupboard beside his and handed it to me, with all the pride and delicacy that might be afforded by the Archbishop of Canterbury handling the Royal Crown, to celebrate the conclusion of my indentureship.

The pot and contents stank something fearful, and at first I thought he had used it in lieu of his chamber pot (which as is usual had not been emptied for several days) but on examination I could see that it was the foul looking Leeches which were responsible for the unpleasant stink. I suspect that the Leeches were brought in by Osbert Gibbon, a pot boy from the Peacock Inn who, I know for a fact, collects the Leeches he sells to us from the stagnant pond adjacent to the cesspit at the Everard Blossom's stinky farm. Osbert is a professional liar, a Thief and a rascal on his good days and although he is but 14-years-old, he already has signs of the pox, caught I have no doubt from one of the Barmaids at the Peacock, neither of whom are better than they ought to be and both of whom are reputed to be willing to blow the grounsils with any man who can spare one and a half farthings. They both have suppurating sores on the lips that are visible to all and sundry and there are doubtless matching sores present on those lips which are not so immediately on show.

On close examination of my graduation gift, I could see that at least four of the Leeches were dead and putrefying, and it is not my intention to begin my work as a fully qualified Doctor by using putrefying Leeches so I fed them to the cat which did not seem to mind the putrefaction and ate them with relish, smacking his lips with apparent delight.

Dr Challot, customarily never entirely sober, was not too drunk to remind me (as though it were necessary) that according to the terms of the Apprenticeship which my naïve but well-meaning father signed for me when I was 16-years-old, I am obliged to work as his practice Assistant for ten more years or until one of us dies. If I wish to leave this employment I must pay Dr Challot a penalty of 30 guineas. The chances of my ever acquiring 30 guineas are about as remote as the chances of Queen Victoria summoning me to the Palace and begging me to stick three brace of my putrefying Leeches upon her Royal personage.

As Dr Challot spoke, I tried to work out whether or not he had acquired an additional chin. Several editions of that notable feature had already been published and it seems that there has not yet been an end to it. If Dr Challot had been blessed with friends I suspect that even they would have agreed that despite his shortage of stature there was probably too much of him.

Five years ago my father handed over 100 guineas for me to be indentured. This which was the sum total of his savings and when he died two years later there was not one penny left to me. I have no doubt that my father meant well but I would have much preferred it if he had not Apprenticed me but had merely handed me the 100 guineas. Still, one road is as good as another when you have no particular destination in mind.

As an Apprentice, I received free board and lodging. My board consisted of a small room in the attic which I shared with a large and ever expanding family of rodents and my keep, shared with the cat, was a barely edible diet of Turnip soup and stale bread. I once worked out that in five years I had drunk 1,478 bowls of Turnip soup.

My circumstances have now changed considerably for during the period of my Assistantship I will be entitled to keep one quarter of the fees collected for my labours when treating existing patients of the practice. In theory, one third of the remaining three quarters will go for the purchase of medicaments and for the upkeep of the surgery premises, and the other two thirds will go to Dr Challot to be spent on essentials such as wine, beer and the two gorbellied and ever-drunken strumpets who he ambitiously describes as Professional Nurses when making up patients' bills. There is a clause in the contract which gives me the right to keep all the fees which are paid in relation to the care of new patients and all fees paid in respect of new treatments which are my own invention. I suspect that Dr Challot would have smiled when this clause was inserted for, since there are no other Doctors in the village of Muckleberry Peverell, all existing citizens are already, ipso facto, patients of Dr Challot's practice.

And the chances of my inventing a new treatment seem as remote as the aforesaid likelihood of my being invited to attend Buckingham Palace with my new pot of Leeches tucked under my arm.

All things considered, I would have doubtless been much better off if I'd taken a job as a school master. My cousin, Archibald Pikelet, who took a degree at Oxford after three years of idleness, and who is now employed as a master at a small school in Somersetshire, receives 75 guineas every quarter day and is provided with a free cottage in the school grounds. He also receives free victuals and all the fuel, candles and tea he requires. He has his own gardener, cook, usher and valet – all paid for by the school. He is responsible for teaching just 12 boys and has an assistant master to help him with essential beatings and with his modest and undemanding chores. Oh, that my father's aspirations for me had concentrated on a career in teaching rather than in medicine.

Still, looking on the bright side, even if I am unable to dream up any new treatments, or find any new patients, I will now be comparatively rich, for during the period of my Apprenticeship I was (in addition to my board and keep as mentioned above) paid an honorarium of three shillings a month from which I was expected to purchase all my clothing. I should now be considerably better off than I am at present. And I will, at least, be able to avoid any more of the meals prepared by Mistress Swain.

Mistress Swain, the resident housekeeper, boostering servant, cook, slut and Butler is a large, rather shapeless woman. I have no idea of her age and my best guess is that she is somewhere between 30 and 90 years of age. She is, I suspect, one of those women who has always looked old. She probably looked 40 when she was 20, not because she had had responsibilities thrust upon her but because of some inner and ungodly forces. Dr Challot once told me that she keeps her husband's pickled head in a box by her Bed and puts it on the pillow at night but I have no knowledge of the truth or otherwise of this allegation for she has her own room in the attic and I have never even seen the door opened, let alone ventured therein.

Dr Challot pays Mistress Swain nine shillings a week, plus two frocks and one coat a year though I don't think she has received the frocks or the coat since I was first Apprenticed. She also gets her lodging and her victuals but she has to find her own tea, sugar and gin. She has one afternoon free every month, to do with as she wishes, and the whole of every Mothering Sunday, from dawn to dusk, is her own. I was surprised when I learned how much she receives for I have never thought Dr Challot to be a generous man, nor a spendthrift one, and these are moderately better terms than I would have expected from him. A weekly income of nine shillings is very close to the sort of sum an established male servant might expect. Come to think of it I have heard some complaints from male servants that female servants are, in many cases, getting paid sums which are close to their own emoluments.

At Last Christmastime, for a treat, Mistress Swain made an iron potful of Turnip soup. She claimed that she had added a small carrot to the soup but I saw no sign of this in the portion with which I was supplied. And I could not tell the difference by taste though to celebrate the season, the Turnip soup had a sprig of mistletoe floating in it. The stupid woman clearly did not have the sense to know that the mistletoe plant is poisonous. I removed the mistletoe and flung it to the ground but since some of the berries appeared to have been crushed into the soup, I was too timid to drink the concoction and lay that night in such acute hunger that before retiring for the night I ate two tallow candles. Despite this, during the night my stomach rumbled with such anguish that I crept downstairs to the consulting room where I ate three ounces of the liquorice powder and glucose which we use for pill rolling, and all the rancid milk-meats, cocoa butter and gelatine mixture which we use when manufacturing Suppositories and Pessaries. I would have eaten a bowl of stale pap, made from bread and sour milk, but by the time I'd scraped the green off the pap there was almost none of it left. I hunted around for more candles but there were none. Remembering that Mistress Swain, who occasionally toyed with the principles of cleanliness, sometimes had soap in the kitchen I scraped mutton tallow from the wooden sink in the kitchen and ate that.

When I got up the following morning, I expected to find the stupid woman dead at the Table, poisoned by the damned mistletoe berries, but she was snoring loudly. She later told me that she and Dr Challot had drunk every drop of the soup and had much enjoyed it. I regard this as additional evidence that neither of them is human.

'What about the mistletoe?' I asked her.

'Oh, we shared that between us,' she replied. 'The little white berries were especially juicy – rather tart, we both thought, but very juicy. We enjoyed them so much that I went out in the snow and picked another sprig from one of the trees in the orchard.'

Both Dr Challot and Mistress Swain consume large quantities of Alcohol (in his case anything which has inebriating qualities and in her case ale and ale alone) and I can only assume that it was this which preserved them from the deadly effect of the mistletoe parasite. My determination, were it ever to be asked for, would be that they are both so pickled that they are immune to poison of any kind. I suspect that if I were to feed them a diet of arsenic and strychnine they would both flourish.

Half an hour after eating the putrefying Leeches, the cat was violently sick on the carpet in the consulting room. Fortunately, the pool of vomit was nicely contained in one area and it was easy to step over it.

January 2nd

This evening I moved my person and my scant belongings into what I am assured is the best bedroom at the Peacock Inn. If it truly is the best then I am glad not to have the worst. Still, I have no real complaints. The bucket which catches water from the hole in the roof is large enough to require emptying no more than once a day even in moderately heavy downpours. I have taken the room as my own on a permanent basis.

'So, you're a proper Doctor now then!' said Henry Youngblood, the Publican. For a moment I thought he was being polite but he laughed in a plainly sneery sort of way. Travellers who have not met him before often complain that he says everything with a sneer and it is believed by some that this is in part because he has had a facial palsy for some years now and in consequence has a lop sided appearance which is accentuated strangely when he smiles. However, it is also true that he sneers a good deal and I had absolutely no doubt that he was sneering on this occasion. He is a raw, cruel brute of a man.

I do not much like Mr Youngblood and look forward to the day when he develops an ailment which requires a serious Purging. He is an elderly and corpulent fellow, in his 60s, with mutton chop whiskers and no hair whatsoever upon his head. There is hair inside his skull aplenty for he has a bushel of hair growing from each of his ears but none, not a single hair, appears to have the strength or the courage to emerge from his scalp. On Sundays and at Christmas he wears a wig which he bought second hand at an auction. The wig, which he claims cost him two shillings, came from the estate of the widow of a judge and when Youngblood wears it, he always behaves as though he has acquired the former owner's legal brain. The wig is one of those grey curly ones which judges wear when they are sitting in court. It looks mighty strange on the head of a Publican.

'That I am, sir,' I answered, with an attempt at modesty which I confess I did not feel. I was very proud of my new status.

'Stranger things have happened, eh?' he said, addressing the remark to his wife.

'I expect they have,' Mistress Youngblood replied meekly. She looked at me, as though apologising for her husband, smiled and blushed lightly. I glanced at the Publican to see if he had noticed the smile and the blush but Youngblood would not notice if the roof fell upon his head.

Mistress Youngblood is a handsome, full-figured, well-shaped woman in her 30s and as unlike her husband in nature as chalk is to cheese. She has dancing brown eyes and wears her hair up from her neck in a style which shows off that feature to its best extent. She has a gentle, kindly nature but her husband can be a violent man, especially when he has over-indulged in his own ale. If he considers that she has failed to laugh heartily enough at his witticisms, he is likely to give her what he calls a 'good slapping'. She has a black eye more often than not.

'Name three!' said Youngblood, slapping his thigh at what he clearly regarded as a good jape at my expense. 'Name three stranger things that have happened!'

I smiled thinly, as though I found his witticism sharp, but I held my tongue and silently decided that when he needs to be purged I will add double or even triple mustard to the mixture and I will not warm the brass nozzle before the insertion. Youngblood is, like all bullies, a veritable coward and I am certain that when I have my brass nozzle a foot up his rear and I am pumping away with the Purging Fluid the damnable fellow will lose not a little of his arrogance.

'Got you there, eh?' he said, looking at his wife. 'That was a good one, eh? A good one?' He guffawed unpleasantly, and I felt a shudder of distaste in my bosom as I thought of his unfortunate lady, as delicate a Maiden as was never rescued by a Lancelot, having to spend long, dark nights lying underneath such an unwholesome brute. Mistress Swain once told me that Youngblood had bought his Wife from a tinker. He had, according to Mistress Swain, paid two shillings and half a pig for her.

'Let me know if you'd like a good Purging,' I told Mr Youngblood. 'I'm having a special offer this coming week – a double Purging and a mustard Enema for half the price of a single purge.'

The creaky dotard is always looking for a bargain and so looked surprisingly enthusiastic. I live in hope. Little does the oaf know that I would pay him for the joy of ramming the nozzle of my biggest and best brass Enema syringe up his posterior.

'I'll throw in a close shave,' I offered, hoping to persuade him to accept my offer.

But he was not to be persuaded and stalked off without a reply.

Mistress Youngblood led me upstairs to my room. She was wearing a skirt of glaucous green and a shallow blouse of mummy brown and she lifted her skirts as she mounted the steep and narrow staircase, giving me a generous view of her stockinged ankles and calves. I fancied she lifted the skirts a few inches higher than was absolutely necessary. She may no longer be in the first blush of youth but I swear she has the daintiest calves and the ripest Arse in the whole of England. As we mounted together I was reminded, that Mistress Youngblood's buns may not be freshly baked but there are none superior in the county. Moreover, she is a woman who knows well how to take advantage of her assets.

Customers in the bar regularly drop small coins from the change they receive so that they can enjoy the good view down the apparently depths of Mistress Youngblood's seemingly bottomless cleavage when she bends down to help me pick up the coins.

My new room, so very different to the squalid attic room which was my home at Dr Challot's, is well-served with furnishings which though maybe not new are stoutly made and serviceable. There are curtains for the windows, and the room contains a four poster Bed with velvet curtains which, although they could do with a wash, were made with good material and have been neatly darned. The Bed is, I am assured, filled with oatflight, the chaff of oats, which makes a lighter and more comfortable filling than sawdust or straw and is preferable to the down, feathers, wool and horsehair often used since it is reputed to be less popular with bedbugs or mice. There are two horsehair stuffed Chairs in the room (one which is comfortable and the other which is not and which I shall save for visitors), a small Davenport which I shall use as a writing desk and which comes together with ladder back Chair which has one leg shorter than the other three, a Washstand with Bowl and Jug, a Pine Table and a Wardrobe made of Walnut. The Jug has a crack near the spout but Mistress Youngblood assured me that the vessel serves perfectly adequately as long as it is not filled too generously. There is a fireplace, which has a surround decorated with rather flamboyant blue and white tiles. Mistress Youngblood assured me that the chimney draws well and will be kept lit from the first day of October until the last day of March. The tiles, I am told, are Dutch and come from a town called Delft of which I had not previously heard. Mistress Youngblood told me, with some pride, that the tiles cost one shilling and a halfpenny for the six, so heaven only knows how much it cost to put them over the whole of the hearth. I have no idea why anyone would do this.

I am to pay six shillings a week in rent, five shillings a week for victuals and nine pence a week to have my linen laundered.

'Are there many rats?' I asked.

'None up here,' replied Mistress Youngblood firmly. She spoke with such certainty that I believed her. 'Not so much as a mouse. We keep three cats and never have to feed them.'

I was deeply impressed by this. In Dr Challot's grubby establishment, I rarely went to Bed without having to heave a rat or two off my pillow and shake their droppings off my coverlet.

'Will you be conducting medical examinations in your room?' asked my landlady.

'Oh, I don't think so,' I replied. 'Well, that is to say I hadn't actually planned to do so. But if you have no objection…'

'No, no, I would have no objection,' said Mistress Youngblood. 'It would be very convenient to have a medical man in the house – available at any time for our customers.' She fluttered her eyelashes and lowered her voice. 'Especially such a young one, and such a good looking one too.'

I found myself blushing.

Is there hope for me here, I wonder? I dare not even suppose. She is a magnificent looking woman and an excellent cook to boot

Moving my belongings from Dr Challot's attic room and taking them across to the inn, was no great a burden for all that I owned was easily wrapped into a bundle made within my spare shirt. If I had tied the shirt bundle onto a stick I would have been able to provide a good interpretation of Dick Whittington, though I was content to travel without the companionship of Dr Challot's cat.

'I suppose you think you're too good for us now that you can call yourself Doctor,' snarled Mistress Swain upon my departure. I was sorely tempted to give her a good crack on the side of her exceedingly fat head but I had my hands full with my shirt parcel under my left arm and my new Leech jar in my right hand. 'The Publican's Wife will have you in her Bed within a week,' she bawled as I hurried away.

When I had unpacked my bundle and placed my new Leech jar on the Table, I went downstairs and ordered supper.

I ate a plateful of Neck and Breast of Venison, half a Ham pie, a roasted Udder which I did not take to, and two slices of cold Tongue. The landlady, Mistress Youngblood, offered me a pheasant but she said it had been hung for a week too long and she thought it would take an hour to pluck out the maggots. I was too hungry to wait. I also had a large slice of saffron cake. With my meal I drank two quarts of the best ale and afterwards a large glass of malmsey. I had never drunk malmsey before, it being a drink previously too much of a price for my purse, but I fancy I could acquire a fair taste for it.

I was relieved not to be asked for any payment since I had but a fourpenny piece in my pocket. I overheard the landlord, Mr Hector Youngblood, tell his Wife that since I am now a qualified medical man I shall soon be rolling in money. I also heard Mistress Youngblood express the thought that if her husband was correct I would make a good match for one of their Daughters. They have three Daughters and it is good to have been alerted to this crafty plan for the three young women are not ones to give a tight-trousered fellow a pain in his groin.

The eldest Daughter, who is called Ursula, looks as if she has been training hard to become a prize fighter. She is reputed to have once knocked out a travelling tallow salesman with a single blow to the ear. He had mistaken her for one of the Barmaids and had offered her a three penny piece for services above and beyond the pouring of ale. The word in the village was that she was not entirely averse to the concept of a subsidised coupling and was offended not by the nature of the offer but by the size of the payment he had proposed. The tallow salesman remained unconscious for two hours and when he left the inn the following morning, and called at the surgery to obtain an order for candles, he asked me why the Church bells were ringing so loudly on a Thursday morning. I told him that the bells were not ringing but he complained that he could hear them very well.

The second oldest Daughter, called Faith, is said to be generous with her favours and is known in the village to be a trollop. It is said around here that a man in Muckleberry Peverell doesn't have to go to Church to have Faith since she can be readily had for the price of a pint of ale.

The youngest Daughter is a simpleton known as Elsa who does little but eat and drink.

When the Landlord's Wife had left, I placed my bundle on the Bed and explored my new accommodations.

I was pleased to find a pot provided for night-time comforting and relief. I was less pleased to see that the pot, which had been recently well-used, had not been attended to by the Chambermaid and stank almost as much as my leeches.

January 3rd

I was woken by a Chambermaid bringing in kindling and coals for my fireplace. I stayed in Bed for I have no Nightshirt and did not wish to frighten the girl.

'Are you awake, sir?' she shouted in a voice which would have woken the dead.

'I am,' I replied. She was a weedy little thing with long butter-coloured hair and very pale skin as though she spent very little time out of doors. I was surprised she had so much voice in her. 'What's your name?'

'My name is Nell, sir. But everyone calls me Nellie. Shall I bring your hot water for shaving, sir?'

I said that this would be splendid.

I had, in truth, not expected to be given hot water for washing or shaving. At Dr Challot's I had been accustomed to shaving in cold water. I always filled my own jug last thing at night, and in the winter it was often frozen solid by morning. It was on account of this that last wintertime I grew myself a beard from mid-December until late February.

When the girl had scurried out to fetch the water, I leapt out of Bed and pulled on my trousers in order to preserve the niceties of my person. I was, I confess, more than a little conscious of my new status as an Apothecary and Surgeon.

'Shall I ask the boot boy to attend to your boots, sir?' Nellie asked when she returned.

I said that this would be a good idea although when she took away my boots I did fear for a moment that I might never see them again. The boot boy, who is reputed to live on a diet of dry toast and mead, supplemented by scraps he takes from plates returned to the kitchen, is not a being to be trusted with a man's life let alone his boots.

I had hardly finished shaving when the girl reappeared with a laden tray upon which lay enough food for a coach party of eight. I have no idea how the girl managed to carry it. There was no towel in the room so I dried my face on a corner of one of the Bed curtains. The material smelt of bad Tobacco and cheap scent. I hate to think how much Rogering and Prigging has been done in the Sheets which appear not to have been changed since the Michaelmas before last.

When I checked my new Leech jar I was dismayed to see that the lid had slipped off and half of the remaining Leeches had gone. I searched the Bed and found two under my pillow but of the rest there was no sign. I also noticed that the Leech jar has a crack in it from top to bottom. In truth it was not the generous gift I originally thought it to be.

I made a mental note to demand new Sheets and a towel from Mistress Youngblood while she and her rogue of a husband are still of the belief that I will soon be wealthy, a ready husband for one of their well-used Daughters, and keen to be of assistance to their fuzzled clientele.

'What's this?' I demanded, examining the contents of the tray which the girl had lain down on my Table. It seemed scarcely possible that so much food had been brought for one person's fast breaking.

'It's your breakfast, sir,' said the Maid. 'The landlord said that if you need more you're just to shout. He also said to tell you that the brewer has put extra yarrow into the ale.'

The tray contained a plate of cold ham and beef, a roast cow's tongue, a roast udder, three Cambridge sausages and two fried eggs, half a pigeon pie and a whole roast mallard. To wash it all down there was a quart tankard of yarrow enhanced ale.

Midway through my meal, young Dick the boot boy appeared with my boots.

'I've given them a light wipe, sir,' said Dick, who is as big a Ruffian as Osbert the Ostler's boy, and, like him, a master of snide remarks and behaviour. I suspect the two of them must be related for I swear they both have rancid Blood in their damned Veins. 'But I didn't dare give them too hard a rubbing in case they fell apart,' he added, somehow managing to sound obsequious and offensive at the same time. He held up the two boots with one hand and with the other drew attention to the fact that one of the soles had become quite detached from the upper leather. He flapped at the sole with his fingers.

'Stop that!' I said. 'You'll damage the damned things yet further.'

He sniggered in an unpleasant sort of way and stopped flapping at the sole.

It occurred to me, for the first time, that my new status as a medical practitioner was not going to protect me from people like Dick, Osbert and the blackguard Youngblood.

'I appear to have misled my best boots,' I lied, feeling myself redden.

'I can lay my hands on a nearly new pair for you, sir,' he said. 'Nice boots fit for a gent like yourself. And they look about your size.'

'And how much would this nearly new pair of boots cost me?'
'Sixpence.'

I rummaged in my trouser pocket and found a fourpence piece. 'I'll give you fourpence if they fit me,' I told the young Varmint.

He picked up my battered boots, hurried out and returned less than a minute later clutching a nearly new pair of black leather riding boots. They were the best looking boots I'd ever seen and I tried them on with some eagerness. They were a little loose but nothing that a few Sheets of Newspaper couldn't remedy. He held out his hand and I dropped in the four pence piece. The coin disappeared into his trouser pocket with alarming speed. The new boots were an excellent exchange for my old ones and four pence. Stupidly, it did not occur to me to wonder where the boy had obtained a pair of boots of such good quality.

When I had finished as much of my breakfast as I could force down, Nellie the Maidservant returned to collect the tray. I'd left half the pigeon pie and most of the cow's tongue. I had, however, succeeded in emptying the bucket of ale.

'I hope you weren't cold last night, sir,' said the Chambermaid adopting a strange manner which I suspect she may have thought seductive. 'I used to have an arrangement with Mr Parkins who had this room before you.'

'What sort of an arrangement?' I asked, not for a moment expecting the answer I received.

'For two pence a night I slept in his Bed and kept him warm,' she told me. 'For more than just the warming he paid me another penny. I could provide the same service for you, sir. I could keep you warm every night except Saturdays.'

'What happens on Saturdays?' I asked. I noticed for the first time that she had unfastened the top three buttons of a filthy chemise. Her chest, quite devoid of dumplings, was as flat as a hymnal book cover.

'The Reverend Standorf's Wife goes to stay with her mother in Lower Leatherwallop at weekends and so I keep him company on Saturday nights. He gives me a shilling if I'm extra obliging.'

I stared at her in astonishment. I fear my mouth gaped open in fly catching mode. The Reverend Standorf is as prim and proper as the proverbial Maiden aunt. He likes to present himself as a thorough man, honest and reliable whichever way you slice him. I had long harboured some doubts about the man but I never suspected he enjoyed such a secret life.

'That cannot be true!' I said.

'It's as true as I'm standing here,' insisted the girl, with a surprising air of defiance. She thought for a moment. 'I can prove it to you!'

'How?'

'He has a third nipple and currently a large bite mark on his thigh,' she replied. 'He likes to be bitten,' she explained with a shrug.

'I can't possibly know if that's true!' I insisted.

'You're supposed to be a Doctor, aren't you?'

'I am a Doctor!' I replied, not liking the use of the word 'supposed'.

'Then find a way to persuade him to undress,' she said. 'You'll see that I'm right!'

'Which thigh?' I asked. 'Left or right?'

She thought for a moment and touched her own left thigh. 'This one,' she said.

'The left?'

'If that's the left one.'

'You don't know which is which?'

She shook her head.

'How old are you?' I demanded, quite shocked by this revelation. I could not help but think she looked too skinny to provide any warmth, even for a Clergyman.

'I've been told I am eighteen, sir. But I am well taught and neither Mr Parkins nor the Reverend Standorf has never made complaints. The Reverend Standorf, in particular, who is an unusually demanding man with quirks, has always expressed himself well satisfied.'

I looked at her in astonishment. I did not think she was as old as she claimed. She didn't seem like any fizgig I'd ever met but did seem surprisingly experienced for her age. It occurred to me to hope, for his sake, that the Vicar used a good, solid tortoiseshell condom rather than one of the flimsy linen ones.

I told the young dollymop that if I felt cold I would request a copper warming pan. 'Can you read?' I asked her out of curiosity, wondering in which direction her learning lay.

She shook her head. 'No one ever took the trouble to learn me.' She seemed subdued and I fancied there were tears in her eyes. 'The landlady charges an extra four pence a night for a warming pan,' she replied, struggling for defiance. 'You'd save tuppence if you had me keep you warm instead of a warming pan.'

'I will buy myself a flannel Nightshirt,' I retorted, quite shocked.

As I went downstairs, about to leave the Inn on my way to Dr Challot's home to see whether anyone was ailing, dying or in need of shave, I heard a commotion in the snug.

'I left the damned things outside my bedroom door to be cleaned,' shouted an angry looking fellow in smart breeches and a dark purple frock coat. I could not help noticing that his feet and calves were shod only in white silk stockings. There are few things more comical than a fellow dressed as a gentleman from the knees up but having only white silk stockings from the knees down – especially when the right stocking has a large hole in the heel as this had. The pistol poking out of the man's coat pocket was rather less comical.

'Can't imagine where they've got to, sir,' wheedled the landlord. 'Maybe burglars climbed up a drainpipe and stole them?'

'I'll shoot the bastard Thief when I catch up with him!' said the man, laying a hand upon the butt of his pistol. He didn't shout but said it in a very flat, dull sort of way which made it considerably more frightening than if he had shouted. However, I have to say that apart from an acute shortage of boots, he looked to be a rollicking sort of fellow; the sort of chap who might have been the life and soul of the party under rather different circumstances.

Suddenly, I felt a hand tugging at my coat. I looked down and there stood Dick, the boot boy.

I knew immediately what had happened, of course. The little Varmint had stolen this fellow's boots and sold them to me. I was about to box his ears when I realised that I needed to do something about the boots I was wearing. I stepped back away from the doorway into the snug. I immediately felt Dick lift my left boot into the air. I looked down and saw that he was using a rather deadly looking penknife to lever the heel off the boot. When he had done this he put the knife and the boot heel into his trouser pocket. I stared at him uncomprehendingly for a moment before I realised why he'd done what he'd done.

'I'll fix it back on for you tonight, sir,' whispered Dick. And with that he was gone. I stepped out of the shadows and limped and hirpled back into the hallway where the man in the white, silk stockings saw me.

'Halt, sir!' he cried, in a voice that was not easy to ignore. He strode over to where I was standing. 'Are those my boots, you Varmint?' he demanded.

'They are not, sir!' I replied, with more bravado than I felt. 'And I resent your tone and the implication. I am a medical man, sir, not a boot thief.'

'They look damned fine like my boots,' said the man.

'Do your boots have a heel missing?' I demanded.

'Of course they don't! They were purchased just last week from Jermyn Street in London. Brand new boots! They cost me six guineas the pair. And the heels were nailed on damned tight, sir.'

Marvelling in part at the very idea that someone might spend six guineas on a pair of boots and in part on the fact that the six guinea boots were now on my own feet, I lifted my left foot into the air and showed him the place where the heel should have been. 'I lost the heel three days ago,' I told him. 'I have not yet had the time to have my damned boot-maker make the necessary repair.'

'Hrmph,' said the bootless fellow without much interest or any sympathy.

'I saw a fellow galloping off with a spare pair of boots hanging from his saddle,' I said. 'Perchance he was the Thief and they were your boots.'

'How long ago was this?'

'Half an hour or so,' I said.

'Which way did he go?'

'He took the road to the West,' I said, surprised at my own skill at telling a tale. It occurred to me that if things went awry with medicine I could perhaps tread in the footsteps of Mr Defoe, Mr Dickens and Mr Thackeray and fashion myself a living out of words. I had recently been much taken with the weekly instalments of Mr Thackeray's *Vanity Fair* and as a boy had been a keen reader of Mr Defoe's tales. I had for several months been a keen reader of Mr Dickens's monthly serial entitled *The Personal History, Adventures, Experiences and Observation of David Copperfield the Younger of Blunderstone Rookery (which He Never Meant to Publish on Any Account)* though I confess I had it in mind that I might have been able to invent a more palatable title.

'Ye gad, sir, this is a vile place, a vile place!' complained the fellow with stockinged feet. 'What is the world coming to when a man cannot leave his boots outside without having them stolen?' He looked down at his feet. 'How can I chase the fellow with no boots?'

'Maybe we can find an old pair for you to wear,' said Mr Youngblood. 'I'll call for the boot boy.'

'I found this pair, sir,' said Dick, appearing as though by magic, and holding up my old pair of well-worn boots. 'I was going to take them home for my father who has been walking unshod for six months but I can let you have them, sir. Tuppence a boot, sir?'

'There's your explanation, sir,' said the landlord. 'The Thief what stole your pair left this sorry pair behind.' He paused for a moment. 'Maybe it was merely a case of mistaken identity,' he suggested. 'It must be said that in the dark one pair of boots can look much like another.'

Five minutes later the stranger, with my old raggedy boots on his feet, was on his horse chasing after the imaginary miscreant. And Dick, the crafty rascal, had another fourpence in his pocket.

'Do you know who that was?' asked Mr Youngblood in an awed whisper as the stranger disappeared in a flurry of dust, shouting over his shoulder that he would never return to an establishment which allowed a decent man's boots to be stolen.

'I have no idea,' I replied. 'Other than that he appears to be considerably upset.'

'That was Paul 'Two Pistols' Hanham,' whispered the landlord. He crossed himself, something I have never seen him do before. The name meant nothing to me. 'The Highwayman,' explained the landlord. 'They say he has killed seven men in robberies and another two in duels.'

I gave silent thanks that one pair of black leather boots looks much like another and hurried out of the Inn.

It was a bengy day with swullocking weather as far as the eye could see and as the ice-cold air hit my face, I closed my eyes and unsuccessfully attempted to suppress the expression of the wind that lay within. Indeed, it did not escape my knowledge that the wind within was as strong as the wind without. I was conscious that I was as full with food as a rich tinker's goat and suddenly found myself feeling rather discombobulated. It was doubtless the result of my trying to cram such an unusually large breakfast into a stomach shrunken by an unbroken diet of Turnip soup. And I had a suspicion that the pigeon pie may not have been quite as fresh as it might have been. Suddenly, my head was spinning like a top and before I knew what was happening, my legs failed me and I fell backwards onto the cobbled courtyard. I have seen men succumb in this way after treating themselves too generously to ale and spirits but I knew this could not have been the case, my having consumed no more than a quart of ale at breakfast time, and that doubtless watered down.

The damnable notching I sustained on the tegument over the Occiput bone at the back of my head did not feel too serious but I nevertheless Bled like a stuck pig at a country fair. The Bleeding soaked into the back of my shirt and collar and was not abated without I put on my hat. The damned thing, which I purchased from Jauncy Withergow's widow, is too tight by a size and usually mortally uncomfortable but the tightness ensured that it suppressed the Bleeding most effectively. I fear I shall have to keep my hat on until nightfall. This is not a good start to my first day as a qualified medical man.

When I got to Dr Challot's, I noticed that the pool of cat vomit had finally disappeared and although the carpet appeared damp it was definitely clean. I congratulated Mistress Swain on having found the time to remove the obnoxious hazard.

'Oh, I didn't clean it up,' she replied haughtily. 'He doesn't pay me enough to clean up cat sick. I was going to use it to thicken up the Turnip soup but next door's dog came in and licked it all up.'

I was not sure whether or not the reference to the Turnip soup was meant in a jocular fashion and I am fearful relieved not to be taking any more meals in Dr Challot's house.

'I see you started the drinking early in the day, like himself upstairs,' said Mistress Swain, turning her head and holding her nose with her fingers as though to indicate that my breath offered evidence of over-indulgence.

Not for the first time I considered the woman a dire hypocrite for she is a committed maltworm and I have never known her to be truly sober. Most evenings she sleeps in a Chair beside the kitchen fire because she is too inconvenienced by Alcohol to be able to drag herself up the stairs. I always gave thanks when she slept downstairs for she snores like a snuffling sow and her attic room was directly next to my own.

'I took a little refreshment with my breakfast, that is all,' I told her haughtily, and regrettably started with a severe dose of the Hiccups. It is difficult to remain dignified when with the Hiccups, so I asked the wretched woman if there had been any patients calling or sending for assistance.

'There's one in the dining room, biting his hat sitting awaiting your arrival,' Mistress Swain told me coldly. 'Plus the Leech man from Allenstein and Marienwerder called in but he said he'd come back in two days.'

Allenstein and Marienwerder is a company of well-known Leech suppliers. Their Leech jars are always decorated with a coat of arms above which are the words 'Suppliers of Fresh Leeches to the Aristocracy'. The aristocratic customers who purchase their Leeches are not named.

Suddenly, I remembered that two days earlier I had promised to make a contraceptive pessary for Mistress Wiltshire. Her husband, who is an able seaman in Her Majesty's Navy, had been at sea for two years and is due to return home within a week. Mistress Wiltshire is not keen to have more children and requested that I make a pessary which she could rely upon to protect her from what she calls Conjugated Consequences. He is apparently not enthusiastic about condoms though the ones made out of tortoiseshell are said to be most effective.

Using a new recipe, which I had based on a foundation recipe obtained from a recent edition of the 'Provincial Medical and Surgical Journal', I had prepared a pessary from glycerine and cocoa butter. I had added nutmeg, Tobacco and ground orange peel to the glycerine and cocoa butter and then, acting on a whim I had added a little senna, some soap shavings and a good portion of gentian root. I had also added a good portion of duck fat and ear wax to help give the pessary a better shape and form.

I must admit that I was well pleased with the finished product which, at 150 grains, was rather larger than usual but impressively formed. I'd rather hoped that Mistress Wiltshire might return wanting one or two pessaries if her husband had an extended shore leave.

'Did Mistress Wiltshire call in to collect her pessary?' I asked.

'She called in but wouldn't take it,' said Mistress Swain. 'She said it was bigger than her husband's lobcock and that she'd never get it inside of herself. I must say I sympathised with her. I've seen some lobcocks in my time but I've never seen one with the girth or length of that thing. It was bigger than those parsnips we had the Christmas before last.'

'I made it specially for her!' I protested. 'It took me half a day to prepare.'

'Well, she didn't want it; said she wouldn't have it inside her.'

'I hope her husband puts a pudding in her!' I snapped crossly, wondering what the devil I could do with the unwanted pessary.

Mistress Swain leant forward, peering at me as though something about me seemed strange but she couldn't quite work out what it was. Eventually, the bit of her brain that wasn't soaked in gin started to function and she asked me if I were intending to remove my hat.

I haughtily told her that I would remove my hat when I found myself in the company of a lady and instructed her to send the Patient in to see me.

Feeling rather pleased with my witty retort, I hurried into the consulting room which, in theory, I share with Dr Challot. In practice, he is rarely in a fit mood to tear himself away from his Bed in order to do any consulting. During the last twelve months I doubt if he has been in the consulting room more than half a dozen times though he will emerge occasionally to remove limbs (an activity which he enjoys) or attend aristocratic patients (who appear on our doorstep but irregularly).

'Why are you limping?' demanded Mistress Swain, speaking to my back as I headed for the consulting room. I ignored her. She obviously hadn't noticed that one of my new boots had no heel attached.

The Patient awaiting me was our local Constable, a bearded fellow in his 40s called Tobias Blomfield. He looked tired and full of anxiety. He is a determined valetudinarian, a large man but a shy and surprisingly gentle sort of fellow.

Constable Blomfield used to be a carrot and mangle salesman until he was appointed to his current post; a position he obtained partly on account of his having large fists and partly on account of the absence of any other applicants. His Wife is a midget and well-known local egg-cracker.

'I've been counting them as best I can, Doctor,' said Mr Blomfield. 'And I reckon as I've only got 23 left. I've been eking them out, withholding them you might say, but my Wife is threatening to go elsewhere for satisfaction. She says the baker's boy has offered to give her all the diddling she requires. Do you know how it might be possible to get some more? I have a little money saved and I am willing to pay.'

Puzzled, I asked him what the devil he was talking about.

It took some time to drag the story out of him but it appeared that he had attended a meeting organised by a certain Reverend Cedric Cadwallader, and had subsequently read a religious tract written by the man's wife, Henrietta Cadwallader. As a consequence he had come to believe that a man can only cleave the pin 300 times in his lifetime and that a man who puts himself about and distributes his oats too freely will run out of orgasms at an early age.

The Constable confessed that since he heard the news, he'd been counting off his orgasms on a sort of 'cleave pinning calendar' as recommended by Mistress Cadwallader. He produced a piece of paper on which he had made a large number of pencil marks.

'They add up to 277,' he told me. 'So I've only got 23 left. I had to estimate how many I'd used up when I was younger because in those days I didn't know there was a limit.' He shook his head rather sadly. 'When I was a lad I was dung reckless,' he confessed.

I stared at him, astonished and bewildered.

'I reckon I must have used up more than two thirds of my allotment with my sister Elspeth,' moaned Mr Blomfield. 'I cleaved the pin a good deal with her.'

I was a trifle startled at this admission.

'She was three years older than me,' continued Mr Blomfield. 'And she had appetites but didn't want to do it with her boyfriend because she wanted to be a virgin when she married.'

'A virgin?' I said, surprised. 'How can she have been a virgin if you were diddling her regularly?'

'Well if she'd not done it with him she'd be a sort of virgin wouldn't she?'

'I suppose…,' I began.

'Anyway, I used up a good many then, when I was still too young to appreciate what I was doing,' continued the Constable. 'Of course, I didn't know about the Reverend Cadwallader in those days.'

'Cadwallader?'

'The Reverend Cadwallader. The gentleman I mentioned. He's a preacher and a Reformed Baptist, a great gentleman and a fine orator. I heard him speak at a chapel in Longton. He travels about the country with his message. They say he speaks somewhere every single evening.'

'And what precisely did he say?'

'He warned that man has only an allotted capacity for loving and that a man who is licentious will run out of his orgasms before he is 30 years of age. He says he has met men who were fully spent before they were 20-years-old.'

'Oh, that's all nonsense,' I told him, naively believing that he would accept my reassurance at face value. 'There are no limits.'

'No, no, it isn't so,' he insisted. 'Mr Armstrong has medical support. He reached into his jacket pocket and pulled out a small leaflet. He unfolded the paper and handed it across the desk to me. At the top of the leaflet was printed the name 'Reverend Cadwallader', accompanied by an engraved drawing of a stern looking fellow with huge mutton chop whiskers and cold, hard, fanatical eyes that seemed to burn right through my skull.

The heading at the top of the leaflet was printed in thick, black type.

'Your Joys are Numbered'

The rest of the leaflet was made up of a stern warning to boys and men.

I turned the leaflet over. On the other side there was the same name and the same scary looking engraving of the fellow's face but this side of the leaflet was taken up with supporting quotes from half a dozen medical practitioners and a dozen or so men and women who told their dernful stories in crisp paragraphs.

'No Man or Woman can Afford to Ignore the Warnings of the Reverend Cadwallader,' wrote Doctor Merridew of Wimpole Street. 'The Body is Limited in Many Ways and a Man's Very Manhood is At Risk Unless He Heeds the Reverend Cadwallader's Warning.'

A Doctor O'Hearn of Manchester wrote an almost identical note of support, adding that only by following the advice of the Reverend Cadwallader could a man hope to preserve his Virility.

'I ran out of my Manly Pleasures when I was just 22 years of age,' said a doleful Mr J.K. of Huddersfield. 'Now I will never know the Joy of Fatherhood.'

'As a boy I was too free with my God Given Strengths and now I am bereft,' said Mr P.R. of Chelsea.

'My husband sowed his oats in Foreign Fields and now there is no Seed remaining for Crops at Home,' said Mistress H.L. of Derbyshire.

There were many more similar testimonials.

'You've got to help me Doctor,' said Mr Blomfield, when I handed the leaflet back to him. 'Do you think there might be a remedy available?' He seemed distraught as he carefully folded the leaflet and put it back into his pocket.

'What does the Reverend Cadwallader recommend?'

'He says that a man can only refresh his strength by joining his Church.'

'Well that doesn't sound too high a price to pay.'

'You have to attend his meetings once a week for a year and then, at the end of a twelve month, you regain another 25 orgasms,' said Mr Blomfield.

'And is there a donation to be made?'

'Oh yes, of course. The pastor says the Lord expects a minimum donation of five shillings a week. It's for the furtherance of the Lord's work and the Reverend says it's also a penance.'

I did the sums in my head. 'So if you give him five shillings a week for a year you can resume satisfactory relations?'

Mr Blomfield nodded.

'That's 13 Sovereigns for a very limited enhancement!'

'A large sum,' said Mr Blomfield miserably.

'And you believe this nonsense?'

'Oh yes,' said Mr Blomfield. He seemed rather shocked that I had asked the question.

'Does the Reverend have many supporters?'

'The night I attended, the hall was packed. People were standing in the aisles.'

'Are his meetings always that busy?'

'Oh yes. I'm sure they are. I spoke to a man from Stratford. He had travelled around the country following the good Reverend. He said there were always big crowds wherever he spoke.'

Cynically, it seemed to me this scaremongering preacher had created a rather profitable market for himself. He had found a way to scare his congregation and a way to promise them the redemption for which he had aroused a yearning. I had little doubt that his warnings proved effective simply because those in his congregation accepted the Reverend's dire prognostications. If a man is told that he is going to be impotent then impotent he will probably be.

'Can you suggest anything a little cheaper?' asked the Constable.

'It's all nonsense,' I said, pointing to the leaflet. 'There's no scientific validity to the fellow's claims.'

'I'm afraid you're wrong, Doctor,' said Mr Blomfield, with certainty but appropriately apologetically. 'Read what all those Doctors have to say! They wouldn't tell lies, would they? They're Doctors!'

I confess I didn't quite know what to say to this. I was pretty certain that it would not be difficult to find Doctors eager to promote any cause, however implausible, if they were encouraged in their deceit by the prospect of a handsome, five guinea fee. I was pretty certain that Dr Challot, for example, would endorse horse shit as a remedy for rheumatism if someone gave him two shillings and a bottle of gin.

I spent some time trying to convince the Constable that the Preacher was talking rubbish, since if what he'd been told were true then every other man would probably be impotent before he wed. Suddenly, Constable Blomfield took a half Sovereign out of his waistcoat pocket and held it up for me to see. The half Sovereign glittered in a small ray of sunshine and I swear I could see the young Queen Victoria winking at me in an unexpectedly seductive way. 'Come and hold me!' was the message I received. 'Put me in your pocket.'

And it occurred to me that I really ought to do what I could to help alleviate the poor fellow's anxieties. I reminded myself that it is, after all, a Doctor's duty to do everything he can to make the path easier for his patients as they stumble along life's rocky road.

'I would be very happy to pay for treatment,' murmured Mr Blomfield. 'There must be a remedy you Doctors know of; a remedy you use yourselves perhaps?' He winked conspiratorially.

'Ah,' I said, nodding my head, as though in understanding. 'Maybe there is a remedy I can provide for you.'

The poor fellow's eyes lit up as hope surged in to push aside the despair.

I paused before saying more and looked about me as though nervous that we were being overheard. I leant forward until I was no more than a foot away from him. 'You must swear not to tell a soul about this. If you go about talking, gossiping and boasting I will have every rancid fool in the county queuing at my door.'

'I understand, Doctor,' he nodded, with a very serious look on his face.

'I can give you a special remedy to enable you to cleave the pin a good deal more,' I whispered.

'How much more?' he asked. 'How many times more?'

I mumbled a bit at that because I didn't have the foggiest idea what to say, though it occurred to me that the fellow would be happier if I gave him some certainty.

'Another 100 times,' I told him. 'The treatment I'm going to give you will ensure that you can do it another 100 times.'

His eyes lit up. And then he frowned. 'What happens after that, Doctor?'

'When those 100 orgasms have run out you will need to return for another treatment.'

He nodded.

'You understand?'

'Oh, yes, Doctor, I do. I understand. I will count them.'

'You will need to keep a record lest you forget. Can you write?'

'I can make a mark on a paper.'

'Then make a mark every time you cleave the pin. Can you count?'

'Only up to five, sir.' He held up a hand.

'Bring the paper to me when you think you've used up your number and I'll do the counting for you.'

'Thank you, Doctor.'

'And next time I will have to charge you a full Sovereign.'

'Right you are, Doctor.'

'The treatment I'm about to give you is an expensive one and the ingredients are rare. I would usually have to charge five Sovereigns. In London they would pay 20 Sovereigns for this remedy. I dare say I could find patients prepared to pay as much as a full 50 Sovereigns for the chance to cleave the pin another 100 times. That's a mere half a Sovereign per cleaving.'

'This half Sovereign is all I have,' muttered Mr Blomfield. 'I had to sell my cow and my eldest Daughter to raise that.'

'Your eldest Daughter is the one they call Violet?'

'That's the one, sir.'

'How much did you get for her?'

'A florin.'

'Just two shillings?'

'Aye. Two shillings.'

'To whom did you sell her?'

'To a fellow who works on a farm,' replied Constable Blomfield. 'I never caught his name. He seemed a nice enough young fellow though he had a wall eye, no teeth, a gammy leg and, to be honest, was not right at the front of the queue when God was handing out brains.'

'Violet was a virgin?'

'Oh yes, sir. Apart from myself, of course.'

'Of course.'

'And her brothers,' he added.

'Naturally.' I nodded but frowned. I knew the girl. She was a nicely plumped creature of seventeen or so. It seemed too small a price by far. The farm labourer might not have been right at the front of the queue during the handing out of brains but Blomfield had been diddled. I thought it reprehensible that a father should sell off his Daughter for such a miserable sum. The girl must have been mortified to know that she was valued so low.

'You think I could have got more?' asked Constable Blomfield.

'You could have asked for half a crown,' I told him. 'Perhaps as much as three shillings.' I thought for a moment. 'Mind you, Jake Aldborough sold his Wife for one shilling and sixpence and was glad to get that.'

'She was an old woman.'

'Nearly 40,' I agreed.

He nodded. 'An old woman,' he repeated. 'And she was fat, ugly and fierce-some bellicose. I would have thought her expensive at a shilling and not much of a bargain at half a groat.'

Poor Blomfield, clearly annoyed that he could have perhaps sold his Daughter for more money, looked glum for a moment before brightening a little. 'I have two younger Daughters,' he said, more to himself than to me. 'They're both much prettier. And I daresay I could get a good price for the Wife.'

'You're not going to sell your Wife are you?'

'I don't think I'll sell her unless I have to,' he said. 'She keeps a good house and is a fair decent cook.' He thought for a moment. 'Yes,' he said, 'she's a fair decent cook. And a good warm body with well sized dugs.'

He didn't say anything about loving her or feeling any affection for her. I got the impression that if I'd offered him five shillings in cash, there and then, he'd have sold me what was left of his family without a blink.

'What sort of treatment will it be?' he asked. 'Is it Medicine to drink? I don't like pills.'

'A suppository,' I told him.

I have no idea why I said this.

I could have made up a bottle or medicine, rolled him a pill or prepared a powder in a sachet. But somehow a suppository seemed more appropriate. And I admit now I think I liked the idea of giving the uncaring wretch something he would have to stick up his arse.

Also I knew I had something handy which I could give him now. This would mean that he would not have to wait for the treatment and I would not have to wait for the half a Sovereign.

'What's a suppository?' he asked with bright innocence.

'You stick it up your nancy,' I told him.

'Up my nancy hole?'

I nodded. 'Up your nancy hole.'

'Can't you give me a bottle of green medicine? Like that stuff you gave me for my sore throat?'

'It has to be a suppository,' I told him firmly.

'How far up must it go?' he asked. His voice was a little higher pitched and shakier than it had been and he had not yet seen the size of the suppository I had in mind.

'A full finger length,' I told him sternly. 'More than a finger length would be better. Put it well in and keep pushing. The further up it goes the nearer it will be to the base of your tallywag.'

He nodded as though this made good sense to him. I was pleased it seemed to make good sense to one of us.

'You can get your Wife to put it in if you prefer,' I told him. 'Do you have a billy club?'

'Oh, yes, Doctor!' he replied, taking a nice and smooth piece of mahogany a foot or so long out of what must have been an especially lengthened trouser pocket. He fondled it lovingly.

'Splendid! Your Wife can use that to push the suppository into place,' I told him. 'Just make sure she ties a long piece of strong string to the handle of the billy club.'

He stared at me, uncomprehendingly.

'So that it doesn't disappear with the suppository,' I explained. 'She can pull the billy club out with the string if she lets go of it.'

He looked at me, and then down at the billy club which he no longer seemed to regard with quite the same affection as a few moments earlier. It heartened me to think that the Wife he had been prepared to sell so cheaply would have such fine entertainment.

'Do I need to tell her what the suppository is for?'

'That's up to you. But why not? If she's been feeling deprived she'll surely be enthusiastic about the procedure.'

Constable Blomfield nodded, realising that this made sense.

'Just give me the half Sovereign,' I told him sternly.

He handed me the coin. I bit the edge of it to check it was real, and slipped it into my waistcoat pocket. I then opened the drawer in my desk and took out the pessary which Mistress Wiltshire had rejected and which I had now arbitrarily renamed a suppository. After all, there is no difference between the one and the other except the purpose and the destination.

Constable Blomfield stared at the suppository as though he couldn't believe his eyes. 'It's huge!' he said at last. 'It's bigger than a good sized parsnip.' There were tears forming in his eyes as he looked at the device.

'It's beautifully shaped, firm but soft and pliant,' I told him. 'You or your Wife will have no difficulty in getting it into place.'

I wrapped the suppository in brown paper, tied a string around it and handed it to him. 'You and your Wife can make the beast with two backs 100 times with what's in that package!'

'Will it work only with the wife?' he asked anxiously. 'I do sometimes like to roger the Maid. And there's my two Daughters as well, of course.'

'It'll work with anyone,' I promised him. 'Except perhaps Mistress Swain!' I added, in jest.

He stared at me, looking terrified.

'It was but a joke,' I explained. 'I didn't intend you to take it seriously.'

The poor fellow looked relieved. He held the package tentatively, as though nervous of its power, and then he left.

I wished I could have been a fly on the ceiling of their bedroom when his Wife struggled to force the suppository into its new home.

When Constable Blomfield had gone, anticipating a certain soreness but also doubtless looking forward to a few weeks of active satisfaction, I took the half Sovereign out of my pocket and examined it. What a pity it was, I thought, that I would have to hand it over to Dr Challot and receive just a quarter of its value in return.

Suddenly, I remembered that according to my contract I did not have to pay Dr Challot any of my earnings which came from new patients or from new remedies which I had invented.

The half a Sovereign was mine. It was the first gold coin I had ever owned.

And, moreover, if I sold another of the suppositories the next coin would be mine too.

I would have danced around the room if I'd had a partner.

As it was I hurried off to the Peacock Inn to celebrate my new found wealth with a bottle of malmsey and a large eel and pigeon pie – with the eels nicely spitchcocked. I may not have had a dancing partner but I swear I danced all the way to the Inn. Or, rather, I danced as well as a man can dance when one of his boots has no heel.

The first thing I did when I got there was to tell Dick to put the heel back onto my boot. After it had been done, however, I was so accustomed to limping that I felt curiously unbalanced. Still, I had no real cause to complain. I had half a guinea in my pocket and a new pair of boots on my feet.

Most important of all, I had succeeded in getting through the day without being shot by 'Two Pistols' Hanham.

January 6th

With some considerable reluctance, I climbed the staircase to the first floor and knocked on Dr Challot's bedroom door.

'Who is it?'

'It's me,' I replied. 'Dr Bullock.'

'What the hell do you want?'

'There's a Patient downstairs who is something of a puzzle,' I said.

'What's wrong with her?'

'That's the problem,' I admitted. 'I don't know.'

'What do you mean you don't know?' demanded Dr Challot, sounding exasperated. My employer is an impatient man, easily roused and nicely ripened, I fear, for a seizure. He has no great affection for work and if he ever wrote his autobiography it would be called 'But not Today'. However, the world of literature is likely to be spared such a tome for he is barely able to make a cross in lieu of a signature and if he is required to write a note he merely scratches the pen around and across the parchment as though the squiggles he makes have a meaning. 'All Doctors' handwriting is illegible,' he remarks if anyone wonders what his meaningless hieroglyphics might mean.

'I haven't been able to make an accurate determination,' I admitted.

'Come in and stop shouting through the damned door,' bawled Dr Challot suddenly. 'I can't abide people who shout through doors.'

When I entered the room all was much as I had expected.

Dr Challot was sitting up in Bed with a tray of food remnants on his lap and two dollymops lying one each side of him. Although Mistress Swain makes regular meals, Dr Challot does not always eat them – sometimes preferring to have his meals sent in from a nearby pie and ale house. The pies are reputed to be made with horse meat but Dr Challot seems to find them tasty enough – and preferable, no doubt, to another bowl of Mistress Swain's interminable Turnip soup.

The dollymop on his left, a redhead called Fanny Church who is the ratcatcher's eldest Daughter, was picking at a huge piece of overcooked beef with her fingers. The other trollop, the one on his right, a brunette called Kitty Fisher, was picking pieces of crust from a pie. She too was eating with her fingers. Both of them were quite naked as far as I could tell and seemed not in the slightest put out by my presence. Dr Challot refers to them as nurses but as far as I am aware they have neither qualifications nor experience in that particular area of expertise and their professional skills lie in other directions.

'What the devil do you want, damn your hide?' demanded my employer who was, I realised, sporting a brand new wig. Either that or he had a ferret sitting on the top of his head. 'What do you mean you can't make a determination? I thought you were supposed to be a Doctor. Aren't you now a Doctor? Didn't I give you a Leech jar to celebrate your licensing as a practitioner?'

'Yes, indeed you did. And thank you for the Leech jar. It was very welcome.'

'And the Leeches. There were Leeches in it. Good Leeches – still got plenty of suck in them.'

'Indeed so, the Leeches are splendid,' I lied. Dr Challot had not been downstairs for some time and so would not have been aware of the cat's unfortunate experience.

'So what do you want, damn you? It better be important, you can see I'm busy having my breakfast. And when I've eaten, these two nurses will expect a good diddling.' The dollymops duly giggled at this.

'I'm afraid I am really not sure what's wrong with Mistress Maitland,' I confessed. 'I haven't been able to make a determination.'

'Augusta Maitland? She is the patient you are talking about?'
I nodded.

'What the devil do want a determination for?'

Suddenly, without any provocation on my part, Dr Challot plucked a roast potato from a plate on his tray and hurled it at me. I ducked and the potato hit the wall behind me with an unpleasant squishy sort of sound. Dr Challot laughed and the two women snickered. They sounded like a pair of horses whinnying.

'I read a book in which the author claimed that a Doctor should always make an accurate determination before treating a patient,' I told him. 'I believe that in London the fashionable Physicians now refer to it as 'calling up a diagnosis'.'

'Of course, you must always make a determination!' exploded Dr Challot, who has a deep rooted suspicion of London Physicians, an even deeper rooted suspicion of fashion and a muggle man's loathing of all things scientific. 'But it doesn't matter a damn whether it's the right determination or not. If your patients think you don't know everything they'll think you know nothing. Where do you think we would be if patients thought we didn't know what was wrong with them?'

'But I really don't know what is wrong with Mistress Maitland,' I protested. 'What if I say that she has one thing when in reality she has another quite different thing?'

'What damned difference does it make, what you say she has? It's the treatment that matters, and the treatment will doubtless be much the same whatever the devil you tell her.' He held up three fingers because he is determinedly innumerate as well as illiterate. 'What treatments are there? Name them, damn your ignorant hide!'

'Bleeding, Purging, Cupping and Herbing with elixirs, powders, melt wafers and rolled pills,' I said instantly, for I had learned my lessons well and knew all the treatments as well as any Doctor. I confess I felt rather insulted to be tested like this; particularly in front of a pair of bangtails. Not that they were listening. With Dr Challot occupied in talking, they were far too busy filling their grubby faces with food from the breakfast tray.

'Exactly!' Dr Challot used his now redundant fingers to pick up another potato. This one he popped into his mouth. 'So what's this damnable mystery woman complaining about?'

'She says she feels weak and that she's noticed some swelling in her lower limbs.'

'Do you mean her legs?'

'Yes, sir, her legs!'

'Well damned well say what you mean when you say it. I don't want any of that fancy twaddle in this practice, do you hear me? An arm is an arm, a leg is a leg and the head is the head. That's your basic anatomy for you.'

'Yes, sir.'

Dr Challot turned to Kitty. 'What do you call the frayed bits at the end of your legs?'

She looked at him and frowned as if he'd asked her to recite the Lord 's Prayer in Latin. 'I didn't do any schooling, sir,' she said.

'I know you didn't. What do you call the frayed bits at the end of your arms?'

She looked at him and frowned. He lifted his hands in the air and wiggled his fingers. 'These things! The bits that you use to hold onto the cockhead as you're preparing to give it a good suckle!'

'My fingers?'

'Exactly right. So what are the frayed bits at the end of your legs called?'

'I know, I know!' said Fanny, leaping about so excitedly that she fell out of bed. 'Those are her toes.'

'That's my girls,' said Dr Challot. He put a hand on one of Kitty's breasts. 'And this? What's this?'

'That's one of my dairy queens, sir!' she replied proudly.

Dr Challot, still clutching Kitty's well-formed dug, turned to me. 'These girls know as much as you do!' he cried with a pleasant cackle. 'Anatomy is very simple. Where did you get this complicated 'lower limb' stuff from?'

'I read it in a book, sir.'

'Another book! A book again! Is that all you can do with yourself? Read books? What the devil have you been reading books for? You don't see me reading books, do you?'

'No, sir.'

Dr Challot, was given his training by his well-ripened uncle, an idle, pox-ridden fellow who was renowned, among other things, for being proudly illiterate. As far as I am aware, Dr Challot himself has never read a book of any kind, thick nor thin.

A wise uncle of mine once told me that if you don't know what you don't know then you don't know anything and if my uncle knew of what he spoke then Dr Challot knows nothing. He does have a very small collection of books on the shelf in his consulting room and this he calls his library. Both volumes in his library are nicely bound in leather but I cannot see that they offer much in the way of help to a medical man. One book is a Bible and the other is a copy of the 1839 edition of Bradshaw's Railway guide. Dr Challot used to point to them with pride, describing them as his professional library, though I never saw him even touch them, let alone open them. Indeed, there would be little point since he cannot read. He always asks me to read the flyers left by Leech Drummers, usually saying that he had mislaid his pince-nez. He certainly has no Latin. When Sir Benedict Ponsonby, the Physician and a rich, evil, snooty bastard if ever there was one, sends along prescriptions to be made up, Dr Challot never makes any effort to study them but just makes up one of his favourite mixtures, or rolls up a dozen pills. (Sir Benedict, like all Physicians, is allowed to charge for making a determination but is not allowed to prepare or dispense medicines.) To be fair, Dr Challot can tell from Sir Benedict's dog Latin scrawl when he's supposed to make up a bottle of medicine and when he's supposed to prepare a supply of pills or a wafer, but the rest of it is as much of a mystery to him as it would be to a blind man.

Even if Dr Challot could read, he wouldn't be able to see what he was looking at because he's as blind as a bat. A few years ago he bought a pince-nez from a traveller but he won't wear the thing because he says he's worried he will wear it out if he uses it too often. He won't even wear the pince-nez when he is treating patients and this has led to some confusion, disappointments and embarrassments. For two years he insisted on treating Squire Ludwig Drinkwater as pregnant because the fellow was so fat that he had grown what appeared to be massive dugs and had acquired a huge belly which hung down so far that his delicacies were well hidden and quite out of sight. 'Face facts! You're a woman and you're pregnant!' he bawled at the poor fellow and would not be dissuaded from this conclusion.

'Where did you find this book of yours?' demanded Dr Challot.

'I bought a stone and a half of assorted volumes from the Carter,' I replied. 'He got them from a house sale and though it's true that the greater number of them are Bibles, mostly well bound in good leather it has to be said, there was one book on anatomy among them. It was nicely printed on good paper and therefore obviously of good quality and reliable.' I hesitated. 'I thought a row of books would be impressive if displayed upon a shelf or in a cabinet.' For two months I had kept them in a box in my room in the attic but now they resided on the davenport in my room at the Inn.

'Baaa,' said Dr Challot, dismissively. 'Books are la-di-da nonsenses and the cause of most of the troubles in the world. What did you pay for them?'

'Tuppence for the stone and a half,' I replied.

I learned some years ago that you can buy books much more cheaply if you buy them by weight rather than by title. Hector Nodorf, a Carter and Rag Dealer who has premises no more than half an hour's drumble distance from Muckleberry Pevrell, sells vast quantities of books by the pound. He buys his stock from the libraries of landed gentry who have died.

'And from where did you get a spare tuppence to waste on books?'

'I gave Phineas Turner, the Saddler a shave and a good Purging,' I explained.

'Don't forget my sixpence!' said Dr Challot immediately. He may be illiterate but he can work out how much he is owed in but a moment. He knew that if I had earned two pence from the Saddler then his share of the fee would be sixpence.

'I won't,' I promised.

'Madness,' muttered Dr Challot to no one in particular. 'You've learned nothing, have you? Still, books will doubtless make good burning if we run low on logs. Are they thick books? Lot of pages?'

'Some of them are,' I agreed. 'The Bibles are very thick and should produce good heat.'

'That's good then. Not so bad.' He thought for a moment. 'And you could be right at that. A row of books could give us a flavour of good learning.' Dr Challot picked up a piece of gammon which he had suddenly spotted and stuffed it into his mouth. 'Maybe I should buy a pound or two of books from Nodorf. Have you had Mistress Maitland unclothe herself?'

'Not fully, no. I have examined those parts of her extremities which can be reached but there were no symptoms in those parts of her that remained clothed and so...'

'Ye Gods, you're a bone brained knucklehead!' interrupted Dr Challot. 'Have you learned nothing from my tutelage? The woman will think you a very poor Doctor if you haven't laid your hands on her parts – especially the nether parts. What sort of charge can you make if the woman retains all her clothing and returns home from a visit to her Doctor with her stays still buckled as tight as they were when she left home? She will think you a very poor excuse for a medical man. She must bare all and have good cause to blush before you can venture a determination.'

Abashed, I promised that I would do this.

'Balderdash and bodkins, you goose, you half-witted booby! Undress her, poke her about a bit and then just give her a damned good six pence worth of Purging.'

'But she wants to know what I think is wrong with her!'

'Bloody cheek of the woman,' roared Dr Challot. 'Do I have to get myself out of Bed and attend to the damned practice myself? The world has gone to pot. Patients wanting to be told their determinations? Whatever next? Tell her that you know but that it'll be another half a guinea if you are required to tell her. Tell her that patients have a right to expect their Doctor to keep his secrets safe.'

I headed for the door.

'And mend your damned head and stop limping,' added Dr Challot. 'Patients aren't impressed if they see their Doctor limping about like a sailor with the woodworm. They'll think that if you can't fettle yourself, you can't be much of a Doctor! Eh, sir? Eh? What do you say to that?'

I didn't say anything. I was busy limping down the stairs and trying to fit my damned hat back onto my damned head to stop the damned Bleeding. The boot boy had used nails which were half an inch too long when putting the heel back onto my boot and I was in agony when I walked. Moreover, all the excitement had caused the Bleeding on my head to start again and I feared that I'd lost so much Blood that I was beginning to feel slightly light headed.

I hope that my hat is not too badly stained with Blood. A new one will cost three shillings and sixpence, a sum I cannot possibly afford.

As recommended, I insisted that Mistress Maitland remove all her clothing (a task which took a good half an hour) and subject herself to a damned good inspection. She blushed and tittered a good deal. When I had finished, I gave her a bottle of Purging medicine and a bottle of the dark green medicine to polish her emptied bowels.

Before she left, still blushing, she asked if she should return for another examination to check that the medicine had worked its wonders.

When I told Mistress Maitland that she could send a Maid for two more bottles of the medicine she seemed curiously disappointed. I fear she does not understand that apothecaries make their money by providing medicines and not by examining their patients. The fact is that we can make just as much money simply by repeating a prescription.

January 9th

Baron Biddulph of Bloxwich rode his black steeplechaser around Muckleberry Peverell today, and in celebration of his birthday gave half a groat to every fourth poor person in the village. Since he is a skinflint who pays wages so low that most of his employees can barely afford to eat, this is hardly an act of Christian charity. The custom, an annual event, invariably manages to cause much discomfort and unhappiness.

I happened to be standing in the street as he rode past and he threw me half a groat which I instinctively reached out and caught.

Startled, and not a little insulted, I tossed the half-groat piece to Pippin Babberly, a professional mute who worked for several local undertakers as a silent mourner and who was standing on my left in hopeful expectation. He had not received a coin.

Unfortunately, the fellow who was standing next to Babberly, an unemployed fellow with a dozen children and only two wives to look after them, who had also been left out of the Baron's largesse, punched Babberly on the nose and grabbed at the half-groat.

Babberly managed to hold onto the coin but suffered a black eye and a broken nose.

I set the nose for him and charged him half a groat since I knew he had the money. I told him it served him right for fighting.

He complained that he was no better off than he had been at the start of the day.

I pointed out that he was also now no worse off than he had been and that he was, indeed, better off in that he would now not acquire the head thumping megrim he would have doubtless ended up with after spending the half-groat on cheap gin.

January 16th

I have been invited to dinner with Mr Ephraim Gengolphus. The invitation was something of a surprise for I am not accustomed to being sent invitations to dine with the local gentry.

Mr Gengolphus is a huge, crude brute of a man who owns a large farm and is a man of some influence in the area. His lady Wife, Mistress Verity Gengolphus, is a pleasant enough woman and a very effective breeding machine. Ephraim and Verity have been married for 11 years and according to Dr Challot, Mistress Gengolphus has been pregnant for ten of those years. The couple have had 14 children (including one set of twins) and all of the children have been named after members of the Royal Family. Unfortunately, since the couple have had more children than Her Majesty has produced, they have had to duplicate some of the names. So, they have produced three Vickys, five Berties, an Alice, two Alfreds, one Helena, a Louise and an Arthur. Of these, just two Berties, one Vicky and a Helena have survived. It is well-known that Mr Gengolphus has, for some years, been angling for a baronetcy and I suspect he believes that by advertising his loyalty in this way he will achieve his ambition more speedily. Every time a child is born and christened, Mr Gengolphus sends a note to Buckingham Palace to apprise her Majesty of the latest show of respect. Still, ambition is a natural and largely laudable phenomenon: even borborygmi aspire to become clamorous eructations or merry expressions of flatulence.

Sir Newton Poppleford and Lady Lettice Poppleford were the other guests, along with their Daughter Miss Phyllis Poppleford, who is an accomplished harpsichord player and who rides to hounds. She looked far gone with child but she told everyone that she was cursed with a good deal of wind as a consequence of eating an uncomfortable surfeit of melons. I heard Mistress Gengolphus whisper to her husband that if the girl's blessing were truly the wind then she will in due course surely produce the devil of a fart.

Sir Newton is short, rotund and so red faced that he looks for all the world like an overripe tomato about to burst his skin and fire flesh and seed in all directions. His wife, Lady Lettice, is exceptionally tall and as thin as a sapling. She is habitually stooped as though bent over by a strong wind, or some other force of nature.

Miss Phyllis, who could never be owned to be pulchritudinous, and who has the features and the personality of a permanently bereaved sow, has recently become engaged to be married to Mr Staple Fitzgaine-Bickenhall, a neighbouring farmer whose estates are extensive and who also has a large house in London. Mr Fitzgaine-Bickenhall is 63-years-old, exceedingly short (no taller than a 12-year-old child) and the possessor of very poor eyesight. According to Mistress Swain, whose knowledge of such matters is extraordinarily precise, he is not believed to be the origin of the afore-mentioned swelling which, if not a result of eating too many melons, may well have been a consequence of one of Miss Poppleford's many close but transient friendships with hunting folk around the county. Mr Fitzgaine-Bickenhall was not present, having travelled to Devon to purchase a new bull.

We started dinner with two fine boiled cods and fried sole in oyster sauce. We were then served sirloin of beef accompanied by pea soup and orange pudding. This was followed with a wild duck each and a forequarter of lamb with salad and mince pies. We finished the meal with Plumb Cake and other tasty pulpatoons. We started dinner at 3 p.m. and were still eating at 6 p.m. We then rested for an hour before having supper. At half past six Mr Gengolphus said he felt peckish and so he ate a whole rabbit to himself. The rabbit had been basted in beef fat.

'I am once more with child,' announced Mistress Gengolphus quite suddenly.

'Is there any way to stop them coming?' asked Mr Gengolphus. 'We think we have a sufficiency now. We thought quite a lot of them would die off but too many have survived. We must breed very healthy ones. I asked Sir Richard Lovelace, my neighbour, if he knows of anything we can try. He and his Wife have six and haven't had a fresh one for five years. I wondered if he was perhaps being served by one of the kitchen Maids but he says not; he says he now buggers his Wife and that's put a complete stop to the births. He and his Wife say they both find it a perfectly satisfactory solution. Unfortunately, my Wife, Mrs Gengolphus, has the piles which rather get in the way of such a solution. The infants came forth by the front passage but the back passage seems to have suffered in sympathy.'

At this point I realised why I had been invited to dinner.

'It is doubtless all the pushing,' said Lady Poppleford. 'As a gal I was taught never to push but whenever I gave birth I was always encouraged to push. They shout at one to do it and so somehow one feels obliged.'

'I blame the first two,' said Mr Gengolphus. 'The more recent ones have been fired out with some speed.'

'Mr Gengolphus is unusually well built in the conviviality department and so gaining an entry to the tradesman's entrance would be unduly painful even without the piles,' added Mistress Gengolphus. 'I have known very few better endowed gentlemen than my husband, though my grandfather was exceptionally well built in that region and when young I did once pleasure a donkey at a Hunt

Ball, but that is quite a different kettle of fish, of course. Would you like more veal, Doctor?'

'Just a little,' I replied.

'Another sausage?'

'That would be splendid, thank you.' I turned to her husband. 'I could let you have some linen condoms,' I suggested.

'Tried 'em,' he replied, pulling a face and shaking his head. 'We bought half a dozen from a tinker but they were too damned tight, uncomfortably so, and we wore always 'em out before completion.'

'Mr Gengolphus is very vigorous,' explained his wife.

I suggested a tortoiseshell sheath might be a sturdier alternative.

'Oh, I tried one of them,' said Mr Gengolphus now pulling a face as though he'd bitten into a lemon. 'My lady Wife wasn't too taken with it and nor was I.'

'It reminded me of the fat candle I used to pleasure myself with when I was a girl,' said Mistress Gengolphus. 'It was very cold and unyielding. The Vicar used to supply me with altar candles in return for certain favours.'

'It was like paddling with me riding boots on,' complained Mr Gengolphus. 'Have you ever tried one of those tortoiseshell things yourself?'

I confessed that I had not. I took a bite of one of Mistress Gengolphus's delicious sausages and turned to her. 'I could maybe try to subdue your piles by the application of a selection of Leeches.'

'Do you think that would work?' she asked, her voice full of hope.

I said I would return the following morning with my Leech jar.

We had been told that Vigo Mountjoy had been hired to play the harp after dinner but there was considerable disappointment when Mr Mountjoy took a Jew 's harp out of his waistcoat pocket and proceeded to attempt to entertain us with a variety of tunes on what we all agreed was a rather sorry looking little instrument. Mistress Gengolphus told us that when she had hired him she had expected he would bring the full sized version. He said he did not have a large harp and would not know how to play one if he was offered one.

'Size is everything,' she said, when dismissing Mr Mountjoy and refusing to pay him.

Miss Phyllis Poppleford then entertained us by playing a harpsichord which was found in an attic room and brought down for the purpose. Owing to her 'wind' she had to sit side saddle on the stool. The playing was not a great success and Miss Poppleford, who burst into tears, said she thought that the harpsichord had been badly affected by damp and was not playing the required notes in the appropriate order.

January 17th

I visited the Gengolphus residence with my pot of Leeches and found that Mistress Gengolphus had prepared for my visit by discarding all of her clothing in the area of concern. When I entered the drawing room she bent herself over the arm of a chaise longue with her voluminous veins offered freely for observation.

I applied three Leeches and although they initially seemed reluctant to take advantage of the offered refreshment, I am pleased to say that with a little encouragement they eventually set to work with laudable enthusiasm. When they had finished their work Mistress Gengolphus invited me to test the aperture. She was quite upset when I demurred, pointing out that I thought it might be considered a breach of professional etiquette.

'My husband won't be in the slightest put out,' she assured me. 'Besides, he is out riding and won't be home for hours. I really would be grateful if you would check that your Leeches have done their work properly.'

I said that I had two other visits to make which were urgent (this was not true) and assured Mistress Gengolphus that I was confident the Leeches had done sterling work and that both she and Mr Gengolphus would be well-satisfied. There is no law which says that a Doctor is ethically or morally bound to have sex with a Patient if she requires him to do so. Indeed, Dr Challot taught me that there are only two rules which a Doctor must obey. The first is that when visiting a Patient in their home you should get your fee before leaving. The second is that in the consulting room a Doctor never hands over the medicine until he has the patient's money in his pocket.

Mistress Gengolphus was, however, quite put out by my refusal to accommodate her request and when I left she ordered me to send in one of the footmen.

'The tallest one would be best,' she said, still lying over the chaise longue with her fulsome Arse on display. 'His todger is quite long but conveniently slender and although usually disappointing would make a suitable testing rod on this occasion.'

I told the tallest footman that his mistress required his services. He seemed neither surprised nor delighted by this information.

When I returned home I decided that my frowsty room needed more books to give it (and me) much needed gravitas.

January 22nd

This morning, in my search for additions to my library, I visited the local marine store, so-called because the proprietor, Hector Nodorf, specialises in selling the jetsam which sailors being back from their travels.

When I arrived, Mr Nodorf had just finished repainting the sign over his shop. His emporium is now called 'Hector's Junk Shop'.

I asked him why he had changed the name.

'Sailors always bring me odd lengths of old rope to sell,' he replied. 'And they call the bits of old rope 'junk'. So, since that's what I sell most of, I changed the name of the shop to suit.'

'Have you stopped selling books?' I enquired, rather disappointed.

Mr Nodorf assured me that he still had books for sale and so I bought a bundle of assorted tomes, sight unseen, weighing fourteen pounds.

When I got the books back to my room and unwrapped the packaging, I discovered that there were two copies of *The Pilgrim's Progress* by that insufferable fellow Bunyan and a ten volume set of works by Pope (a writer whose work I find very dull). Six of the books were identical editions of *Tom Jones* by Fielding. I have read this, and excellent though it is, I see no need to have six copies of the same tale so I gave one copy to Nellie, the Maid, who was excited. It is, she says, the first book she has ever owned.

I have promised her that when I have time I will teach her to read.

January 28th

I had a strong discussion about the values of my profession in the Inn this evening.

The landlord Mr Youngblood, Cedric Potter, a local solicitor and Everard Blossom, a farmer, were all complaining about the poor quality of medical care available in the area. Since Dr Challot and I are the only Apothecaries and Surgeons in Muckleberry Peverell, I naturally found this assertion rather offensive.

Potter is an unnaturally short, fat fellow who seems to spend his days drinking and pissing. Unlike most people, who tend to alternate the two activities, he tends to do the two at the same time wherever he happens to be. He dowses himself with cheap perfume and thinks this hides the smell of piss but the two stinks together merely create a more obnoxious stink than either alone. He is the only solicitor in the area and is solemnly dedicated to hypocrisy. He insists that his housekeeper preserve the niceties by putting two layers of white pantaloons onto the legs of his piano but is reliably reputed to have deflowered far more than his fair share of local virgins.

Blossom owns a farm with cattle and sheep and although he must be rolling in money he is as mean a fellow as I have ever met. He holds up his trousers with twine instead of a belt and his Wife and Daughters have to darn their own clothes. And it is reputed that none of them has had anything new for a decade. When I had to examine Mistress Blossom last month, I could not help noticing that her five layers of underclothing were all heavily mended. Her stays were grey and several of the whalebone struts were snapped.

Blossom, who is as big a rogue as can be found in the county, loans his eldest Daughter to Potter on alternate Wednesdays and in return Blossom is allowed to put 100 sheep on one of Potter's unused fields. Heaven and the girl alone know what Potter gets up to with the girl for his belly hangs down over his nether regions and I doubt if he has had a clear view of anything below his waist for a good ten years.

Mistress Swain, who is a bubbling cesspool of local gossip, claims that Potter, a renowned lallygagger, has offered to marry the other Daughter, the younger and least noisesome girl, if Blossom gives him the freehold to the field his animals occupy, together with another of a similar size which he is known to covet since it has a stream through a corner of it. The stream has never been known to dry up. Blossom is keeping the younger Daughter a virgin in the hope that this arrangement can be completed. I pity any poor Maiden who finds herself permanently trammelled in such a way. The younger Blossom girl is as not as pretty as the older but she is as wide as she is tall and as round as a pumpkin, and Potter has a renowned fancy for plump girls.

'You're no more a man of science than the charlatans and quacks who sell bottles of tonic in the market on Saturdays,' said Potter.

'You're right there,' agreed Blossom, nodding agreement. 'The medicine you practice is no more than black magic. Your remedies are crude, unreliable and downright dangerous.'

'I'd rather die at home than go into a hospital,' said Potter who must have been feeling well to make such a brave, bold claim.

'If you cure someone it's just by good luck,' said Youngblood who was already lion-drunk and had to hold onto the bar to stop himself falling over.

'Mind you,' said Potter, with a smirk, and a nod in my direction, 'I will say one thing for him.'

The other two looked at him and then at me.

'He gives a good shave!' said Potter.

The three of them laughed as if it were the funniest thing anyone had ever said.

I pointed out to the ungrateful Potter that I did not remember him complaining that Doctors were useless when he was plagued by the Boils last September. I reminded him that without the Gunpowder pills I had prescribed he might still be suffering the torment of Job, with pus oozing from so many noxious imposthumes and boil heads that he appeared to be full of the stuff.

I would not mind so much but on his behalf I spent a messy two hours making up pills out of Gunpowder and butter. The damned pills have to be rolled afresh by hand and the rolling requires much care. The previous time I prepared Gunpowder pills, I failed to clean my hands properly before lighting a cigar and suffered badly in consequence. I had been given the cigar by Ladram Ackroyd, whose piles I had annihilated with the handle of my second best bone saw brush. The resulting small explosion left me with scorched fingers, no right eyebrow and a greater respect for the need for safety when handling Gunpowder pills. I remember that Dr Challot, who heard the explosion and came downstairs to see what had happened, laughed so much that he puddled on the surgery floor. Mistress Swain refused to clear up the mess, claiming that it was outside her responsibilities and for a while I thought it would be left to me to find a mop. Fortunately, the cat, which has Catholic enthusiasms but no sense of taste, cleaned up the mess with relish and seemed to take an unexpected fancy to the mixture.

'The boils would have probably gone without your pills!' responded the thankless Potter, overfull of courage and phlegm now that his body has emptied itself of the pus.

I told him firmly that the next time he needed medical help he could take the choice of seeing Dr Challot or ride six leagues to see Dr Montgomery, the fool of an Irish quack whose favourite and only remedy (which he recommends for every disorder imaginable) is the eating of two large Spanish onions.

'Eat two large Spanish onions and call in tomorrow if you are not cured,' Montgomery tells all his patients.

The ones who dare to return and complain that they are still not cured will be told to go away and eat another two large Spanish onions.

I fear the man is a rogue and I strongly suspect that he has some sort of financial 'arrangement' with the local greengrocer. Either that or he has simply heard that onions are fashionable in London society.

(Montgomery is one of those practitioners who are forever leaping on some new medical fashion. Two years ago he offered to make determinations by studying navels. This so-called science is known to its enthusiasts as omphalomancy, though it is a branch of medicine which I believe should be defined under blatant quackery. Montgomery also practices gyromancy. He forces his patients to walk round in circles until they fall down and subsequently makes his determinations according to where they land when they fall. Finally, I have heard it on good authority that he also listens to the intestinal gurgling of his patients – a practice which he dignifies with the name gastromancy.)

I pointed out to the ungrateful Potter that medical science does not stand still and that the Gunpowder remedy, which was fashionable until a month ago, has already been surpassed by a more sophisticated solution to the problem.

Hercules Tomkins, a Drummer who brought a new range of bone saws around for my inspection, confided that a Doctor he visits in Lichfield has had great success with a boil remedy which consists of rendered leaf lard to which has been added beeswax and burgundy pitch. Our practice already has three perfectly good bone saws but I was so delighted with this new remedy that I promised that we would buy a fourth on his next visit. I also gave him a good, close shave with a newly honed razor and scissored his hair so that he can more easily put a mustard Poultice onto the ringworm which marks his scalp. The wise fellow rarely removes his hat. I also persuaded Mistress Swain to give him one of her disgusting and infamous bow wow mutton pies. This one was, I believe, made with a mongrel which was found dead in the street after being seen eating a rancid rodent.

The Drummer afterwards declared it to be the tastiest pie he'd eaten in a quarter. 'Rich and full of flavour!' was his verdict. I'm not surprised it was 'rich' for the damned dog had been dead for a week when Mistress Swain picked it up to turn into a pie.

Potter, who is a sly fellow, as everyone knows and as befits one in his scurrilous profession, asked me for details of the new remedy to which I was privy. Naturally, I was not fool enough to tell him.

Potter, who suffers from boils several times a year, was subdued by my refusal to tell him about this new remedy and although he did not apologise I could tell that he was regretting his previous remarks. He bought another round of drinks without having to be reminded that it was his turn.

I had thought that Youngblood might have been a little less caustic in his observations since I live under his roof and he must know that I will, when Dr Challot gets round to paying what he owes me, hand over ready cash for my room and board. But Youngblood is always drunk after six of an evening and he and Blossom, the fool of a farmer, were joined as brothers by their cocky intemperance and unjust contempt for my profession.

I stood my ground like a proud Englishman and argued, foursquare and unrelenting, that the care of the sick has in this century attained new heights and that modern scientific medicine is so advanced that it is difficult to see how and where any improvements could possibly come. I stated firmly that patients and Doctors will look back upon 1850 as the day when scientific medicine reached an unsurpassable peak. I told them we are now living in the future.

None of this was an exaggeration.

We are, without a doubt, living in an unprecedented time of scientific and social progress. It is difficult to see what is left to be invented or how man can progress further, both in general terms and in my own chosen field of speciality, the world of medicine. From now on I rather think that any so-called progress will simply be change for the sake of it, rather than in serious hope of offering any improvement. How can you make a better Leech than the ones we currently have at our disposal?

January 29th

I spent some time preparing an inventory of the advantages of modern, scientific medicine and produced the following pieces of indisputable evidence in support of my claim:

Good Surgeons can perform amputations so quickly that it is difficult to imagine that it will ever be possible to remove limbs more speedily. I myself once managed to remove a leg, above the knee, in just five seconds under a minute and a half. The leg had been fractured and if left in place would have been a painful encumbrance. With a wooden stump and a pair of crutches, the man was up and about less than six months later. It is reputed that a Dr Benson, who has a large practice in Whitechapel, once succeeded in removing a man's leg in 31 seconds. Here is plain evidence that surgery has almost reached the peak of the possible – though I accept that the sub 30 second amputation is probably not far away. Those cynics who complain that medicine is not a science should know that every Barber-Surgeon I have ever met is well aware of the value of a sharpened blade when performing amputations. The best men can now boast a post-amputation survival rate approaching 50% which was unheard of just a decade ago. I met Dr Benson once. He showed me how to sharpen my knives by stropping them on the sole of my boot. He also amused and delighted a group of us by removing his frock coat and allowing us to examine it. The coat was so crusted with old Blood and dried material that when Dr Benson removed it, he was able to stand it by itself in a corner of the room. Dr Benson wields both saw and knife so speedily that he has on three separate occasions removed the fingers from assistants who have failed to move out of the way with sufficient enthusiasm. Unfortunately, he has had cataracts and the palsy for two years now and his surgical skills are not what they once were. My own surgical skills are locally regarded as excellent and I can think of no better evidence of this fact than that both our village butchers regularly pay me to cut up the carcasses of cows, pigs and sheep.

In our practice, three out of five patients who have major surgery are still alive 48 hours after their operation. It is true that half of those will die in the following week but it is clearly absurd to expect this success rate to be improved upon very significantly.

Specially designed mouth gags for stifling the screams made by patients in the operating theatre are so effective that folk in the next room are sometimes quite unaware that an operation has taken place at all. In primitive days, Surgeons used to hit their patients on the head with a wooden mallet in order to quieten them and keep them subdued. Such methods are now confined to practices in very rural areas. These days more sophisticated practitioners quieten their patients with Alcohol and Laudanum and ensure that they keep still by employing the services of three or four strong assistants. As Mistress Standorf mentioned, I have heard of Surgeons experimenting with chemicals such as Ether and Chloroform to quieten patients but both these substances are toxic and may result in the Patient dying at the conclusion of a successful operation. What's the point in being able to amputate a leg in less than a minute if the Patient is killed by the drug used to put him to sleep? Only publicity seekers use these dangerous substances. It is much safer and more sensible to use well-tried, traditional remedies. By putting a dozen or more Leeches onto a patient's body before surgery, it is possible to remove the volume of Blood so significantly that Bleeding after surgery is dramatically reduced. There is no doubt that the Leech, not the dog, is man's best friend. Drummers regularly bring round fresh Leeches in addition to Poultices and Plaisters. If Leeches aren't available, it is possible to remove Blood from the system by the process of scarification – using small blades to cut into the skin. The latest equipment available is a spring loaded Scarifier which contains no fewer than 16 blades. Dr Challot always recommends removing three pints of Blood from a Patient before surgery. When this has been done, the amount of Bleeding after the operation is very much reduced.

It is now increasingly uncommon for more than three patients to be put into one Bed in provincial hospitals. For the payment of a small extra fee it is sometimes possible for patients to have a Bed entirely to themselves. In most Poor Hospitals, the Sheets are changed every month regardless of whether they are stained with Blood, pus or other bodily substances. This seems an optimum arrangement. Changing the Sheets more frequently would be a bitter inconvenience for staff and patients and of no value to anyone except, possibly, the local laundresses.

It is perfectly possible to stop Bleeding after surgery. Post-surgical Bleeding can be ended by cauterizing a wound with a hot iron or by pouring boiling oil onto it. Both these methods work extremely well. It is impossible to see how any other remedy could be more effective or less troublesome to the Patient who is, in any case, often unconscious by the time this procedure is performed.

We now have several powerful drugs which can be used to help patients. Digitalis, taken from the foxglove, is effective against the dropsy. Mercury is of inestimable value to those who have carelessly over-indulged in the bedrooms of whores and who now wish to rid themselves of the unbidden consequences. Laudanum, a tincture of opium, is such a wonderfully effective medicine, useful in the treatment of almost all ailments, that it is impossible to consider it ever being surpassed as a universal remedy. Many Doctors now recommend that everyone above the age of 12 take a regular daily dose of Laudanum in order to help them stay healthy. A good dose of Laudanum will eradicate pains, coughs, sleeplessness, nervousness and scores of other conditions. It seems to work particularly well, and to be more palatable, when mixed with other substances including musk, amber, belladonna, usky, gin, brandy and cayenne pepper. One major advantage of Laudanum is that patients find it immensely palatable. I myself have a number of patients who swear by it, take it daily and say that they wouldn't be without it. All this from something as simple as the opium poppy! (I have heard some critics suggest that the opium products are addictive. What utter nonsense!) We can now prepare safe and effective medicines in many different forms. Medicines should look frightening, stink to high heaven and taste like pus from the devil's pox. Most Doctors have a favourite brew which they make by the gallon and give for a wide variety of ailments.

Using cloves, hops, senna, gentian root or orange peel we can produce medicines in single dose vials. Since powders in individual doses can be difficult to take (unless placed on rice paper and turned into wafers) we make hand-rolled pills containing useful herbs, using cocoa butter, glycerine, liquorice, glucose, gelatine, ear wax or saliva to hold the ingredients together. The mixture is rolled into a tube, cut into sections and hand rolled into pills of varying sizes. The pills so made can be varnished or covered in gold leaf.

Excellent and efficacious plasters and Poultices can be made using a wonderful paste made with linseed, olive oil and lead oxide. The paste is put onto chamois, leather, silk or sheepskin and cut to size. A good Poultice will be solid when cold but flexible at body temperature. Poultices can be used a dozen times or more.

We can now give patients an Enema with a jet of water powerful enough to strip the rectal mucosa clean of all toxic materials. The Patient sits on a brass nozzle and with the aid of a hand or foot operated pump and a few yards of flexible tubing, the Doctor squirts several gallons of water into the lower reaches of the intestinal tract within seconds. It is possible to purchase portable Enema sets which have ivory fitments and can be carried in a smart mahogany case.

Hearing aids used to be clumsy, ugly things made out of cows' horns. Modern conversation tubes are much more elegant and can be made out of ivory or silver. To avoid unpleasant odours and stop themselves being infected with fleas, it is now possible for Doctors to buy a hearing tube which is one and a half yards long. Who would have dreamt of such a thing a decade ago? The single tube monaural Stethoscope, invented by a French fellow called Laennec, is now widely used by Doctors. Dr Challot has two of these devices. One is small enough to fit into a silver clip inside his hat. The other is about three feet long, and I am allowed to use it when I am required to listen to the chest of a Patient who is infested with fleas. (I confess I cannot hear much through this piece of equipment but some of my patients live in hovels where the clothes and bedding are visibly jumping with fleas and the inability to hear is acceptable in those circumstances.) Even if nothing can be heard through the Stethoscope, the instrument helps give the Doctor an aura of scientific knowledge. Many of my patients regard the Stethoscope as a treatment. More than once, a Patient who has been Stethoscoped has sat up, cured, within seconds of my placing the far end of the instrument on their chests.

Surgical tools are infinitely better made than they were just a few years ago. Most Doctors now carry a pocket set of matching knives. I have seen sets sold in a leather covered case lined with velvet. Large amputation knives are so well made and hold a sharp edge so well that they are invariably borrowed by the cook and disappear into the kitchen. It is possible to buy a bone saw with ebony handles, and most Surgeons who use a bone saw will use a bone brush to clean away the bone dust from the teeth of the saw. It is possible to buy ear scoops, for removing wax from the ears, which are made from the finest silver. Catheters designed for opening venereal strictures affecting the flow of fluid down the channel from the bladder are also made from silver and sold in telescopic form so that they can be more easily fitted into a Doctor's bag.

January 30th

I took my list of medical improvements to the public bar this evening and started to read it to my three critics of yesterday evening.

Sadly, however, I was no more than half way through the list before my three companions took to drowsing. Potter was soon snoring and sounded like a pig who has consumed two peck of over-ripe apples. I woke them all by announcing that I was offering to buy another round of drinks, together with pickled eggs for all, on sole condition that they now agreed with me that medical care had never been better, that Doctors are more effective than at any time in history and that it is pretty well impossible to see how and where any serious improvements in health care could possibly be made.

To my delight, my proposal was met with enthusiasm and shouts of approval. I woke the Barmaid, who had also nodded off, and ordered the drinks and pickled eggs for all, the sum for which to be put on my rapidly bloating account. After three more rounds of mead and pickled eggs I felt weary and headed for my bed.

As I headed out of the bar and into the corridor on my way up to my room, I found myself face to face with Mistress Youngblood who was returning from the kitchen. 'Your defence of modern medicine was most convincing,' she whispered. In the public bar I could hear her husband and two travellers wrawling about the appalling state of English roads. Mistress Youngblood put her hand on my arm and I felt a physical thrill throughout my body. The woman, although of mature years, is zaftig and extremely attractive, surprisingly winsome even, and was wearing a very low cut bodice which exposed her milky white dumplings to my admiration and caused much surprised stirring in my loins. 'I do so very much admire a man with a loud intellect and the ability to express himself with distinction,' she murmured.

And with that she was gone, disappeared completely as though magicked away by one of those Music Hall performers who draw rabbits and doves from their headgear. And as she hurried off, I fear I heard her laughing merrily to herself. The woman is a tease and has no respect.

I ascended the stairs to my room and cursed myself for being a slow-witted nincompoop. I should have done what Dr Challot would have done: taken the woman in my arms, dragged her up the stairs, whipped out my twig and berries and taken her without further ado. Her husband was too drunk to have heard her cries, if there had been any, and her protests would in any case have been inspired only by natural modesty and inevitably short-lived.

When I reached my room, alone and without comfort, I discovered that the damnable Maid had not replenished the fire and nor had she filled the scuttle. The room was as cold as a witch's dugs. I undressed quickly, pulled back the curtains around my Bed and climbed between the Sheets hoping to find the Warming Pan had been placed in position. Still not having a Nightshirt (for I had not found the time or the spare groat to buy one) I clambered into Bed in the suit given to me on my birth. I was startled when I discovered that the Bed was already partly occupied. My first thought was that the rogue Youngblood had rented out my Bed to a Drummer but my suspicion was entirely unfounded for a little exploration showed that the Maid who had previously offered to do the blanket hornpipe with me was sprawled akimbo. She was quite naked and fast asleep. When I tried to push her off the mattress and through the curtains she complained bitterly without waking and so I left her where she lay. Not being possessed of any linens for protection from the pox I suspect she carries within her quim, for despite her years she is assuredly more bangtail than Maiden, I eschewed the very modest temptation and eventually went to sleep myself.

February 1st

When I woke this morning I had a fierce ache in my temples and the contents of my bowels seemed to have turned to water. I also had a terrible, urgent desire to use the piss bowl beneath the Bed. The ale which Youngblood sells is so adulterated with yarrow, fish bladder, bog myrtle and ground ivy that it contains more poison than a bucket of yew berries. The only good thing that can be said for it is that it is cheap. I made myself a vow that in future I would avoid the ale he sells and to stick to mead and malmsey. Now that I am a properly qualified medical man, I can afford to look after my health a little more carefully. If Dr Challot ever pays me what he owes me (an increasingly doubtful prospect) I should be well able to afford a better quality of gut-rot.

I had been awake for two minutes before I realised that I was still sharing my Bed with Nellie, the slutty young Chambermaid who had been asleep in the Bed when I had retired last night.

Moreover, it appeared that we were both quite naked. I quickly lifted the Sheets and in some terror examined my lobcock for sores, pustulence or any other sign of poxification. However, the damned thing was quite shrunken and useless and I could see no sign of it having been of any service to me during the night and nor, to my great relief, could I see visible sign of disease. I quickly realised that this was of modest comfort for the interval between the moment of joy and the first signs of dismay can be a lengthy one. I cursed myself for not kicking the strumpet out of the Bed and leaving her to snore on the carpet. My relief was briefly enhanced when I was able to fill the Pisspot without yelping in pain. But nevertheless what a bitter thing it would be if I had rogered the girl but had not been aware of it and had no memory of the encounter. It would be like enduring the consequences of food poisoning without any memory of enjoying the meal.

I gave the girl a nudge in her bony ribs to waken her.

'Where's my breakfast?' I demanded. 'And why did you let the damned fire go out?'

'I'm sorry,' she said, sleepily. 'But I warmed your bed, didn't I?' She smiled at me but made no effort to get out of bed. Instead she put her arm onto my chest and started to slide her hand down towards more rewarding territory. To my horror I felt a reaction in the area.

'What are you doing?' I demanded.

'The same as last night,' she replied.

I could not help but notice that she no longer put a 'sir' onto the end of her remarks.

'What do you mean?'

'Don't you want to have me again?'

I grabbed her hand and tried to remove it but she was clinging fast, in the way that a baby will grasp a thumb and will not let go.

'We didn't do anything!' I told her. 'You were asleep when I got to bed. I left you where you were because you were asleep.'

'You woke me in the night,' she said. 'And now you owe me three pence.'

'Three pence? You said you would charge me two pence!'

I remembered this because I remembered her telling me that the landlady charged four pence to have a warming pan put into the bed.

'I said it was two pence to warm you and an extra penny if you buttered my bread.'

'Buttered your bread? What are you talking about?'

'That's what the Vicar calls it,' said Nellie. 'Sometimes he tells me he is going to butter my bread and sometimes, when he is tired of buttering my bread, he likes to do a little basket making.'

'Basket making? What are you talking about? Why do you make baskets with the Vicar?'

I was genuinely puzzled by all this.

With a great effort I succeeded in freeing myself from her grasp. I leapt out of bed. The girl slid out after me, grabbing at me in a no doubt desperate yearning to boost her earnings. I assumed that if she succeeded in getting me back into Bed she would up her demand to four pence. I could not but notice how skinny and bony she was. She looked almost skeletal and I could count her ribs without any difficulty.

I grabbed my clothes and hurriedly dressed. 'I'll give you three pence if you tell me the truth,' I offered. 'Did we really butter any bread last night?' I felt stupid using the phrase which the girl had introduced into my mind.

She used her two hands in a vain attempt to cover her nakedness and looked at me in what I suspect she thought was a coy and seductive manner. 'Don't you remember?' she asked.

'No! I don't remember anything. Now tell me the truth! And stop using that silly buttering the bread phrase.'

'You promise that you'll give me three pence?'

'Yes!'

'Let me see the three pence.'

'I'll have to owe it to you. I don't have three pence at the moment.'

'I'll tell you when you've given me the three pence,' she said. She started to dress. It did not take her long because she wore very little and her clothing consisted of little more than a rag of a chemise.

I reached out and grabbed her by a skinny arm. 'If you don't tell me the truth I'll tell Mistress Youngblood that you stole my purse.'

The girl paled at this. She knew the consequences for thieving. A Maid at the White Hart had been transported for stealing a stick of celery from her employer's kitchen. Nellie didn't know that I didn't have a purse, and that if I'd had one I wouldn't have had anything to put in it.

Suddenly she started to cry.

'We didn't do anything, did we?'

She shook her head.

I breathed a huge sigh of relief and sat down on the edge of the bed.

'Don't you fancy me?' she asked. 'Am I too young for you? Too skinny?'

'You're a very attractive girl,' I told her. 'I just wanted to know the truth.'

'You were too drunk,' she said suddenly. 'I tried to make it stand but it stayed dangling and of no use.'

'It can happen,' I said, defensively.

'It did happen,' she said bluntly but simply and without malice. 'I have never known it before but it did happen.'

'It doesn't happen with the Vicar?'

She shook her head. 'Never.'

'Oh.'

'I haven't got the pox,' she said suddenly, as though she'd read my mind. She pulled up her chemise and exposed herself to me. 'Look!' she said.

'I don't need to look,' I said, turning away.

'Please look,' she insisted. There was a change in her voice and I could tell that she was holding back tears. 'You think I'm pox ridden, don't you?'

'Of course I don't,' I said softly.

'Please look.'

I examined her and found, rather to my surprise, that she appeared quite free of the pox or any other lurgies.

'See? I'm clean aren't I?'

'You are,' I said.

'So do you want to do it now? You can have the first one for nothing.'

'Thank you, but no,' I said, declining her offer.

She looked at me with her head to one side. 'Do you prefer making baskets with young boys? I have brothers of different ages. You can make a basket with one of them for tuppence.'

'No!' I said firmly. 'I do not prefer boys. Not of any age.'

'You would prefer to prig Mistress Youngblood,' she said suddenly. 'I have seen the way you look at her.'

'No!' I cried, alarmed at her perspicacity.

'She may tease you with her ample dumplings but she will never make the beast with two backs with you,' she said firmly. 'She prefers to sleep with young girls. When her husband is drunk she sometimes takes me to Bed but she gives me only a farthing.'

I stared at her shocked, my world falling apart. It appeared this young Chambermaid was far more worldly-wise than I am.

'Tonight then,' she said firmly. 'We'll do it tonight.'

'We will not!' I shouted. 'Now fetch me my breakfast and bring some logs before I freeze to Death.'

'Can I just sleep in your Bed?' she asked, turning as she reached the door.

'Why are you so keen to sleep in my Bed?'

'Because at home I have to share a Bed with five brothers and I get no sleep at all.'

'Ye Gods! That's awful.' I was genuinely appalled, but not appalled enough to pay her two pence to allow her to share my Bed.

'You can sleep on the floor beside my Bed for the night, if you wish, but I'm not paying you a penny,' I said, feeling sorry for the girl. 'I will allow you one blanket and one pillow and if you ensure the fire is lit before we go to Bed you will be warm enough.'

'All right,' she said, apparently accepting this suggestion.

'But you must promise me something.'

'What's that?'

'You're not to go sleeping with other men.'

'Why not? Are you jealous? You want me for yourself?'

'Don't be silly,' I said.

I had no idea why I had said this. The odd thing was, I think, that there was, despite everything, a curious charm about her which I wanted to preserve before it was too late.

'What about the Vicar?' she asked.

'Not the Vicar and not your brothers either.'

'I'm not to make the beast with two backs with anyone?' She seemed astonished and intrigued by this.

'No. No making the beast with two backs at all.'

This seemed marginally more acceptable terminology than the silly bread buttering nonsense. I hesitated and then continued. 'If you promise not to sleep with anyone I'll teach you how to read and write.'

'You will?'

I nodded.

'You promise?'

I nodded again.

'How much will you pay me?'

I frowned. 'What do you mean?'

'How much will you pay me to learn how to read and write?'

'You should pay me to teach you,' I said.

She laughed. 'Don't be silly!'

I sighed. 'I'll pay you half a farthing for every lesson. And when you can read a page from a book and write a simple sentence I will give you half a Sovereign.'

'A Sovereign! Give me a Sovereign when I can read and write.'

I laughed at her impertinence. It didn't seem likely that I would ever have to pay out the Sovereign and so I agreed.

A moment later she let herself out of my room and I heard her hurrying down the stairs. To my astonishment, she appeared to be singing to herself.

It occurred to me that I must have taken leave of my senses.

February 7th

I emerged from the consulting room this morning and found Dr Challot waiting for me in the hallway. 'I will need you with me tomorrow afternoon,' he said sternly. His speech was slurred and he appeared to be having difficulty in both concentrating on what he was saying and, at the same time, standing upright without support. 'If you can spare the time,' he added rather sarcastically.

It was the first time I'd seen him dressed and downstairs for over a week. His clothes were filthy dirty and he reeked of Alcohol and vomit. He had attempted to cover up the stink by drenching himself with cheap perfume, doubtless from a bottle borrowed from one of his 'nurses'. I wasn't sure which was the most offensive: the stench of the perfume or the underlying stench of an unwashed body and clothes stained with pus, Blood and dried vomit.

Much of the pus, Blood and vomit (but by no means all of it) had come from a Patient we had operated on together a month earlier. The operation to relieve a large abscess had been a failure since Dr Challot's enthusiasm had resulted in him slicing through not one but two large arteries. Blood had spurted out so violently that the stains from the splashes could now be seen on the consulting room ceiling. Dr Challot did not seem unduly perturbed by this. He always found it surprisingly easy to bear the suffering and hardships of others; indeed, he did so with great fortitude.

'You require my assistance for an operation?' I asked.

I could think of no reason why he would require my assistance other than for some sort of surgical procedure. I looked at his hands, which were shaking, and hoped I could somehow persuade him not to take up a knife. If he insisted on doing the cutting himself then the Patient would have very little chance of surviving and my fingers, indeed my arm, would be at risk. I had heard it rumoured in the Peacock Inn that the local undertaker had bought himself a new chaise and two fine black horses with the money made from burying Dr Challot's mistakes.

'For an interview,' said Dr Challot. He wobbled slightly and caught hold of a door frame to hold himself upright. 'Now that you're qualified and beginning to spread your wings I am considering taking on a new Apprentice.'

For a moment, I was slightly surprised by this. I was relieved that we would not be operating together but startled at the prospect of having a third pair of hands in the practice. I didn't think Dr Challot was likely to be keen to take on the responsibility of training a new student. I realised that the reason I was being invited to attend the interview was that I would almost certainly be the one doing most of the work.

'The boy is called Mourdant Mort and his father Clarence Mort wrote to me asking me to take the boy under my wing,' continued Dr Challot. 'I knew the father when we were both young but haven't seen him for some years. We grew up in Aston Magna and he is now a very successful Tobacco importer. He also has a number of shops in the City and a textile factory somewhere up in the North of England.'

'What does he sell in his shops?'

'Watch chains, dolls, books, cutlery, hat boxes, umbrellas and the more flamboyant variety of patent medicines – that sort of thing.'

I was surprised that Dr Challot was prepared to do business with a fellow who sold patent medicines. As long as I have known him he has had a low opinion of the merchants who sell such nostrums. When a rag shop an hour distant started to sell an invigorating tonic, Dr Challot began a rumour that the tonic was made with water contaminated with cholera. The fellow went out of business in a week.

I had always thought that my employer disapproved of patent medicines on scientific grounds but I now realised that this was a foolish error. Dr Challot only cared about money and he regarded the sale of patent medicines as a threat to his livelihood.

'Young Mort's father is highly thought of,' said Dr Challot, 'and, I believe, quite a force in the business world in the City. Unfortunately, I have heard that his factories have been sorely affected by Lord Shaftesbury's inequitable Factory Act.'

Three years earlier, Lord Shaftesbury had introduced a widely criticised Act of Parliament which restricted the working hours of women and children to ten hours a day. The Liberal Party, whose members opposed the introduction of limits on working hours, had done their damnedest to stop the bill being passed but the legislation had been voted through and had damaged the earnings of factory owners.

'He is also an MP and I hear quite likely to receive a knighthood for wheedling and deception,' added Dr Challot. He sighed. 'He is, of course, as bent as a three groat coin and therefore admirably suited to become a carpet-knight and to be awarded a senior position in the Government.'

'I find it appalling that so many of our politicians are crooked,' I said, naively and pompously. 'Most of our politicians seem to have taken up politics to enrich themselves.'

Dr Challot peered at me as though realising for the first time what an idiot I was.

'Why the hell else would anyone go into politics?' he demanded. He laughed. 'I'd be very surprised if old Man Mort didn't have a peerage before he's finished.

Dr Challot told me that the son, Mourdant, our Apprentice to be, had been offered a career with his father but had, to his great credit, expressed a wish to pursue a medical career.

'My original thought was that the extra responsibility and workload involved in taking on an Apprentice would be too much for us,' said Dr Challot. 'I explained to Mr Mort that our practice is a thriving one which lays great demands upon our shoulders. However, I fear that I allowed myself to be convinced by the father's earnest request and my own sense of responsibility to the community.'

It occurred to me, but I did not say, that it was the fact that the two men had not met for some years which probably explained why the father was prepared to entrust his son to Dr Challot's care.

'How old is the boy?' I asked.

'He's 18 years of age but I understand from his father that he is a mature young man who can read and write and manage his tables with great facility. I am told he also speaks a little Latin and some passable French. He was tutored at home.'

'And his father can pay for the son's training?'

'I have been assured that the boy is bringing 500 guineas in gold to pay for his education.'

I blinked but didn't say anything. This was a huge sum of money and it was no longer difficult to see why Dr Challot had allowed himself to be persuaded to accept young Mort as an Apprentice .

'Since you will be sharing some of the responsibility I am prepared to make a payment of 25 guineas to you,' said Dr Challot.

'Thank you,' I said, astonished.

On the surface this seemed a modest sum, making no more than five per cent of the total, but it nevertheless seemed to me to be surprisingly and uncharacteristically generous of my employer. I was, after all, tied to the practice until I could find enough patients of my own to set up in practice elsewhere. I wondered if Dr Challot's kindness was a result of his drunken state but rather suspected that there would be a catch. Dr Challot has often told me that he regards kindness as a sign of weakness but I have known crapulence to temper his usually hard heart.

'You will, of course, receive your 25 guineas when the boy has completed his training and has qualified.'

And there, indeed, was the catch.

Dr Challot's brain might well have been thoroughly addled with drink but the part which looked after his financial interests had clearly survived the daily onslaught and was still present, to the fore and ready, willing and able to defend his purse. I could not help but be impressed by his use of the phrase 'of course', as though it were normal practice to delay a payment in such a way. I wondered how keen Dr Challot would have been to take on the new Apprentice if Mr Mort had offered to hand over the 500 guineas on completion of the boy's training.

I didn't say anything to this but it seemed clear that since the boy's Apprenticeship would last five years there would not, I suspected, be much, if anything, left of the 500 guineas by the end of that period. Dr Challot would have spent the entire sum on liquor and strumpets before six months were over, and I had about as much chance of seeing my 25 guineas as of waking up and finding that I had been made a Fellow of the College of Physicians. In fact, it seemed to me that giving 500 guineas at one time to Dr Challot was as foolish as handing him a knife and showing him precisely where and how to stab himself so as to do the most damage.

'Our new Apprentice is due here at two o'clock tomorrow afternoon,' said Dr Challot. 'I'd like you here if you please.'

'Have you already agreed to take the boy?' I asked.

'Subject to interview, subject to interview,' said Dr Challot, as though this were open to question.

If the boy had five hundred guineas in gold with him then I knew that the chances of Dr Challot turning him away were beyond remote. The interview would be a formality.

'I'll be there,' I promised.

'While you're here, what do you think of these?' asked Dr Challot. He moved towards a small Table in the hall and took from it a brown paper parcel. The parcel had already been opened and the string hung loose. Opening up the parcel he removed a cheaply made clay box. It was made in the shape of a spittoon or spitting box.

'It looks like a spitting box!' I said.

'That's exactly what it is,' replied Dr Challot. 'It's a portable, disposable spitting box. The Leech man brought this one in yesterday.'

'It looks rather cheaply made,' I said.

'Exactly! They cost four pence each to buy but we can buy them wholesale for tuppence apiece.'

'Are you suggesting that we buy them and sell them?'

'Precisely!' said Dr Challot. He sounded curiously excited. 'They're perfect for travellers. You take one of these with you on the coach or the train and simply toss it out of the window when you've filled it up.' He held up the spitting box so that I could examine it more closely. 'If you sell them to our patients you'll get a penny a box. That's fair, isn't it? A penny for you and a penny for me? And they're a bargain compared to Dr Dettweiller's Portable Spitting Bottle.

I had never seen one but knew that Dr Dettweiller's Bottle was a solidly made ceramic and pewter spittoon sold for use by coach travellers.

'Isn't throwing them out of the window a bit rough on anyone who happens to be walking past at the time,' I enquired.

'Oh, don't worry about passers-by,' said Dr Challot with a dismissive wave of a hand. The Leech Drummer reckons an Apothecary in Surrey sells 20 of these a week. That's 40 pence profit a week! In a year that's...what?'

'More than 20 pounds.'

'There you are! Twenty pounds a year for doing next to nothing.'

'Isn't it a bit demeaning?' I asked. 'We're Doctors, not spitting box salesmen.'

'You'll soon change your tune when you get your next bill from the Peacock Inn!' snapped Dr Challot. 'These disposable spitting boxes are going to be all the fashion soon. You mark my words. People will be buying them to use at home when they're having dinner or sitting in front of the fire. You can hold it on your lap and use it whenever the fancy takes you. No need to aim at a spittoon the other side of the room.'

I looked at him, looked at the spitting box he was holding and felt rather low.

'Is this really what the medical profession has come down to?' I asked myself. I had never seen myself as a purveyor of spitting boxes. We are living in the 19th century, for heaven's sake, a century of progress and scientific knowledge, but Dr Challot sometimes gives the impression that he is still marooned in the 18th century.

'So, what do you think?' asked Dr Challot, eagerly.

'Excellent!' I replied, feeling cowardly as well as low. 'I'm sure they'll be hugely successful.'

'We can send our new Apprentice round the local inns and taverns with a sample,' said Dr Challot.

He belched and I was enveloped in a nauseating cloud of stale beer.

February 8th

Dr Challot and I had been sitting waiting for half an hour when Mistress Swain knocked on the dining room door to let us know that our prospective new Apprentice had finally turned up.

'Dr Mort is here to keep his appointment as arranged,' said Mistress Swain attempting to sound like a Butler and failing miserably.

'Well, send him in, send him in,' said Dr Challot impatiently. 'Don't keep the fellow waiting.'

I then remembered that the young man would be bringing with him a purse containing 500 guineas in gold. I had no doubt that Dr

Challot would, if required to do so, have uncomplainingly waited a week for the apprentice to turn up. I thought it odd that Mistress Swain had referred to our new student as Dr Mort but assumed that this was merely a slip of the tongue.

Mistress Swain stood aside and then, as the newcomer started by her she stepped back and, to my absolute astonishment, made a rough attempt at what I believe she intended to be a curtsey. It was a clumsy attempt, and one which would have garnered guffaws if it had been offered at court, but there was no doubt that it was nevertheless intended to be a curtsey. I had never before seen Mistress Swain show any sign of deference to anyone. She would have been more likely to throw a pie dish at my head as to curtsey upon my approach and she treated Dr Challot with all the respect a fishwife might show her drunken sot of a husband.

'Good afternoon to ye both!' the primpit newcomer cried as he burst into the room. He had a chubby, prognathous face which made him look young and innocent; something of a pigwidgeon. I thought he looked like a fat boy who had outgrown his age rather than a man who had simply grown fat as a result of years of good eating. Well equipped with strut and swagger he came in at a rare pace, removed an expensive looking black top hat and tossed it carelessly on to Dr Challot's desk. He moved with the self-assurance of a Prince or, I confess it occurred to me right from that moment, like a spoiled brat whose only achievement has been to accumulate expectations and a vast library of shoes and waistcoats. His hair, neatly parted in the middle fell in ringlets over his ears. He was dressed in what was clearly a very fashionable outfit and I immediately got the impression that he regarded himself as a mashing fellow; more than something of a dandy. He wore a black frock coat with a pink rose pinned to the lapel, grey trousers with a stripe down the side and a heavily embroidered and highly coloured waistcoat. There was a gold stick pin in his cravat, which was a fairly startling canary yellow, and the stick pin carried a pearl as big as a horse pill. Without waiting to be invited to do so he slumped down in a Chair, sprawling as though at home, letting out a bushel of air and cocking one leg over the arm of the Chair. He wore patent leather shoes not boots and these were of the highest quality and polished so well that they could have served as mirrors. The white silk stockings he wore would have drawn envious eyes from any woman. To be honest, the confusing result was that it looked as though three people had got dressed and then decided to undress, take pot luck and share the resultant pile of clothing.

I made a small bet with myself that the fellow hadn't ever shined his own shoes. Nor, I hazarded a guess, was he the sort of fellow to tie his own cravat or button his own waistcoat. I noticed that he wore yellow gloves with large rings, worn on top of the gloves, decorating several of his fingers.

'Gadzooks!' the newcomer cried. 'Am I utterly fandoogled? I am indeed, sir.'

Having made himself comfortable, he sighed extravagantly, as might a man who has run two leagues in someone else's shoes, patted his belly and grinned. 'One can feed damnably well round here, eh?' Judging by the size of the fellow, he was certainly accustomed to feeding well. He may have been only 18 years of age but he had the belly of a man with twice that number of years of solid eating behind him.

'Oh certainly so,' said Dr Challot, ingratiatingly. 'This is an excellent part of the world for fine eating establishments.'

Since Dr Challot hardly ever ventured out of his home, except on those rare occasions when he deigned to visit a Patient at home, I wondered how on earth he could have come by this quite erroneous information. The pies he had sent in from the local pie shop could hardly be described as defining fine eating. However, there was never any doubt that he could, if the moment seemed to him to require it, be nauseatingly ingratiating.

'Splendid roast shoulder of mutton,' said the young man. 'Two veal cutlets, plate of cold tongue and a dish of frilled potatoes followed by six hard boiled eggs and a large Plumb pudding with brandy – all washed down with three large pitchers of cyder. Damned fine snack!'

He patted his stomach as though congratulating its efficiency in dealing with this small feast.

'Hadn't eaten a morsel since breakfast.' He laughed heartily at this. 'Absolutely ravenous, as you can imagine.'

I got the impression that the visitor was grateful that it had recently become fashionable for all men and women to take a meal at midday, in order to break up the long hours of abstinence which had previously been the norm. Even in my lifetime I could remember the time when it had been customary for working men to take their breakfast between 10 a.m. and noon and to not eat again until dinner whereas the aristocracy, and those who aspired to the aristocracy, enjoyed meals at regular intervals throughout the day, sometimes allowing the end of breakfast to run into the start of luncheon, the end of luncheon to crash into the start of afternoon tea, the end of afternoon tea to be hurried only to allow time to change ready for dinner and for dinner to be concluded at something of a rush in order to leave time for a decent supper before bedtime.

'I ate at some Inn or other,' said Dr Mort, as I must now call him, though it stuck in the craw. 'I did not note the name though doubtless it has one.' He laughed at this modest pleasantry. 'My residence is not yet ready and my man is up at the house chivvying up the people there. He's a good, reliable fellow. He'll have everything shipshape before dinner.'

The more he said the more he seemed an overbearingly cocky young fool. I was somewhat reassured by the thought that today's cock is likely to find himself reduced to being tomorrow's hat decoration.

'I am Dr Challot to whom, sir, you are to be indentured,' said my employer. 'And you, sir, must be Mr Mort?'

Dr Challot did not bother to introduce me and I did not trouble to introduce myself.

'Dr Mort, I think now, eh?' said the newcomer with a confident smile. 'Since I am joining the medical profession I must henceforth be Dr Mort wouldn't you say? What? Eh?'

'Well, it is customary for a fellow who is still a student to retain the title of Mister until he has graduated and qualified,' said Dr Challot, rather tentatively.

'Oh, surely not!' said the young Mort. 'I don't think I should wish to be a student of medicine if I could not call myself Doctor!' He looked very put out and if he had been a young girl I would have said that he was pouting. He seemed absolutely certain of himself, brimming with enough confidence for a Parliament full of politicians; quite certain of who he was and where he was going.

'Well, I daresay no harm would be done if you were to assume the title at the outset rather than the conclusion of your career,' said Dr Challot, clearly alarmed at the prospect of his 500 guineas walking out of the door in Mr Mort's pocket. 'So, indeed, Dr Mort it shall be.'

I confess I did feel well-aggrieved at this. It seemed to me that allowing the fellow to call himself Doctor before he had attended one patient, taken part in an operation or learned one thing about pill making was an insult to myself and all those others who had had to wait five years before acquiring the title of 'Doctor' before our names.

'Jolly good,' said Dr Mort. 'My father knows a good many people and he says that the Government will soon be bringing in legislation requiring medical practitioners to be licensed. But father has been advised that the legislation will not be retrospective. All of those practitioners who are already calling themselves 'Doctor' will automatically be entitled to a licence and therefore allowed to carry on practising their profession.'

'Is that so?' said Dr Challot, who seemed as surprised by this news as I was. He has often expressed himself sorely tried by any sort of paperwork and had frequently expressed the opinion that lawyers must buy their parchment by the acreage. The idea of Doctors having to obtain some form of licence terrified us both. I was terrified lest I be unable to afford the fee. He was terrified lest the authorities require practitioners to have mastered the twin arts of reading and writing.

'You are very young, sir,' I said, feeling it was about time I introduced myself into the conversation.

'Oh, but I always say that age is less important than character,' the apprentice retorted immediately, not even glancing in my direction. My dislike turned immediately to loathing.

'You didn't have to arrange your own residence,' said Dr Challot. 'We have accommodation here for you; a room available for your exclusive use. And you are welcome to share our table.'

'Good heavens above, you are too kind,' said Dr Mort. 'But no, thankee all the same. I have rented a house in the district. One of father's people found it for me. A modest place, just eight bedrooms and the ballroom is woefully inadequate for decent entertaining, but it should serve the purpose for the moment. And I've hired a cook. One of the French fellows. He used to be with the Duke of something or other.'

'Very good,' said Dr Challot who was clearly impressed and doubtless hoping that he would receive an invitation or two to dinner. 'Splendid!'

'Now on which days of the week do you suggest we conduct our educational programme?' asked Dr Mort.

Although young he was, I realised, wise enough to keep his gold coin upon his person until the terms of his engagement had been properly agreed.

'I would expect to see you Monday to Friday,' said Dr Challot. 'From ten in the morning until such time as your attendance is no longer required. And I would hope you would be available on Saturdays and Sundays.'

Dr Mort laughed as if Dr Challot had cracked a rather fine jest. 'No, sir! You tease me, I suspect. Did my friends put you up to this? Lord Dundee, eh? It sounds his sort of jape. I couldn't possibly spare you so much of my life. I have other things to do; so many other demands on my time.'

Although he was but half a dozen years younger than me, it seemed to me that young Dr Mort came from the new generation of young citizens who are overfed with expectations and skimpy with appreciation and any sense of responsibility or obligation. I could not help but feel that he might be happier and more replete with contentment if he had fewer expectations. Like all those of his age and rank, Dr Mort seemed to think only of himself. It occurred to me that self-absorption might not be the most appropriate characteristic in a man of medicine.

'No, sir. I am in earnest,' said Dr Challot, as firmly as he was able. I noticed for the first time that although he had shaved, probably for the first time in a week, he had failed to remove a large portion of egg yolk from his coat.

'Cannot possibly manage Wednesdays or Fridays,' said Dr Mort. 'I'll be out hunting or off with the beagles. Or training me horses, don't you know. Horses are a rare responsibility. Wednesdays and Fridays are spoken for, sir. I've brought half a dozen horses down here with me. And the beasts need to be ridden. Have to balance me work and me life, don't you know.'

'So what about Mondays, Tuesdays and Thursdays?' asked Dr Challot, back pedalling with commendable speed.

'Pick the one you choose and I'll warrant to be here with you on that day!'

'I was hoping to see you for more than one day a week.'

'One and a half,' said Dr Mort. 'I'll compromise with you. I'll give you one and a half days a week and I'll work as solid as any fellow. The thing is, you see, that I believe, and I know the old Pater agrees with me on this, that a young fellow must find a fine balance between his working time and his living time. I need time to find myself. After all, all work and no play make Jack a damnably dull fellow, eh what?'

He turned to me, apparently noticing me for the first time. 'Fetch me a dish of coffee, will you, there's a good chap? Make it good and strong. Just a dash of milk and stir it up well with a clean spoon to make a good froth. I do so love a good froth on me coffee. Do ye have Cuban?'

I stared at him but did not stir.

'May I introduce Dr Bullock, my junior partner,' said Dr Challot, belatedly introducing me. 'I trained him,' he added, as though I were a performing dog who would, if properly encouraged, balance a ball on my nose.

'Bollocks, eh?' said Dr Mort, laughing. 'Good name for a Doctor! Bollocks.' He laughed a good deal.

'It's Bullock,' I said. 'Dr Bullock.'

'I shall call you Bollocks for that is far more entertaining.'

It occurred to me, but I did not say, that the name Mort was far more notably eccentric for a medical man.

'So, do ye have Cuban coffee? Get away with ye and fetch me a cup! Pop half a dozen cloves into the pot. I take my coffee with one third milk and don't forget to swish it around with a spoon to make a froth. And don't ye forget to add a little cinnamon to the cup.' He mimed the action he wished me to make in order to turn the milk frothy. 'If you stir with vigour and make a good lather, the cinnamon will float on the top and look damnably palatable. Do you have any avocados?'

'Avocados?' I muttered, never having heard of the damned things and not knowing whether they were fish or fowl. 'We have biscuits.'

'Pity, pity. Avocados are all the rage in the London coffee houses and estiminets. Still, I don't suppose you country bumpkins get up to London all that often, do ye?'

I stared at him in astonishment. My loathing had now gone up a notch and morphed into simple hatred, largely because even though he knew that I was medically qualified he seemed determined to treat me as a servant.

'Well, if ye have no avocados, bring a few fancy cakes back with you,' said Dr Mort. 'It seems hours since I last ate a morsel.' He patted his belly, burped and laughed uproariously as though this were the funniest thing in the world.

'Oh yes, we certainly have Cuban coffee,' said Dr Challot who did not, I knew, know anything about what went on in the kitchen. He certainly didn't know what sort of coffee Mistress Swain purchased apart from the fact that whatever it was it would be the cheapest stuff available. 'We never drink anything else here. You like cloves in your coffee do you?'

'In the pot, sir, in the pot,' said Dr Mort. 'I am a great believer in the efficacy of coffee. Cleanses the stomach of phlegm, chases away fumes from the interior of the head. And damnable good for the bowels, let me tell you. The cloves bring out the flavour. In Piccadilly this year they wouldn't sell you a coffee without putting cloves in the pot.' He laughed at the very thought. 'I must tell you, a pal of mine horse whipped a fellow within an inch of his life for bringing him a coffee without cloves or cinnamon. Can you believe the cheek of the knave?'

Crossly, I got up, left the room and hurried to the kitchen where I found Mistress Swain eating jellied eels and drinking ale. 'We need coffee,' I said. 'It must be Cuban and the new fellow wants cloves in the pot and cinnamon sprinkling on top of foamy milk. And he also wants a plate of fancy cakes.' I turned and left without giving her a chance to reply, knowing that I could rely on her to deal most effectively with our new student.

'I hope you won't miss the London cafés,' Dr Challot was saying, as I returned to the drawing room.

'No, no, not at all!' cried Dr Mort. 'I'll be there Saturdays and Sundays and probably once or twice in the week. We're a pretty fast crowd, don't you know. We call ourselves the New Generation on the grounds that we're the start of something new and very special. *The Illustrated London News* ran a big article about us all the other day. And a journalist fellow from *The Times* interviewed me.'

'But you will be here as agreed?' enquired Dr Challot, rather tentatively.

'Oh yes, absolutely! Got to do me studies. Complete me education!'

'Have you always had an interest in medical matters?' asked Dr Challot.

'Oh no, not at all,' replied Dr Mort. 'But my father insisted I take up some sort of occupation. He wanted me to join him in his business but I can't go into trade, can I? My friends would be appalled. So I compromised and decided to become a Physician.' He leant forward. 'But there is one stipulation I must make.'

'Yes?' said Dr Challot.

'I don't want to have to see any ugly people or poor people or folk with nasty looking rashes or broken bits and pieces.'

I looked at Dr Challot. He looked at me.

'It would upset me too much,' he said, quite earnestly. 'As a young fellow, my tutor always said I was a sensitive sort of chap – and that I shouldn't be exposed to unpleasant things.'

'So, what sort of patients did you envisage looking after?' asked Dr Challot.

'Oh, young, pretty ones. Women, of course.' He thought for a moment. 'Teenage girls, girls in their 20s, women in their 30s if they're handsome, nicely appointed and well turned out.'

Dr Challot and I just looked at him, not quite knowing what to say.

'That's the attraction of the game, eh?' said Dr Mort with a laugh. 'As a Doctor you can tell these girls to remove their clothes and damnit to bits they will because they'll expect it from you won't they? Then you can see what's what and take a free taste of what's on offer as it were.'

'You don't want to see male patients at all?' enquired Dr Challot.

'Good grace, no, sir! What do you take me for? I've no interest in looking at men and even less interest in looking at them without their clothes on.'

'And no poor or ugly patients or patients who seem obviously ill?' I added.

'Absolutely right!' said Dr Mort with a nod. 'You two fellows can look after the elderly, the broken down and the worn out. I'm not in the slightest bit interested in any of the old people. I don't want to be wasting my time with anyone over the age of 30, by and large. Save, as I said, for any women you have in their 30s who are damned fine pretty and shapely. I'll take the girls and the young women. What do they call it? Specialism, don't they? That'll be my speciality.'

'Do you prefer to see just young girls and spinsters?' asked Dr Challot.

Dr Mort looked at him as though puzzled.

'Would you be prepared to see young, married women?' explained Dr Challot.

'Oh certainly, most certainly! I'd pretty well say that I almost prefer the married ones in a way. All the fellows will tell you that I've never minded a woman with a little experience of life – never taken against a girl just because she has a husband tucked away in the country, looking after his estates, or off in some foreign parts fighting for Queen and Country.'

'Do you not feel any sense of responsibility towards your patients and their families?' I demanded, realising as I spoke that I sounded rather sanctimonious.

Mort just laughed. 'I can always beg forgiveness and explain it was a misunderstanding,' he said, with a wave of his hand. 'I find it much better to do whatever I will and apologise after if it be necessary.'

Just then there was a devil of a bang as Mistress Swain kicked open the door with one of her hobnailed boots and entered clutching a large, wooden tray upon which stood the coffee pot, three cups (two of which had broken handles), no saucers and a jug of cold milk which stank and was clearly rancid. There was also a chunk of bread and a small earthenware pot of jam. The bread looked solid and stale and I could see where green mould had been scraped off the crust. Mistress Swain put the tray down on the Table and gave a toothy sort of grin and an exaggerated attempt at a clumsy curtsey in Dr Mort's direction. 'I'm afraid we 'aint got no cakes, fancy or otherwise,' she said, apologetically. 'But I've brought some bread and some jam if you're hungry.'

Dr Mort looked at the tray in horrified astonishment.

'We don't have none of that "cubic" coffee and we don't have any cloves or cinnamon,' said Mistress Swain, pointing to the coffee pot but addressing Dr Mort. 'So since you like your coffee spicy I put in a large piece of ginger and two tablespoons of good pepper.'

'You put ginger and pepper into the coffee?' I asked incredulously.

'No cinnamon and no cloves,' replied Mistress Swain. 'I asked Mistress Elworth next door but she didn't have any either. She 'aint never seen no cinnamon though she says she might have a handful of cloves round about Christmas time. She suggested the ginger and I thought of the pepper myself. It was almost as good as the best pepper. And the coffee is made with best acorns. We were out of proper coffee but Mistress Elworth had some acorn coffee she had bought off a gypsy and I begged some for your Highnesses. I did ask her if the acorns were Cubic but she didn't rightly know and didn't like to say without knowing.'

Dr Mort seemed nonplussed for a moment. 'And the jam? What variety is the jam?'

'It's pig jam. A lovely recipe. I borrowed it from Mistress Elworth next door. Made with leftover bits of pig all boiled up nicely. I'll have to take back the pot when you've finished with it.'

'Thank you, Mistress Swain,' said Dr Challot, hurriedly. 'That will be all for now, thank you.'

When she had gone, curtseying and shuffling out backwards as though in the presence of royalty, Dr Challot turned to his new student. 'Living out here in the country, we sometimes have difficulty in obtaining supplies,' he explained.

'What an adventure this is!' said Dr Mort, his face frozen in a rictus of astonishment and terror.

'So, when would you like to start your Apprenticeship?' asked Dr Challot. Without being asked, he poured coffee from the pot into the three cups and placed the one with the handle in front of Dr Mort.

'Oh, I think next Tuesday would be soon enough, don't you?' said Dr Mort. 'A friend of my father's, a fellow who runs an emporium in Harley Street, is sending down a carriage with some supplies – a listening tube, a pot of Leeches and so on. And some boots. I ordered two dozen pairs of new boots in case I have to do riding through rough country and get them scratched.' He picked up the cup of coffee, sniffed it, as a dog might sniff a strange hound, and took a delicate, rather ladylike, sip. He grimaced and put the cup back down. 'I must tell the fellows at my Club about this! What did your woman say? Ginger and pepper?'

'I believe so,' said Dr Challot. 'Well, now that we've established how we will operate together, shall we complete the preliminaries?'

Dr Mort seemed surprised. 'The preliminaries?'

'I believe there is a payment to be made, for the training period.'

'Oh yes! Almost forgot about it.' Dr Mort reached into his coat pocket and pulled out a large, black, silk purse which he tossed onto the Table. It fell heavily, with quite a clatter and Dr Challot's eyes lit up at the sound.

And with that Dr Mort stood up, picked up his hat and with a small bow to Dr Challot and a promise to be knocking on our door at the crack of noon on the following Tuesday, he departed.

He ignored me completely. For all the notice he had taken of me I might as well have not been there at all.

'What a splendid fellow,' said Dr Challot, when he had gone. 'A real asset to the practice. A gentleman, and beautifully dressed. Did you see the label inside his hat?'

I admitted that I had not seen the label inside his hat.

'Made by Lock and Co of St James Street in Piccadilly,' said Dr Challot with awe. 'They made hats for Admiral Lord Nelson and Beau Brummel. I dare say you can't buy a hat there for less than four guineas. For all I know it may be more. And did you see the way he just tossed the hat down as though it had cost no more than a standard piece of headgear at three shillings and sixpence.'

'He seems rather immature,' I said, rather pompously.

'He's a young man,' said Dr Challot. 'He's not yet cast his colt's tooth.'

I stared at him.

'Still sowing his wild oats,' explained Dr Challot. He leant forward confidentially. 'I have high hopes that he will bring some smart new patients to the practice.'

I thought this about as likely as Queen Victoria popping in to have one of our famous rancid butter Enemas but I said nothing.

Still, on the bright side, it did seem that Dr Mort would not be requiring a good deal of training or supervision.

And who knows, maybe if Dr Challot and I both live long enough, I might one day receive the 25 guineas I've been promised.

February 15th

'I need a repetition of this prescription,' said the patient, a tall, well-built, distinguished looking fellow, draped in an expensive cloak and wearing a large, black hat which gave him a rather sinister air. He thrust a piece of paper at me. I looked at him carefully for it seemed to me that I recognised him. And the voice seemed familiar. A moment later I knew where I'd seen the fellow before. The knowledge turned my bowels to water.

I opened the paper, written on expensive paper but well creased and worn, and examined it. The paper was indeed a prescription, written and signed by Sir Lemuel Tanqueray, a well-known Royal Physician who lives and has a practice about twenty leagues away.

'The prescription instructs you to sleep with a fresh young Maiden three times a week,' I said, having read the slightly surprising content.

'It is for my health,' said the man.

I looked at the prescription again. The prescription was due to expire in two days' time. I handed it back to the patient.

'You are Mr Arbuthnot Trout?'

'I am.'

'Why have you not gone back to see Sir Lemuel?' I asked. 'Would he not renew your prescription?'

'He is away hunting with a Royal party,' replied Mr Trout. He seemed rather aggrieved. 'I was passing this way and asked for the name of an alternative Physician.'

'I am but an Apothecary,' I said.

'No matter,' he said, dismissively, with a wave of a hand. 'The one is much the same as the other.'

'I cannot provide you with the Maidens,' I told him, as I hunted in a drawer for a piece of notepaper. Eventually, I found a piece upon which I wrote a renewal of the prescription. I signed it with rather more of a flourish than is usual when I sign my name.

'That is no matter, no matter!' he cried, waving a hand dismissively. 'I can find the Maidens with no trouble. This note is merely to satisfy my wife. She has been somewhat critical of my needs but accepts them when they are authorised in this way.'

I handed the piece of paper across the desk. The Patient read it, twice, folded it and put it, with the original signed by Sir Lemuel, inside his coat.

'Is this satisfactory?' demanded Mr Trout. He took out a purse and counted out ten Sovereigns which he placed in a neat pile in front of me. 'It is what I usually pay Sir Lemuel.'

'Most satisfactory,' I agreed. 'Perfectly copacetic.'

And without another word, Mr Trout turned and departed. Moments later I heard his horse galloping away.

It was no small relief to hear him go. And I was relieved that I had not needed to stand for who knows, maybe the fellow would have recognised his boots.

Mr Trout was none other than Paul 'Two Pistols' Hanham, the Highwayman whose boots I was now wearing.

Since Mr Trout (or Mr Hanham) was a new Patient I did not feel any obligation to mention the transaction to Dr Challot.

I put the ten guineas into my two largest waistcoat pockets.

The coins clinked and felt very heavy and comforting.

February 17th

Patent medicines are enormously popular (and profitable). New products came onto the market with astonishing frequency.

Here is a list I have compiled of some of the best known medicaments currently available:

Barkers Liquid of Life for patients suffering from the weariness, Atkinson and Barker's Infants' Preservative for sick Babes, Blinblow's Eucalyptus and Stramonium Cigarettes for Chest Troubles such as Asthma and Bronchitis, Bunter's Nervine for troubled Nerves, The Buxton Rubbing Bottle for all Ailments between A and Z, Congreve's Elixi, Do-Do Pastilles for Sore Throats, George's Gravel Pills for Kidney Stones, The Infants' Friend and Jackson's Febrifuge for Fevered Infants, Mrs Johnson's American Soothing Syrup for Coughs and Chest Infections, Langdale's Compressed Self-Aid Peppermint Tablets for Indigestion, McClure's Crescendo Vitamin Tonic Syrup for a hundred varieties of Tiredness, Mother Siegel's Digestive Syrup for Intestinal Ailments, Nurse Harvey's Mixture for the Patient one degree under the weather, Page Woodcock's Wind Pills for Flatulence, Father Pierre's Monastery Herbs for giving good health back to the Sickly, Barclay's Ointment for the Itch (for those with Skin conditions), The Poor Man's Friend for those Ailing but unable to afford an Apothecary or even a Wise Woman, Dr Williams Pink Pills for Pale People and a variety of products with no particular purpose: Dr Solomon's Balm of Gilead, Simpson Seaweed and Celery Tablets, Ramsey's Medicated Spice Nuts, Huxham's Tincture of Bark, Dalby's Carminative, Daffy's Elixir and, last but by no means least, Cephalic Snuff.

And if all else failed, there was always Lydia E Pinkham's Vegetable Compound, popularly known as 'Lilly the Pink' and renowned as 'the greatest remedy in the world'. Oh, and the ever reliable Dr Morris's Gargling Liniment 'for all ailments of man and beast'.

The contents of some of the remedies on sale are alarming, to say the least.

For example, Dr Brinkley's Medicinal Cordial with Tartar Emetic contained a mixture of spiders' webs, pigeons' Blood, Spanish fly, ants' eggs, hoof of elks, spawn of frog, dung of horse pig and peacock and ground human skull. The good Dr Brinkley sold 20,000 bottles of his Cordial every year, from a room in Charing Cross which he described as 'temple of health'. Who knows how all these medicaments will act with or against one another?

And Dr Holliday's Reliable Tonic was made with a potent mixture of human ear wax, saliva and human fat. I have no idea of the source of the human fat or, indeed, any of the other ingredients.

It is my considered view that anyone brave enough to take one of these nostrums well deserves to be cured of whatever ailed them.

February 19th

Dr Challot asked me to assist in treating a Patient this morning. He said he would pay me 30 pence if I did so. This seems miserly and was therefore to be expected. To avoid unpleasantness, I agreed to assist since I hoped to learn something new. Dr Challot told me that he was intending to try out a new procedure which he had heard about from the Blind Drummer who sells us jars and bottles suitable for the storage of medicines.

The Patient turned out to be Mr Youngblood, the Innkeeper and my landlord. Dr Challot has decided that he is suffering from an Elevated Pressure of the Blood which must be reduced. Dr Challot told me that he made the determination because Mr Youngblood is both ruddy cheeked and prone to be rich in dander.

The new method of lowering the Pressure of the Blood which Dr Challot intends to try is called Extreme Blood Letting and is, allegedly, much faster than using Leeches or scarification. According to the Blind Drummer, it also offers a way to make an accurate measurement of the pressure under which the Blood is circulating.

'You must first lie down upon the couch,' said Dr Challot, addressing Mr Youngblood. 'I will then make an incision in your left radial artery. The Blood in the arteries is under far more pressure than the Blood in the veins and when I make the cut your Blood will shoot out across the room. Dr Bullock will measure the furthest reach of the Blood as it spurts out of your artery. I will allow the artery to pump Blood for three or four minutes and I will then seal the cut with hot tar.'

Mr Youngblood seemed remarkably sanguine about the procedure he was about to undergo and I wondered if he might have prepared himself by drinking a surfeit of beer.

'How will we know if the procedure has been successful in lowering the Blood pressure?' I asked.

'That is the brilliant part of the procedure,' said Dr Challot. 'We will take advantage of the fact that Mr Youngblood has two radial arteries. Once the hot tar has sealed the cut in Mr Youngblood's left radial artery, I will make an identical cut in his right radial artery. We can again measure the distance the Blood travels when it spurts out across the room. If the procedure has been successful, the Blood from the right artery should travel a shorter distance than the Blood from the left artery.'

This made excellent sense to me and so we proceeded with the operation without further ado.

I am delighted to report that it was an immediate and dramatic success, the Blood from the left arm having travelled 22 feet and the Blood from the right arm having travelled just 17 feet.

Dr Challot and I both agreed that this diminution in the distance the Blood had travelled proved that the Blood pressure must have fallen, thereby dramatically reducing the chances of Mr Youngblood having a seizure. The only unfortunate thing was that it proved difficult to seal the right radial artery, and several pints of Blood had spurted over the horse hair sofa in the consulting room before we were able to halt the flow.

Nevertheless, Dr Challot pointed out that if reducing the Blood supply a little was good then it stood to reason that reducing it a great deal must be very good.

I helped Mr Youngblood home for he was rather dizzy and unsteady after his ordeal. He was, nevertheless, enormously grateful and promised me a double helping of Plumb tart this evening.

February 25th

There is no doubt that Mr Rowland Hill's invention of the scheme popularly known as the Penny Post has improved life in a number of ways.

It is, for example, now possible for a housewife to write to the butcher at 10 of the morning to demand information on the meats available and to request his recommendation, to receive a reply by post in the early afternoon, to put details of her requirements into the late afternoon post and to receive a parcel containing her order well in time to cook the evening meal.

But the advertising material which now comes in daily is rapidly becoming a considerable nuisance.

In the post this morning, I received three letters promoting pill making equipment, two leaflets advertising Leech jars and a note from a fellow claiming to have a supply of the best Leeches in England. 'Our Leeches suck faster and harder than anyone else's or your money back!' Another Leech supplier promised me a free bottle of port if I chose to purchase two dozen Blood suckers from him. And the London Mercury Company is promising me a reduced price on Mercury for all varieties of the pox.

March 2ⁿᵈ

Miss Zahlia Colefax came into the surgery and demanded that I provide her with a certificate of virginity. A surprising number of patients attend and request such certification and not all can be considered obvious candidates for confirmation.

'It is for my fiancé,' she explained. 'He has requested that I provide him with a certificate prior to our marriage next month. We are to be married by the Bishop of Winchester.'

She did not seem in the slightest bit put out by her fiancé's pre-nuptial requirement.

'But you have two children!' I pointed out. 'Am I not to assume that these were produced in the normal way?'

'Oh yes indeed they were,' she answered. 'But although he has been eager to anticipate our nuptials I have not had the more intimate variety of relations with my fiancé and so in that regard I must surely be considered a virgin.'

'Does your fiancé know that you have two children?'

'Oh yes.'

'And how does he think they came into being?'

'I told him they were the result of immaculate conceptions,' replied Miss Colefax. 'He is a very religious man and understands and accepts these matters.'

I declined to provide the certificate, thinking it dishonest and being unwilling to take advantage of her fiancé who must be something of a half-wit.

March 7ᵗʰ

Dr Mort turned up just as I was beginning to think that we would see no more of him.

Dr Challot and I were in the consulting room examining a new batch of dead toads which had just been delivered by our usual toad man. Dr Challot was preparing to toss the toads into a pail of cows' urine to soften them up a little.

'Ah, come in, sir,' said Dr Challot, as Dr Mort appeared on the threshold. 'What seems to be the problem? What can my colleague and I do for you?'

'It's Mr Mort,' I whispered. 'The new Apprentice.'

Dr Challot took his pince-nez from his waistcoat pocket, slipped them onto the bridge of his nose, tilted back his head and peered at the newcomer as though he were a dog he was considering purchasing. It was, I think, only the second time he had used his pince-nez since he is frightened of wearing them out.

'Mort, you say?' he said to me.

'Mort,' I agreed. 'He paid you a fee for an Apprenticeship.'

'Dr Mort,' corrected the newcomer, rather petulantly. 'You said I should be called Dr Mort.'

'Ah yes,' said Dr Challot whose memory had returned at the mention of money. 'I remember now.' He patted his coat pocket and the coins he had placed therein jingled merrily. I was surprised and delighted to see that he had not yet succeeding in spending the entire fee. 'You're young Mort the new Apprentice, if memory serves me right.'

'That's right,' agreed Dr Mort who seemed to have exposed himself to the joys of the zythepsary and was well disguised by beer. 'But do please remember that I am to be addressed as Dr Mort.'

'Dr Bullock and I were just engaged in a conference to determine the treatment of the Duchess of Piddlehampton,' said Dr Challot, who was clearly rather taken aback at young Mort's manner.

My employer lies so well that for a moment I found myself wondering who the Duchess of Piddlehampton might be, and why I couldn't remember what was wrong with her or why we were contemplating treating her.

'Oh, ah,' said Dr Mort. 'The Duchess of Piddlehampton, eh?' Splendid.' Our new Apprentice was clearly a fierce-some snob.

'We have here a sample of the Duchess's urine,' said Dr Challot, indicating the bucket of cow piss standing on the Table.

Dr Mort stepped forward and peered into the bucket which contained at least two thirds of a gallon of still warm piss. The dead toads had not been dropped into the bucket.

'She is an ample pisser,' explained Dr Challot.

'I should say so,' said Dr Mort, clearly impressed.

'We have a number of ways to assess the integrity of a patient's piss,' said Dr Challot pompously, 'but the most valuable is still the simple savouring with the tongue.'

Dr Mort looked at him, clearly startled.

'I stick my finger into the piss, hold it there for a minute and then insert it into my mouth and suck it dry,' explained Dr Challot. As he said this he dipped a finger into the bucket, held it there, and then pulled it out. 'All you do next is stick your finger into your mouth, suck off the piss, hold it there and check the taste.'

'Ye Gods!' said Dr Mort, looking horrified. 'Is that really necessary?'

'Invaluable,' insisted Dr Challot. 'Piss tasting is a crucial part of medical training. You cannot progress in the profession until you can do a decent piss taste.'

With some considerable ceremony, he placed his finger into his mouth, closed his eyes as though concentrating, and left the finger in place for a minute or so while he sucked and nodded. 'Definitely too much sugar and light on the liver salts,' he said. He turned to me. 'See what you think, Doctor?'

I did exactly as Dr Challot had done.

'I agree,' I said eventually. 'The liquid is very low on liver salts and quite certainly blessed with far too much sugar.'

'Your turn,' said Dr Challot to our new Apprentice. 'Dip the finger right into the bucket, twizzle it around, get it nice and wet and see what you think.'

Dr Mort paled. 'Is this truly necessary?' he asked.

'Essential,' said Dr Challot sternly. 'You can't continue with your training until you're an accomplished piss taster.'

With clear distaste and noticeable reluctance, Dr Mort dipped a finger into the bucket, lifted it out and stared at it.

'Don't wait too long!' snapped Dr Challot, pointing at Mort's finger. 'All the piss is dripping off the end.'

Dr Mort closed his eyes and put his finger into his mouth.

'Can you taste the sugar?' asked Dr Challot.

'I believe I can,' admitted Mort.

'But not enough liver salts?'

'Indeed, I believe not.'

Suddenly, Dr Challot burst out laughing. He didn't laugh often but when he did so he made quite an alarming sound. He bent almost double, slapped his thighs and staggered around the room in such a state that I feared that he would collapse.

'What ails ye?' demanded Dr Mort.

Dr Challot held up his index finger. 'This is the one I dipped in the bucket,' he said. He paused to laugh again. 'And this is the one I sucked!' He held up his middle finger.

Puzzled, Dr Mort stared at Dr Challot and then at me.

'But how did you taste the piss?'

Dr Challot and I laughed so much we could not answer.

'I declare that if I laugh more I shall piss my breeches!' said Dr Challot.

March 11th

Nathan Biggin is not the brightest candle on the chandelier. Indeed, he is not bright enough to be the village idiot. He earns a very modest living by taking part in hopping races in a number of Public Houses in our part of the country.

Last year Biggin volunteered, for the third time in his absurd life, to be the Fool in the village Autumn Fire pageant – an event that has been celebrated in Muckleberry Peverell for 500 years.

I have no idea what the Autumn Fire pageant is intended to celebrate (there is probably some pagan theory behind it) but the principle event involves the tying of a man dressed as a fool to the branch of a tree. A fire is lit underneath the dangling man and wet rags thrown onto the fire to produce a large quantity of smoke. The man is left dangling in the smoke for as long as possible. Eventually, the fool is cut down and allowed to drop into the fire. The hope is that when he falls into the fire, he will have the strength of body and balance of mind to scramble away.

It is widely understood that no one ever agrees to play the Fool more than once.

No one, that is, except Nathan Biggin.

The idiot has agreed to play the Fool for the third year running. If the man was required to live by his wits he would surely die.

Unfortunately, a group of villagers decided that it would be more fun if Biggin were drunk when tied to the tree and so they supplied him with copious quantities of cyder. The result was when he fell down into the fire he forgot to scramble away but lay there, on the hot ashes, laughing hysterically. When he finally scrambled out of the fire he tripped on an old root, fell and broke his leg in two places.

The leg obviously had to be removed but since I did not have my bone saw with me, I borrowed an axe from Cuthbert Fazackerly. The axe was not well kept, and indeed quite dull, and it took three hard blows to sever the damaged limb. Mr Fazackerly and two other labourers were needed to hold Biggin down while I operated and we had to stuff Biddy Fluke's used pantaloons into the fellow's mouth to stifle the screaming. (Biddy Fluke is a well-known local bangtail who was practising her profession up against an oak tree at the time. Her pantaloons were lying on the ground, brazenly abandoned and just the thing for use as a mouth gag.)

As I was amputating Biggin's useless limb, I heard several spectators betting on the outcome of the operation. The favoured bet was that Biggin would be dead within 24 hours. When I had finished my work, which had I thought been efficiently done, I placed half a Sovereign on his surviving between two and three days.

March 19th

Many of the villagers in Muckleberry Peverell are closely related by marriage and it sometimes seems to me that this may have something to do with the fact that the district is well populated with idiots.

Today I heard that Perdita Clutterbuck, a local 15-year-old hussy wench and halfwit, has been found guilty of non-payment of a four shilling debt to the baker. The magistrate has ordered that she must pay within two weeks or be whipped from Exeter to Budleigh Salterton.

The hapless wench was brought to see me by her mother who asked me to speak to the magistrate.

'Perdita is a slow girl,' she said. 'She has never been quite like others but she is a well-meaning girl, generous to a fault. She can neither read nor write and she has a great affection for currant buns which I cannot afford to buy for her. I have asked the Baker not to sell her anymore but he won't listen to me.

After I listened to her sad tale I went with her and the girl to the Magistrate's home to plead for leniency. After I'd finished my pleading, the Magistrate announced that in view of my pleading he would change the punishment he had prescribed.

'She must pay within one week or be whipped from Exeter to Budleigh Salterton and back again,' he said gruffly. 'Slow wittedness is no excuse for not paying your debts.'

With Mistress Clutterbuck in tears and her Daughter staring glumly at the ceiling as is her wont, I started to protest but was warned that if I said anything else the punishment would be increased still further. It seemed cruel beyond comprehension. We are all separated from madness and lunacy by fine lines. There is a fine line between self-sufficiency and reclusiveness, another between reclusiveness and hermitry and yet another between hermitry and misanthropy.

As we left, I told Mistress Clutterbuck that if the Magistrate ever came to me with an Illness of any kind, I would prescribe a double strength mustard Enema to be delivered with my brass ended Enema pump. I told her I would also insist on giving him such a good Purging that he would find himself emptying his innards at both ends.

Mistress Clutterbuck was more than mildly mollified by this and thanked me deeply.

And having recently received a handsome payment from the Highwayman, I gave Mistress Clutterbuck the four shillings with which to pay the debt to the baker. I also promised to see the Baker and tell him that I will report him for selling mouldy bread if he gives any more buns to the Clutterbuck girl.

My ten guineas have now almost disappeared. By the time I had paid the landlord for my lodgings, there was very little left.

I lost the half guinea I wagered on the outcome of Nathan Biggin's amputation. I am woefully annoyed. He died in 19 hours and his brother is reputed to have made a killing on this sad outcome.

I should have learned by now that it is dangerous to wager on the outcome of any medical procedure.

March 22ⁿᵈ

A boy of about nine or ten wandered into the consulting room followed by a very large woman who appeared to be wearing several coats. The boy, an impudent looking fellow, was smoking a clay Pipe with a cracked bowl.

'Oh excuse me, your worship, I'm sure,' said the woman, who introduced herself as Mistress Biddy Fluke. 'It has taken us two hours to get here and it is now time for Jethro's mid-morning visit to Nature's Public House. He becomes mortally upset if I deprive him his natural sustenances.'

And so saying, with surprising dexterity, she removed not three but four coats before unfastening the buttons of her blouse. Once this was done she pushed down a grey and tattered camisole and pulled out one of a surprisingly large pair of well stuffed dugs. A small piece of lace attached to a few inches of the camisole was all that remained to show that it had once been a fine piece of underwear. Even without the clothing she was still a very large woman. She herself did not appear to have been unduly deprived of nourishment.

With her left hand the woman offered up a hugely swollen right nipple to the boy who took his Pipe out of his mouth, bent his head and began to suck away as though his life depended upon it. The nipple was as big, as brown and as gnarled as a labourer's thumb. It had clearly seen a good deal of use.

'He has to suck hard,' explained Mistress Fluke as the boy attacked the dug with gusto. 'It takes him a minute or two to get the milk flowing.'

With her right hand she pointed down towards her groin. 'I have a worrisome rash down below. It itches like the very devil and I cannot see down there. Would you take a look for me?'

While the boy took his milk, the mother pulled up her Bristol red skirt and a bewilderment of petticoats, yanked up a huge fold of surplus abdominal fat and finally succeeded in exposing her nether regions.

'You take a good look, Doctor!' she said.

'You have lice,' I told her immediately.

'I knew it!' said Mistress Fluke with surprising vehemence. 'It was that Silus Baxter. I knew there was something amiss with him. Scratch, scratch, scratch all evening he was.'

'You should shave the area and apply some medicinal vinegar,' I told her.

There is in fact no difference between medicinal vinegar and the variety used for culinary purposes but by calling it 'medicinal' we can charge five times as much per bottle.

'You do it for me, Doctor,' said Mistress Fluke.

The boy was still slurping away, alternately sucking on the proffered dug and puffing on his pipe. Looking at him more closely I thought he was perhaps older than I had originally surmised. He was, I suspected, probably 13 or 14 years of age. He was, however, not the oldest I had seen still at the breast.

'You want me to do the shaving?' I asked, slightly surprised.

'You're a Barber Surgeon aren't you?' said the woman. 'I'll hold up my belly so that you can get at the scene of the crimes.'

With a half-hidden sigh, I found my razor, wiped off a few meat fibres, gave it a stropping, and shaved Mistress Fluke's pubic area. It annoys me a great deal that Mistress Swain sees fit to use our surgical implements in the kitchen. When I had finished the shaving, I dowsed the area liberally with vinegar. Mistress Fluke then re-clothed her lower self and roughly pulled the boy from what must have been a now empty dug. He was reluctant to stop.

I asked for sixpence for the shaving and the medicinal vinegar but the woman only had three and a half pence so I reluctantly accepted that in full payment. It seemed a very small recompense for the nature of the labours involved.

April 4th

The weather has been surprisingly warm for the time of the year and also rather muggy. I talked about this with a bunch of villagers who were taking evening refreshment in the Public House where I reside.

Vigo Fitzmountjoy, a retired Saddler who had to give up skilled work when he lost a hand and who now helps out in the Peacock Inn stables, though precisely what he does there is probably as much of a mystery to the Ostler as it is to the rest of the world, claimed that he had heard it said that the mugginess was caused by all the train smoke being puffed out into the atmosphere. He says the smoke has changed the temperature of the air around us. He said there had been a meeting in London where experts had agreed that within two years at the very most, the planet will spontaneously ignite and we will all be roasted to Death in a ball of fire.

Theobald Standish, a baker, asked Mr Fitzmountjoy how the experts had arrived at the meeting. Mr Fitzmountjoy replied, without any apparent embarrassment, that they had mostly travelled to the meeting by train. Mr Standish remarked that if the experts were right then their meeting had probably shortened the planet's life expectation by a week.

Mr Fitzmountjoy, ignoring Mr Standish's remark as 'inconvenient', added that there was clear evidence that trains racing through the countryside were responsible for an increase in the incidence of spontaneous abortions among cattle in fields next to the tracks. He said that several farmers he knew had stopped using the fields which were closest to Railway tracks to protect their cattle from this eventuality. He also said that there were Doctors in London who believed that Railway travel was a major cause of the dropsy. He did not know the names of the Doctors who believed this but he insisted that they were most reputable men of science.

Lumpy Darbyshire, a professional mourner, said it had been hot and muggy long before trains had been invented so how did these so-called experts explain that.

Mr Fitzmountjoy could not provide an adequate explanation so we took him outside, put him in the stocks and threw abuse and ripe fruit at him for being a scaremonger. As we did this, Mr Stevens pointed out that somewhere in Mr Fitzmoutjoy's lineage there must have been a bastard. He explained that since the 11th century, the surname prefix Fitz has always denoted illegitimacy. He said that when William IV was still the Duke of Clarence, he had fathered ten illegitimate children with a mistress called Dora Jordan and that all the children had been named FitzClarence.

Mr Standish pointed out that royalty had always been a randy lot and that King Henry I had fathered 20 bastard children with six different mistresses.

I did not see much point in this discussion about his antecedents but putting Mr Fitzmountjoy into the stocks was the best entertainment I have had for a month, and a sound antidote to those who claim that life in the country is not culturally diverse.

After we had finished throwing all the rotting fruit we could find, we left Mr Fitzmountjoy where he was for a while and, since he is almost certainly descended from a bastard, repaired to the pub for refreshment.

Throwing fruit always exhausts me and gives me a thirst.

April 9th

'Your husband has died,' I told Mistress Augusta Maitland.

'He's dead, you say?' She seemed surprised but not particularly distressed. 'How long has he been dead?'

'I would say a week or so at the very least.'

'I thought he was quiet,' said Mistress Maitland thoughtfully. 'It wasn't like him to be so quiet. He was usually complaining about something or other.' She paused and frowned. 'Are you absolutely sure he's dead?'

'Positive, I'm afraid.'

The old fellow was starting to decay and it was possible to be certain he was dead by smell alone. I was sad to see him go for he had been a colourful character, famous for two things.

First, his was one of the first homes in the country to have specially built indoor water closets. It was generally agreed that this was a gloriously eccentric thing and that having a water closet inside the house was clearly a health hazard. Never one to do things by halves, Mr Maitland had installed two water closets inside his house.

There was one downstairs and one upstairs. Both emptied through pipes into a large pit in the vegetable garden and it was rumoured that since the pit had been dug, the Maitland's gardener had produced the biggest cabbages, marrows and Turnips in the county. It is certainly undeniable that the produce he had grown had won many first prize trophies and certificates.

Second, although he had always been a keen carriage driver, and had once held the record for driving a four in hand from London to Bristol in under four hours, the late Mr Maitland had recently taken a deep affection for trains. In his final years, he had customarily paid the Railway company to allow him to travel on the engine platform alongside the driver and the fireman. Once he was safely ensconced on the platform, and the train was out of the station, Mr Maitland gave the driver a guinea to allow him to drive the train. He did this at terrifying speeds, sometimes amusing himself by finding time to throw lumps of coal and glowing gleeds at people and houses as they passed. On one occasion, Mr Maitland had ridden inside the train, pretending to be a ticket collector, and had physically thrown people off the train simply because he did not like the look of them. 'You are too ugly to travel on my train,' he roared at those whom he ejected. I remembered all this because there had been quite a fuss at the time. Two of the people whom he had physically ejected from the train had subsequently died from the injuries they had sustained and Mr Maitland was reputed to have had to pay 30 guineas to the local magistrate, and five guineas each to the relatives of the travellers who had died, in order to have the case against him dismissed and the affair hushed up.

'Him being dead would explain why he's been off his food,' said Mistress Maitland.

'I would think so,' I agreed.

Mistress Maitland nodded thoughtfully for a moment. 'Well, that's wonderful news,' she said at last.

I looked at her, surprised and puzzled. To be honest, it was not the reaction I had been expecting.

'Your husband has passed away,' I shouted, thinking that perhaps she was deaf and having difficulty in hearing me.

'Still gone, is he? Well, that's wonderful! Marvellous. Now I can sell this damned barn of a house and travel to Italy.'

I stared at her.

'I've always wanted to go to Italy,' she explained. 'I hear the weather is warmer there. I think I'll go tomorrow. I've lived in this damned house for more than 30 years and I've always hated it. My husband's late parents lived here. And his grandparents.'

The Maitland home was a large, rather splendid house with two or three hundred acres of land around it. On the downside it was undoubtedly impossible to heat during the winter months. Even with half a dozen fireplaces blazing away, the place was freezing cold.

I looked at her in horror. 'But you have to bury your husband before you can go anywhere!' I reminded her.

The whole business of burying a deceased person takes some considerable time. Indeed, it is usually necessary to keep a body in the house for twelve days or so. Relatives and friends take it in turns to sit up and keep the deceased company. Much gin is drunk and there are strict social rules about how a funeral is organised and how the bereaved must behave afterwards. A widow is expected to wear her weeds for a year and then slowly abandon the crepe trimmings and start wearing black silk. A woman seen out of the house in black silk in under a year would be regarded as unacceptably flighty. By leaving for Italy, the widow Maitland would doubtless escape all these restrictions but she would also shock all her friends and neighbours, not to mention any relatives still alive.

'My solicitor can deal with all the funeral nonsense,' replied the widow, with a dismissive wave of a hand.

'What about the sale of your house?'

'He can deal with that too,' added the widow Maitland with a firm nod. 'I shall go to London, take a cabriolet to Dover and a boat to France.' She thought about this for a moment. 'No, damnit,' she said suddenly. 'I'll take a four wheeler, a growler, and be damned to the expense.'

April 14th

I was called to the Red Dragon yesterday evening to attend to Hieronymous Scroggs who had fallen off a Table and broken his right leg.

Mr Scroggs is a professional dancer. His speciality is to put twelve eggs on the top of a Table, allow himself to be blindfolded and to proceed to dance a hornpipe jig around the eggs without stepping on any of them.

It is a form of entertainment which was popular with both the Saxons and the Normans. Chaucer, an author long deceased, used to call these dancers hoopesteres.

Egg dancing can be most profitable, and skilful exponents are often rewarded with good sums of money by the spectators.

Since Mr Scrogg's leg was broken, I had no choice but to remove it. I did not have my saw with me so since it was raining, I borrowed an axe from the landlord and performed the operation in the scullery. I am delighted to say that although the axe badly needed sharpening, I succeeded in removing the damaged portion of limb with just three blows. Three customers had to hold the fellow down and to quieten his screams we had to stuff his stained and shapeless felt hat into his mouth. Since this is the second time I have had to remove a limb without my bone saw, I made a note to myself to carry my bone saw with me at all times. Using an axe is hard labour and I put my shoulder out today.

This morning, I visited the Patient and was well pleased to see that he was still alive. He was, however, not well endowed with good spirits complaining loudly that with only one good leg he would no longer be able to perform a creditable hornpipe.

'Hop, sir!' I told him. 'Hopping is very popular. Just lay down your eggs and hop around them.'

This cheered him no end for he remembered that a man in the North of England was reputed to be able to make up to fifty shillings for an evening's good hopping.

But he complained about his hat having been ruined and when I presented my bill for a guinea he insisted on deducting three shillings and sixpence, the price of a new felt hat.

April 22nd

I attended a medical forum on Leeches which was held at an Inn in Reading and organised by a Leech selling company called 'Pettigrew's – Purveyors of Prime Leeches'. Their slogan, printed on the side of their Leech Jars, is: 'You Can Rely on Pettigrew's – Our

Leeches Suck Longer and Harder than Anyone Else's Or Your Money Back'.

When first invited to attend the forum, I had expressed little interest in the event but the seller's local Drummer, a man called Mr Bartholomew, who dresses like a funeral walking man apart from the fact that he always wears a greasy, black bowler hat with a navy blue band around the crown, offered to arrange for me to be picked up by a cart and pair and promised an entertaining as well as educational event.

Pettigrew's had hired the large room at the Blue Ball Inn and there were two dozen of us in attendance. The meeting began with a lecture from an Apothecary who had been brought from London to explain why Leeches are the preferred method of exsanguination. He had compared three patients who had been treated with Leeches with three patients who had been treated with scarificators and cupping glasses. Two of the three patients who had been treated with Leeches had survived but all three of the patients who had been treated with scarification had died.

A stern Apothecary whom I did not know, asked the lecturer, whose name by one of those strange coincidences which occur in life was Pettigrew (the same as the Leech selling company), if he had any information about the diseases from which the six patients had suffered.

'I don't see how that could be of any relevance,' responded the lecturer rather stiffly. 'The only point of any significance is that all three of the patients who were subjected to scarification were, within less than a week, staring up at the lid of a coffin whereas within the same time period two of the individuals who had been treated with Leeches were up and about and enjoying life. That's a 100% failure rate for scarification and a 66% success rate for Pettigrew's Leeches.'

It was generally agreed that the lecturer's presentation had been thoroughly convincing and an Apothecary who had travelled all the way from Lichfield proposed a vote of thanks which was duly seconded and recorded.

There was only one other lecture. This, which was given by Mr Tarbuckton, a representative of the company, included a lengthy explanation of why Pettigrew's Leeches were far superior to their competitors and immensely to be preferred over wild Leeches taken from a local pond or sold by travellers or gypsies.

'If you purchase Leeches from Pettigrew's you will be able to rely on the quality of the creatures you employ,' explained Mr Tarbuckton. 'Moreover, since Pettigrew's Leeches are accredited and guaranteed taken from clean running water supplies, you can rely on them for high quality Bleeding. Regular articles about our Leeches in the popular press mean that many patients ask for Pettigrew's Leeches and will accept no others. A recent investigative article which appeared in *The Times* newspaper, explained just why a Leech taken from clean, river water can provide a superior and safer service to a Leech taken from dirty or stagnant water. It was revealed that one of our competitors, who I will not name, was taking Leeches from a stream which was thick with sewage. The article attracted a good deal of interest. The discerning Apothecary can, therefore, charge two or even three times as much when he is providing Pettigrew's Leeches as when providing Leeches with lesser provenance.'

Finally, after telling a lengthy but amusing anecdote about an Apothecary in Wolverhampton who had tried using garden snails instead of Leeches, Mr Tarbuckton announced that the company was initiating two new promotional policies to encourage sales.

'First,' he said, 'we are introducing what we call a 'Be Given a Free Leech If You Purchase a Leech' policy. This means that if an Apothecary purchases two dozen Leeches, we will supply him with four dozen Leeches. He will pay for just two dozen Leeches. The other two dozen Leeches will be free of charge.'

He went on to explain that the company was also initiating a three for one returns policy for what he called 'tired' Leeches.

'There is no doubt,' he said, 'that a Leech which has been well utilised will become sluggish and unwilling to take on more nourishment. This can seriously impair a Leech's performance. But here at Pettigrew's Leeches, we always try to go one step further than the competition and so if you return a dozen bloated Leeches to our Drummer he will, at absolutely no charge, replace them with four entirely fresh, hungry Leeches.'

We all agreed that these two innovations were excellent news and very welcome and I made a note to recommend to Dr Challot that in future we should use only Pettigrew's Leeches.

We were then invited to move from the room in which we had been meeting into the Inn's dining room. This splendidly furnished room had clearly been hired exclusively for Pettigrew's guests.

As an amuse bouche we were immediately offered small pieces of hot lobster which were, so I was told by the comely young wench who served me, cooked in bouillon and covered with a mixture of yolk of egg, liqueur brandy, cream, madeira and herbs. The serving wenches, and there were a dozen of them, were delightfully attired in very low necked puffy sleeved frocks which I was later told were popular uniforms in German beer cellars. The comely servers had clearly all been chosen for their appealing and substantial features.

I had never seen such an array of Alcoholic beverages. The Inn keeper, obviously at Pettigrew's expense, had supplied a hogshead of cyder, pipes of both port and Madeira and apparently unlimited supplies of both strong beer and small beer. There was also a good supply of gin.

The meal consisted of eight courses.

We began with a rissole made with capon breasts, calves udders, marrow, bacon, herbs and all fried in lard to give a nice brown colour. We were then served a whole roasted goat, stuffed with plums and spiced stuffing and served with neat's tongue and slivers of goose. This was followed by a roasted swan, a quarter of a boar and a sufficiency of venison, plover and snipe. I tried to make a note of everything placed before me but could hardly keep up with the onslaught of food. I did jot down that for the fish courses we were served sturgeon, crayfish, carp, pike, trout and elvers. There was also an excellent pigeon and rook pie of which I had three helpings.

After a short break we were served a variety of puddings including saffron cake, gingerbread, marchpane, nectarines, custard and warden pie.

Throughout the meal we were served sack, malmsey and muscadine – all imported from foreign parts such as France or Germany.

The meal took five and a half hours to serve and to consume and I do not believe that men have ever dined more thoroughly or been served by more delightful waitresses. Towards the end I noticed that seven of my colleagues were missing. Coincidentally, seven of the waitresses had gone too, though I quickly realised that with fewer of us at the Table the girls had probably been sent home since there were less of us to serve.

As I left, to be taken back home by the same cart and driver who had brought me, I was handed a large Leech storage jar; a delightful thing with a domed perforated lip to prevent the creatures climbing out. I was also presented with a small, portable Leech jar in a pewter box to carry inside my medical satchel. The pewter box has both Pettigrew's name and my own name engraved upon the side and is a most pleasing item which must have cost a considerable sum. The Leech business is clearly a profitable one.

The whole evening was a very instructive and most educational experience.

I arrived back home very late that evening feeling that my excursion had been most worthwhile.

Unfortunately, I was kept awake for much of the night by gurglings and rumblings in my stomach which also caused me some considerable discomfort and occasioned a number of visits to the courtyard lavatory where I emptied myself from both ends on several occasions.

Young Nellie, bless her kind heart, asked if I had managed to eat anything while at my conference, or if my determination to feed my mind had left my body quite forgotten and unattended.

When I confessed that I had consumed an inelegant sufficiency of foods rather richer than those to which I was accustomed, she suggested that if I were, in consequence, suffering from a contused stomach and bewilderment of the bowel I might remedy the situation by taking additional refreshment. I am constantly amazed by her understanding of the human body and I quickly agreed to her suggestion. After visiting the kitchen, she presented me with a dish of cold pigeon pie served with a mound of cold, battered and buttered Turnips. When, with her constant encouragement, I had succeeded in demolishing the pie and the Turnips she suggested that I added a good layer of strong beer to the substance in order to encourage a speedy recovery from my plight.

I entertained high hopes that this fulsome remedy might ease my symptoms but sadly and inexplicably I fear that if anything my condition deteriorated still further and I spent the rest of the night curled up in a corner of the room waiting to die. For several hours I was more than mildly disappointed when this relief was not forthcoming.

April 29th

I was invited to a medical forum dealing with scarifators. The meeting, actually described as a 'Congress', was organised by a company called Hooklebury's Patent Scarifators.

I was, at first, sceptical and reluctant to agree to attend. However, I was, eventually persuaded to keep the day free of appointments when the Drummer, a greasy, middle aged fellow who wears a frock coat which saw its best days several decades ago, explained that I would learn a great deal about the future of scarification and be paid a guinea merely for attending.

'Leeches are dangerously out-of-date,' he insisted. 'The modern Apothecary no longer uses them. Today's man of medicine favours scarification when a Patient needs Bleeding. It is the scientific route to efficient exsanguination. '

The Drummer added that there would be an excellent meal after the lectures had finished. I told him that I was not to be easily bought by the prospect of a bowl of soup and a chunk of bread but he assured me that the meal, which would consist of nine courses together with wines, would be prepared by a French chef from the Savoy Hotel in London.

And it transpired that the Drummer's promise contained not a whiff of exaggeration.

The meeting was held in the upper room of the King's Head Public House and I was delighted to see that many of the fellows whom I had seen at the Leech demonstration were present to learn about scarification. I found it reassuring to know that so many of my colleagues were so eager to learn more about the practice of their profession that they were prepared to give up so much of their time in the cause of education. I am sometimes heartened by the nobility of my fellow professionals.

One fellow to whom I spoke, a Dr Jasper Prout, told me that in the last month he had been to 11 of these affairs. 'I save a fortune on food and eat much better than I could afford to myself,' he told me with a wink.

After a short lecture about the danger of using Leeches (the lecturer explained that the amount of Blood they consume cannot easily be regulated and pointed out that they are such unprepossessing creatures that many patients, particularly high born ladies, find the whole idea of applying Leeches quite upsetting) there was a demonstration of the Hooklebury Scarificators.

Two volunteer guinea pigs (both plump Maidens in their late teens) stripped to the waist and, dressed only in white cotton bloomers, were subjected to extensive scarification on their arms and chests. Both volunteers (who I assumed were being well paid for their part in the proceedings) smiled and joked throughout the display. As the Blood dripped it was caught in special silver containers so the floor coverings were not soiled.

This exhibition was followed by a short lecture by Mr Hooklebury himself.

He showed us several sets of scarificators.

His top selling premium set, which costs 100 guineas and was, I suspect, well outside the range of affordable items for those of us present, is a very fine looking set of 16 spring loaded blades which can be used to make small cuts in the skin. The blades, equipped with ivory handles, come in a solid silver scarificator case designed by Paul Ambroccio who, we were told, is an artist of some renown. The cases, decorated with enamelled flowers, are especially made by Asprey's of Bond Street. There is no doubt that the whole business of scarification is very clean and tidy. In addition to the 16 spring loaded blades, the premium set of blades sold by Aspreys also contains 16 small glasses packed into a leather box.

The scarification process is, of course, precisely the same as with more ordinary products. The Apothecary heats each glass over a candle before placing it onto the skin which has been efficiently lacerated by one of the scarficator blades. The vacuum created pulls Blood into the glass. This is science in the true 19th century style.

Mr Hooklebury claimed that his scarification equipment can be used without any risk of Blood spilling onto clothing or Bed linen.

I was very impressed.

It is difficult to see how medicine can progress any further than this. Indeed, as one of the apothecaries present commented, it seems as though we have moved so far forward that we are already living in our own future.

According to Mr Hooklebury, his top of the range scarification sets are used by nearly all Physicians and Surgeons including, he claimed, the ones who attend Her Majesty at the Palace.

There was then some discussion.

An Apothecary from Birmingham, whose name I did not catch, commented that he had been shown a copy of a book called *Mistress Beeton's Book of Household Management* in which the author had recommended Bleeding as an activity which could be done at home without the trouble and expense of calling in a professional. The author apparently recommended using a lancet to initiate Bleeding and provided useful advice on how to avoid Blood dripping onto carpets, rugs and sofa coverings.

An Apothecary who had read the same book said that in his view the best advice Mistress Beeton gave was to remind her readers that they must remember to stop the Bleeding when they thought the time was appropriate.

This caused much merriment and many ribald comments were passed at the expense of Mistress Beeton.

There was some discussion about whether home Bleeding would be a serious threat to our business, and a fellow from Winchester remarked that he had started a rumour in his neck of the woods that two patients who had followed Mistress Beeton's recommendation had Bled to Death because they cut too deeply and either didn't remember to arrest the Bleeding or didn't know how to do it effectively. It was agreed that this was an excellent notion and an Apothecary from Paddington said he would write a letter to *The Times* warning readers of the hazard associated with home Bleeding.

Dr Ferdinand Teague, an Apothecary from North of London, said he had a Patient who used to insist that Blood from his scarification cuts be allowed to drip onto a bucket so that he could put it on his roses. Apparently the fellow was a keen gardener who claimed that he had won numerous prizes for his roses at his village flower and vegetable show. This was thought to be good information.

An Apothecary from Oxford, called Dr Potter, said he once had a Patient who liked to have his wife's Blood drip into a saucepan so that his cook could incorporate the Blood into meat dishes. The Patient said the Blood gave the dishes extra body and a richer taste. Unfortunately, on one occasion, the wife, left alone for twenty minutes, fell asleep and when the husband and the Apothecary returned to the room they found one of their dogs, a Great Dane called Jack, enthusiastically licking the Blood from the skin as it leaked from the woman's arm. Deprived of the Blood for a steak and kidney pie he had ordered his cook to prepare, the husband reached for his shotgun and mortally wounded the dog with a single shot. The wife, woken by the gunshot, leapt into the air, had a heart seizure and died moments later.

After this sombre story there was silence for a while before the staff of the inn brought in the food and wine for our meal.

There was a special strength local mead for those who requested it and two bottles of wine for each of us (both bottles were of French origin, one red and one white) and the meal was, as before, served by an ample number of waitresses. Indeed, we had a waitress each to make sure that our needs did not go unfulfilled.

There were, as promised, nine courses.

I had with me a small notebook and I jotted down details of all the food we were served, checking with my waitress for information when I wasn't certain of the nature of the dish I had been given.

First course: trout roe pie which was served with eels baked in marzipan. This was quite wonderful. If I had to eat one thing over and over again for the rest of my life this would be my selection.

Second course: pheasants' breasts in a sauce made from truffles and mushrooms. A trifle rich for my taste.

Third course: fried trout tails with whitebait. Too fiddly.

Fourth course: crusty topped sparrow and ptarmigan pie. Too many bones.

Fifth course: individual pies made of breasts of capon minced with cows' udders. Monsieur Anatole, the cook, came out with this course which was I gather his pièce de résistance though to be honest it was not my favourite item on his menu. He called the pies bouillands and I had to ask him to write down the name for me. I found the whole thing rather rubbery for my taste though the cook assured me that the ingredients had been boiled for two hours before being placed in the pie. He told me that the pie also contained cloves, butter, vinegar, sugar, cinnamon, tripe, mugget and cocks' combs.

Sixth course: a tart made from fish spleen, a boar rissole and capon livers wrapped in cauls. Rather bitter and too strong tasting for my liking.

Seventh course: a whole roasted francolin each. Excellent. Very tasty.

Eighth course: bone marrow pasties. Extremely handsome delicacies which are undoubtedly full of nutritious qualities.

Ninth course: the meal was rounded off with spotted dick pudding, served with lashings of brandy and egg custard. The pudding was the best I have ever tasted and the brandy and egg custard was magnificent.

And finally, bottles of port, cigars and little packets of Pipe Tobacco were brought round by our individual serving wenches. I noticed that several of my colleagues took handfuls of cigars and as many of the packets of Pipe Tobacco as they could grab and thrust them into their coat pockets.

One fellow, an Apothecary called Norbutt Wainscot, who hailed from Berkshire, even succeeded in cramming the bottle of port he had been given into his jacket. I suspect that he must have had special pockets made, larger and stronger than the usual variety, to accommodate such items.

Mr Wainscot, who had already consumed a good deal of Alcohol, told me that he drank only for his health. He said he had good, reliable evidence that a generous supply of Alcohol will improve a man's health and life expectation. Always eager to expand my medical knowledge I asked him about this.

'I'll give you an example,' he said, leaning closer and generously giving me a chance to share a lungful of second-hand breath that was powerful enough to strip the skin off a cow. 'A chap I know fell down a flight of stone steps last Saturday evening. A long flight of steps, made of quarried stone. Not a rug in sight. And do you know what? The fellow didn't hurt himself one little bit. Not one broken bone. No Bleeding. Not even a bruise. Tore a hole in his breeches, bruised his hat and lost his tiepin but his person escaped entirely unscathed. And do you know why?'

I admitted that I did not.

'The fellow was as drunk as a polony,' he said, stabbing a podgy forefinger in my chest and giving me another chance to taste his breath. 'As drunk as a lord. So pickled he could hardly stand upright. That's why he was unharmed when he fell down the damned stairs. And you know what that means?'

I admitted that I did not.

'That means I have an investigative medical mind!' said Wainscot. He tapped his skull with the knuckles of his right hand. 'Finest medical brain in Britain resides in there!'

I took a step back and waited; there was clearly more to come. I blinked to keep him in focus for I confess I was more than a little tiddly myself and he appeared to be moving from side to side and drifting in and out of focus.

'Why do you think the fellow didn't hurt himself?' asked Dr Wainscot.

'He fell onto a cushion?' I suggested.

'The Alcohol, sir! The Alcohol protected him from harm. If he hadn't been protected by Alcohol he'd have broken every damned bone in his damned body. I've seen people fall down shorter flights of steps and die from the consequences. It was the Alcohol which saved him.' Wainscot beamed with pride and jabbed me again with the same podgy finger. 'You've not heard that before, have you?'

I tentatively said that I had heard it said that a man who is drunk can fall over without hurting himself because he is relaxed and falls without becoming tense but Wainscot pooh poohed and tut tutted impatiently.

'No, no, no that's all superficial nonsense,' he cried. 'The fact is that Alcohol acts as a preservative. If you put a dead rat into a vat of Alcohol it will be preserved indefinitely. That's the point you see! Alcohol is a marvellous preservative. The greatest medicine ever discovered. The stuff protects and preserves. It is a gift – given to us by God to shield us from all harm.'

I felt privileged to be allowed to share this discovery.

'If Alcohol protects us from the consequences of falling down a flight of stone steps,' continued Dr Wainscot, 'it stands to reason that it will protect us from damage caused by other things. It will keep the heart healthy, the lungs in fine fettle, the spleen and the liver in tip top shape and the brain functioning like a machine.'

'Gadzooks!' was all I could manage in response to this.

'Gadzooks indeed. You might well say 'Gadzooks'.'

Dr Wainscot took the bottle of port from his pocket, removed the cork and drank a quarter of the bottle at a single gulp. He replaced the cork and put the bottle back into his pocket. 'Can't share this with you,' he said. 'Need it myself to protect my body. You'll have to get your own. Vitally important to keep the body's Alcohol levels sufficiently high. Allow the Alcohol level to drop and you expose yourself to untold dangers. The body must be protected at all times. Do you know how I make sure my patients are well protected?'

I admitted that I didn't.

'I make them walk along the edge of a rug,' he said. 'If they can walk in a straight line they're dangerously exposed and urgently need more Alcohol. That's the trick! I shall be writing a paper for that new journal they're putting out,' he said. 'What's it called? 'The British Medical Journal' or some such pompous title. It'll make my name.'

He suddenly stopped and glared at me.

'Don't you go thinking you can steal my thunder by writing it before me,' he said. 'Anyway, you can't. I have all the evidence and the knowledge.' He tapped his head. 'It's all tucked away safely up here. Biggest and best brain in Britain!' He then lurched away, tripped over a dog and fell onto his face.

The dog, a neutered mutt, either mud coloured or needing a wash, sniffed at the unconscious body and investigated it fully before deciding to piss all over him. It then wandered off.

When we left the Congress we were each given our guinea, a pound of sugar plums and a leather pouch into which three complimentary scarificator blades had been placed. There was room in the pouch for two dozen blades and I, like my fellow attendees, purchased a couple of extra blades, though they were very expensive.

It seems to me that Leeches are a thing of the past and scarification is definitely the way forward. It is clearly scientific medicine at its very best. Since it is obvious to anyone that we will always have to bleed our patients, and that Bleeding will be the treatment of choice for many specific ailments as well as for all uncommitted symptoms, it does seem to me that we have no choice but to embrace the process of scarifiction.

It is a wonderful feeling to be living in the future.

May 2nd

The Leech Drummer came. He had somehow found out that I attended the Congress on scarification last week and was as sore as a pickled dog. He seemed to regard my determination to educate myself as some sort of insult to himself, his company and the entire Leech industry. He pointed out that Leeches have been used for many centuries and were well favoured for their Blood sucking skills by the ancient Egyptians. He took the opportunity to remind me that I had recently accepted his company's generous hospitality. I felt my face redden when I noticed him staring pointedly at the scarifier case which was standing on the desk in front of me. The rather splendid Leech case with which I had been presented by his employer was, at that moment, sitting snugly in my medical satchel.

It had previously been my intention to send the Leech Drummer on his way but he somehow managed to make me feel swamped with feelings of guilt.

How do you explain to a fellow that he is working in a dying industry and that Leeches are very old-fashioned whereas bladed scarification is the way of the future?

In the end I was so consumed by a potent mixture of guilt and pity that I bought three dozen of his best quality Leeches.

It seems that in medicine there are age old customs which will die hard.

And I have to admit that we do have patients who prefer to be Leeched than scarified. Indeed, we have three patients who require Leeching once a month and who regard the process as calming and beneficial both mentally and physically.

May 7th

I spent a merry evening playing shoveh'penny, a game which was enormously popular with Henry VIII, though it is said that as a young man he much preferred pole vaulting.

There is no little irony in the fact that Henry VIII, who was keen on jousting and arranged for wives, monks and political enemies to be executed favoured indoor sports associated with Public Houses. He banned contact sports of all kinds, saying that they were too violent and too dangerous and he preferred shoveh'penny to all other sporting activities.

The great playwright William Shakespeare wrote about the game with enthusiasm and under its various names (push penny, shovegroat and shovelboard are the best known) this is probably the most popular game of our modern era.

Most Public Houses and Inns have their own teams and play competitively against neighbouring teams. Inevitably, therefore, betting and cheating are popular.

The Peacock Inn Table, one of the largest in the area, is 29 feet long and two feet wide. It has an unvarnished walnut top on an oak base with oak legs and woe betide anyone who lays a tankard on the surface.

Sadly, players are not always loyal.

One of our best players, Tobias Hinchcliffe, was recently lured away to an Inn in the next town where, it was rumoured, he had been offered a payment of a guinea a week just to play shoveh'penny for the Inn's team.

The Inn is one of our most prominent competitors in the local league and this treacherous act resulted in much ill-feeling.

By a cruel coincidence, the traitor was attacked one evening as he went home from the Inn. All of his fingers were broken and it seems that his career as a shoveh'penny player is now over.

May 12th

I was called to see Squire Hercules Figbotham this afternoon.

Squire Figbotham is a bad tempered old fellow of 74 years who has been ailing for many years. A vituperative quidnunc he has done nothing with his life except steadily become older, though this is, it must be admitted, an achievement at which he has excelled and at which he has shown considerable skill. A minute here, a day there, a week here, a month there and they all add up.

'Look after the minutes,' he once told me in a rare moment of comparative lucidity, 'and the years will look after themselves.'

Dr Challot insists that Squire Figbotham is only alive because he is too stupid to know how to die.

His housekeeper, Miss Haverhouse, who looks after the squire and a twelve room house by herself, called for me because the old fellow had refused point blank to get out of bed.

When I examined him I found that his heart was fluttering like a butterfly on a summer's day. There was no rhyme nor reason for the irregular beating. I gave him digitalis leaf but it made no difference. He refused my offer to use the scarification knives on him so I tried half a dozen good Leeches but they didn't help either.

'Am I dying, Doctor?' he demanded at last. He picked up a speaking trumpet and held it to his right ear, indicating that my reply should be directed into the trumpet.

'Oh no, not at all,' I replied as cheerily as I could be. I have never mastered the art of talking into a speaking trumpet.

'There's no need to shout!' he roared.

'I'm sorry. I thought…'

I waited for a moment while he struggled to find his teeth which had been expelled by the roar and which were now caught in a fold of his nightgown. When he had recovered them he slipped them back into his mouth. They looked to be wooden and clumsily carved.

'Tell me the truth you blackguard!' he suddenly shouted, so loudly that I fell over backwards and knocked my Leech jar off the bedside Table.

'Well, you're not well,' I admitted.

I bent down and struggled to pick the Leeches up off the floor and to get them back into the jar.

'The damned gardener's boy could have told me that, you idiot! What the devil are you doing down there?'

'Picking up Leeches.'

'Have we got Leeches in here? Good God man. Are you sure they aren't slugs?'

'I brought the Leeches with me,' I explained.

'You brought Leeches into my bedroom? What sort of buffoon are you?'

'I'm the Doctor,' I shouted into the trumpet. 'You have some of the Leeches on your chest.'

'Is that what they are?' He looked down at his chest, where the Leeches were busy sucking his Blood. 'I thought they were lawyers

– all sucking out my Blood. Are you trying to kill me? Tell me the truth or I'll rip off your damned impertinent hide and use it as a rug. Am I dying?'

I took a deep breath. 'I'm sorry to have to say that you are dying,' I told him.

'Thank the Lord for that!' he said.

'I beg your pardon?' I said, as I put the last of the spilt Leeches into their jar.

'I said: 'Thank the Lord for that!'. Are you deaf as well as stupid?'

'I was just surprised that you were thanking the Lord for the fact that you are dying.'

'You'd be thanking the Lord if you were me. I'm just glad it's nearly over.'

'What?'

'Life! I've had enough of it. Someone else can have a go. There must be people queuing up to be alive. I never did learn the damned bassoon.'

'I beg your pardon?'

'You are deaf aren't you? You can have my speaking trumpet when I've gone. It's been in my family for three centuries. My great great great grandfather used it. It's got solid silver and ivory accoutrements and there's a pewter case for it somewhere. I never use the case because it weighs half a ton if it weighs a grain. The case that is. Tell my lawyer I said you can have it. Do you play the bassoon?'

I thanked him for the offer of the speaking trumpet, though I had absolutely no intention of speaking to his lawyer since I cannot see myself having a great need for such an item, with or without silver accoutrements. I also admitted that I did not play the bassoon.

'Nor do I. Always meant to learn. Don't know why. Just a whim. Too late now. Too late for a lot of things. Too late for everything.' He paused and closed his eyes as though day-dreaming. 'I'd have liked to play the bassoon, though.'

I gave him a large dose of Laudanum and went downstairs to tell the housekeeper that her master would probably not be long for this world. As I descended, it occurred to me that if there was a pewter case for the speaking trumpet I should, after all, speak to the lawyer.

Miss Haverhouse, the old fellow's housekeeper was in the kitchen washing dishes. The remains of what looked like a pint of weak milk stood on the draining board.

'I'm not surprised and not sorry,' she said, wiping her hands on her pinafore. 'He's a man who has been overfull of misery for many a year and I can tell you, Doctor, that there'll be many a dry eye at his funeral.'

She certainly didn't seem in the slightest bit upset that her master was standing on the step outside Death's door and I cannot pretend I was surprised. The world is over-populated with mean-spirited, grotesque scolds whose main ambition in life is to spread unhappiness, and Squire Figbotham would be on anyone's list of the most egregious examples.

'Would you like a glass of posset?' she asked, nodding towards the jug on the draining board.

I have never liked posset and never understood why anyone would want to mix ale and milk. I thanked her and declined.

'I'm never without a glass close by,' she said. 'It's the only thing my stomach can take.'

I gave her the name of a good undertaker and left her with a bottle of Laudanum to give her master. 'Give Squire Figbotham some of this if he wakes and is in pain,' I told her. 'It'll ease his passing.'

'That'd be just a waste of good medicine,' she retorted, taking the cork out of the bottle and pouring a third of the contents straight down her throat. 'There I go,' she gasped, taking the bottle from her lips. 'I dare say that'll help settle my stomach even better than the posset. What did you say it was?'

'Laudanum,' I told her.

'Oh splendid,' she said, and poured half of the remainder straight down her throat.

'Shall I send a boy round with another bottle?' I enquired.

She belched loudly and handed me the empty bottle. 'Better send two,' she said. 'Here, you can have this empty one back.'

May 18th

Early this morning Miss Haverhouse sent word via the gardener's boy that Squire Hercules Figbotham had got out of Bed and was outside in his Nightshirt shooting the heads off all the stone statues that stood in his garden.

When I got there I found, to my astonishment, that the message I'd received had been entirely accurate. The grounds of the house were full of headless statues and Squire Figbotham, who was quite naked apart from his filthy Nightshirt, was wandering about his rose garden clearly looking for something else to shoot. He had a wild eyed, disappointed look about him.

I have often heard it said that we should respect our old people, for they have accumulated much wisdom and acquired a good deal of knowledge.

No one who had ever met Squire Figbotham would talk that way.

'You should go indoors,' I shouted, for he did not have his speaking trumpet with him.

'Why? Are there more statues there?' He stared at me, as though trying to recollect where he'd seen me before. 'You're younger than I expected,' he said. 'You're a damned site younger than you used to be.'

'Actually I think I'm older than I was,' I said.

'Answer the damned question,' he shouted. 'Are there more statues indoors?'

'I don't think so but you have no shoes on your feet and the weather is cold for the season.'

'My feet are damnably cold,' he said, looking down at them. They were an unpleasant shade of blue.

'Will you go into the house, sir?' I asked.

I wondered what the devil was wrong with him. He did not appear to be with drink. Maybe he had acquired some version of the pox. Or perhaps he had eaten too much rhubarb. He showed no signs of meaditis or any other form of intoxication.

'Are there any statues to shoot indoors? I'm rather taken with shooting the heads off the damned things. They stare at me and never say a damned word. Can't stand being stared at by people who never say anything. The damned things remind me of a Wife I once had.'

'Let's go indoors and get you something warm to drink,' I suggested, making sure I didn't stare at him.

'I don't want to drink! I want to shoot.' Holding his gun in his right hand he put his left hand into his Nightshirt pocket and rummaged around. A moment later he pulled out an empty hand. 'Have you got any cartridges?' he asked. 'I'm out!'

I confessed that I had no cartridges, apologised for this regrettable shortcoming, and suggested that there might be some inside the house.

'Let me tell you something, young man,' he said. 'There are only three things you can rely on in this world. There will always a dead fly in the ointment, there will always be an inky blot threatening to besmirch some part of your eschucheon and you will never have enough cartridges.'

Remembering his remarks the previous day, when we had both thought him about to step onto the barge to take him across the River Styx, I asked if he would like to go indoors to play the bassoon.

'What the devil are you on about?' he demanded. 'Why would I want to play the damned bassoon? I haven't got one and I don't want one.' He stared hard at me for a moment. 'You're the deaf fellow, aren't you? I remember now – you're the fellow who came round sprinkling slugs on my carpet and wanted to steal my speaking trumpet?'

'I'm the Doctor,' I shouted. 'I came to see you yesterday because I thought you were ill. And they were Leeches not slugs.'

'Leeches or slugs – who cares? Disgusting creatures. You can't shoot 'em and you can't eat 'em. Do you eat Leeches? Do you eat slugs?'

'No, sir, I don't.'

'Then why sprinkle the damned things around my bedroom? Are you mad?'

'No, sir, I'm not mad.'

'You're the damned Doctor aren't you?'

I admitted that I was, indeed, the Doctor.

'And now it appears you've come to see me again? Why? There's nothing wrong me. I've never been better. I'm not paying you just to come round, sprinkle slugs around my bedroom, steal my speaking trumpet and talk about bassoons. You Doctors are just like lawyers. You take every opportunity to come round and jabber away so that you can send me an extortionate bill for jabbering.'

With that he marched off into the house and headed straight for his gun room where, it transpired, he kept whole boxfuls of ammunition; quite enough cartridges for a man to start a small war.

'I think perhaps you should put the gun away,' I shouted as I followed him and watched with horror as he reloaded the gun and stuffed three boxes of cartridges into his nightgown pocket. 'Put some clothes on and have something to eat and drink.'

'Are you trying to sell me food and drink now? I don't want any. I want to shoot the damned statues. There may be more of them around the place. I shot all the blackbirds. I could only get 23 of 'em. Not quite enough for a pie, eh?'

Just then I noticed his housekeeper, Miss Haverhouse, standing behind him. I noticed that she was holding a large, iron frying pan.

'Can you persuade Squire Figbotham to get dressed?' I asked her.

'Why do I want to get dressed?' he roared. And with that he put down the gun and tore off his Nightshirt, leaving himself totally naked. He then picked up the gun again.

It occurred to me that in the same way that not all young men are bold, handsome and strong, not all old men are wise and erudite.

'Do you feel in good spirit?' I asked him. 'For your age,' I added.

'How the hell am I supposed to know how a man of my age is inclined to feel?' he demanded.

'He'll be better off if he has a sleep,' said Miss Haverhouse and with that she swung the frying pan as high as she could and bashed the old man on the back of his head. He went down like a stone.

'Good heavens, Miss Haverhouse!' I exclaimed. 'Have you killed him?'

'Not likely,' she said, apparently quite uninterested in whether she had or not. To my astonishment she pulled up her skirts, pulled down a stocking and pushed her right leg forward in such a way to draw attention to her knee.

'While you're here, Doctor,' she said, 'would you take a look at my knee for me?'

It wasn't difficult to see what was wrong with it. The knee was red, angry looking and the size of a football.

'I've tried cow dung,' she said. 'But it didn't make no difference.'

'Cow dung?'

She sighed in that way people sigh when they thought they were talking to someone sensible and suddenly discover that they're talking to an idiot. 'You take a shovelful of cow dung, put it on the fire and roast it,' she explained, 'and you then wrap it in a towel or a pillow case and bind it round the bad joint.'

'And it didn't work?' I said, doing my best to express surprise. I find myself less and less alarmed by the extraordinary beliefs of my patients. I would not have been surprised if she had put the roasted dung into a pie and eaten it with a Turnip mash.

'Not this time,' she admitted. 'It usually does,' she added quickly. 'And this were darned good smelly stuff from Buttercup. She's one of our best producers.'

'Of milk?'

'Dung.'

'Well I never!' I said sarcastically. 'Fancy the old cow dung treatment not working. Let me take a look at the knee.' I bent closer and peered at the knee. It was definitely red, angry looking and swollen.

'So, what are you going to do about it?' demanded Miss Haverhouse, as though it was my fault that her knee was inflamed and deformed.

'You haven't tried swallowing a small frog, have you?'

'No, I haven't! I don't hold with those old-fashioned remedies.'

'Swallowing a frog used to be a very popular remedy for joint problems,' I reminded her. 'As long as the frog was alive when swallowed.'

When I first started my Apprenticeship, Dr Challot had regular visits from an old fellow we called the frog man. He used to bring us live toads as well as live frogs but these were, apparently, more difficult to get hold of. I don't know why but we never referred to him as the toad man. Today, we obtain our frogs and toads from a reputable supplier. They're all dead when he brings them. I don't know what happened to the old frog man.

'Never tried it myself,' she said. 'My mother did it once or twice.'

'Did it help?'

'No it didn't. It didn't do the frog much good either.'

'I'll make up some medicine for you. You can collect the bottle from the surgery later tonight.'

'Will it cure me? I'm not going to walk all that way if it doesn't cure me.'

'It'll cure you,' I assured her. 'Meanwhile, put a piece of flannel over the knee and run a hot iron over it half a dozen times. Not hot enough to burn, just hot enough to be unpleasant.'

'A hot iron?'

'A hot iron.'

'What'll be in the medicine?' she asked, suspiciously.

'It'll be a mixture of one ounce of sulphur, eight drams of cream of tartar, a small spoonful of treacle , a pinch of brimstone, one ounce of rhubarb, one dram of gum guiacum and a pound of clover honey,' I told her.

I don't usually like telling patients what is in their medicine lest they write it down and make it up themselves. But Miss Haverhouse can neither read nor write and I knew darned well that even if she heard what I'd said she wouldn't remember it for more than half a minute.

'You take a teaspoonful every morning and another teaspoonful every evening,' I added. 'If it isn't better in ten days come and see me at the surgery.'

She disappeared, swinging the frying pan as though it were a club of some kind. As she did so I noticed that she was deliberately banging the frying pan against the side of her swollen knee. It seemed to be a tic and, surprisingly, it didn't seem to bother her unduly.

'Do you always bang your knee with the pan when you walk about? ' I called after her.

She turned. 'I do,' she said, rather impatiently.

It didn't seem to occur to the stupid woman that constantly banging her knee with a heavy frying pan might have made it red and swollen.

Making a mental note to put extra rhubarb into the mixture I prepared for her I bent down and examined the still unconscious Squire Figbotham. He was out cold but was breathing and had a pulse and seemed, therefore, to be still alive. He was far too heavy for me to lift alone so I found an old horse blanket and covered him up. Both the gardener (who appeared to be at least 150-years-old) and the gardener's boy (who appeared to be about six-years-old) refused to help me lift their master upstairs to his bedroom so I left him where he was and went back to the Peacock Inn where I enjoyed a nice piece of overcooked beef, a large plateful of frilled potatoes, three boiled eggs and a couple of jugs of malmsey.

After eating, I found that I had split my trousers. I have had the pair for only three years but they have become damnably tight about the Arse region. I fear they must have shrunk. It has been raining a good deal recently. Unless I can find a way to ensure that I never offer my rear outlook to my patients, I must buy another pair for I think the damage is so extensive that the trousers are beyond repair. I think it would be unseemly for me to back out of the room every time I leave a Patient and going upstairs backwards at the Peacock Inn is out of the question for the staircase is exceedingly steep and narrow.

I rode to Dr Challot's surgery where I made up the bottle of medicine for Miss Haverhouse.

'Did you know you'd split your trousers?' demanded Mistress Swain as I hunted in a cupboard for the requisite ingredients.

'I did, thank you.'

'I can see your flannel underwear,' said Mistress Swain. 'There's a split in them too so I can see your pink Arse.'

'Thank you Mistress Swain!' I snapped, attempting to shield my rear with the tails of my jacket.

I was fierce-some annoyed for this news meant I would have to buy another pair of trousers and another flannel undergarment in addition. In view of all these additional expenses, I decided to increase my charge to Miss Haverhouse from nine pence to a shilling and to send Squire Figbotham a bill for half a guinea. Since both were already patients of Dr Challot I would have to pay three quarters of the money over to him. It took me twenty minutes, half a pencil and the backs of two old Leech brochures to work out that my earnings for the day would be approximately thirty four and a half pence. It would not be enough to cover the cost of the new trousers and new flannel underwear which I need to purchase.

My financial outlook is not rosy. I desperately need to find more new patients who require the medication I sold to the hapless Constable Blomfield.

I have heard it said that the level of a man's happiness is the sum of his achievements minus his expectations.

If that is the case my happiness is now well into negative territory.

May 19th

I was called again to see Hercules Figbotham. A passing drayman left a note requesting my attendance, informing me that the squire had tried to shoot his gardener with his shotgun.

In the note, the housekeeper said that she thought that the Squire was disguised in liquor but with the advantage of several years of medical education behind me I couldn't help wondering if the unfortunate fellow might not be suffering from a mental disorder of some kind.

When I arrived at the house, Mr Figbotham was standing on the roof, stark naked, and singing hymns. He refused to come down until I promised that he could have a Plumb Pudding for his supper and a quarter of a pound of Pigtail Tobacco to smoke afterwards. When I had promised him these things, he completed the negotiations by adding that he also wanted a hogshead of Cyder all for himself.

After he had climbed down, which he did with surprising ease, I settled him down with a large draught of Laudanum, which he drank without any hesitation.

I instructed the housekeeper to make a Plumb Pudding and obtain the Tobacco and the Cyder lest he wake up and be disappointed by their absence. I also strongly suggested that the squire's shotgun be hidden in a cupboard.

May 24th

Mr Josiah Rossetti, a lawyer and acquaintance of mine suggested that I needed a hobby and said he thought I should take up fishing. He lent me an old rod and suggested that I try fishing in one of the ponds in the grounds of his home. He said the largest pond was well stocked with fish and was home to several magnificent pike.

This afternoon I decided to try my new hobby but after spending an hour sitting beside the lake I was bored. Not wishing to tell my acquaintance of my failure, I hired a passing labourer to sit beside the pond and do my fishing for me. I told him that I would pay him tuppence for every fish he caught, up to a maximum of three.

When the man came to my room at the Peacock Inn and handed me three fish, I happily paid him the sixpence I owed. I was so delighted that I took the fish along to Mr Rossetti's home to show him my catch.

'Did you catch these in one of my ponds?' demanded my friend. I fancied I heard a note of scepticism in his voice.

I said that I had.

'But these are mackerel,' said Mr Rossetti, after glancing at the fish.

'Are they?' I said. 'I fancied they might be pike.'

'They are mackerel,' insisted Mr Rossetti with what I fear sounded like a smidgeon of a sneer. 'They are salt water fish.'

For a moment I was stuck for an answer.

'It has been very windy recently,' said Mistress Rossetti who was standing nearby and who had been listening to the conversation. 'Maybe the fish were blown off course and landed in our pond by mistake.' Mistress Rossetti, who is at least 20 years younger than her husband is a delicately featured girl who has masses of blonde curls and who always reminds me of a bisque doll.

Her explanation sounded convincing to me but Mr Rossetti seemed to be sceptical.

I don't think he and I will ever be anything more than acquaintances.

No true friend would have been prepared to make me look foolish in front of his wife.

May 29th

Mistress Clarissa Humbug died. She negotiated the final stages of her life as though picking her way through a bed of nettles. But however ill she has been she had never stopped working. She took in washing and dealt with several bundles of the stuff every day. She was also renowned to be the fastest potato and strawberry picker in the county.

When she had gone I stood on one side of her Bed with her husband standing on the other.

He looked at me and there were tears in his eyes; they were flowing down his cheeks and dripping onto the Bed coverlet. A tear splashed onto his dead wife's wrist.

'Who is going to look after me now?' he whined pathetically. Mr Humbug is a selfish, lazy boor and I stared at him, finding his raw expression of self-pity difficult to believe.

'She did everything,' he explained, as though an explanation were necessary. 'She did the shopping, the cooking, the cleaning and the washing. She dug the garden and mended the clothes. She chopped and brought in the firewood and cleaned out the fireplace.' He stared at me, almost accusingly. 'So who is going to do those things now, eh? Who is going to look after me?' He stared at his Wife and there was anger in his eyes. 'You had no right to up and go and leave me!' he said. He clenched and raised a fist and for a moment I thought he was going to hit her but slowly he unclenched and lowered the fist.

'I'm sorry for your loss,' I said softly. 'She was a hard-working woman.'

Mr Humbug, who could not have been described as a hard-working man, looked across at me, as though noticing me for the first time. 'Do you know where she kept the cyder?' he demanded. 'I could make short shrift of a pint of cyder.'

I admitted that I did not know where Mistress Humbug had kept the cyder and without saying anything else I left the bedroom, the house and, I hoped, Mr Humbug's life. The wretched fellow has been a wastrel all his life; a parasite living off his wife's labours.

I shall have to find some way of getting in touch with the Humbugs' six children. There are three girls and three boys. The girls are called Brie, Camembert and Roquefort, after French cheeses, and the boys are named Stilton, Wensleydale and Cheddar after English cheeses. I do not know why this should be but I can only assume that one or other of the Humbugs had a stirring penchant for cheese.

The children all left home before they were 15 years of age and rarely reappear though I believe that Camembert was seen at the house last Mothering Sunday.

June 2nd

The eldest Humbug boy sent word that neither he nor his siblings would attend their father's funeral. He has changed his name from Stilton to Gloucester. I sent a message back pointing out that it was their mother who had died. The boy replied that it didn't matter who had died, they would not be returning for the funeral.

Deaths in the village appear to be coming thick and fast.

Old Figbotham finally worked out how to die. I have no doubt that he and his former housekeeper will both be relieved.

June 5th

It is some time since I was visited by Constable Blomfield and sold him the massive suppository which I had originally made as a pessary for Mistress Wiltshire's voluminous cock alley.

Since then I have found myself suddenly rising curiously popular with the male members of the local community – a surprising number of them wanting me to provide them with one of the special suppositories I had given to the Constable.

It appears that, quite contrary to my request that he keep quiet about the remedy, Mr Blomfield has spread the word of his treatment further and wider than I had envisaged.

The first to turn up in the surgery was Mr Josiah Rossetti, the lawyer who embarrassed me when I turned up at his house with three fish which I claimed to have caught in one of his ponds – the ones which I thought were pike but which he claimed were mackerel.

'I've come for one of those enhancement things you sold Constable Blomfield,' he whispered. 'To, put up the back passageway in order to increase my orgasm storehouse.'

I told him that I was afraid that I didn't have any more of the suppositories available but that if he really wanted one I'd make one up especially for him. 'It'll cost you a guinea,' I warned him. (Since he was an acquaintance, I'd have charged him half a guinea if the scrunch bowelled bastard hadn't mortified me in front of Mistress Rossetti.)

'That's all right, Doctor,' said Mr Rossetti, without turning a hair. 'Constable Blomfield did say it would be a guinea for a treatment to give me 100 priggings. Is that right?'

I said it was.

He took out his purse, which I could not help noticing was surprisingly full, and pulled out a guinea piece. He looked at it, thought for a moment and took out a second coin. 'I'll take two of them, please,' he said. 'That should last me two months.' He thought again and removed a third coin. 'And I'll take a third one for a good friend of mine,' he added.

I told him to come back the following day to collect the three Arsefills.

When he'd gone, I looked at the three coins for a moment, and jangled them together, before putting them into my waistcoat pocket. Such wealth!

And before the clock had struck noon, two more men and three gentlemen had come into the surgery requesting the very same thing. I took their guineas and dropped them into a waistcoat pocket. At this rate I would need to buy myself a decent purse or have my waistcoat pockets enlarged and strengthened.

I spent the rest of the day, and a good part of the evening, making up more suppositories.

I contemplated making these smaller than the first one I'd produced but decided that if I made them smaller, the patients would probably be disappointed. It occurred to me that the pain and trouble involved in manipulating a rather large suppository into a rather narrow opening, and subsequently into and along a confined space, might well be part of the mystique. So I made these suppositories just as large as the original one had been. After all, pain and fear give us humility, humanity and understanding and these are the very essence of civilisation.

No medicine ever works as well as one which looks and tastes foul – as though it had been mixed by Shakespeare's witches in a particularly venomous mood.

June 8th

Mistress Clarissa Lambert, the butcher's Wife, came to the surgery and after subjecting me to an ache by ache description of her corns that lasted a full twenty minutes and would have weakened the tedious Mr Thackeray's resolve, finally came to the point.

'My nipples are too small,' she complained, producing the two items for my consideration. She did this almost as if by magic.

I told her they looked perfectly healthy and aesthetically acceptable but she was not convinced, reporting that her husband said they were so small that he couldn't find them in the dark. Eventually, I told her to dip her nipples in a saucer of cold gherkin water for twenty minutes every evening before bed.

'I don't think I'll be able to get both nipples in one saucer,' she complained.

I told her to use two saucers or to dip the nipples consecutively rather than concurrently.

She seemed bewildered by the choice so I told her to use two saucers and dip the two nipples at the same time.

She went away well pleased with this suggestion and since I had not dispensed any medicine and am not by law allowed to charge for a mere consultation, she offered to send round two fowl and a string of sausages a yard and a half long. I thanked her and told her that this would be most satisfactory.

Mr Pippin Babberley, my next patient, is a bachelor who works as a Drummer for a corsetiere. He is of medium height but still manages to look as round as a football. He complained of a mole on his chin but since the mole had obviously been in position for the whole of his life (45 years if he was to be believed, though he looks a good decade and a half older) it was clear that this was not the real reason he had come to the surgery.

'What else is on your mind?' I asked, having had my offer to remove the mole with a sharp knife declined.

The man frowned. 'How did you know there was something else on my mind?' he asked, clearly impressed.

'I have a small skill in the area of clairvoyance,' I told him. It is, I think, always wise for a Doctor to retain some elements of mystery and one has to do everything within one's power to retain an air of superiority.

Mr Babberley went a little pale.

'Have you ever been out to dinner and been disappointed by the fare on offer?' he asked.

I confessed that I had attended one or two dinners which had been disappointing.

'Or gone to a dinner where they serve portions that wouldn't satisfy a blowfly? You spend the evening feeling hungry and by the time you get home you're ravenous. You'd eat a chunk of stale bread and a piece of mouldy cheese?'

I laughed and nodded.

'I have to go to a good many dinners in my line of work,' said Mr Babberley. 'There are business dinners and dinners with customers. Sometimes I go to three or four of the damned things in a week. It's where I do a good deal of my business.'

I offered a little sympathy.

'But a year or two ago I found a solution to this continuing problem,' he told me. 'Before I go out to dinner I eat my ordinary meal.'

'You have your dinner before you go out to dinner?' I asked, astonished.

'Exactly.'

'Don't you find you're too full to eat the second dinner?'

'It depends,' replied Mr Babberley. 'If the second dinner is good I can eat it and enjoy it. But if it's dull, badly cooked and unappetising I just move the food around on my plate and leave it without feeling hungry.'

I nodded. It did not seem such a daft idea after all.

'Well, six months ago I took that philosophy into another area of my life,' said Mr Babberley.

He paused, as though uncertain as to how to continue with his tale. I nodded encouragingly.

'I am a bachelor, Doctor, but I have the needs of a married man. I travel a good deal and have never found myself able to settle down, acquire a home, a dog, children and a wife.'

I did a little more of the nodding which seemed to be serving me so well.

'In my line of work I meet a good many ladies,' continued Mr Babberley. 'Some of them are single, some of them are widowed and some of them are married.'

'And you romance some of these ladies?'

'I do, sir, I do,' said Mr Babberley. 'And from time to time I receive a proposition which I find irresistible.'

'Is there a problem with this?' I asked him.

'Even at my age I still find it difficult to know if the evening is going to reach a successful culmination,' said Mr Babberley. He paused. 'If you know what I mean.'

I said I thought I did know what he meant.

'And when an evening fails to reach the high point to which I had previously aspired, I find myself a little let down.'

'Frustrated?'

'Exactly!' cried Mr Babberley, clearly pleased that I understood his predicament.

'And you are hoping that I can offer some solution to your problem?'

'Oh no, thank you, sir. I have found the solution myself.'

'Ah,' I said, thinking that the solution could not have been too difficult to come across.

'You remember what I was telling you about going out to dinner?'

'I do indeed.'

'I have been following a similar route in order to avoid any possible frustration resulting from my romantic encounters.'

'You have a meal before you meet a woman?'

'No, sir, no sir. I found a more appropriate solution. I hire myself a Whore for half an hour before I go to meet the lady,' said Mr Babberley. 'I find this reduces any sense of frustration but it also dampens expectations, makes me less desperate and helps if the evening doesn't work out quite as hoped. Strangely, it also seems to increase my chances of success with my companion.'

'Your lack of desperation is perhaps enticing?'

'I think that may be the case, sir. The ladies, feeling that they are not being pursued with sufficient vigour, may themselves become the pursuers.'

'You seem to have found an excellent solution to a unique problem,' I said.

'I thought so, Doctor,' said Mr Babberley. 'Unfortunately, one of the Whores with whom I consorted turned out to be less fresh than I might have hoped.' He stood up, pulled down his trousers and brought out on display the most unpleasant looking member it has been my misfortune to view. The whole thing was as covered with warts as Cromwell's face.

'What can you do with this?' he enquired. 'I've tried everything I can think of. I've rubbed it with a raw radish and I've rubbed fresh pig's Blood onto it. I even rubbed a piece of raw beef over it and then buried the beef.'

I nodded wisely. I never fail to be surprised by the nature of the remedies favoured by my patients. Radishes indeed! How the devil does a fellow rub a raw radish on his twiglet?

'Can you help?' he asked.

'I can indeed,' I assured him. I gave him a mixture of acetic acid and tincture of steel and told him to rub the liquid on each of the warts in turn.

'How often should I do it?'

'Twice a day for three days,' I told him.

'It smells of vinegar,' he said, taking the top off the bottle and sniffing.

'Indeed,' I said. 'It is but a coincidence.'

He paid me a guinea and went away happy.

June 15th

Queenie Nelson, a local Whore who was sitting on a stool at the bar, suddenly turned and slapped William Bacon full on the face. The sound of the smack sounded like a pistol shot.

'What the devil was that for?' demanded William, who now had the imprint of the Whore's hand on his right cheek.

'You squeezed my Arse as you passed behind me!' complained the Whore.

'So what?' demanded William. 'It was hanging over the edge of your stool.'

'You shouldn't do that!' complained Queenie. 'Not unless you've paid.'

'Why the devil not?' demanded William.

'Yes, why not, it's big enough for squeezing!' demanded Thaddeas Prout, who was sitting nearby.

'She's got her future behind her!' said someone else.

'He shouldn't have done that should he?' said Queenie to Mr Youngblood, who was behind the bar.

'What the devil are you talking about?' replied Mr Youngblood. 'Why shouldn't he squeeze your bum if he wants to? Maybe he was just sampling the goods? There's plenty of Arse to be squeezed.'

Everyone laughed at this except Queenie who slapped Mr Youngblood's face.

Mortified, Queenie's husband, who was sitting on the stool next to her, told his Wife to go home, find his largest belt, sit in the kitchen with her Arse bare and await his return. She slunk off in shame. Mr Youngblood, his face quite red where Queenie's hand had connected with his cheek, called to the magistrate who was sitting in a Chair by the fire and demanded action.

The magistrate, Lumpy Darbyshire, looked up and immediately sentenced Queenie to be put in the stocks for the day. Mr Darbyshire used to be a mourner but unexpectedly came into a small estate and a sum of money and was in consequence recently appointed a magistrate.

It was widely agreed that the magistrate had been unduly lenient and that this was a result of the fact that he had drunk two bottles of port and one and a half of malmsey.

June 16th

The beating of Arses seems to be all the rage at the moment. When I arrived at Dr Challot's house I found Mistress Swain sobbing and howling in the hallway. She was rubbing her posterior and, given the size of the feature, this was an activity which required some considerable expenditure of effort.

'The Doctor has a brittle sore head this morning!' she managed to say when I asked her what ailed her.

'What's wrong with him?'

'I've no idea. He has his coach whip with him. He chased me round the kitchen five or six times and beat my poor Arse more times than I could count. They were good smacks too. There'll be wheals there. I shan't be able to sit for a week.'

I have never had any affection for Mistress Swain, nor indeed she for me, but I was shocked by this revelation. Dr Challot has never been known for the undue beating of women.

'Look!' she cried, and without warning she pulled up her skirt and several petticoats and, holding them aloft with the one hand used the other to pull down her pantaloons. 'You're a Doctor. Tell me what you see!'

For a moment or two I was so startled that I could not bring myself to speak. The sight of Mistress Swain's naked posterior was not one for which I had prepared myself. I was as full as a goat and began to wish that I had eaten a smaller breakfast and had, in particular, eaten a few less sausages and eschewed the second helping of pigeon pie. But I could see that the wretched woman was not exaggerating for the success of Dr Challot's ministrations was clear to see; the twin white expanses of Mistress Swain's more than ample buttock cheeks were marked with singular red stripes where the coach whip had scorched the dimpled skin. There were some flecks of Blood along two of the stripes.

'Do you see?' she asked.

'I do,' I confirmed.

'Am I marked? My cheeks? Has the whip left marks?'

'It has,' I agreed.

'Oh my, oh my,' said Mistress Swain. 'Whatever will he say?'

I told her that she could cover herself and she pulled up her pantaloons and allowed her petticoats and skirt to drop.

'I don't expect he'll say anything,' I said. I had never known Dr Challot apologise or express regret for his actions.

'But he'll say something when he sees the marks upon me,' insisted Mistress Swain.

'Don't show him,' I suggested.

'Don't be daft!' she said. 'How can I avoid him seeing?'

I frowned. I was puzzled. 'Just don't show him!' I repeated. 'Keep your pantaloons up and your skirt down.'

'And just how is the poor devil supposed to find his way into cock lane with my skirts down and my pantaloons up?'

'Dr Challot?' I said, startled. I was genuinely startled by this thought. It had never once occurred to me that Dr Challot might be rogering Mistress Swain. Indeed, I confess it had never occurred to me that anyone might be rogering Mistress Swain.

'No, you young fool!' she said with an unpleasant loud snort. 'Mr Youngblood.'

'Why would Mr Youngblood want to find his way…' I stopped as I suddenly realised the implication. 'You are being rogered by the innkeeper?'

'Once a week for seven years,' she said, not without a certain pride. 'And he will not be pleased to see stripe marks on my lilywhite Arsc.'

'Couldn't you perhaps wait until dark?' I suggested. 'Or somehow keep him from seeing the part with the marks?'

She thought for a moment. 'Won't be easy,' she said. 'But I suppose…if…'

I left her contemplating ways to hide her soundly marked Bottom from her lover and entered the drawing room wherein I found Dr Challot pacing up and down the room hitting items of furniture with his coach whip. Two small walnut Tables and a mahogany torchère had been tipped onto their sides. A vase lay on the floor, shattered into a hundred pieces.

'What the devil's the matter?' I demanded.

He turned to face me and his face was purple with rage. 'I was tricked!' he said. He raised the whip as though about to strike me with it. I picked up one of the small walnut Tables which lay on the floor and held it aloft in my defence. I remembered having seen a lion tamer confront a beast with a Chair when the circus last came to Muckleberry Peverell. 'Tricked!' he repeated. 'Tricked by a damned Baker!'

It was without doubt the fact that he'd been tricked by a Baker that annoyed him as much as having been tricked.

'Who's tricked you?' I asked. 'Mr Standish?'

Mr Theobold Standish was the only Baker I could call to mind. He and his Wife run the bakery in Muckleberry Peverell. He is an old fellow but a striking man; proudworthy, tall and well-built and now well into his forties. His wife, a diminutive body, is meek, like a mouse and has a soul which seems corroded by anxiety. He bakes the bread and buns and she deals with the customers.

'Yes, that bugger Standish.'

'How did he trick you?'

'He owes me a guinea and a half for the operation I performed on him six months ago.'

I remembered the operation. I had assisted Dr Challot by helping to hold the Baker still. It had been a tricky operation for the Baker was a powerful man who did not take kindly to being restrained; it was, I remember, as tricky as trying to catch a dead spider in a bath tub full of water. We'd had to bring in two men from the stables and even they hadn't been enough to hold him still. In the end, Dr Challot had brought in Mistress Swain and told her to sit on the fellow's face so that he could not breathe. Within a minute and a half the hapless fellow had become unconscious.

'We should use you more often,' I remember Dr Challot telling his plentifully endowed housekeeper. 'Your fat Arse would make a splendid sedative.'

'Has he not paid his bill?' I asked.

'He refused to pay!' said Dr Challot, his face becoming increasingly purple.

Standish had, I recalled, been kicked by a horse and left with a fracture of his left leg. A bone below the knee had broken through the skin and amputation had been the only possible answer. We had removed the wretched man's leg and arranged for him to be provided with a wooden replacement carved by Onions, a local carpenter we invariably used for the purpose. Onions made most of the wooden limbs we fitted and Phineas Turner, a competent Saddler made the leather cup and straps to hold the limbs in place.

(Turner does good work when he is sober so it is always important to make sure that he does the work required of him before midday. We also knew not to buy anything from him which was made on a Saturday since he always get fearsome drunk on Fridays and everything he made on a Saturday would invariably fall asunder well before the following Monday.)

I could understand why Dr Challot was annoyed. We'd had to pay the two men from the stables a farthing each. It was true that we'd sold the amputated leg for a farthing to the Sheriff, who keeps four wild boar as pets and always needs cheap food for them, but that still meant that we were out a whole farthing.

'Have you threatened him with a whipping?' I asked.

'Have you seen the bugger?' demanded Dr Challot indignantly. 'Even with one and a half legs he's a powerful fellow. He's as big as the Blacksmith and twice as unpleasant.'

Dr Challot had a point. Standish was a formidable looking man. All the kneading of bread had given him arms like hams. He could have taken on the Blacksmith in an arm bending contest.

'So couldn't you come to some arrangement?' I asked. 'He must have something you want?'

When patients could not afford to pay his bill Dr Challot often took payment in kind or in some other material way. He had two pigs and half a dozen sheep in the field behind the house and Langford, one of the smallholders in the village had been bringing in a cartload of Turnips every month for as long as I could remember. I couldn't even remember what Langford's debt was for. I don't think Dr Challot could remember either and it's quite possible that Langford himself had long ago forgotten why he delivered the free Turnips. It was the paying of this debt which explained why my diet had consisted almost exclusively of Turnips for so long.

'I did come to an arrangement,' replied Dr Challot. 'The damned Varmint has three Daughters and I agreed to take two of them in exchange for the debt.'

'Ah!' I said, nodding.

Two of the Baker's Daughters were comely enough, though since their father was a Baker and they had unlimited access to his wares they were rather on the plump side, but the third, even plumper, had no teeth, a wall eye and ears like jug handles. I'd heard that Standish used to rent her out for half a farthing a time and even at that price she was no bargain. 'Didn't he keep his side of the arrangement?'

'He tricked me!' insisted Dr Challot. He whipped two vases off the mantelpiece and sent them crashing into the hearth. 'He sent the jug-eared one as half the pair though I expressly demanded the other two.'

'That must have been annoying,' I agreed.

'She has no teeth so she wasn't entirely useless,' said Dr Challot, reflectively. 'I closed my eyes and wrapped a scarf around her head.'

'Very wise,' I agreed.

'I asked for the three but he bargained me down to two,' said Dr Challot. 'And the rogue double tricked me.'

'How?' I asked, now definitely not understanding.

'This morning the Daughters dressed, put on their bonnets, thanked me and headed for the stairs,' explained Dr Challot. 'I'd understood that they were a sale not a loan and so I locked them in my bedroom. And at ten o'clock sharpish there was a banging on the front door and Standish was there demanding the return of his property.'

'He thought he'd merely loaned them to you for the night?'

'He did! He did! Can you imagine the impertinence?' demanded Dr Challot. 'Those two were hardly worth a guinea and a half but I thought I could hire them out as 'nurses' for a year or two when I wasn't using them. But as a loan the two together were not worth a fourpenny piece for the night.'

I could now see why Dr Challot was in such a bad temper.

'You didn't have anything in writing?'

'I trusted the fellow!' said Dr Challot. He stared at me. 'Go round there and demand the return of the wooden limb we had made for him. I paid a shilling and sixpence for that.'

'He hasn't paid for it?'

'Not a penny for anything! He said I could have the one with the jug ears for another four Wednesday nights but he wouldn't budge further than that. You have to go round and get the limb back. When he's standing on one leg he might be a touch more amenable.'

'I'm not going round there,' I said.

I knew the strength of the Baker. It was true that on one leg he would be hampered, and it might be possible to push him over, but I'm not as big a fool as I was when I was younger and I wasn't going to be the one to try unbuckling the wooden limb.

'You're a coward!' shouted Dr Challot.

'You can call it cowardice,' I retorted. 'But I call it self-preservation. I know the strength of the fellow.'

With that I left the room. Behind me I could hear the still furious Dr Challot whipping yet more innocent furniture. I closed the door.

'Is he still in a rage?' asked Mistress Swain.

'If he emerges from the drawing room I strongly recommend that you put a breadboard down your pantaloons,' I told her.

I returned to the Peacock Inn and ordered a plate of jellied eels and a bottle of malmsey. I hope I manage to persuade Dr Challot to part with some wages soon for my bill at the Peacock must be mounting at a rare pace.

I do sometimes despair about my employer's lack of any sense of morality. To confiscate a man's wooden limb because he has failed to pay a debt might be entirely reasonable for a lawyer or a tailor but seems to me to show a lack of compassion venturing fearful close to unacceptable in a medical man.

June 20ᵗʰ

Tobias Blomfield, the dray driver (and younger brother of our local Constable), came into the surgery and announced that he was so depressed he was thinking of killing himself. 'I have a darkening mulligrub and am determined,' he told me. 'I am going to cut my throat.'

'That will produce a fearsome amount of Blood,' I told him.

'You think so?'

'A large amount. Tell me why you want to kill yourself. Then we will discuss how I can be of help?'

'You will help me?'

He seemed surprised.

I explained that on the Greek island of Cos, citizens who had valid reasons for ending their lives were invited to state their reasons in public. If the reasons given were sufficiently convincing, a local magistrate would give them a cup of hemlock and invite them to drink it in public. I thought that if I offered to help him kill himself he might lose his enthusiasm for the idea.

He told me he thought his Wife was being rogered by the Vicar.

I sympathised but was not surprised. Mistress Blomfield, a keen member of the congregation, has a reputation for flirting and the Vicar has a reputation for more than flirting.

'Who told you this?'

'Queenie Nelson the Whore,' Mr Blomfield replied. 'She mentioned it last night when I was paying her.'

Mr Blomfield had clearly not heard the phrase about the sauce, the goose and the gander.

'Do they still put a stake through a suicide's heart?' asked Mr Blomfield. 'My uncle killed himself and they put an oak stake through his heart. It was his eleventh attempt and he was beginning to think of himself as something of a failure.'

'No, I don't think so,' I assured him. 'Do you love your wife?'

'Not at all,' replied Mr Blomfield. 'But it's a matter of pride.'

'Have you spoken to her about your suspicions? Have you confronted the Vicar?'

'No, I haven't,' admitted Mr Blomfield. 'I've spoken to neither of them.'

'But you want to kill yourself?'

'I've been thinking of it.'

'And you want my advice on the best way to go about it? When were you thinking of doing it?' I opened my scalpel case and put it out on the desk.

Mr Blomfield seemed surprised, even startled by the sight of my scalpel case. 'Well, I might not do it just yet,' he said. I opened the scalpel case. Mr Blomfield stared at the open scalpel case and started to fidget. He was suddenly rather keen to leave.

'Maybe you should have a word with the Vicar before you go any further with this,' I suggested. I rather fancied the idea of the Vicar being confronted by an aggrieved Blomfield.

Mr Blomfield said he agreed that was a good idea. He then hurried off.

I hope I will hear no more about his plans to kill himself.

June 22nd

I have been teaching young Nellie, the Maid at the Peacock Inn, how to read and write for some little time now.

To my astonishment and delight, she is already capable of reading short passages of text from the latest instalment of the current monthly serial by Mr Charles Dickens. I had previously purchased this for my own entertainment and I had lent it to her. She picked up the rudiments of reading and writing in no time at all and has turned out to be as smart as a whip-mark. Who would have guessed it? She has reminded me that I now owe her a Sovereign for I recklessly promised to pay her this if she learned to read and write.

'Where does Mr Copperfield live?' she asked me.

I explained that the story she was reading had been made up by Mr Dickens and that none of the people described in the book actually existed. She was rather alarmed by this revelation for she had been so taken with the tale that she had almost come to regard the people as friends and was genuinely looking forward to being able to meet them one day. The realisation that she would never be able to talk to such well-drawn characters as Steerforth and Peggotty upset her. However, she brightened up when I explained that next month there would be another instalment of Mr Dickens's story and that she would, in consequence, be able to continue reading about these people's lives.

'So he makes up all the things he writes about?' she asked.

I admitted that was the case.

'So he is telling lies?'

'In a way you could say that,' I agreed. 'But it is generally agreed that when an author writes a story which is untrue he is behaving quite within normal moral boundaries. A lie which an author tells in the prosecution of his profession is no more than a taradiddle.'

'Has Mr Dickens written about other imaginary people?' she asked. 'If so I would like to read about them too.'

I showed her a copy of a book called *Pickwick Papers* which I had in my possession and also a copy of a book called *Vanity Fair* by Mr William Makepeace Thackeray. She was much taken with the fact that the heroine of *Vanity Fair* is a young girl called Rebecca Sharp though I explained to her that Miss Sharp was a girl of rather low character and almost no virtue and therefore not one to seek to emulate. As I said this I suddenly remembered that Nellie had not led a blameless or sin free life and that her regular Saturday evening dalliances with the Reverend Standorf had hardly been conducted out of love but, rather, for the small sums of money which she had earned by sharing her affection. I took back the copy of *Vanity Fair* and suggested, instead, that she read *Pickwick Papers* when she had finished with the current instalment of *David Copperfield*.

Nellie's writing too has come on apace and she has learnt to copy out sentences and paragraphs from *David Copperfield*. She has a readable and mature hand which is very legible and does not look in the slightest unsteady or untutored.

I am beginning to realise that she has more of a future than one might expect from her previous experience of making fires and Beds and emptying Bed pans.

She has assured me that she no longer shares the Vicar's Bed and that she has, indeed, abandoned that part of her life completely.

June 27th

Mr Blomfield, the Constable's brother, came to see me again. He said that he had confronted the Vicar about his alleged relationship with Mistress Blomfield.

'He has agreed to pay me sixpence each time he sleeps with my wife,' said Mr Blomfield.

'And you are happy with that?'

'Oh, yes,' replied Mr Blomfield. 'I think that's a very decent, very fair price. And since Queenie Nelson only charges tuppence I will be well in hand.'

Mr Blomfield says he now has no intention of killing himself. Indeed, he seemed in a very good humour and, thanks to the compensation he is receiving, has clearly come to terms with being a cuckold.

June 30th

I was called to see Sir Ebenezer Biddulph who is, I believe, a nephew of Baron Biddulph of Bloxwich.

The footman brought a note explaining that I was being summoned because Sir Staple Fitzgaine-Bickenhall, (a member of the Royal College of Physicians) was away treating one of the Queen's cousins.

When I arrived, the Butler made me go to the back door before he would let me in. I was moderately offended by this. Sir Ebenezer's family made their money out of coal and have no real reason to lord themselves over everyone else.

He (the Baron, not the butler) has a dusky complexion (his mother was reputed to be a Moroccan dancing girl) and a voice crammed full of privilege and inherited money. He screamed at his servants and told me that it is the only way to get them to work well. He boasted of eating two large bowls of onion soup every evening for his supper. It is perhaps no surprise that Dr Challot (not famed for his sense of humour) once described Sir Ebenezer as a dark and windy knight.

'I'm thinking of adding another wing to the house,' he drawled boastfully. 'But where do I put the damned thing? I've got a west and east wing. I could put a north wing on the east wing I suppose.'

The house already has 34 bedrooms and I cannot imagine why he could possibly want more.

Sir Ebenezer complained of colic, headaches, a rash on his upper leg, toothache and the need to get up five times a night to pass water. I feel he has been storing up ailments so as to get the most out of a single consultation. I told him he needed a good Blood-letting to take the strain off his organs and got my revenge for being forced to use the tradesman's entrance by removing three pints of his Blood and spilling most of it on the carpet.

Although disgustingly rich, Sir Ebenezer is renowned for failing to pay his bills and so I refused to leave the house until he had paid my three guinea fee. He grumbled a good deal but was fuzzled and enfeebled by the Blood-letting and so I was able to insist that he parted with the coins.

July 2nd

This morning I received a call to visit Miss Euphemia Standorf who is the only Daughter of the Reverend and Mistress Standorf. The Reverend Standorf, whom I had never met in person, is, of course, known to me as a skin-close acquaintance both of Nellie, from the Peacock Inn, and of Mistress Blomfield.

The Reverend and Mistress Standorf have two sons, both huge, hard drinking fellows who have only half a brain between them and who mould themselves on the memory of John Mytton, a wild hunting man whose legendary, disrespectable activities they ape with relish. There are no other Daughters. It is, perhaps, for this reason that Euphemia is the Apple of her mother's eye. (The Vicar's Wife has only one eye. The other eye was lost many years ago in a hunting accident which involved an errant Bloodhound, a temperamental stallion and a blackthorn bush.)

I am moderately acquainted with the family and have no doubt that Euphemia has some good qualities but she seems to me to be the most snobbish person I have ever met and any good qualities she might have are well hidden. She is reputed to have once demanded smelling salts after an Ostler at the Lion Inn had the temerity to address her directly. Jokes have to be deconstructed and explained to her in such detail that any humour which might have been present is completely removed.

Physically, she is quite possibly the ugliest brute of a woman I have ever laid eyes on. She has a broad, high forehead, a chin that juts and a nose that is more than a little reminiscent of Mr Punch. She is a large woman, in width if not in height. A visitor who complimented her on the size and shape of her bustle was shocked and confounded when assured that she was not wearing one.

'We asked Sir Benedict to call,' said Mistress Standorf, the Vicar's Wife and Euphemia's mother, when I arrived. 'Unfortunately, he was unable to come. His secretary sent a message to say that Sir Benedict is attending to an ailing Duchess at the Palace.'

It seems that the local physicians spend a good deal of their time attending to members of the Royal Family. The only safe conclusion is that the Royal Family are not, on the whole, in the best of health.

'So, we had to call for Dr Challot,' said Mistress Standorf, making it quite clear that they regarded this as shamefully unsuitable to their station.

I nodded.

'And Dr Challot was also unavailable.'

I agreed with this. I did not consider it seemly to mention that Dr Challot was unconscious with drink and lying in Bed with two drunken strumpets for company. When I left, the three of them had been snoring loud enough to awaken the long dead.

I find myself taking on more and more of the responsibilities for the practice and my daily life is full of confusions and necessary deceits. As a result, my hours are ruined by baseless anxieties dragged forward from yesterday and backwards from tomorrow, tomorrow's tomorrow and ad infinitum. Some days I feel that the weighty responsibilities I am expected to bear are too much for a young practitioner with relatively little experience. I had hopes that Dr Mort might take on some of the practice responsibilities but we have not seen hide nor hair of the fellow since our first meeting.

'So it appears that we must make do with you,' said Mistress Standorf.

'I fear so,' I agreed.

'Oh but he looks much younger and more agreeable than Sir Benedict,' said Euphemia. 'And I cannot abide Dr Challot. He always smells of cheap wine and whatever may ail me he always insists that I unbutton my blouse so that he can examine my globes.'

'Euphemia!' said her mother sharply. 'You should not use that word in mixed company.'

'But this gentleman is a Doctor,' said Euphemia. 'He must be aware that ladies have globes or bosoms. I only mentioned Dr Challot's peculiarity because last time he visited he insisted on examining my globes at some length even though I was complaining of a pain in my foot.'

'Maybe Dr Challot thought that your upper parts were affecting your foot,' said her mother. 'I believe that the human body is more complex than we non-medical folk may sometimes realise.'

'What is the problem?' I asked, anxious to get to the heart of the problem before the day had dribbled away in a meaningless discussion of Euphemia's globes. 'How can I be of service to you?'

Euphemia giggled a little and pointed to her chest. 'I fear that this time an examination of my bosom might be entirely necessary,' she said. 'I have a cough and I suspect that my poor lungs may be suffering from what I believe is called congestion.'

Feeling rather embarrassed after the previous comments about Dr Challot, I invited Miss Euphemia to loosen her upper garments so that I could place the listening end of my Stethoscope upon the various parts of her chest.

The undressing took twenty minutes or so and I was required to act as a ladies Maid and to assist in the untying and unhooking of some of her under garments. These were rather voluminous and made of a variety of calico of a strength and thickness usually associated with the variety of canvas favoured for the manufacture of military tents. Underneath Miss Euphemia's dress there lay five petticoats, a crinoline cage, a camisole bodice, a corset cover, a boned set of stays, and a linen chemise.

Once the various layers of clothing had been removed, I performed the necessary percussion and auscultation and made a determination of congestion of the chest cavity. As I had been taught, I naturally decided to apply Leeches to counteract the difficulty. Bleeding really is the only logical answer to congestion.

My original determination was that Euphemia's condition was an ailment requiring twelve Leeches but applying the first eight to her bare back proved so troublesome, and so fraught with unwanted excitement on her part (I had never known a Patient become so excited at the application of the Leeches), that I decided that eight Leeches would be acceptably sufficient, particularly since the Leeches I had selected were the best Blood-hungry suckers I had available; all being nicely fresh and thirsty for refreshment. Unfortunately, the Leeches were slow to start sucking and Euphemia's congestion made no immediate improvement.

Things were complicated by the fact that Mistress Standorf, who had entered the room to act as chaperone just as I had finished assisting in the unrobing process, had fainted and was lying on the floor.

She later claimed that she had been overcome with emotion when she had seen me helping to undress her Daughter. However, I had doubts about Mistress Standorf's claim to have fainted since when she subsided to the carpet she did so rather slowly, first lowering herself onto her knees and then onto her back, and somehow managing to make sure that she had a soft cushion neatly positioned beneath her head to act as a pillow. This display of the vapours did not seem to me to be the normal way for a fainting personage to collapse onto the floor. Before 'fainting', she also managed to ring the bell for a Maid and when the Maid arrived, Mistress Standorf instructed her to stand behind a screen so that she could hear but not see the proceedings.

With the Maid in position, Mistress Standorf cried out several times, saying things like: 'Woe, woe is me for I am fainting and cannot see what is happening to my poor Daughter'; 'I am fainted and waffy and my Daughter is unclothed and in the hands of a young man – forsooth she is ruined unless they marry' and 'The shock to my system is such that I am collapsed and unable to protect my Daughter's reputation'.

Foolishly ignoring this strange display, which I mistakenly and innocently took to be nothing more than a mild case of the hysterics, I decided to take out my cupping apparatus to supplement the Leeches.

However, on seeing the cups and the heating equipment Miss Standorf began to shake with terror. I therefore abandoned this plan and took my scarification knives out of my bag, taking care to ensure that Miss Standorf did not see what I was planning to do. I was rather proud of the scarification equipment I was using at the time for the device I had selected consisted of no fewer than 16 spring loaded blades – all designed to cut into the skin at the flick of a single lever.

Unfortunately, despite my best efforts, Miss Standorf caught sight of the Scarifier and her response was immediate and considerable.

'Oh my, oh my,' she cried. 'Oh I think I shall faint at the thought of it. It is so much larger than I anticipated. Indeed, the thing is so large that I do not think I shall be able to bear you putting it into my body. But if you feel you must plunge it into me you must feel free to go ahead and do what you will with me.'

Having decided that scarification was a necessary accompaniment to the Leeches I set the Scarifier in action.

'Oh, my!' she cried. 'My how it hurts at first.'

'It will be easier in a moment,' I assured her.

'It seems so painful. The moment of the first pricking sends my whole body into a state.'

'It is to heal you,' I told her in my most reassuring voice. 'And it will go only a little way into your body.'

'Oh you must not worry yourself about my feelings,' said Miss Standorf. 'You must put it into me as deeply as you feel necessary.'

To my surprise she began to hyperventilate and to moan and make a great deal of noise. 'Oh Mama,' she cried, turning towards the place where she had last seen her mother, 'I thought I would faint at the start but I am being brave am I not? It is a monstrous large thing and it hurt to start with but as it goes deeper so I am getting accustomed to it.'

She moaned a good deal more and raised her arms and cried out once or twice. 'Oh, Mama, it is not as painful as it was at the beginning. Oh my word, I feel a warmth all over my body. I am shivering with excitement. It is a very strange feeling. Have you ever experienced anything like it, Mama? It is not at all unpleasant.'

'Oh my, oh my Good Lord, oh my,' said a strange voice. I looked around but could see no one.

When I put away the Scarifier, took the Leeches from Miss Euphemia's body and wiped off the Blood with the cloth I keep for such purposes, she began to sob a little. I had a little difficulty wiping away the Blood since the cloth I was using was rather thick with crusted fluids of one sort or another.

'Oh, thank you, Doctor,' said Miss Standorf, reaching out and grabbing my leg. 'That was quite wonderful. You have worked wonders upon my body. I feel a new person already.' She squeezed my thigh with a grip which could have burst the pips from a lemon.

'Oh my, oh my,' said the strange voice again. This time when I looked around I saw the Maid peeping around the edge of the screen.

Miss Standorf's mother, who had, until this moment been seemingly unconscious, suddenly made a most remarkable recovery. She leapt to her feet, coming to her Daughter's side and helping her to re-clothe. As she struggled with a myriad buttons, bows and mysterious little catches, Mistress Standorf looked at me with her one eye and I felt most uncomfortable. (Mistress Standorf has a glass eye in lieu of the eye that is missing and it is such a good replacement that I am never truly able to tell which eye is the real one and which is the glass one.)

The Maid, a toothy creature of indeterminate years, had been instructed to emerge from her hiding place in order that she might also assist with the dressing of Miss Standorf and she now gave me a very strange look. She had eyebrows which looked as though they had been knitted out of several dozen spiders.

'I suggest that you lie still for a while,' I told Miss Standorf. 'You should relax for an hour or two. It has doubtless been a tiring experience for you.'

'Oh, indeed I will need to rest,' said Miss Standorf with a contented sigh. She reached out and took my hand. 'Oh thank you Doctor. That was most wonderful. I was but a child before but you have made me a woman now.' She lifted my hand and with a grip of iron placed it on her full bosom. 'Feel my heart!' she instructed me. 'How it pounds does it not? It is your doing.' I tried to remove my hand but she added her other hand and I found the force of her two hands impossible to overcome. She lowered her eyes and looked at me in what was, I suspect, supposed to be a coquettish way but which merely managed to draw attention to her wall eye. 'If you feel that you will need to repeat this treatment I think I will be brave enough to allow you whatever access to my body you may feel you require.' She paused. 'No,' she said after a moment's thought, 'I will definitely be ready and available to you. You have opened me and I shall never be closed to you.'

'Oh I think one treatment should be sufficient,' I told her hurriedly.

'Maybe later this evening,' she suggested, ignoring my remark. 'I shall without doubt be sufficiently rested by then and available once more to you. Or you may assuredly come at any time tomorrow. I will assuredly be at your disposal whenever you feel the need. You must do with me what you will. My body is your slave in this and any other matter. Indeed, I shall lie abed and await your coming.' She turned to her mother. 'I don't think there will any need for you to chaperone me now you are aware of Dr Bullock's generous intentions, do you, mother?'

'If you think not,' said Mistress Standorf. She paused and examined me again. Once again I wasn't sure which eye was looking at me and which was merely sitting there in her eye socket, as unseeing as a child's marble. 'I am sure we can trust the Doctor now that he has made his intentions so vividly apparent.' She looked at me with an intensity I found more than a little unnerving. 'I will have a word with the Reverend Standorf.'

It was at that point that I began to feel that there could be problems lying ahead.

As I descended the Vicarage staircase, the Maid who had been in the room during my treatment of Miss Euphemia walked beside me.

'I am cursed with the same condition as my mistress,' she murmured, unbuttoning her blouse, apparently in readiness. 'Would you recommend the same treatment for me?'

She seemed perfectly well as far as I could tell and she was certainly not suffering from congestion of the lungs. I apologised and told her that my Leeches were too full to be of any use for another day at least.

She did not seem well pleased but in any case I could not think it likely that she would have the wherewithal to pay for treatment.

July 6th

'You need to be at the Feathers Inn in Snodbury Parva this afternoon,' said Dr Challot. 'You'll be needed there for most of the afternoon. Take half a stone of goose fat with you. If you need more goose fat the local Vicar will find it. He will provide you with all the eggs you need. We were only asked to supply half a stone of fat.'

Puzzled, I asked him why I needed to take so much goose fat.

'To put on the burns,' explained Dr Challot, as though talking to an idiot. 'And remember to pour egg whites on really badly burned bits to relieve the pain and stop the screaming. Just the whites, mind you. Put the yolks into a cup and bring them back with you.'

'I know how to treat burns,' I retorted. 'But why are we expecting so many burns?'

'Because it's Burning Trousers Thursday,' replied Dr Challot, once again as though he were speaking to a complete idiot. 'Dr

Branwell Jones, the local practitioner is in Bed ill. He has a recurrence of his meaditis and can't attend.'

'Meaditis?'

'He's drunk too much mead. He brews the stuff himself and it's twice as strong as anyone else's. His Wife sent a message with their coachman to say that he fell out of Bed last night and she can't move him.'

'Do I need to call in to see him?'

'No, no. He'll wake up in a day or so. If he doesn't recover we'll bury him, say a maudlin goodbye to a fellow practitioner and take over his practice.'

'Do we get paid for attending this event?'

'There's an attendance fee of a Sovereign. Make sure they pay as soon as you arrive.'

I assured him that I would do this. 'But what the devil is Burning Trousers Thursday?'

'The villagers hold it every year. It used to be held on the first Thursday after Epiphany,' said Dr Challot, his voice dripping with disdain. 'But it always rains in January and you can't hold a burning trousers race in the rain so a century or so ago it was moved until a date later in the year. It's one of those mad pagan festivals. The villagers at Snodbury Parva have been doing it for four centuries and they're all so stupid over there that if any of them survive that long they'll doubtless be doing it for another four centuries.'

He paused, sighed and shook his head.

'There's a lot of in-breeding there,' he said thoughtfully. 'Since 1750 everyone in that village has been related to everyone else. These days brothers marry sisters with impunity for there's no fresh Blood available for miles around. I know of two Daughters who married their fathers. Still, none of this is of any account other than that it helps explain why there are so many idiots in Snodbury Parva.'

Dr Challot explained that the Burning Trousers tradition had begun in 1456 when the local Vicar, a man called the Reverend Sheldean Pearce, fled a house fire and ran, with his trousers ablaze, along the main street before diving into the village horse trough in an attempt to extinguish the flames. Although it took place at night, the Clergyman's run along the main street attracted a number of spectators. The poor fellow died a week later of substantial burns and the event was celebrated the following year when a Patient from the local lunatic asylum responded the local Publican's offer of free mead to anyone who repeated the run. The lunatic, known to posterity only as Daft Davy, soaked his trousers with tar and deliberately set fire to them before racing along the same route that the Reverend Pearce had taken all those years ago, before plunging into the same horse's trough. Local lore has it that the idiot managed to drink fourteen free pints of mead before succumbing to his burns. The publican more than covered the cost of this inducement since many of the spectators retired to the Feathers Inn to refresh themselves.

Not surprisingly, given the fact that the village was full with folk whom it would be wildly over-generous to describe as half-wits, the event has become a tradition. Once it has started, an English village tradition is impossible to Stamp out, however ludicrous and dangerous it might be. The only change that has taken place over the years is that these days there is no limit on the number of contestants.

Such oddling events are quite commonplace throughout England.

The villagers of Ottery St Mary in Devon have been carrying burning tar barrels through the streets since 1605. The citizens of Gloucestershire have been engaged in annual shin kicking contests since about the same time, and shin kicking is one of the most popular events at the Cotswold Olimpick Games. Burnt skin and bruised shins are considered a negligible price to pay to preserve proudly sustained English traditions.

Every community in the country seems to have its own curious, local practices.

Here in Muckleberry Peverell we celebrate the exploits of Guido Fawkes on November 5th and on May Day there is Maypole dancing but we also have our own special and, I believe, unique traditions.

So, for example, on the eve of the Winter solstice every year we celebrate Duck Apple Night. And we celebrate Old Florrie's Night every May 18th.

On Duck Apple Night a hundred apples are thrown into the River Florrie and local men have to dive in and retrieve as many as they can before the apples disappear over the weir and are lost in the lower reaches of the river. Since the event is always held in

December, the river is invariably in full flood and there are usually one or two drownings.

On Old Florrie's Night, three young male virgins are stripped naked and tied to sycamore trees on the edge of the churchyard. Local female virgins are invited to throw old eggs at them. Eggs are stored for a month or so before the night and the stench afterwards is pretty dire. I confess I have never seen much point in this particular event since there are no prizes and no punishments but the event is more popular than you might imagine. Every year, there are some noisy discussions about the entitlement of some of the egg throwers. On several occasions it has been suggested by critics, usually anonymous, that unsullied virgins wishing to throw eggs should be required to produce medical certificates proving their status and, therefore, their right to take part. On more than one occasion there have been slaps and hair pulling after the event when woman have been accused of taking part when they had no right to be throwing eggs. Last year, a woman who was betrothed to one of the targets became incensed when a disappointed rival had thrown eggs at her fiancé, clearly aiming at an area twixt waist and knees, and had caused considerable injury in consequence of having come supplied with two dozen hard boiled duck eggs as ammunition. This was strictly against the rules.

Another year, a fellow who was hit by a stone (painted white to look like an egg) needed a considerable amount of stitching. I remember him because after I stitched him up I discovered that the fellow had no money. After Dr Challot threatened to remove the stitches, his grandmother eventually paid us two pigeons, a small bottle of home-made lavender water and a sack of green logs.

Still, hard boiled eggs notwithstanding, we don't have anything quite as reckless and hazardous as Burning Trousers Thursday.

Dr Challot, who told me that he had stood in for Dr Jones, the local Physician, on two previous occasions, explained that the event is now open to all men over the age of 14 and that the race takes place between the Lychgate outside the Church of St Gwenn of Quimper and the horse trough in the village square – a distance of approximately three furlongs.

The burning house from which the original run took place was never rebuilt and the Lychgate is the nearest site available.

'The stupid bastards cover their trousers with tar and stand in a line,' explained Dr Challot. 'Behind each of them there stands a woman with a lighted taper – usually a Wife or a mother believe it or not – and when the Huntsman blows his horn, the tapers are applied and the trousers are set alight. The men all race up the street in an attempt to reach the horse trough before any of the others. The first one into the trough wins the race and suffers least. The losers must rely on being dowsed by having bucketsful of water thrown over them.'

'Do any of the competitors ever die?' I asked.

'Not so many these days,' admitted Dr Challot. 'There are invariably a couple of Deaths but these days the men of the local fire brigade stand ready at the finish and have their buckets filled with water. Six years ago there were no Deaths but that, I think, was something of an anomaly and may have had something to do with the poor quality of the tar which was used to soak the trousers.'

'And is there a prize?'

'The winner receives half a hogshead of watered beer and a new pair of red velvet trousers,' replied Dr Challot. 'The red velvet trousers are surprisingly much prized and the winner can usually be seen wearing them for years after the event.'

And so I set off for Snodbury Parva with my churn of goose grease, a heavy heart and young Nellie who came with me for the day out and brought a loaf of bread, two pounds of cheese, a pound of butter, some fruit and two bottles of cyder. (I had given her a shilling for these victuals.) Nellie, clutching our pique-nique in a large basket, rode upon my horse while I walked beside.

'I feel a proper lady,' said Nellie who confessed she had never ridden a horse before. She had borrowed a bonnet from Saphire Swain, the Daughter of Mistress Swain who is a Whore, and rather to my surprise it occurred to me that to the unknowing eye Nellie looked every inch a daphlean and not in the slightest a bawdy or a marmulet.

The Burning Trousers Thursday event was something of a disappointment for those for whom the smell of burning flesh acts as an amuse bouche. One of the competitors had the notion of thoroughly soaking a pair of long under-trousers in water and wearing them underneath his burning breeches and he was either generous enough to share this secret with his fellow competitors or naïve enough to allow them to discover his secret ploy.

Only two of the competitors spurned the idea of wearing wet under garments and the result was that very little flesh was burnt. Sadly, the two who had run their race with burning trousers, but without water-soaked under-things, were two of the slowest in speed as well as in wit and they both suffered severe burns below their waists. I smothered the burns with goose fat but both men developed the shivers and collapsed. One of these unfortunates died that evening and I heard the following morning that the second had also succumbed to his burns.

Despite these disappointments (it was generally agreed that soaking under-garments in water was out of order and three days later the Organising Committee disqualified all those who had protected themselves in such a way, leaving one of the deceased competitors to be crowned the victor) Nellie and I had a splendid day out. We found a quiet spot by the river for our pique-nique.

As I was handed my fee of a gold Sovereign, the Chairman of the Organising Committee congratulated me on my engagement to Euphemia Standorf. Since this was the first I had heard of the engagement I was rather taken aback. He then congratulated me on having such a good looking mistress.

I was about to correct him but when I saw the look of quiet delight on Nellie's face as being described as my mistress rather than my maid I could not spoil such a splendid day with a cruel denunciation.

However, the gossip about my engagement to the Vicar's sloomy Daughter rather spoilt an extremely pleasant day.

July 12th

The Duke and Duchess of Beaufort came through Muckleberry Peverell and caused considerable excitement.

An advance party consisting of an Under Butler and two Assistant Footmen arrived two hours before the Main Party in order to make arrangements for a stop for Luncheon. The Duke and Duchess themselves were travelling in a procession of five coaches, with a total of 24 members of staff in attendance.

The landlords of the two local Inns had been most assiduous and desperate (some would say quite pathetic) in their attempts to persuade His Grace's Under Butler, a snooty young fellow of around 25 years, that their establishment would offer the best facilities.

Mr Oliphant, the proprietor of the Red Lion Inn, promised that he would provide a private sitting room, without charge, and a seven course meal for one and a half guineas a head with Alcoholic Refreshments included in the price. He also offered to make his stables available to the Duke's coachmen for a knock-down price of half a guinea a horse (this being, in truth, something akin to ten times the price he would have charged any ordinary traveller not of the nobility).

Representing the Peacock Inn, Mr Youngblood responded by promising the travellers a free sitting room for the Duke and the Duchess, a free bedroom (in case the Duchess wanted to rest a while), another dining room for the travelling staff and a nine course meal for a modest one guinea a head with wines, beers and spirits at usual prices. His price for horses was also half a guinea a beast.

I was present in the Snug during the negotiations and heard Mr Youngblood, a crafty fellow if ever I knew one, offer a modest cash inducement of five guineas in gold pieces to the Duke's Under Butler if the Peacock Inn was selected for the stopover. When the Under Butler seemed to be wavering, Mr Youngblood called over his wife, who had changed into her lowest cut gown, and it was clear that she was being tossed in as an extra inducement and offered to the Under Butler as an incentive.

When the arrangements had been agreed (and the Peacock Inn selected for the stop) one of the Assistant Footmen rode back to the main party to pass on instructions to the coachmen.

Everyone waited for the Ducal party to arrive.

When the Duke and the Duchess finally arrived at the Peacock Inn, they climbed down from their coach and, with hardly a moment's delay, passed straight into the Inn. This was much to the disappointment of an assembly of locals who had gathered to gape. Two young people whom I did not recognise, both of whom were the same sort of age as Dr Mort, had brought scraps of paper and pencil stubs with them so that they could record the moment for posterity. The young man was tall and very skinny. The girl who accompanied him was short and very skinny.

In a blatant attempt to garner attention, Mistress Swain, who had kicked and pushed her way to the front of a small crowd in the Peacock Inn's courtyard, waved both hands and yelled 'Hello Your Duchessness!' while assaying a most ambitious curtsey. The waving and the curtseying unbalanced her severely, which resulted in her falling backwards into a puddle of mud. The fall, accompanied by a loud splash and a flurry of disordered petticoats and other miscellaneous and unidentified undergarments, caused Mistress Swain some considerable annoyance and not a little embarrassment but provided the assembly with a very great deal of amusement.

During all this excitement, the two who had brought pencils and paper continued to sketch away. Afterwards I looked over their shoulders and saw to my astonishment that each one had drawn themselves watching the Duke and Duchess disembark from their coach. The Duke and Duchess, being in the background, were hardly visible. 'Why have you drawn yourselves?' I asked them both. Initially, they seemed startled by the question which clearly puzzled them. 'I will make copies of my drawing and send them to my sisters and cousins,' said one as though this were an explanation. He dug into his jacket pocket and pulled out a neatly folded piece of paper. He unfolded it and showed it to me. It contained a drawing of a young girl standing in front of a large building. 'What is it?' I asked. 'The girl is my sister Effie and the building you can see behind her is St Paul's Cathedral.' The building was hardly visible.

'Do you do this sort of thing a great deal?' I asked.

'Oh yes,' replied the young man.

'We're always looking for new experiences,' said the young woman.

'And when you find something interesting, do you always make drawings of yourselves standing in front of it?'

'Of course,' said the woman. 'There would be no point otherwise, would there? We have to prove that we were there.'

Our bizarre conversation was interrupted by Mr Youngblood who came hurtling out of the Peacock Inn as though the place were on fire. 'Oh there you are, Doctor!' he cried. 'Thank heavens I've found you.' He paused for a moment with his hands on his knees, trying to get his breath. 'You must fetch Dr Challot immediately.'

Mr Youngblood was wearing his grey, curly second hand wig, the one he bought from a judge's widow for two shillings. He looked as if he ought to be appearing in a comedy by Molière, the French playwright.

'Is someone ailing?' I demanded.

'The Duchess does not feel well,' replied Mr Youngblood. 'Her Maid says she has been taken poorly. You must fetch Dr Challot.'

As he spoke, the Duke's Under Butler came down the stairs buttoning up his trousers. He had a huge grin on his face and his eyes seemed glazed.

I was, I confess, more than a little offended by Mr Youngblood's instruction that I should fetch Dr Challot. I pointed out that I was already present and that since I was a qualified Doctor I was perfectly capable of attending the Duchess by myself.

'Her Maid says that two Doctors are required,' said Mr Youngblood who had taken his hands off his knees and was now wringing them. He seemed to be so distressed that he was close to tears 'Apparently, the Duchess always sees Doctors in pairs,' he added. I suppose he was upset at the prospect of the Duchess actually dying in one of his rooms. Feeling sorry for him, I said that I would fetch Dr Challot and bring him back with me.

'Hurry, Doctor,' pleaded Mr Youngblood. He paused, and you could almost hear his brain ticking over. 'I'll have something very special sent up to your room this evening.' As he spoke, Mistress Youngblood came down the stairs. She looked very hot and flushed and was trying to arrange her hair which had come undone. I could not help noticing that the top three buttons of her blouse were all unfastened and the remainder were in the wrong buttonholes. It looked as though she had dressed in haste.

It was thirty minutes before I returned with Dr Challot. It took me most of that time to sober him up and help him dress.

'What the devil is the hurry?' he demanded as two of his nurses pulled on his trousers while I helped him into his shirt. I didn't recognise the two nurses and didn't have the faintest notion what their names were. There is a high turnover among Dr Challot's resident nurses. He seems to tire of them easily and ruthlessly discards used nurses in the way that other folk discard soiled and unwanted bandages.

'The Duchess of Beaufort is asking for two Doctors.'

'What's wrong with her?'

'I haven't the faintest. All I know is that she is demanding two Doctors.'

'A Duchess, eh?'

'Yes.'

'How much do you think we can charge a Duchess?'

'Doesn't it rather depend on what's wrong with her?'

Dr Challot rolled his eyes and looked at me despairingly. 'Have I taught you nothing?' he demanded. 'With a Duchess it doesn't matter what's wrong with her! Whether she has a hangnail or a broken leg we can charge her the top rate.'

'What is the top rate?' I asked.

'Ten guineas,' he replied. 'At least ten guineas.' He attempted to button his trousers. 'There's two of us so that's twice times ten guineas.'

'Twenty guineas?'

He looked at me admiringly. 'Do you think so? Twenty definitely sounds better than ten. We'll make it twice times twenty guineas.'

'No, I meant…' I began, trying to explain.

'That's 40 guineas,' he said.

'We cannot possibly charge 40 guineas!' I protested.

'Of course, if we have to go back again that'll be another forty guineas,' said Dr Challot. 'Does my breath smell?' he asked, breathing heavily into my face.

'It does,' I replied, when I had finished coughing and spluttering. His breath stank.

He turned to one of the nurses. 'Go out into the garden and pick me a bunch of mint.' The nurse pulled on a filthy petticoat and hurried off barefoot to complete the errand.

'Do you think we should take the nurses with us?' Dr Challot asked me. 'It might make us look more professional. We could charge extra for them? Another five guineas apiece do you think?'

The eyes of the nurse who remained lit up. 'Five guineas?'

'Half a guinea for you,' said Dr Challot quickly. 'The five guineas is a professional fee to be charged before expenses.'

I looked at the nurse. She looked to be in her mid-twenties and was stark naked. She stood with hands on hips and posed proudly, attempting to push out a very large bosom as though offering it for inspection and possible sale. 'If the Duchess doesn't need us perhaps the Duke will,' she said with what I suspected was an attempt at a pout.

'Good idea,' said Dr Challot. 'You two get dressed and we'll send for you if we need you. Try to wear something that looks clean and respectable.'

'I haven't got anything clean and respectable,' said the nurse. 'Nor has Florrie. You'll have to give us money to buy something new.'

With a sigh and great reluctance, Dr Challot took a two shilling piece out of his pocket and tossed it to the girl. 'That's for both of you,' he said sharply. As he spoke, the first nurse, whose name was apparently Florrie, returned holding a bunch of sage leaves.'

'I said mint!' said Dr Challot, examining the sage which he'd been handed.

'What are we supposed to buy for a shilling each?' demanded the nurse with the two shilling piece.

'Try Hector Nodorf's junk shop. Tell him you want something smart and fashionable.'

It seemed to me unlikely that the two nurses would find anything clean, respectable, smart and fashionable in Hector Nodorf's junk shop but you never know.

'And remember that I don't want you coming back with something that makes you look more like a couple of Whores than you are.'

'Very nice, I'm sure!' said the first nurse, pulling a face.

'What does mint look like?' asked the second.

'Oh, it doesn't matter,' said Dr Challot. 'There isn't time.' He stuffed a fistful of the sage leaves into his mouth and chewed them. He turned and breathed into my face, still chewing on the sage leaves. 'What do I smell of now?'

'Stuffing,' I replied.

The two nurses giggled.

'Better than smelling of cyder, I suppose,' sniffed Dr Challot. He pulled a face and spat the chewed leaves out into one of the disposable spit bottles which stood on his side Table. We had never managed to sell more than half a dozen of them and now had stocks of the damned things stored all over the place.

The two of us then hurried off to the Peacock Inn to attend to our important patient.

'Have you ever treated a Duchess?' I asked him, as we walked.

Dr Challot thought about it for a moment. 'I've treated a couple of baronets,' he said. 'And an MP.'

'But no Duchesses? No Dukes?'

'I don't think so,' admitted Dr Challot reluctantly. 'But underneath their fancy clothing, they're just the same as everyone else but richer, aren't they?'

'What do we call a Duchess?' I asked. 'Your highness? Your eminence? Your grace? Your graceless? Your majesty?' I wished we had Dr Mort with us. He would have known.

'Don't have the faintest,' admitted Dr Challot with a shrug. 'I shall simply call her Mistress Duchess.'

'Do we bow?' I asked. 'Mistress Swain tried to curtsey when she saw the Duke and Duchess arrive at the Peacock.'

'I'm not bowing for anyone,' said Dr Challot firmly.

When we got to the Peacock we were met in the doorway by Mr Youngblood who was, if anything even more nervous than he had been when I'd left him.

'Where have you been?' he demanded anxiously. 'The Duchess's Maid has been down at least six times to see where you were!' I could hear screaming but it seemed to be coming from the stables.

'We're here now,' said Dr Challot, making an effort to stand firmly upright and to enunciate clearly.

'Good Lord, what have you been eating?' demanded Mr Youngblood, catching a face full of Dr Challot's breath as he burped rather loudly.

'Sage,' I explained for him, as he added a second burp to the first as though in competition with himself. 'Freshly picked sage leaves.'

'If you wanted to cover up the cyder why didn't you chew some mint leaves?'

There didn't seem to be any point in trying to explain.

'Well, are you going to stand here gossiping or are you going to take us up to our patient?' demanded Dr Challot, who had finished burping and, in view of the fact that he was about to become a Doctor to the aristocracy, was now overflowing with a new sense of importance. I could tell he was already thinking of how best he should advertise his new position. Maybe he would have a coat of arms placed above the doorway? Or, perhaps he would confine himself to a new set of visiting cards with 'Medical Advisor to the Duchess of Beaufort' inscribed in gold.

'Who is that screaming?' I asked Mr Youngblood.

'One of the Duke's coachmen has fallen and broken his leg,' replied the landlord as he ushered into the inn and up the stairs. 'And he has been kicked in the groin by one of the Duke's horses. Perhaps you'd take a look at him afterwards? He seems to be in a good deal of distress? You can hear him screaming.'

Dr Challot and I paused on the stairs. I couldn't help feeling sorry for the fellow. A coachman with a broken leg doesn't have much of a future.

'Something has to be done!' I said, listening to the screams. 'I'll go and see if I can do something to assist the poor fellow.''

'No, no, no!' cried Dr Challot. 'Her Highness requires two Doctors and two Doctors she must have.' He turned to Mr Youngblood, the hapless landlord, who was no doubt by now wishing that he had allowed his rival to win the right to look after the Duke and the Duchess. 'Go and stuff a rag in the coachman's mouth,' he snapped. 'I can't be treating the Duchess with that row going on. We can find our own way upstairs. Which room is Her Majesty in?'

'Certainly, Doctor,' said Mr Youngblood. 'The Duchess is in the second bedroom on the right.' He hurried off to find a rag with which to silence the coachman's screams.

'That's my room!' I called after him as I suddenly realised the significance of what he'd said.

'I needed all my rooms,' replied Mr Youngblood, over his shoulder. 'I'll only charge you half price for today's board.' And with that he was gone.

Moments later we were standing outside my bedroom. A flunky dressed in a red and gold uniform and wearing a powdered wig was on guard.

'Dr Challot and Dr Bullock to see Her Majesty,' said Dr Challot.

The flunky didn't say a word but tapped on the door. Half a second later the door was opened by a worried looking Maid. 'Are you the Doctors?'

Dr Challot replied that we were, indeed, the Doctors.

'Come in,' said the Maid. She turned to the flunky. 'Tell the innkeeper to send someone up with a menu so that His Grace can decide what he wants for supper.'

Without a word the flunky nodded and disappeared.

'Her Grace is in a lot of distress,' whispered the Maid. 'She thinks that she has perhaps been rather shaken about in the carriage.' I looked around the room and could see none of my possessions. A very large man wearing an absurdly large wig was sitting on a Chair at my writing Table. And a very large woman in a silk dress was lying on top of my bed. I couldn't help noticing that she hadn't even bothered to remove her boots.

'Ah, that's a problem with which we are well versed,' said Dr Challot. 'Most of our patients do a lot of travelling about by coach.' He somehow managed to sound both pompous and ingratiating at the same time.

'Are you the Doctors?' enquired another woman, whom I assumed to be a more senior Maid. She was considerably older than the first one and would clearly not see 30 again. Her dress seemed a good deal more expensive. She was as thin as a post and had a golden pince-nez pinned to her dress with a gold chain. She had a large and well-presented bosom with generous grounds.

'We are,' replied Dr Challot. 'I am Dr Challot and this is Dr Bullock. Are you Her Majesty's Maidservant?'

'I am Lady Honoria Wellbeloved,' replied the woman, clearly put out. 'I am the Duchess's Lady of the Bedchamber and Personal Secretary.' She talked as though she had her mouth full of curried eels and when she moved she did so tentatively, as though she had a prize winning courgette stuck up her bum and was frightened that it might fall out.

'Beg your pardon, your majesty,' said Dr Challot, who had gone very red. 'Forgive our error.' He reached to remove his hat, realised he wasn't wearing one, and bowed so far down that I feared he might never be able to rise again. I followed his example and bowed, though with rather less enthusiasm.

'Her Grace is suffering from a problem with the very lowest part of her lower back,' said Lady Wellbeloved.

'I'm so sorry to hear of it,' said Dr Challot. 'May we examine her Grace?'

'I will enquire,' said Lady Wellbeloved. She moved a few paces closer to the Bed and addressed the Duchess. Although we were standing only a few feet away I couldn't hear what was said.

'You may approach,' she told us eventually, after much muttering.

We approached my Bed and I could see that the woman lying on the coverlet was even older than I had at first suspected. She had what looked like half an inch of make-up on her face and her hair was pinned in such an extraordinarily complex way that I suspected it must have taken an hour or two to prepare.

'Would your Grace be kind enough to share with us the details of her discomfort?' asked Dr Challot, holding his hands together as though praying.

'She's got an attack of her damned flaming piles,' roared the Duke suddenly. 'Haemorrhoids. Her arsehole looks like a basket of ripe raspberries. She's had 'em for years – caught 'em from sitting on cold saddles when out hunting. They always get worse when we travel. It's all the bouncing about. She sits on six cushions but it makes no damned difference.'

'Oh dear,' said Dr Challot. 'I am sorry to hear of it. May we look?'

'Look at her piles? Of course you can if you feel the need and the idea takes your fancy. Can't imagine why you'd want to, though. Seen one set of piles you've seen 'em all in my view.' He turned to his Wife the Duchess and ordered her to pull her dress up and her under-things down.

'What the devil was all that screaming about downstairs?' he demanded.

'One of your Eminence's coachmen appears to have broken his leg,' said Dr Challot, apologetically.

'Is that all? Hell of a lot of noise for a broken leg. Some of these people never think of others, do they?'

'I believe he was also kicked in a delicate part of the body by one of your Highness's horses.'

'Well he was making a lot of noise about it.' The Duke paused, and cocked an ear as though listening. 'He seems to have stopped, thank God.'

'I instructed the landlord to put a rag in the man's mouth,' said Dr Challot.

'Damned good idea,' said the Duke. 'Why the devil didn't someone else think of that?' He thought for a moment. 'Though, it might have been quicker and easier just to shoot him.' He paused as though thinking. 'We don't shoot enough people in this country,' he added.

Dr Challot looked very pleased with himself and the praise he had received.

'Could be dashed inconvenient,' continued the Duke, who had clearly now had time to think. 'Will you have to take his leg off? Can he drive a coach with one leg? I was only planning to stay here for a couple of hours. How soon will he be fit to drive the coach? Damned thoughtless of the fellow to break his leg when it's dashed most inconvenient. Why couldn't he break it yesterday when we were back at the Palace? Can I get a replacement?' demanded the Duke. 'Are there are any spare coachmen around here or do we need to send back for one?'

'Oh I feel sure that it will be possible to find a spare coachman,' said Dr Challot, responding quite well to this barrage of questions. 'I haven't seen him yet so I don't know if we'll have to remove the leg.'

'Well, we'll get a new fellow,' said the Duke, making a decision. He turned to a man in a military uniform, a fellow I had not previously noticed. 'Take the uniform off the useless coachman and put it on the new one. Just find a fellow that fits the uniform.' He thought for a moment. 'And if there's Blood on the uniform make sure it's washed off. I can't abide coachmen with Blood on their uniforms.'

'Certainly, your Grace,' said the military man. He saluted and clicked his heels.

'And if the fool with the broken leg survives make sure he's horse whipped. That should teach him a lesson for being damned inconvenient.'

'Certainly, your Grace. I will see to it myself.'

Just then there was a tap on the door. The door was opened and Mr Youngblood entered. 'I've come to take the food order,' he told Lady Wellbeloved.

'I'm rather shy of exposing my lower regions to strangers,' said the Duchess, clearly addressing her husband. She was lying on her stomach and she now pulled her pantaloons back up.

'They're Doctors!' roared the Duke. 'They see lower regions all the time. I'd show 'em my lower regions without a qualm.' He stood up and tried to unbutton his trousers but fell back into his Chair. A valet standing nearby rushed forward and rushed back again when he saw the Duke had settled safely back down.

'Still…' said the Duchess.

'Turn yourself over and pull your things down,' ordered the Duke. 'It's not as if any of these fellows are gentlemen!' He turned towards the door. 'Are you the fellow come to take our food order?'

I found the Duke's remark about us not being gentlemen rather insulting, though technically not inaccurate, but thought it better not to say anything in protest lest he have me shot or horsewhipped.

'I am, your Highness,' said Mr Youngblood. 'I am Mr Youngblood, landlord of the Peacock Inn. We met when you arrived.' He tried to bow but a complete failure to understand the principles required, added to by one wobbly knee and a pair of bowed legs, meant that the movement ended up more of a curtsey than a bow.

'Maybe the two medical men could both be blindfolded,' suggested Lady Wellbeloved.

Dr Challot and I looked at her and then at each other. 'Oh, I don't think that…' began Dr Challot.

'Seems fair enough to me,' agreed the Duke. 'The pair of 'em can examine the raspberries by having a feel of 'em. No need to look at 'em as well, is there? Are you happy with that Agnes? Do you object to the fellows having a feel of your regions?'

'No, no,' said the Duchess. 'That would be perfectly acceptable.'

Lady Wellbeloved walked across the room to a small travelling trunk and removed two long strips of white linen. She handed one to each of us. Realising that these were the blindfolds we were supposed to wear I wrapped mine around my eyes. I assumed Dr Challot had done the same.

'Have you got any venison?' demanded the Duke.

'Certainly sir,' said Mr Youngblood.

'We'll take a haunch of venison, three dozen oysters, a roast hindquarter of pig, half a dozen fowls, a fatted goose and a cold ham for nibbling. Have you got a good, large ham?'

'If you will stand on the two sides of the Bed I will place your hands on the Duchess's buttocks,' said Lady Wellbeloved. She took me by the arm and led me around the Bed so that I was standing on the far side of the Duchess. She took my hand and placed it on a round globe of flesh which I took to be one of the Duchess's buttock cheeks. As I moved my fingers across the hillock, I found myself touching another set of fingers and realised that my hand had met with Dr Challot's hand approaching from the opposite direction.

'You first,' I said, pulling back my hand.

'No, no, you first,' insisted Dr Challot.

'Hurry up!' snapped the Duchess. 'It's damned chilly in this godforsaken hovel. Winter draws on.'

'You've got no drawers on at all, my dear!' laughed the Duke. 'No drawers on at all.' He laughed at his own small jollity.

I replaced my hand on the Duchess's skin and explored until my fingers slid into the crack between her cheeks. It wasn't difficult to find the haemorrhoids. They were bigger and firmer than any I had ever previously encountered. As the Duke had implied they felt like a small basket of raspberries. I tried to squeeze a finger between the raspberries but the Duchess struggled away from my finger with a series of little yelps.

'Oh yes, sir, we have venison,' agreed Mr Youngblood who was apparently either oblivious to what was going on across the room or was suppressing his curiosity with great effect. 'And for pudding?'

'Not done with me first course yet,' said the Duke. 'Bring me some rump beef, a large platter of mince pies and some frilled potatoes.'

'Certainly, your worship,' replied Mr Youngblood. He spoke as I think he thought a man should speak when addressing a Duke.

'Grace!' snapped the Duke. 'Say grace you fool.'

Mr Youngblood hesitated for a moment. 'For what we are about to receive...' he began.

'No, you blithering idiot!' cried the Duke. 'You address me as 'your Grace' not 'your worship'.

'Certainly, your Grace,' said Mr Youngblood.

There was a yelp from the Duchess.

'What are they doing to ye?' demanded the Duke.

'One of them is trying to push his finger into me rump's inner portions,' reported the Duchess.

I knew the digit in question wasn't one of mine so I assumed it belonged to Dr Challot.

'Do you like it or does it hurt?'

'It hurts like buggery!'

'Then tell the bugger to stop it,' said the Duke. He thought for a moment and repeated his instruction. 'Did ye hear that?' he demanded. 'A good jape, eh? Tell the bugger to stop the buggery.'

It was apparently considered that it was safe to show appreciation of this jollity and loud, appreciative laughter followed immediately.

'Is that the innkeeper you've got there?' asked the Duchess.

'He's taking the food order.'

'Is he blindfolded?'

'No, no, he's not blindfolded. He's just an innkeeper. I'll ask the beggar if he can see you. Can you see my wife's Arse from where you're standing?'

'Oh no sir,' said Mr Youngblood. 'Hardly at all.'

'There you are,' said the Duke. 'He can't hardly see your arse, though I'd have thought it large enough to see from the other end of the county.' He laughed loudly at his own remark. But this time no one else laughed, probably because they were not certain that the size of the Duchess's Arse was a suitable subject for general laughter.

'That's all right then,' said the Duchess, apparently appeased by the reassurance and untroubled by the Duke's playful remark.

'Have you got nice puddings?' the Duke demanded, now presumably addressing Mr Youngblood again. Being blindfolded meant that it was difficult to follow the path of the various conversations going on. 'Spotted dick? Something with treacle? A Plumb tart?'

'Oh yes, sir,' said Mr Youngblood. 'We can supply spotted dick, treacle pudding and a Plumb tart. And to drink? What would you like to drink?'

'Stop rushing me you idiot. I'll lose me train of thought. How is your spotted dick? Not too much dick? I like lots of spots. Decent sized ones too.'

'There are spots aplenty, your grace. I have received no complaints about the lack of spots and my good lady attends to the dick herself.'

'Good. I'll take a helping of that. And I want an apple tart too.'

'We have apple tart but I'm afraid we have no raspberries, sir. The raspberries are out of the season.'

'Damn your eyes I don't want raspberries. My Wife has raspberries. She's got more than enough raspberries for both of us. Bring us a pipe of port and half a dozen bottles of your best champagne.'

'Certainly, your Majesty, your Grace. I apologise. I thought I heard raspberries were mentioned. Where would you like to be served?'

'In here, you fool, in here, of course. Bring the food on trays.'

'Certainly, your Grace,' said Mr Youngblood.

There was a sudden squeak of surprise from the Duchess.

'The raspberries appear to have disappeared,' said Dr Challot.

The Duchess started to breathe a little more rapidly.

'There are no raspberries, I fear,' said Mr Youngblood. 'It is the wrong season for raspberries.'

The Duchess started to moan a little.

'Where did this moonling come from?' yelled the Duke. 'Him and his damned raspberries.'

'Is any of this food for your entourage?' asked Mr Youngblood, who was obviously slightly cumpuffled.

'Damn your eyes of course it aint!' roared the Duke. 'It's a snack for me, me Wife and me wife's Lady of the Bedchamber. They look like a pair of damned horses. Look like horses and eat like them.' He paused. 'Probably taste like 'em too!' He then guffawed loudly.

'And for the others?' asked Mr Youngblood.

'What others?'

'Your servants, sir? How would you like me to feed your servants?'

'Have you got soup?'

'Yes sir.'

'Something cheap and filling? What the devil are you moaning about Agnes? Is that Doctor fellow still playing with your raspberries?'

The Duchess continued to moan.

'The passageway now seems quite clear,' said Dr Challot.

'I fear that the Doctor may have inadvertently misapplied his fingers,' said Lady Wellbeloved, who sounded very close and was apparently standing near to Dr Challot.

'Has he indeed? Where's he misapplied them to?'

'I don't much like to say,' said Lady Wellbeloved.

The Duchess, although lying face down and stifled somewhat by the pillow, was now moaning much more noticeably.

'Ah! Is that damned fellow finger fiddling me wife's muff?'

'I believe so, your Grace.'

'I thought it sounded that way. You'd better take the damned blindfolds off 'em,' said the Duke. 'Need to let the fellow see what he's doing before he unbuttons his trousers by mistake.'

'We have Turnip soup, your Majesty,' said Mr Youngblood. 'I could serve it with bread. That makes a very filling meal.'

'That'll do very well. How much is the bread?

'Today's bread, very fresh, is tuppence a loaf, your Majesty.'

Lady Wellbeloved removed my blindfold. She had already removed the blindfold from Dr Challot who, I could see, appeared embarrassed and now had both hands tucked firmly behind his back.

The Duchess, who was plainly quivering and still breathing rather heavily, suddenly spoke. 'Why have you stopped your examination?' she demanded. 'Get on with it, Doctor. Get on with it.'

Dr Challot, with surprising reluctance, put his hand back onto the Duchess's buttock and slid it across towards the piles which I could now see for the first time.

'Not there, you fool!' said the Duchess. 'Back where you were.'

Dr Challot, his face now deep red with embarrassment, and no doubt fear, put his hand back where it had been and continued with the examination he had so recently interrupted.

'And yesterday's bread? How much is yesterday's bread?'

'A penny a loaf, your Majesty.'

The Duchess' moans now reached a crescendo.

'Haven't you finished fiddling with my wife?' demanded the Duke.

'Nearly done, I think, your Majesty,' said Dr Challot.

'Yesterday's bread will do fine. They can dip it in the soup. You don't have to give them fresh bread for that.'

'How many loaves?'

'Two will be plenty. And who was that woman who met us when we arrived?'

'Which woman would that be, your Highness?'

'Comely woman of a decent age. She wore a white frock with huge milk jugs hanging out of the top of it.'

'The woman with blonde hair?'

'Didn't notice the colour of her hair you fool. Does she have hair? Blonde you say? Just saw the jugs. Caught the eye. Could hardly miss 'em. A grand display.'

'That would be Mistress Youngblood, my wife,' said the landlord, not without a certain amount of pride. 'She is a well-developed woman.'

'Well send her up next time. She's a damned sight better looking than you are.'

'Certainly, your Grace.'

'And tell her not to keep going on about raspberries.'

'No, your Grace. Certainly not your Grace.'

'If I enjoy my snack I might roger her afterwards. Does she like a good rogering, your wife?'

'Oh yes, your Highness. She's very agreeable to a sound rogering.'

'Not got piles has she?'

'Oh no, your Highness.'

'Not got the pox?'

'Oh no, your Highness. She's very clean in all departments.'

'Splendid. If she stinks badly, tell her to have a bath. And find me another bedroom. It looks as if the Duchess is going to be using that Bed for the rest of the day. I like to have room to move about when I'm doing me rogering.'

'Certainly, your Highness,' said Mr Youngblood. He backed away until he reached the door. A Maid opened it for him and he scurried away. A moment later I heard him hurrying down the stairs.

'Has that damned Doctor done playing with my wife's muff?' demanded the Duke.

'I believe he has completed his examination,' said Lady Wellbeloved.

'I feel much better now,' said the Duchess. She sounded calm and relieved.

'So what are you going to do about my wife's damned piles?' demanded the Duke.

'May we consult, your Highness?' asked Dr Challot.

'Consult away. But hurry up and get on with it. Why does that landlord fellow wear a judge's wig? Is he a judge?'

'I don't believe he is a judge,' said Lady Wellbeloved. 'Although I suspect he may have purchased the wig from a judge.'

'Looks bloody silly on a Publican,' muttered the Duke. 'He's another fellow who needs to be shot.' He paused and thought for a moment. 'Damned fine looking wife, though.'

Dr Challot hurried round to the side of the Bed where I was standing. He was very red in the face and sweating considerably. I don't know whether this was through excitement, embarrassment or fear of retribution though there seemed no reason for fear that since the Duke did not seem to have been inconvenienced by his error. 'What do you recommend?' Dr Challot asked me.

'We could tie them,' I suggested.

I had read in a journal that one way to tackle haemorrhoids was to tie string or wire around them, thereby cutting off the Blood supply. The theory is that the haemorrhoids will eventually die and fall off.

'Too many of them,' said Dr Challot, illustrating his viewpoint with a shake of his head. 'There are too many piles and they're too large. What do you think of applying lesser celandine ointment?'

I said that I thought this seemed a good idea. Lesser celandine is also known as pilewort since it helps reduce the size of swollen piles.

'Two Leeches, a strong purgative and twice a day treatment with lesser celandine?'

'The Duke and Duchess won't be able to travel for two days if we use a strong purgative,' I pointed out.

'Good news for us,' whispered Dr Challot, who could obviously hear gold guinea pieces clinking into his pocket. 'We can visit four times a day. Four times a day for two days. Twenty guineas apiece so that's…'

'We could also try rectal dilation,' I suggested. It was a remedy I had read about in one of the new journals.

Dr Challot, who had clearly not heard of this remedy, frowned in confusion. I suspect he was trying to multiply forty guineas by four and then by two days.

'We push a small dilator in between the piles, take it out and replace it with a slightly larger dilator. We keep using larger and larger dilators until the Patient cries 'Enough!' or a large aperture appears and the condition is cured.'

Dr Challot looked doubtful. 'It sounds damnably painful! Does it work?'

'I don't have the foggiest idea. But Dr MacMillan, a fellow with a practice in Harley Street swears by it. He says that pain is the body's way of talking to the brain. He is something of a scientist and reckons that the dilation also cures insanity.'

'I'd rather my body didn't bother talking to me at all,' said Dr Challot. 'But I can believe it would cure insanity.' He thought for a moment and chuckled. 'But if it cures insanity we should stuff the largest one we've got right up the Duke's arse.'

Eventually, we agreed to dilate, use two Leeches, try a strong purgative and apply a specially prepared ointment of lesser celandine sold by a Drummer at a guinea a pot.

'Just make damned sure we don't lose the Leeches!' said Dr Challot. 'Put 'em next to the arsehole and they'll like as not disappear. Leeches cost too much to lose up someone's Arse – even if she is a Duchess.'

'I'll tie a bit of string around them,' I promised. 'Then I can always yank them out if they disappear into the darkness.'

We told the Duchess that we would go away and return the following morning with the appropriate remedies.

'How long do we have to stop here?' demanded the Duke.

'At least 24 hours,' replied Dr Challot. 'Maybe a little longer.'

'Goddamnit!' cried the Duke. 'Do you mean we have to stay here the night?'

'I fear so, your Highness,' said Dr Challot.

'Eh well,' sighed the Duke. 'Let's hope that woman with the big jugs provides me with good entertainment.'

On my way downstairs, I was told by Mr Youngblood that he had temporarily moved me into a small room in the attic. He was not the slightest bit apologetic about this.

When we left the Peacock Inn, Dr Challot went to the consulting rooms to find and prepare the ingredients and equipment which we would need for the Duchess's treatments. I went to find the coachman who had been injured.

It was near dark outside and gloomy inside the stable. The injured coachman had been laid out on a truss of straw which had been placed in such a way to make a rough sort of bed. He was lying there quite alone.

'I'm the Doctor,' I told him, just managing to avoid the almost statutory 'What can I do for you?' with which we Doctors tend to greet all our patients.

There was a stifled, gagging sort of reply and when I leant closer to him I could see that the poor fellow still had the gag in his mouth. As instructed, Mr Youngblood had pushed a large and rather filthy piece of rag into place in order to stop the fellow screaming. I removed the rag and the coachman gasped and breathed heavily several times.

'What happened?' I enquired.

'Some idiot stuffed a rag into my mouth!' explained the coachman. He held out his hands so that I could see that they were tied. I assumed that Mr Youngblood had tied the fellow's hands in order to prevent him removing the filthy gag.

I cut the rope and freed his hands. 'What happened before the idiot stuffed the rag into your mouth?'

'I fell off the coach and broke my left leg,' he said. 'And while I was on the ground one of the horses trod on my bollocks.'

I looked down at his legs. He was absolutely right. The left leg was broken and a piece of bone was sticking out through the skin and the man's trousers.

'It's broken isn't it?' he said.

'It is, I'm afraid.'

'Will it have to come off?'

'It will. The bone is sticking out. I'll have to remove it. But I can recommend a carpenter who will make you a decent peg leg.'

The man was quiet. 'His Grace will never hire a coachman with one leg.'

'Why on earth not? You can still drive a coach.'

'I would look woefully asymmetrical. His Grace is very keen on symmetry.'

'Maybe he will be able to find you other employment?'

'Not when he sees the damage my bone has done to the breeches.'

I could not think of a suitable reply but I was not surprised to find that the Duke would worry more about a pair of damaged breeches than about the man who had worn them.

'What about my bollock?' he asked. 'It feels as if it has been crushed.'

I examined his balls and found that the left one was, indeed, completely crushed and clearly quite without purpose.

'I will have to remove the crushed one,' I told him. 'But the other one seems fine and should continue to function perfectly satisfactorily.'

'His Grace will not be pleased,' said the coachman gloomily. 'I fear my bone has completely ruined the uniform breeches.' The poor fellow was far more worried about the damned breeches than his own woeful condition.

'Damn the breeches!' I said, rashly. 'His Grace will have to order another pair.'

I told the man I would have to go to the consulting rooms to fetch my saws, a bottle of Laudanum and a couple of assistants to hold him still while I removed the damned leg.

I am becoming tolerably good at removing limbs though generally speaking I find arms, being thinner, much the easier limbs to amputate. I may not be as fast as some of the London Surgeons, specialists in this sort of work, but several of my patients have survived for more than a week after surgery and I am still tolerably proud of this.

July 13th

The Duke's coachman, the poor devil who had a broken leg and who had been kicked in the groin, died in the night.

Dr Challot was mortally aggrieved since he had bet two guineas that the man would last three days. I was mildly flattered by his confidence.

We took away the man's leg since he no longer had any use for it, and Dr Challot has arranged to have the flesh stripped off and melted down for pill making.

After breakfast I saw a man with a bad cold in his bowel. He was rich in curmurings and had been farting a good deal. He complained that his farts smelt rotten and having been witness to his ventuosity, I can confirm that his complaint is justified.

I put three Leeches on his abdomen and placed a treacle Poultice on his head. He is tolerably well-off so I charged him half a guinea. I am becoming pleasantly accustomed to having guinea and half guinea pieces in my pocket.

Dr Challot and I then returned to the Peacock Inn prepared to treat the Duchess's raspberries. We had dilators, medicine and Leeches all ready and prepared, and Dr Challot had put on a fresh shirt and a waistcoat which pretty well covered most of the Blood stains on the front of the clean shirt. To our dismay we found when we got there that the Duke, the Duchess and their entourage had all left the Inn and had continued on their way. It seems that Bed rest had soothed the Duchess's condition. The Duke had not paid our bill and Dr Challot is beyond fury. We have not even been paid for the amputation of the coachman's leg. All we have to show for our efforts is the leg itself – worth a groat and a half at most.

Still, there is good news. Their departure means that I can return to my room. The attic room in which I slept last night was very small, cold and dark. Nellie said she saw three bats and a rat.

July 19th

I received a request to visit the Vicarage and with a heavy heart I set off to see what was required. I had assumed that I had been asked to see Euphemia and was, to say the least, feeling nervous. I wondered if I could get away with examining her without actually touching her. Maybe, I thought, I could stand at the end of the Bed and make a determination on the basis of her reported symptoms. I knew that many of the country's leading Physicians, esteemed members of the College of Physicians, had gone for decades without ever actually touching a patient. They thought it beneath themselves to have to bend over a sick Bed and lay hands, or even the distal end of a Laennec's tube, onto a sickly patient. Indeed, most of them were too frightened of catching fleas to do anything quite so reckless.

But my fears turned out to be unfounded.

'Your Patient is in here, Doctor,' said the butler, having led me up the stairs. He knocked gently on the door before opening it.

And to my surprise my Patient turned out to be the Reverend Standorf himself. He was lying abed, wearing a white Nightshirt and a maroon nightcap.

'What ails you?' I asked, now feeling quite cheery in consequence of my relief.

'It is my throat!' he replied, though the nature of the reply, the rasp and hoarseness, rather made the words he spoke superfluous. He had a long, red, woollen sock wrapped around his throat.

'What is wrong with it?'

'It's sore.'

'Whose idea was that?' I enquired, pointing to the sock.

'It was at the housekeeper's recommendation,' he replied, clearly speaking with difficulty. 'The sock has been worn. And it contains a rasher of bacon, as she recommended. It was placed there three days ago but sadly the remedy has failed to work. I have a sermon to preach in two days' time.'

'That sock business is all rather old-fashioned nonsense, I fear,' I told him firmly. 'Put out your tongue!'

He did as I asked.

'Ah, the tongue is discoloured,' I told him. 'And your throat is inflamed.'

'I told you that!' he said, rather rudely I thought.

'With respect, sir, you did not. You told me that your throat was sore. That is a symptom. I have told you that it is inflamed. That is a determination.' I was quite well pleased with myself.

'So, what are you going to do about it?' he demanded. 'Do you propose to offer me a treatment in addition to a determination?'

'I shall treat you with flowers of sulphur,' I told him. 'Do you have writing paper available?'

'In the writing desk,' he replied, pointing to a large desk beneath the window.

In a pigeon hole I found some printed notepaper. I opened my satchel and took out a small bottle of flowers of sulphur; one of the medicines I always carry with me.

'What the devil is that?' demanded the clergyman.

I told him.

'And the notepaper? What is that for? Do you intend to make me eat paper? Or are you going to write off for assistance?'

'No, no. I intend to use the notepaper to enable me to direct the sulphur into your throat where it can penetrate the tissues.'

I confess I found myself wondering whether or not a few Leeches and a little scarifying might not be called for. Or, more profitably perhaps, a double dose of a powerful Enema.

The Vicar looked sceptical.

'Unlike your old sock this is a scientific remedy,' I told him. 'It is well known among members of my profession that sulphur is the treatment of choice for a sore throat.'

Having made a funnel with the piece of notepaper, I poured a little of the flowers of sulphur into the funnel. I then blew hard. Unfortunately, I had folded the paper a little tightly at the cone end and the powder, not being able to go down into the throat, blew back into my face, making my eyes sting and causing me to cough a good deal.

'Have you done this before?' asked the Vicar.

'Many, many times,' I told him, though in truth this was not entirely accurate since I had used the sulphur remedy only once before.

'Never let a Patient know that you are inexperienced in the provision of a particular type of treatment or in conducting a particular operation,' Dr Challot had told me, early in my training. 'You must exhale confidence. A Patient will recover far more speedily if his Doctor exudes confidence and certainty.'

On my second attempt, I succeeded in blowing some of the sulphur down the Reverend Standorf's throat. Some of it, to be sure, blew back into my face but I was pleased to see that a goodly proportion of it had disappeared down his throat.

'When will my throat be repaired?' he demanded, after he'd finished coughing.

'In two days,' I told him firmly. I put the bottle of sulphur back into my bag. That was something else that Dr Challot had taught me. Precision in medicine is everything. If you tell a Patient that he will get better but you aren't sure when, then the chances are that he will never get better. If you tell him that he will recover in two, three or four days he will recover in two, three or four days.

Suddenly, I remembered something that Nellie had said to me.

'I now need to examine your legs,' I told him. I pulled the Bed Sheets down, revealing the Clergyman's body, clad only in traditional nightwear. 'Please pull up your Nightshirt.'

'Sir!' he said firmly. 'I am naked underneath my clothing. I am a grown man. A Clergyman. I am not some young girl, eager to display her portions to your lascivious gaze.'

I couldn't help wondering if he was talking about his Daughter. It appeared that he perhaps knew her better than I might have thought possible.

'Sir, it is essential that I examine some portions of your nether regions. There is a syndrome which I must disqualify from my differential determination.'

'What syndrome?'

'It is newly discovered and does not yet have a name,' I said. 'But the sore throat is always accompanied by a mark on one of the thighs – usually the left.'

'What sort of mark?' demanded the Vicar, who had paled noticeably.

'To the uninitiated it can take on the appearance of a bite mark,' I told him.

'There is no need for any examination,' insisted the Vicar. 'I have no such mark on either thigh.'

'It is something that the untrained eye can miss,' I told him with a confidence that surprised me. 'If it gives you great discomfort to allow otherwise you may shield your most personal departments with some item of cover.'

'Is this essential?'

'Indeed it is. The mark is the first sign that the infection had spread,' I told him. 'I would be remiss if I did not check to see whether there are any signs that it has done so.'

With a snort of mild protest, the Clergyman lifted up his Nightshirt and placed his hand on top of his twig and berries. I lifted the Nightshirt a little higher and there on his chest was the third nipple which Nellie had told me was there. I peered closely at his thighs, looking for the bite mark which she had reported would be present.

And to my astonishment there it was! A large bite mark in exactly the position she had described to me. I pulled a magnifying glass from my coat pocket and leant forward. The Vicar's grip on his twig and berries tightened. The glass had been a small gift from a Leech salesman. It had the words 'Pilkington's Leeches Suck Better' engraved on the handle but by holding the glass firmly I was able to hide this.

'Oh there may be a birthmark on my thigh!' he insisted, as though the memory had suddenly come to his mind. He had gone very white, so white that he almost disappeared against the Bed Sheets. 'The mark has been there all my life. I was born with it.'

I examined the bite mark and touched it gently with the tip of a finger. 'No, I think not,' I said. 'This is no birth mark.'

He looked down at his own lower regions and stared at the bite mark as though it were something he had never seen before. 'Oh, goodness!' he said, weakly.

'I am sorry to say that I fear this may be a sign that the infection has entered your Bloodstream,' I told him.

'No, it cannot be! It is not!'

'But how can we be sure? Do you have any other explanation for its presence?'

The Vicar swallowed hard. 'Maybe it is indeed a bite mark.'

'A bite? What sort of bite? An animal of some kind? Do you remember being bitten?'

'It is a human bite mark,' he whispered. 'I am confident of it.'

I looked at him and raised an eyebrow a sixteenth of an inch or so. 'A human bit you there? Were you attacked? Did you call the constable?'

'No, no! There was no need to call for the constable. It was done in a purely playful manner.' He swallowed hard. The pallor had now been replaced by a redness which was spreading across his cheeks and down his throat.

I bent down and examined the bite mark again. 'These are teeth marks?'

'They are, yes they are teeth marks.' He was now as red as he had been white.

'Mistress Standorf's teeth?'

'Ye Gods, man, of course not! My wife's dentures are wooden. She has difficulty in biting a tomato.'

'I thought not,' I said with a nod. It had seemed an unlikely possibility. I really could not imagine Mistress Standorf biting any man on the thigh, unless it was in some sort of self-defence. I straightened myself and slipped my magnifying glass back into my jacket pocket. 'I agree the mark does not seem as though it were made by the teeth of Mistress Standorf.'

He stared at me. 'You can tell?'

'The shape of the mouth is a distinguishing feature,' I said. 'Mistress Standorf has a most clearly identifiable overbite. Any student of medicine could tell you that this mark could not have been made by Mistress Standorf's teeth.'

Though I have never understood the reason for the action, I rubbed my chin with my hand, as I have seen some men of learning do when they are thinking.

'I feel sure that I know these teeth,' I said.

'The bite was made by a young woman who visits me occasionally,' said the Vicar. The confession spilt from him in haste. 'The mark is without doubt a bite mark. It cannot be a sign that my Blood is troubled.'

'A young woman?' I said.

'She visits me from time to time,' he said.

'From time to time?'

'Occasionally.'

'Occasionally?'

'Once a week. My Wife visits her mother at weekends and the young woman visits me on Saturdays. Or, rather, she used to. Her visits appear to have ceased.'

'Ah.'

'The visits were for spiritual reasons,' he said. 'She provided me with relief from my worldy woes.'

'You may cover yourself,' I told him.

'There is no spread of the infection?' He used his free hand to pull down his Nightshirt.

'None.' I pulled down the Sheets.

'Have you now finished with your examination?' It was notable that as he became covered so he regained some of his lost assurance.

'I have sir.'

'There will be need to mention...?' he began.

'Good heavens, no, sir! Everything that occurs between a Doctor and a Patient is sacrosanct.'

'I'm pleased to hear it.'

'How much do I owe you?' he asked, reaching to his right and pulling on the bell to summon a member of his staff.

'One guinea, sir.'

'A whole guinea!'

'The powder is expensive and acquiring the knowledge to use it even more so,' I told him. 'You must send word if you require a second treatment. A subsequent treatment will be merely half a guinea.'

When the Butler arrived, the Reverend Standorf instructed him to give me a guinea piece from the purse on his bedside Table. It appeared that the Reverend did not wish to soil his hands by taking out his own guinea and handing it to me.

I put the guinea into my pocket, picked up my bag, bad them both goodbye and left.

I was still rather shocked that young Nellie, the Maid, had clearly been telling the truth when she had spoken of the nights she spent in the Reverend Standorf's bed.

But it was good to know that the Reverend Standorf and I now shared a secret.

July 29th

Dr Mort arrived with a small King Charles Spaniel dog which bore a smart silver collar. The dog was, he said, a gift for a young woman related to the Duke of Wellington. We have not seen our new Apprentice for some while but he offered no explanation or excuse for his failure to attend the surgery.

Dr Moat boasts that he has acquired a yearning and a strong inclination for the niece of a cousin of the Duke of Wellington and told me he hopes to become personal Physician to the Duke. From what I have heard I consider this a doubtful ambition.

The Duke is not keen on Doctors since that trouble with his ear. Indeed, it is no exaggeration to say that Wellington doesn't much like or trust Doctors.

In 1822, the Great Man's left ear drum was shattered during firing practice at Woolwich. An ear specialist who was brought in, treated the Iron Duke by pouring a strong solution of caustic soda into his ear. 'I don't think I've ever suffered so much in my life,' said the Duke.

I don't blame him for disliking and distrusting Doctors after that.

Dr Mort confessed that he had spent everything he had on the dog's collar which was encrusted with sapphires and rubies and demanded that I lend him £10. I told him that if I had £10 I would lend it to myself. Since I did not have the £10 to lend him I had no choice in the matter. I suspect that Dr Mort is not as wealthy as Dr Challot believes. I wondered if perhaps Dr Mort's father might not have conveyed himself into the suburbs of an uncomfortable financial position.

'I spent myself most commodiously last evening,' he said with a laugh and a wink. My refusal to lend him £10 did not seem to have incommoded him. 'Do you know Astley's Royal Amphitheatre?'

I confessed that I had not heard of it.

'You've never been to Astley's?' he asked, as though I were admitting that I had never drunk mead.

'I have not,' I confessed rather stiffly.

'Great heavens, what a dull provincial life you do lead,' he said. 'It is in London,' he explained. 'Three girls, Kitty, Sue and Polly, known collectively as the Fleming girls, do spectacular trick riding. They leap their horses through fire hoops. It's a most damnably enthralling show. And afterwards you can buy them for the night. Last night I purchased all three for myself. At the time they seemed excellent value for money, though in retrospect the exercise appears to have left me rather light in the wallet. Lord Porchester says that women are like horses, you know.'

'In what way?'

'Both need to be ridden hard. The difference is that women should be put away wet but horses should be put away dry.'

He laughed merrily at this quip.

I resisted the temptation to share my thoughts on his incontinence and extravagance. I am more than ever convinced that Mort is alive only from the waist downwards.

'What's been happening in my absence?' he asked. 'Have I missed anything exciting?'

He laughed disdainfully when he said this, as though he felt sure that there were unlikely to have been any exciting events for him to have missed.

'No, you haven't missed anything,' I told him. 'We've been very busy looking after the Duchess of Beaufort.'

I thought he would have died of envy when I told him this but he simply shrugged and watched with quiet indifference as his dog emptied itself of both departments at once. It is a rare sight to see an animal do this.

'What have you been feeding it?' I enquired, as the dog concluded its emptying.

'A fellow sold me a dozen crab and I wanted to see if they were fresh so I gave one to the dog for breakfast. It appears that the damned crab was not fresh. I will have to tell my coachman to donate the crab to some poor people and give the crabman a damned good whipping.'

'We have not seen you for some while,' I said. 'Where have you been?'

'Oh, I've been with Lady Penelope Fitzwater. We spent a few days together at her father's seat in Somerset.'

I was surprised by this. I had heard talk that Lady Penelope was exceptionally prim in her manner.

'I told her that there are vampires in those parts, constantly searching for virgins,' explained Dr Mort.

I stared at him, puzzled.

'I explained to her that the presence of the vampires meant that the only way for her to be safe was to give herself to me immediately.'

'And she did?'

'Oh yes! With great enthusiasm. I told her that to be on the safe side she should repeat the exercise at regular intervals.

'She believed this nonsense?'

'Oh they always do.'

'You've tried the same trick before?'

'Good heavens, yes. One never wastes a ploy that works.'

'What about the Duke of Wellington's relative?' I asked.

'Oh she is another fish for a different sort of frying,' replied Dr Mort.

'Are you going to clean that up?' I asked, nodding towards the twin messes the dog had made.

'I am not,' he said. 'A servant can do it.' He peered at the dog, clearly attempting to think. Eventually he reached down and unfastened the silver collar which he slipped into his coat pocket.

'There is clearly a fault with this dog,' he said. 'I shall purchase another. Are you certain you cannot lend me a paltry ten pounds?'

I told him that I did not have a paltry ten pounds nor, indeed, any other variety of ten pounds and he stalked off in a sulk.

'Then you can clear up the dog's mess,' he said, before marching off. 'And you can keep the incontinent beast.'

The dog stayed behind and did not appear to be in the slightest bit disappointed to have been abandoned.

'What is its name?' I called after him.

He shrugged. 'I never called it anything,' he shouted over his shoulder. 'Why would one take the trouble to give a name to a damned dog?'

July 30th

Nellie is well taken with the King Charles Spaniel which I was given by Mort. I was going to find the dog a home elsewhere but Nellie insists that we keep it. She has named the creature Charlie since, despite his regal nomenclature, he is a very friendly little fellow.

August 3rd

'The Vicar's Wife has sent their Ostler with a message asking you to visit the Vicarage,' said Mistress Swain with a smirk. 'She gave strict instructions that you should present yourself at the front door.'

'Did the message say if the request was urgent?' I asked.

I was surprised at the suggestion that I use the front door. The last time I'd been to the Vicarage I had made the mistake of ringing the front doorbell. When I had identified myself, I had been sent by the Butler to the tradesman's entrance at the back of the house.

'What's that got to do with the price of fish?' demanded Mistress Swain, who prides herself on her ability to combine irrelevance and impertinence.

'I just wondered.'

'I think you can regard it as very urgent,' replied Mistress Swain looking unbearably smug and pleased with herself. 'The Vicar's Wife sent a message with one of their under-gardeners. Apparently Miss Euphemia Standorf has a need to see you.'

Damn Mistress Swain! Damn her entrails. The wretched woman was looking smug because she knows how, for very excellent reasons, I now loathe visiting the Vicarage. Even the very mention of the name Standorf turns my bowels to wind and water and gives my heart to somersault so violent that I am momentarily convinced that the next beat will be the last. I don't know how much the damned woman has guessed but I suspect she knows more than is good for her. She is, I believe, on good gossiping terms with the Standorf's housekeeper and I also suspect that she may be doing the blanket hornpipe with the Standorf's Head Gardener. Since discovering that Mistress Swain has for some time been regularly rogered by Mr Youngblood, I have had to revise my view of her attractiveness to a certain type of person. Mr Youngblood is a drunk, rarely seen sober, and I believe that the Standorf's Head Gardener may be similarly afflicted by yearnings.

'Maybe she has an itch which requires your assistance,' added Mistress Swain. She followed this with a wink and throaty laugh which curdled my Blood.

The hazard which produces these dire effects and affects my innards so vehemently is, of course, my fear that Euphemia and her Mother have together decided that I would make a suitable husband. This now appears to be the accepted belief locally.

This decision was made without my having contributed to any discussion on the subject and clearly seems to have originated with the examination I conducted, and the treatment I provided, when Euphemia was suffering from a chest complaint a short while ago.

From the way that the Vicar looks at me, over the top of his pince-nez and with a stern and searching look, it is clear that whenever he sees me he is sizing me up to see how I would look standing before him, with Euphemia by my side and a gold ring in my waistcoat pocket. I was very much of the impression that he had received misleading guidance on the precise nature of the visit I had made when his Daughter had been laid low with congestion.

I looked at the clock. 'I think it's probably too late to go today,' I said. 'Perhaps I should delay my visit until tomorrow. The Standorfs will doubtless be taking lunch, having afternoon tea or dining. Or maybe the Reverend Standorf will be preparing his sermon and unwilling to have his peaceful contemplations disturbed by my ringing his doorbell.'

'The message was that you should go very urgently regardless of convenience,' insisted Mistress Swain with another dirty chuckle. 'Young Miss Euphemia seems to think she already has you well under her thumb.'

'Not a bit of it!' I protested.

'The Ostler said to say that you were free to enter by the front door,' Mistress Swain reminded me. 'I think he was referring to the Vicarage rather than Miss Euphemia but I cannot be entirely sure.'

I stared at her wondering why the devil Dr Challot put up with her damnable impertinence.

'Still, at least you can take heart from the fact that she's been very well prepared for her wedding night, and your way has been well rehearsed,' continued Mistress Swain. She took a small box of snuff from her apron pocket, put a pinch into the indentation at the base of her thumb and sniffed it up her nose with, I thought, a good deal of unnecessary noise.

I looked at her, frowning and asked her to explain what she meant.

'Just what I've heard,' she said with a careless shrug. 'You'd probably say it was nothing more than tittle tattle.' She sneezed, blowing snuff powder everywhere including over me, pulled a revolting piece of rag from somewhere in her skirts and wiped her nose with it.

'What sort of tittle tattle?' I demanded.

'Oh, just that she's been consistently well attended to by the under-gardener up at the Vicarage.'

'The under-gardener?' I said, startled.

'You must have seen him. A huge, red headed fellow who is said to be a bit simple minded but a hard worker. I gather he's lain with the Daughter of the house quite regularly and done some of the ground breaking work for you with Miss Euphemia. You might say he has dug his spade in deep and tilled the earth for you.'

Astonished, I stared at her.

'Three times a week for two or three months now,' said Mistress Swain. She paused and wiped her nose again. 'So I hear.' She sniffed. 'Still, they do say 'like mother like Daughter' do they not?'

'What on earth do you mean?'

'Oh, were you not aware?'

'Aware of what?'

'Mistress Standorf has always been serviced by the Under-Footman,' she told me, as if surprised that I did not know this. The Vicar holds services at the Church while his Wife is safe in her Bed being serviced by the Dining Room Senior Under-Footman. They do say that she always appoints the Dining Room Senior Under-Footman herself.' She winked at me. 'And the interview has nothing to do with whether he can carry a bowl of soup without spilling any.' She laughed merrily at this quip. 'When interviewing prospective young men she makes them change into uniform and watches as they do it. Makes them go right down beyond their skivvies.'

'How on earth did you acquire all this scurrilous nonsense?'

'I keep my ears open,' said Mistress Swain mysteriously. 'A good friend of mine has seen her at it more than once. But you need not worry yourself about the Lady of the House for she likes them well built and young but you need to watch yourself with Euphemia. There is word that the Gardener may have planted a seed or two,' she added. 'And if a seed has taken he may have started your first crop for you. He has a Wife with three little ones back home so he's no problems filling a woman's belly.' She winked and cackled again.

Putting aside the question of how Mistress Swain knew that my build, as she put it, was not up to the required standards for Mistress Standorf, it occurred to me that my non-existent relationship with Euphemia was becoming more complicated by the minute. And from what Mistress Swain had told me, I could not help wondering if Euphemia and her mother might not have a very good reason for looking for a suitable husband. If I was not careful I could find myself tied to the Reverend Standorf's wretched Daughter, a cuckold before the fact as well as after, and playing Papa to a red headed, simple minded baby with two green thumbs. I decided there and then that I needed to take the bull by the horns and deal with this misunderstanding before it became impossible to extricate myself from the family Standorf.

'I shall go there immediately,' I told her, brushing snuff powder from my cravat, which had once been pale blue but was now stained as brown as if I had spilt gravy upon it. As I did so it occurred to me that we had still not been paid for my last visit to the Vicarage. I decided that if the opportunity arose, I really ought to bring up the matter of payment. I have often found that it is the people with butlers and other servants who are the most reluctant to pay their Doctor's bills.

Nevertheless, although I had told Mistress Swain that I was heading straight to the Vicarage, I decided to call in at the Peacock Inn for a light snack and a fortifying glass or two of malmsey.

When I arrived at the Peacock Inn, I was surprised to see that Jack the Hopper was in the snug bar. I have had a fondness for Hoppers since I was a boy. I always found them most entertaining. I therefore found myself a spare seat and asked the waitress if there was anything fresh on the menu. I was not averse to delaying my visit to the Vicarage for a short while. The Peacock often has visiting Tumblers and Mime Players but Hoppers are rather rare these days.

'The goose pie is six days old and I spent half an hour pulling out the maggots,' the waitress told me in confidence. 'And you will need a fine sharp set of teeth to bite through the crust.'

I always try to stay on the right side of the serving staff, promising generous tips at every opportunity, for exactly this sort of inside information.

I looked around and could see at least three diners happily spooning up the goose pie as fast as they could shovel the stuff from plate to mouth.

'And the mutton? What do you say about the mutton?'

'Tough,' she replied, wrinkling her nose. 'So stringy I thought of using it to make myself a pair of stockings.'

'So, what do you recommend?'

'I'd take the Tench if I could afford it. Freshly caught, mashed and boiled.'

I fumbled in my pocket, found a penny and passed it to her. 'I'll take the Tench.' She thanked me and hurried off. 'And a half pint pot of malmsey!' I shouted after her.

While I waited, I watched Jack the Hopper earn his dinner, and his supper too.

He took off his shoes and stockings and encouraged the customers to throw glassware onto the floor until the place appeared to be entirely carpeted in broken glass. No one took any notice of Mistress Youngblood who was complaining bitterly about her glassware being smashed.

'I'll lay five shillings he can't hop twice round the room without cutting his foot!' cried Seth, a farm labourer who seems to me to spend considerably more time drinking than labouring.

'Taken!' shouted two voices I didn't recognise.

And so it went.

Within two minutes the best part of five pounds had been wagered. I did not take part in the nonsense and was pleased by my abstinence. I have decided that I regard betting as a fool's game and I can find easier ways to part myself from the little money I have. I confess that if I had taken a bet it would have been to bet against Jack cutting his foot at all. He is the best Hopper I have seen for many a long year.

And true enough, with startling skill and dexterity he succeeded in finding a way around the room without cutting his hopping foot.

When the course had been completed the gamblers, particularly those who had lost their stakes, demanded a rerun and Jack went the other way round the room, using his other foot. Once again he succeeded in avoiding the broken glass. I could not help wishing that I'd placed a couple of small wagers on him. Maybe next time.

As the entertainment finished, the waitress appeared carrying my plate of mashed Tench and my pot of malmsey. It took but one mouthful to discover that the idiot cook had mashed the Tench without first having the good sense to remove the bones. I spat a mouthful of bones onto my plate and spent several painful minutes pulling another dozen out of my cheek and tongue. When the waitress next came my way she had the nerve to laugh and wink at me.

'What sort of trick was that?' I demanded, giving her behind a good whack with my palm.

'Mistress Youngblood offered me a farthing for every bowl I could sell,' she admitted. 'The cook forgot to bone the fish before mashing it.'

'I discovered that!' I retorted.

She then brought me a plateful of roasted Neck of Pork, served with a dish of boiled eggs, half a crusty loaf, a plateful of apple sauce and a block of cheese. I told her I wouldn't pay for these victuals as well as the Tench, and the girl promised that she wouldn't put the items onto my bill. I also requested an additional pot of malmsey.

The Neck of Pork was excellent, the fat nicely crisped around the edges as I like it, and the cheese had a good fighting taste. The malmsey was damned fine and I had a third pot before I left. All of us in the snug sang 'May We Always Have Enough'. I took off my boots and socks and attempted to emulate Jack the Hopper and hop around the room. Unfortunately, I failed and cut my foot so badly that I had to bind it up with a handkerchief loaned me by Ebenezer Lamplight. He did not mind my having the muckender for it was filthy dirty and, he said, had proved impossible to clean even though his Wife had attempted to launder it.

I blamed my failure on the fact that as I hopped, I carried my boots and stockings with me lest anyone be tempted to steal them away, for the snug bar was filled with knaves and varlets as always at that time of day. Who but knaves and varlets can waste away their days in the parlour of a low Inn?

By the time I had finished my meal, it was too dark and too late to ride to the Vicarage so I stayed at the Peacock Inn and ordered more mead.

August 4th

I breakfasted well and drank six pints of mead to give myself confidence for the day ahead.

'Do you think you should be riding, in your condition?' asked the Ostler at the Peacock as I prepared to climb up onto old Bess, the elderly mare which I had brought with me from home when I had first arrived at Dr Challot's establishment to begin my training. Bess had been my Father's Second Best Horse. His First Best Horse had been taken by the moneylenders as he lay on his Death bed. Bess was some years past her prime and was, more often than not, unfit to be ridden. But today she seemed in sublime fettle for a beast of her years.

'What the devil do you mean?' I demanded of the Ostler. 'What, pray, is wrong with my condition?'

The Ostler has become very confident now that he plans to leave his post. He told me the other day that he is weary and plans to retire at Michaelmas. He says he has some savings and plans to live on these, supplemented with a little light thieving. I think this is a dangerous move. Everyone I know who has retired has gone on to die within a year or two. It seems clear to me that the evidence shows that retirement is an option to be avoided if at all possible.

Without waiting for a reply, I climbed up onto the mounting block, put my left foot in the stirrup and in attempting to illustrate my sobriety by leaping up onto the saddle, rather over emphasised the leap and found myself flat on my face on the mud and straw covered cobble stones.

It was, I suppose, my good fortune that the mud and straw provided something of a cushion against the pain which might otherwise have been occasioned by the cobbles for my Pride was the only victim of this Tumble.

'The damned horse moved,' I complained, as soon as I was able to stand. 'Or the saddle was not set properly. Damn your eyes!'

The Ostler was laughing, and two small boys who had suddenly appeared from nowhere and were sniggering loudly. Why is it that whenever something embarrassing happens to me there will always be two small boys present to act as witnesses?

I attempted to brush mud off my jacket and realised it wasn't mud. Bits of wet straw were stuck to my clothing and my hair. There was, I realised, a terrible smell of horse piss about me.

'You're too drunk! Not fit to ride,' said the Ostler, leading Bess back into the stable. 'If you're going somewhere you'd best be safer to take Shanks's pony.'

In reply, I gave one of the small boys a smack around the head as a lesson to him not to snigger at the misfortune of others. Regrettably, the other managed to avoid the back of my hand. I stood for a moment wondering whether I should go up to my room and wash my hands and face. But wanting to set off for the Vicarage without delay I simply washed myself in the horse trough and brushed some of the straw from my body. The unpleasant odour remained.

'They can damned well take me as they find me,' I announced to no one in particular. It occurred to me that the smell of horse piss rather disguised the smell of malmsey which doubtless emanated from my person. It seemed to me that the Ostler's advice was worth following. I decided to leave Bess to her oats.

'You'll be wanting this, I dare say,' said the Ostler, walking after me and handing me my medical satchel which had fallen off my shoulder and landed a couple of yards away. 'Though if you're planning on an amputation I'm fierce-some glad it's not my limb you'll be hacking off.' He laughed. 'I wouldn't put a knife within a chain of your hands in your present condition.'

I damned the vagabond's ignorant eyes, took my satchel from him and set off for the Vicarage on foot.

It was a three mile walk to the Vicarage and by the time I had found my way there, stumbling and swaying a little, for the fall must have banged my head more than I had realised, the sky was heavy with rain. My only consolation was that when the weather lacks clemency, the footpads tend to stay at home. Mind you, no self-respecting, footpad with ambition would have bothered himself if he had seen me staggering past. My clothes were of no quality to start with but my fall had done them no favours.

'Mercy from above, what has happened to you?' cried Euphemia when the Butler had opened the front door and, after a good deal of sniffing and more tutting than I thought was appropriate to our relative positions, allowed me into the Vicarage with obvious distaste and reluctance.

(I have never had much affection for Butlers for they always seem to regard themselves as superior to everyone. The Standorfs' Butler is particularly guilty of this high mindedness and sense of superiority. The damned fellow deserves a daily purging to empty him of his starchy ways.)

'I fell,' I answered her. 'Or to be more precise I was thrown! My damned horse threw me. Moreover, I suspect that the Ostler hadn't fastened the saddle properly.'

'Oh, you poor dear!' said Euphemia. She took a scented handkerchief from a pocket somewhere in the folds of her dress and held it to her nose as she approached me.

'He's drunk!' said the Vicar, who had appeared at her side, as though by magic. 'The knavish fellow is as well-neezled as a Lord.'

'He's a Doctor, father,' said Euphemia, springing to my defence. 'He is a professional man. He cannot possibly be drunk.'

'Maybe he has been experimenting with medicinal gases,' said the Vicar's wife. 'I have read about them in the *Illustrated London News*.'

'What sort of medicinal gases?' demanded the Vicar, with a snort of derision. I had never before heard a snort of derision. This was definitely one; lots of snort and a good deal of derision.

'According to the article I read, they are used for putting patients to sleep during onerous surgical procedures,' said Mistress Sandorf. 'I imagine their main value must be that they reduce the risk of the Surgeon being attacked or bitten by a struggling patient.'

'Oh, good heavens!' cried Euphemia. She put her hand to her heart. 'What dangers you do encounter in your profession.'

'There is apparently a dentist in America who has experimented with something called Ether,' said Mistress Standorf. 'And according to the article I read, there is a Professor in Edinburgh who has used Chloroform to silence his patients' screams.'

'Good heavens!' said the Vicar. 'The Church could not possibly condone such a thing. I hope they do not consider giving the stuff to women in childbirth. To do so would be ungodly in the extreme.'

'These things have not yet reached general usage,' I assured him.

'So, what do you say happened to you?' the vicar enquired.

'I fell off my Bess,' I said, thinking I should offer an explanation for my condition. 'I was almost on top of her and I fell off with something of a clatter. She may have moved.'

'Who, pray, is this Bess?' asked Euphemia, frowning and backing away a yard.

'A damnable creature,' I replied. 'She's as ugly as sin and twice as bad tempered. She's old enough and experienced enough to know to behave better when a man's on top of her and trying to get his legs around her waist!'

There was silence.

'I was on top of her,' I continued. 'My legs were damned near astride her damnit; ready to dig in my heels and be at her and off. Suddenly, I found myself thrown onto the floor without so much as a by your leave. One minute she was still, waiting for me and as ready as always, and the next moment I was on the floor.'

'Oh no!' cried Euphemia, fainting to the floor but being careful to go down gently and to hold up her skirts so that they were not creased. It occurred to me that she must have taken fainting lessons from her mother, Mistress Standorf.

'The damned creature has had enough men on top of her to know to behave better!' I said.

'I think he may be talking about his horse,' said the Vicar drily. 'It is my hope that this is so.'

'A horse?' said Euphemia, lifting her head. 'Is this Bess a horse?'

'What else could she be?' I demanded, impatient at the woman's idiocy. 'She must have stumbled in a pothole. The roads around here are a menace.' I did not like to admit that I had fallen in the courtyard of The Peacock. 'I walked here. I think I'll have the damned beast cut into steaks – though she's probably too stringy to eat outside a stew.'

Euphemia fainted again. Since she was already on the floor this did not require the caution she had previously exercised.

'I'm sure that the Doctor speaks in haste,' said her mother, trying to calm the situation.

'Of course he does,' agreed Euphemia speedily. She sat up.

Mistress Standorf turned to the butler. 'We will take Doctor Bullock into the drawing room,' she told him. 'Bring a bottle of brandy and some glasses. The second best glassware will be sufficient but bring the best brandy since I will have a glass myself.'

To be honest I would have preferred a cheese sandwich or a slice of cold mutton but the prospect of being able to sit down and rest my worn out legs was attractive enough.

I followed the Standorf family into their drawing room and on Mistress Standorf's insistence was handed a large brandy by the butler. 'Brandy is the only thing for shock,' she announced. 'The Doctor has had a painful and shocking experience.'

'Your health, sir!' said the Reverend Standorf, who I noticed had taken a very modest quantity of brandy, hardly enough liquid to cover the bottom of the glass.

'Your health!' repeated the two Standorf women, speaking in unison and waving their glasses in my direction. They were both drinking brandy and impressively they emptied their glasses in a single draught. The butler, who had been expecting this, refilled their glasses immediately. I sipped at mine, thinking that perhaps it might be reckless to take too much brandy on top of the malmsey.

'What is that I can do for you?' I asked Euphemia. 'Are you ill again?'

'Oh you must not concern yourself about my health!' insisted Euphemia. 'It is you we must think about. You are the one who has taken a nasty fall.'

'I just fell off a damned horse,' I said.

We sipped our drinks for a moment in silence. The Vicar seemed to have mastered the art of sipping without ever emptying his glass. I assumed that he had perhaps acquired this skill when doing his rounds of his practitioners. A glass of something here and a glass of something there could otherwise lead to some embarrassment by the end of an afternoon of calls. I suspected that many an aspidistra grew large on unexpected draughts of sherry.

'You must show the Doctor your collection of mechanism protectors,' said the Vicar's Wife to her husband when the silence had become painful.

'Oh no, no…' said the Vicar, with assumed modesty.

'What are mechanism protectors?' I asked.

'I am an amateur collector of unconsidered trifles,' said the Vicar. 'I have accumulated a collection of the disks of paper which are placed within Hunter watches to prevent dust getting inside through the keyhole.'

'Good heavens, how fascinating!' I said.

'I have 37 of them.'

'My word,' I murmured, doing my best to look impressed.

'When will they give you a knighthood?' asked Euphemia, suddenly. She was looking at me when she spoke.

I stared at her, for there seemed to be no reason for this unheralded query. 'Why would anyone give me a knighthood?' I asked, genuinely puzzled.

'Because you are now a qualified Physician now,' replied Euphemia. 'Sir Benedict is a knight and his Wife is Lady Ursula. Every Physician I know is Sir something or other.'

'Well, that's because they're all licensed by the Royal College of Physicians,' I explained. 'I'm an Apothecary and a Barber Surgeon.'

'Is there a difference?'

'Of course there is,' I replied, astounded that the silly woman didn't understand.

'You don't have a license from this College?'

'No.'

'So who gave you a licence?'

'I was Apprenticed to Dr Challot,' I explained. 'When I had completed my Apprenticeship he announced that I could call myself both a Surgeon and an Apothecary.'

'Oh!' said Euphemia, who seemed rather startled by this. 'You have no formal training?'

'Only at the hands of Dr Challot; he taught me all that I know.' It occurred to me that if they had seen Dr Challot as I had seen him over the last few months, when his general condition had deteriorated notably, they might have been unimpressed by my training.

'And you have no official licence?'

'I have no need of a licence.'

'But you are both a Surgeon and an Apothecary? How can you be both?'

'Dr Challot trained me as a Surgeon and taught me how to prepare medicines,' I explained. 'And so I can perform operations and prepare medicines. If Physicians such as Sir Benedict prescribe a medicine for a Patient they must come to someone like me to have it prepared.'

'Surely Sir Benedict is allowed to make up his own medicines?'

'Oh no, not at all. Medicines must be prepared by an Apothecary. The physician sends a request for a medicine to an apothecary and then sends a man to collect what has been prepared. We charge two pence for the bottle of medicine and the Physician charges 10 guineas when he hands it to the patient.'

'But you can prescribe treatments yourself?'

'Oh yes. But although I can charge for treatments I cannot charge for a consultation.'

'And surgery? Cannot Sir Benedict perform surgery? Amputations and suchlike?'

'Good heavens, no! I daresay he would doubtless consider himself above such things.'

'So doesn't that make you superior to Sir Benedict in this regard?'

'Not precisely,' I said, suppressing a burp. 'I don't think Sir Benedict would consider that to be the case.'

'So, what is the main difference between you and a Physician?'

'I live in a small room in a Public House and ride a broken down old nag. A royal Physician such as Sir Benedict lives in a mansion and rides around in a carriage.'

The vicar spoke. 'Am I right in thinking that you are allowed to cut hair and to shave your customers?'

'Oh yes,' I said, thinking how kind it was of the Reverend Standorf to remind me of this.

There was a silence as Euphemia allowed all this to sink in. She seemed grieved by what she had learned.

'Well, you'll just have to join this Royal College of Physicians,' she said at last. 'Daddy knows all sorts of people. He can get you into any club you care to mention. My brothers are both members of several of the best clubs in London. They know everyone who hunts and I am sure there won't be any difficulties.'

'I'm afraid it doesn't work quite like that,' I said. 'You have to go to one of the Universities and take a degree and be presented to the College in the proper way.'

'But you have to have a knighthood,' insisted Euphemia. 'If you don't have one I won't be a Lady. And I want very much to be a Lady. I have always thought that I should very much like to be considered a Lady.'

It occurred to me to mention that there would perhaps be a greater chance of her being considered a Lady if the gossips in the locality were not aware of her having been regularly rogered by the red-headed under gardener.

During a short pause in the conversation I took courage into my hands (the malmsey now having been well supplemented by the Brandy) to bring up the question of our bill.

'I know you won't mind my mentioning this,' I said, hesitantly. 'But I thought I ought to mention my bill for the treatment I have previously provided.'

I was intending to continue with a suggestion that payment would be appreciated but before I could get to the nub of the matter, Mistress Standorf interrupted me.

'I'm so glad you brought that up,' said Mistress Standorf. 'We all wanted to say thank you to you for your treatment of both Euphemia and my husband. We appreciate that it would embarrass you for us to offer you payment, given the circumstances of our current and future relationship, but we did want to repeat that we were and are grateful for your medical services.'

This rather took me by surprise. I opened my mouth to respond but could not think of anything worthwhile to say and so I shut it again.

The Vicar's Wife then suggested that we all play whist.

We played for several hours and I went home seven shillings and six pence the lighter; a sum which I could well afford not to be without.

Both the Vicar and his Wife cheated. Neither of them bothered to hide the fact that they were shigging. I suspect we played with a deck which contained six aces but none of this abundance ever managed to find their way into my hands.

Afterwards I walked back to the Peacock Inn.

It was by now raining heavily.

Still, if I die of the Pneumonia my problems will all be solved.

August 11th

English villages used to have a very good way of telling whether a woman was a witch or not. They would put the accused woman into a ducking stool and duck her, complete with Chair, into the village pond. If the accused woman drowned it was clear that she was innocent. If she did not drown she was a witch and they would burn her at the stake. It was all good fun for villagers looking for entertainment on a Saturday afternoon, though it probably wasn't quite so much fun for the accused woman.

It had long been accepted as an essential precept of the English legal system that an accused person should be considered guilty until proven innocent. Indeed, this way of administering justice was common all over Europe in the Middle Ages. So, for example, in the village of Saint-Severe in France, founded in the 7th century and subsequently famous for hosting a visit from Joan of Arc, the locals had their own unique way of administering justice. They used to hang the accused first and hold the trial afterwards. If the prisoner was found guilty, much time was saved because they had already been hung and probably buried too. On the other hand, if the prisoner was innocent, the ones who had done the hanging would apologise to the relatives and everyone would feel a bit bad about things for a day or two.

We in England are now civilised and do not administer justice in this way these days. I do not know about the French for they are without doubt a more primitive people. But we do celebrate our traditional way of life with a great number of traditional events which had the origins in the arcane backwaters of our legal system. So, for example, we in Muckleberry Peverell celebrate 'Fire Test Friday' once a year. This is a curious celebration which consists of tying a woman to a branch on a tree and lighting a bonfire underneath her. The woman's wrists are tied with rope and the rope tied to the branch above the fire. It is surprising just how many traditional customs involve either fire or water.

Much of the entertainment comes from watching the woman wriggle and twist as the flames and smoke rise higher and higher. (I have to say, by the way, that this event appears to have been misnamed at some stage in its career for these days it is always held on a Saturday.)

Traditionally, Fire Test Friday was our village's equivalent of tipping a suspected witch into the village pond.

The woman who was tied to the tree was being tested and there were only two possible results. If she was burned to Death, or died of the smoke she inhaled, the conclusion was that she was innocent of all the charge laid against her. But if, when the fire went out, she was still alive then the conclusion was that she was clearly a witch. In such a case the woman would be cut down, tied to the stake and burnt alive.

I suppose the system might now appear to have flaws, but in its day it was regarded as a fair and reasonable way to deal with a very real problem. After all, no one likes having a witch living in the village.

Naturally, we no longer use such an archaic process to decide whether or not women are witches, but the event is remembered still and is a day much enjoyed by locals and by villagers from round and about.

The selection process used to choose the volunteer who will be tied to the tree is very simple. The volunteer, always an unmarried woman in her thirties, is selected by a voting system in which only women are allowed to vote. Any woman can put down a candidate's name and it has been said, though never proven, that women sometimes use the event as a way to get back at a rival or to soothe a grudge.

This is the only time in the year when women are allowed to vote for anything and whenever feisty women claim they should be allowed to vote in parliamentary elections, we always point to Fire Test Friday as proof that, in our part of the world at least, women are already allowed a vote in the way things are done.

Moreover, since there are regular complaints of rigged voting, bullying, vindictiveness and downright cheating, this event is often used as a damned good reason for not allowing women to vote in any other form of election.

It was Fire Test Friday today and a woman volunteer was duly selected and tied to the oak tree which we've been using for the test for around three hundred years. One side of the tree has been badly scorched where bonfires have been lit but there is still a large branch, around twenty feet from the ground, which is sturdy enough to be utilised.

For a few decades now, it has been traditional for the volunteer (known on the day as Mistress Fire Test) to be given as much gin as she wants to drink before the event begins. This is done partly to numb her, and thereby provide some protection from burns, and partly so that she can piss onto the flames from time to time if she feels the heat is getting too much for her. The pissing is regarded as one of the highlights of the event and three years ago a woman called Flora Pickleworth managed to put out the fire completely with a sustained burst of pissing that won her a hearty round of applause and a beating from a group of aggrieved citizens. (The fire was restarted and when Miss Pickleworth was cut down she was found to be dead. No one ever really knew why she had died because when Dr Challot and I examined her we found that she was only burnt on the legs and slightly singed above the waist. Miss Pickleworth, an unpopular figure of Scottish ancestry was quickly buried and no more was said about it.)

This year's Mistress Fire Test had been hanging over the fire for nearly twenty five minutes when it was decided to cut her down. She hadn't been squealing much and most of the crowd were bored and wanted to get to their favourite Inn. So Egbert Merrydew, one of the farm lads from Shore-end Farm, shinned up the oak and used his pocket knife to cut the rope holding her to the branch. He came down the tree and we all tottered off to the Inn to continue the celebrations. The Potbury Arms always serves whitebait in jelly and brandy sauce on Fire Test Friday and no one who has ever tasted whitebait in jelly and brandy sauce wants to be late for that.

If you were being picky you could possibly criticise us a little bit for not checking that the damned woman had been able to extricate herself from the fire but any such criticism would be entirely unjustified since having been drinking beer and cyder all afternoon, we were all well anointed with Alcohol. Besides, that's all smoke up the chimney, as they say, and the fact is that after noting that this year's Mistress Fire Test (Miss Tabetha Walton) had safely fallen from the tree, and was almost not in the fire itself, we all hurried off to the Potbury Arms.

Unfortunately, the damned woman was never the brightest star in the sky and she was so sizzled with the two pints of free gin she'd drunk that she didn't move after she'd fallen but just lay there with the whole of one leg still in the fire. By then the fire had pretty well died down and there weren't any flames, as such, just a pile of red hot embers. Still, there is no denying that a limb on hot embers can suffer a goodly amount of damage.

It wasn't until three or four hours later that anyone noticed that Mistress Fire Test was missing from the celebrations. Indeed, we only noticed her absence because at that stage in the proceedings it is customary for Mistress Fire Test to be stripped naked, covered in honey, made to run through the streets carrying a string of pork sausages and finally thrown into the village pond. There's nothing malevolent in any of this, of course, and sending the victim running through the bee hives in Mr Turner's orchard is no longer part of the day, having been abandoned when two women were stung to Death. (The local Bishop rightly said that it might be wise if that part of the event were removed from the proceedings.)

But villagers do still let loose their dogs so that they can chase the sausages. There wouldn't be much point in the sausages if the dogs weren't involved.

It was some time later that we found Mistress Fire Test still lying in what remained of the fire under the oak tree. Her leg was so badly burned that there was no alternative but to amputate it just below the hip. I therefore went back to the surgery to collect a bone saw, a chisel and a few knives.

I wasn't away more than twenty minutes but when I got back I found that a book had been set up on the outcome of the amputation with people betting on how long the amputation would take, whether Mistress Fire Test would survive the operation and, if she died, when it would be.

I was told that I wasn't allowed to bet on how long the operation might take, even though I promised not to look at my watch while I was cutting and sawing. I was however allowed to put half a guinea on her dying within three days of the operation though I was only given odds of two to one since it was generally thought that I had too much of a chance to influence the outcome of the operation and the success or otherwise of my own bet.

Unfortunately, I lost my bet because the damned woman upped and died while she was lying on a wooden Table in the snug at the Inn. I managed to take her leg off in four minutes, which was a pretty good time, but try as I might I couldn't stop the Bleeding and the wretched woman just Bled to Death.

Afterwards, I did rather wonder if it would have been better if I'd removed the limb just above the knee rather than below the hip. But I really don't think that would have made any difference. She wasn't a woman in the best of health. And to be honest she didn't have a great deal to live for so it wasn't too much of a shame.

Later the Vicar pointed out that this was the seventh Death in the last ten years of Fire Test celebrations. No one was quite sure why he made this point since there isn't anything we can do differently that would make the event any safer. As Dr Challot pointed out later, sometimes you just have to accept that life comes with chances and that unless we are all prepared to wrap ourselves up in straw and oatchaff then from time to time one of us will die a little prematurely.

August 17th

'Why are you so gloomy?' asked Nellie.

'I harbour the strongest of suspicions that the Reverend Standorf and his Wife are planning to recruit me as a son-in-law,' I confessed.

'I had heard something of this,' admitted Nellie. 'Does the idea of marrying Miss Euphemia not fill you with pleasure?'

'It does not.'

'There has been much talk of her dalliances with a red headed under gardener,' said Nellie. 'Moreover, I have heard that she may be with child already.'

I looked at her and frowned.

'You are not the father?' she asked.

'Good heavens, no!'

We sat in silence for a while. We were in my room at the Peacock Inn drinking port and nibbling pieces from a Plumb Pie which Nellie had taken from the kitchen.

'Do Miss Euphemia's parents know about your debts?' asked Nellie suddenly.

I looked at her and frowned. 'What debts?'

'Your gambling debts.'

'I don't have any gambling debts.'

She looked at me, smiling.

'In truth,' I said. 'I do not have any gambling debts.'

'I have heard that the Reverend and Mistress Standorf had bad fortune with investments in a Railway company,' said Nellie. 'There was some difficulty with the company and they lost most of their money. Now they are struggling to make ends meet.'

'How on earth do you know all that?'

'One of the Maids in the Vicarage heard them talking. The Reverend was saying to Mistress Standorf that they would have to sell some of their land and sack some of the servants. There has even been talk of the two sons having to find work – though from what I've seen of them neither of them is fit for anything remunerative. They aren't trained and I doubt if either of them could handle a plough or milk a cow.'

'The Maid overheard them saying that?'

'Oh yes. Like a lot of rich people they assume that their servants are deaf or stupid or both.'

'And the Vicar is really in financial trouble?'

'He has already started to charge parishioners who attend the Sunday services.'

'Good heavens!'

'It's a penny for the morning service and a penny and a half to attend the evening service. He calls it a service charge. The Churchwardens are not happy about it.'

'I bet they aren't.'

'And Mistress Standorf is not well pleased with the idea of their selling some land and getting rid of some of the servants.'

'I bet she isn't!'

'So I'm guessing that they would probably not be well pleased to know that Miss Euphemia was planning to marry a penniless Doctor with large gambling debts.'

Suddenly, I saw young Nellie in a very different light. She was clearly far more intelligent than I had previously thought. It had never occurred to me that a strumpet would have such a good brain in her head.

'You think I ought to be honest with them about my gambling debts?'

'It would be the honourable thing to do, would it not?'

'I think you're right,' I agreed. 'Do you think my debts should be large or huge?'

'Oh, quite huge don't you think?'

My word, young Nellie is a bright girl.

September 7th

Hercules Tomkins, the Drummer came in and I bought yet another of his bone saws.

'How is business?' he asked when I'd handed over the price of the saw.

'Not terribly good,' I admitted. 'To be honest, terribly bad would be closer to the mark.'

This was, of course, something of an understatement.

The truth is that Dr Challot is killing the practice. He drinks far too much and often spends all day in Bed with a couple of Whores. Dr Mort, our new Apprentice is even more useless than Dr Challot. He turns up when it suits him and will only see the patients he fancies.

'I hear that Dr Mort spends a good deal of time in Bed with the patients,' said Hercules.

Misplaced loyalty prevented me from commenting but I did not dispute the suggestion.

'I see a lot of that as I travel around,' confessed the Drummer. 'I say it's all down to opportunity. A luscious female Patient goes in to see the Doctor and he tells her to take her clothes off. What happens next is entirely natural if you ask me.'

'I fear someone needs to introduce rules forbidding Doctors from making the beast with two backs with their patients,' I said. I know I'm probably considered a bit of a stick in the mud but it seems to me that practitioners like Dr Challot and Dr Mort are giving the profession a bad name.'

'I've heard they are thinking of bringing in rules,' said the Drummer. 'You mark my words they'll introduce proper qualifications and registration and all the rest of it. Doctors who roger too many of their patients, especially the ones who are unwilling, will find themselves hauled before some sort of court – probably a disciplinary tribunal.'

'Oh, I can't see it going that far,' I said. 'But the authorities are bound to do something. Dr Mort, or someone like him, will sleep with a politician's Wife and before we know it there will be rules.'

'So, have you thought about moving away and setting up a practice of your own?' asked the Drummer.

I admitted that I'd thought about it once or twice.

'But I don't have the money,' I confessed. 'It takes money to start a practice. I'd need a decent consulting room and unless I could buy a practice it would take some time to build up a list of patients. I have no savings and it's pretty well all I can do to pay my bills at the Inn.'

'You need to find yourself a little sideline, Doctor,' suggested the Drummer.

'What sort of thing do you mean?'

'Oh, get yourself appointed as Private Doctor to someone well off. That's the quickest way to make some money.'

'No chance,' I said, sadly. 'Rich people always want to be treated by a Physician; they look down their long noses at people like me – apothecaries, Barber Surgeons, general practitioners.'

'Then find yourself a nice, clever remedy that people have to buy,' suggested the Drummer. 'I know a Doctor in Bristol who has made himself a pretty penny out of selling an ointment for baldness.'

'What sort of ointment?'

'Ah, that's the trick, you see! No one knows what's in it. So no one can copy it. I've heard that it's got 16 different ingredients in it, all mixed up in boar fat. He calls it 'Dr Postlethwaite's Perfect Baldness Remedy'.'

'And what do patients do with it?'

'They rub it on the bald spot every morning and night for six months. Dr Postlethwaite issues an instruction leaflet with every pot of ointment. I've seen one. The leaflet instructs users that they must rub the ointment into the scalp in a clockwise direction and that they must rub for three minutes each time.'

'Does it work?'

'I've no idea. Is it important? People believe in it – that's all that matters. After using the ointment for six months, most men will be able to convince themselves that there's been some hair growth. They won't want to admit they've wasted all that time, energy and money.'

'But what happens if the stuff doesn't work?'

'The Doctor says they probably missed an application. Or they rubbed it in anticlockwise. Or they rubbed it for two and a half minutes one day. What's the worst that can happen? He gives them a refund.'

I told him about the little success I'd had with my remedy for restoring orgasmic ability beyond nature's allotted allowance and explained that I now had five patients who were turning up every month for their orgasm enhancing treatment.

I did not tell him that in every case I had tried, and failed, to persuade the patient that his fears were groundless and that the suggestion that a man's orgasms were limited was a piece of promotional nonsense thought up by a publicity seeking evangelist. In every case the patient had dismissed my reassurance and leapt at my remedy with unbridled eagerness. It seemed that patients simply preferred to accept a little discomfort, and a financial penalty, rather than take their chances. Only when they had been treated did they believe and feel the contentment they desired. If my treatment had any value then the value was, I suspected, in the mind rather than the body. But if it worked and gave comfort to those who chose to use it what harm was done? I had decided to abandon my pointless attempts to persuade prospective patients that my remedy was unnecessary.

'What's it called?'

I had to admit that I did not yet have a name for my remedy.

'You need to spread your wings a bit, Doctor,' said the Drummer. 'You could do very well with that remedy if you took it out across the country; go up into the Midlands, maybe even travel North a way. Visit the university colleges in Oxford and Cambridge – you'll catch a few of the young Bloods there and they're rolling in money.'

'Good heavens! I hadn't thought of that. Do you think there'd be a market outside Muckleberry Peverell?'

'I'll be a sailor's foreskin if there isn't, Doctor!'

'But how would I find new patients? There's no point in just my wandering up to Birmingham or Manchester and just expecting people to find me.'

'Give some lectures,' suggested the Drummer immediately. 'There are Town Halls and Institutes all over the country just crying out for speakers. And once you're down to give a speech, the local press will want to interview you. You rent a room in the biggest hotel in the region, the Railway Hotel by preference and for convenience, and when you are interviewed you make it known that you'll be there for a day or two and that patients who want to avail themselves of your treatment simply have to turn up at the hotel. You can always have some bills printed and maybe a few posters.'

I was so pleased with all the helpful advice he'd given that I bought one of his company's newly patented Superior Bone Saw Cleaning Brushes, specially designed for removing bits of bone from the teeth of the saw and preventing clogging. I now have quite a collection of these brushes.

'You won't regret the purchase for an instant,' said Hercules when I'd paid him for the saw and the Superior Bone Saw Cleaning Brush. 'And good luck with your promotional travels.' He paused for a moment. 'If you will forgive the impertinence I recommend you find a name for your remedy. Something like Dr Bullock's Stiffness Enhancing Remedy. And try to find a celebrity who'll give you an endorsement which you can put on your promotional leaflets.' He thought for a moment. 'I don't suppose you'd consider changing your name, would you?'

'What to?'

'Dr Bollock's Stiffness Enhancing Remedy has a more rounded ring to it, don't you think?'

I told him I'd think about it which indeed I will.

And I shall talk to Nellie before making a decision. She appears to me to have a stout intelligence and a fierce-some clever business mind.

Moreover, I also have high hopes that her suggestion for escaping from the clutches of the Standorfs will prove fruitful.

September 19th

'Since you were last here, Euphemia has purchased a small gift for you,' said Mistress Standorf. 'As a 'thank you' for your ministrations.'

I had responded to another request to visit the Standorfs. Father, mother, daughter and I were sitting in the drawing room.

'Oh yes!' cried Euphemia. She jumped up, put her brandy glass down on a small side Table and rushed out of the room. She returned moments later clutching a very fine Meerschaum Pipe with a huge bowl in the shape of a man's head. The Pipe had a bend in it which gave it a very curious look and, judging by the colouration it had been well used by its previous owner. It occurred to me that it would not have cost the guinea that we might have expected if our bill had been paid. I had no idea of the cost of a second hand Pipe but I doubt if the market flourishes quite as successfully as, say, the market for second hand pearls or diamonds.

'Here you are, my dear!' she said, handing the Pipe to me with what I thought to be unwanted reverence. 'Smoking a Pipe will give you gravitas when you are dealing with your patients. I have seen Sir Benedict smoke a Pipe similar to this one.'

I didn't quite know what to say. I have always loathed pipe smoking, considering it smelly, messy and rather affected. The silly girl seemed to think that taking up Pipe smoking would ensure that I would be elected to the College of Physicians and that a knighthood for me and a ladyship for her would follow as a matter of course. These seemed large expectations for a Pipe.

'I have a pot of Tobacco in my study,' said the Vicar. 'I will fetch it so that you can try your new Pipe now.' He levered himself out of his Chair and disappeared.

Weakly, I thanked his retreating form.

'Now that we are to be married you must not ask any of your female patients to undress for you,' said Euphemia. 'I cannot bear the thought of you seeing pretty, young ladies in a state of dishabille. And the thought of you touching any of their intimate parts drives me quite to distraction with jealousy.'

'But...' I began.

'And if you must, really must, do this terrible thing, I insist that you promise me that you will keep your eyes firmly shut at all times when examining any woman under the age of 40!' She stood up and moved her Chair closer to mine. She placed a hand on my arm in a very proprietorial manner, as though I were a pet dog. 'You will promise me, won't you?'

I was saved from all this nonsense by the return of the Vicar. He was clutching a large, red pot labelled 'Tobacco'. He put the pot beside me and removed the lid. The smell of the contents made me nauseous. 'Are you having a pipeful?' I asked him. It was only when I'd asked the question that I realised that Euphemia had used the 'married' word when she'd spoken to me.

'Oh good heavens, no,' the Vicar replied, rather sternly. 'I don't take Tobacco. It's a sin in the eyes of God. And I take a small potation of Alcohol only in sociable quantities. I keep the Tobacco for sinners who may feel the need.'

He pointed to the mantelpiece where there was a pot filled with twisted paper spills. It occurred to me, not for the first time, that if you were looking for a companion for an evening of high spirited entertainment, the Reverend Standorf would have been fairly low down on the list of recommended possibilities. I wondered if he had always been such a dreary fellow.

Egged on by both Euphemia and her father, I filled the huge bowl of the Meerschaum with Tobacco, lit a spill from the log fire in the grate and attempted to set fire to the Tobacco in the pipe's bowl. My efforts caused some amusement for it was clear that I was not an experienced Pipe smoker. Eventually, after burning up three spills, I succeeded in the endeavour and immediately found myself wreathed in the foulest smelling smoke it has ever been my misfortune to encounter.

'I'm told it is the best Virginian,' said the Vicar, nodding approvingly as the smoke rose. I sucked at the stem of the Pipe and coughed. It was a struggle to prevent the contents of my stomach from leaving home.

'It's very rich,' I managed to say.

'It will no doubt take a little practice,' said the Vicar. 'But I think that Euphemia is correct in thinking that a good Pipe will give you gravitas.'

Not knowing what to say, I alternately sucked at the Pipe and coughed for a few minutes. It seemed a heavy price to pay for a little unwanted gravitas.

'The Bishop of Fulham is coming for the weekend in a month's time,' said Mistress Standorf suddenly. 'I know you'll be delighted to hear that he's agreed to officiate at the wedding.'

'The wedding?'

'It is a great privilege and an honour to be married by a Bishop,' said Mistress Standorf. 'Though the Reverend Standorf will assist, of course.'

'Isn't it exciting, my darling?' said Euphemia. She leant closer and put her head on my shoulder. She breathed in the Tobacco smoke and seemed to enjoy the taste of it. I found myself wondering if the red-headed gardener was a Pipe smoker.

'You two love birds must get together and plan the wedding,' said Mistress Standorf. 'Though I will be only too pleased to help in any way you think fit.'

'Do you not think we should wait a while?' I suggested. 'To get to know each other a little better?'

'Oh good heavens no,' said Mistress Standorf. 'You don't want a long engagement.'

It occurred to me that if Euphemia was already expecting her first child, the family would not want to wait until the baby was showing. I was now, more than ever, convinced that Mistress Swain's information was almost certainly accurate.

'Do you have a house big enough for a family?' asked the Vicar.

'I'm sure the Doctor has a splendid house,' said Mistress Standorf.

'How many staff do you have?' asked the Vicar. 'And stables? How many horses do you keep? Euphemia will need a coach of her own, of course.'

'To begin with one lady's Maid will be sufficient,' said Mistress Standorf. 'But when your family starts to grow there will be a need for nannies. I have heard of a woman in the village who will make a splendid wet nurse.'

'I have a modest room at the Peacock Inn,' I said. I seemed to remember having mentioned this before. I had the impression that no one in the family heard anything they didn't want to hear.

'Oh how romantic!' said Euphemia, laughing nervously and, I thought, rather hysterically. She actually clapped her hands in what was, I think, intended to display delight.

'Good heavens!' said the Vicar.

'Oh, I don't think that would be entirely suitable,' said Mistress Standorf. 'You could perhaps both live here in the Vicarage for a month or two while you find a suitable home. The Reverend Standorf could perhaps arrange for you to speak to his bankers about a loan. Do you have substantial savings?'

'I'm afraid I have no savings whatsoever,' I said. 'I have only just started to earn a living. As an Apprentice I was not highly paid, though I did have my board and lodgings provided.'

'And your family?' said Mistress Standorf. 'Do they not have money?'

'My parents are both dead,' I replied. 'And my father used the last of his savings to pay for my Apprenticeship with Dr Challot. He was, I fear, not a wealthy man.'

There was an uncomfortable silence for a while. The Reverend Standorf looked at his wife, his Wife looked at their Daughter and Euphemia took a sudden interest in the pattern on the carpet. I began to feel that there might, after all, be some hope ahead.

'I expect to clear my gambling debts within a couple of years,' I lied, remembering what Nellie had suggested.

'Your gambling debts?' said Mistress Standorf. She sounded shocked.

'I had terribly bad luck at the tables,' I said. 'And foolishly I tried to recoup my losses at the races. Sadly, the horses I selected all seemed to be essentially sedentary animals.'

'How much do you owe?'

'Oh, I don't think it's much above £1,000,' I said cheerily. 'Though, of course, the interest keeps mounting because I've been having difficulty paying off the debt.'

There was silence.

'I will have to ask you to pray for my boots,' I said in an attempt to lighten the mood.

They all looked at me.

'I fear their souls are in peril!' I said. I lifted a boot in the air and, with my fingers, showed where the sole had parted company from the remainder of the boot. It appeared that the Highwayman had bought his boots for looks rather than sturdiness. Still, he probably did more riding and less walking.

No one laughed at my small jest.

'To whom do you owe this money?' asked the Reverend Standorf sternly.

'Oh just fellows here and there,' I said dismissively. 'Sadly, I fear, they are the sort of fellows who wager a good deal in a professional way and who are not generously disposed to those who are unable to pay their debts.' I shrugged. 'Fortune has not been kind to me and chance has not been my friend though fortunately my creditors have refrained from expressing their dissatisfactions in the usual way on the grounds that without my hands I would be unable to earn a living and therefore unlikely to be able to repay them.'

'Oh!' cried Euphemia, who looked as though she would like to faint but was refraining from doing so lest she miss the next instalment of what had clearly become something of a horror story.

'What do you mean?' asked Mistress Standorf. 'How do your creditors usually 'express their dissatisfaction'?'

'Usually by breaking a bone or two,' I explained. 'But sometimes they are known to chop off a hand or a foot. Unfortunately, the world into which I have strayed is populated by men who are unforgiving, impatient and violent. I have found, to my cost, that the three do not sit well together. When they attempt to recover monies owed to them they refer to it as 'putting on the bite'.' The Reverend Standorf looked at his Wife again. She looked at Euphemia who had given up on the carpet and was now directing her gaze at a piece of wallpaper to the left of the fireplace.

'Of course, if you felt able to pay off the debts for me I would hope to be able to pay you back over the next few years,' I said.

The Reverend Standorf could not have looked more shocked if I had suggested that we all disrobe so that we could play naked leap frog on the drawing room carpet.

'Oh, I think not, sir. I think not!' he replied. 'That would not be possible at all.'

'I understand, sir,' I said, standing. 'Then I will take my leave of you.' I held my new Pipe out to Euphemia. 'Should I return this to you?'

'Oh no,' she replied, very coldly. 'You may keep it as a souvenir of something beautiful which might have been.' I had feared that there might be tears. But tears, it seemed, were not in her repertoire. She looked at me as though I were something a horse had dropped.

'I shall cherish it,' I replied, putting the Pipe away into my jacket pocket.

Less than five minutes later I was walking home in the moonlight.

It was a mizzly, drizzly sort of night, with the mizzle and the drizzle turning to pikels but I didn't give a damn. An owl hooted as I strode along back to the Peacock Inn.

'And up yours too!' I cried merrily.

Moments later I felt a hot feeling in my side and discovered that the damned Pipe had set fire to my coat. I bent down and splashed water onto my coat from a puddle. I took out the Pipe and threw it into a bush.

Even this mild discomfort and inconvenience was not enough to dampen my spirits. I was delighted to have managed a skilful escape from a dangerous position.

I felt like dancing and found that I could hardly wait to tell Nellie the good news of how well her simple plan had worked.

October 1ˢᵗ

My relationship with Nellie has taken a turn for the better and last night one thing led to the other.

October 4ᵗʰ

Today was Trundling Day.

The origins of this custom are lost in impenetrable pagan mists but Trundling Day always takes place on the day after the second dry day of the month, the dryness of the days being defined by the Trundling Major who is elected every year by his predecessor. This year's Trundling Major, Edgar Bloted Esquire, is 83-years-old, blind, deaf and incapable of coherent conversation. His election was intended as a joke.

The rules are simple. Young, single men between the ages 25 and 30 must take a wooden wheelbarrow and push it through the streets as rapidly as they can. All unmarried women over the age of 25 must stand outside their homes in their best and most comely attire. As each barrow Trundles past, the attendant spinsters must attempt to leap in while the barrow is moving. If a spinster fails in her attempt, or falls out of the barrow, she is not allowed a second attempt. It is considered exceedingly bad form for a Trundler to deliberately tip a Maiden out of his barrow.

Once a spinster has succeeded in her endeavours to board a barrow, the young man behind the handles must Trundle his barrow and contents to the milestone next to the gate into the top field at Huckberry Farm. With the woman still in the barrow, the young man pauses, stands in front of his passenger and says: 'Thou wilt be my Maiden.' He plucks a bundle of grass from the verge and uses this to make the barrow more comfortable by stuffing the vegetation beneath the Maiden's posterior. The spinster does not have to speak though it is customary for there to be some blushing and murmurings of assent, and not a little wriggling, sometimes rather more than is required, as the grass is pushed into place. The Trundler then pushes the barrow to the Church where the Maiden clambers out of the barrow and the now 'engaged' couple go into their Church where they promise to plight their troth.

The 'engagements' and the 'troth plighting' are supposed to be light hearted but the event is usually taken seriously by many young folk. Inevitably, one of the parties will take the whole thing more seriously than it was intended. Three years ago, a Trundler was shot by the father of a spurned Maiden who claimed that she believed she was truly engaged to be married.

In recent years there have been many accusations of cheating, with stories being told of Trundlers pausing outside the homes of favoured Maidens in order to simplify their entry into the barrow.

To stop this happening, roving judges called Prosecutors wander the streets checking to make sure that there is no underhanded behaviour. Two years ago, a local newspaper called *The Intelligence and Visitor* reported that a Trundler had been seen helping a selected spinster into his barrow. Attempts were made to annul the 'engagement' though both parties had rather jumped the gun and the Trundler claimed that he had to help the spinster involved because she was so well endowed with child that she had difficulty in clambering into the barrow.

October 7th

My former fiancée Miss Euphemia Standorf has recovered well from the breach in our engagement.

It seems that on Saturday next she is to marry Canon Cuthbert Fazackerly at the Cathedral in Winchester. Canon Fazackerly, who is a Prebendary at the Cathedral, is as, as fashion seems to dictate among the wealthy, as fat as a pig. Queen Victoria's predecessor, George IV 1820-30, was so fat his belly reached his knees when he removed his stays and this is still regarded as a worthy aspiration among the obscenely wealthy who are clearly believers in the survival of the fattest.

Canon Fazackerly has £500 a year from stocks and £12,000 in gilts. He is reputed to own at least one square mile of farmland in England and to be the Laird of 20 square miles of Scotland where a Laird is ranked below a Baron but above a Gentleman. The fortunate

Canon also has great expectations since his uncle is an Earl with vast estates and a failing heart.

Nellie, who provided me with all this information, also reported that Canon Fazackerly has settled £100 a year on his bride-to-be for pin money. It is widely believed that he will be a father before he expects and it is to be hoped that his skills at arithmetic are too poor for him to draw conclusions about the child's ancestry. Nellie told me that the Canon is a renowned trencherman who is reputed to eat 19 eggs for breakfast every morning. When he was asked why he ate 19 eggs every morning he apparently replied, rather indignantly: 'What, would you have me eat 20 and be condemned as a glutton?'

Miss Standorf will not become a lady just yet (something already way beyond her reach I fear) but she will become rich. And when the Earl dies and the Canon inherits the title, she will become a Countess.

I have no idea how the Standorfs managed to arrange this marriage but some nifty footwork must have been involved.

October 9th

I received confirmation that the Government has plans to introduce some form of registration for all medical practitioners. My initial fears were assuaged when I discovered that all existing practitioners will be allowed to have free registration for life.

Dr Challot went a whiter shade of pale when I told him about the plans. He hates change of any kind and claims that betterment is never a good thing. 'Betterment invariably makes my life more complicated, takes away my rights or costs me money or all three,' he has declared more than once.

'You young whippersnappers get upset when we old folk gripe and criticise as though we know it all but that's because we bloody well do know it all,' said Dr Challot, who is ageing by the day and now looks to be about 106 though I believe he is rather younger than this. 'People forget that we've seen everything twice. You young folk don't understand why we get irritated when idiots come up with hare-brained solutions to problems that don't exist. You may call it intolerance but I call it good sense.'

I pointed out that although a register was to be introduced for Doctors he would have no problems and that, as a practising Apothecary, he would automatically be registered.

'We older folk can see problems arising before they arise,' he continued, not listening to me. 'We've seen the problems all before. When you're young you don't know how badly things can get buggered up. You don't realise that your horse will be lame just when you need it most. You don't know that the smiling banker is likely to be a crook who will steal everything you have. It's why we worry so much. You wait and see, you'll be the same when you're my age. They'll bring in these rules and regulations and before we know where we are it will be illegal for a doctor to roger a patient. And where will we be then, I ask you?'

'I've often worried why old people worry so much,' I confessed.

'We have seen a good deal,' he replied. 'We know how easily things can go wrong and we know how crooked people can be.'

There didn't seem to be anything worthwhile to say to that. It made old age appear rather depressing and I suddenly felt engaged by sadness for it seems that old age must come to all who are fortunate enough to avoid the alternative.

'I'm full up with problems,' Dr Challot sighed, with a dismissive wave of a hand. 'I've had enough. I don't have room for any more.'

I tried again. 'But you have nothing to worry about. You will be legally entitled to register as a Doctor,' I said again.

But Dr Challot wasn't listening. He was too busy emptying a bottle of port wine into his belly.

October 11th

Last Tuesday, Tobias Blomfield, a dray driver with six children and a relative of our Constable Blomfield, was found guilty of stealing three medium sized potatoes from one of Farmer Jessop's fields.

Blomfield is a simpleton (it is a surprise to me that he has succeeded in fathering six children though it has to be said that none of them looks anything like him) and although the churchwarden and three other good minded fellows begged for leniency, Jessop would hear nothing of it, demanding that the sad miscreant be properly published as a lesson to himself and to others. A lesson to others it may be but it will certainly not be a lesson to Blomfield. By the time he is punished he will have forgotten why and within an hour of the punishment he will have forgotten that it took place at all.

Jessop likes to consider himself a gentleman farmer but though he is a farmer he is no gentleman. He is, rather, the craftiest fellow in the county. Last spring he organised a ploughing competition and put up notices inviting men to bring hand-ploughs and to demonstrate how fast they could plough a straight furrow. Each man was told to pay a tuppence entry fee. There was promise of a half a guinea prize for the winner. Eventually, 97 men turned up to compete and Jessop had to make three large fields available for ploughing. I remember leaning on a fence watching the competition with Ebenezer Wentwhistle, a former farm labourer who is well into his eighth decade.

'What's 97 tuppences come to?' he asked me.

I found a piece of paper and a pencil.

'194 pence,' I told him, forty minutes later.

'And how many pence in half a guinea?'

That did not take so long. '126,' I replied in due course.

There was a long silence.

'Am I right in thinking that 194 is a bigger number than 126?'

'It is.'

I found an unused corner of my piece of paper.

'It is bigger by 68,' I told him.

There was another long silence.

'So Jessop made 68 pence profit,' said Ebenezer. 'And got his three largest fields ploughed for free.'

I remember we stood for a while contemplating this and trying to decide (unsuccessfully) whether Jessop was a mean-spirited, grasping bastard to be derided or a brilliant businessman to be admired.

It was, perhaps, hardly a surprise that Jessop insisted that the luckless Blomfield be severely punished for his crime.

And so Jessop, who is also the magistrate, has sentenced Blomfield, who was born a wretch and who will doubtless die a wretch, to be tied to the end of a cart and whipped through the streets by an official hangman.

Once or twice in the past we've used the whipper in from the hunt for this work but it has never been a really satisfactory solution.

There were a couple of cases where the whipping was desultory to say the least. The only official hangman who is available is a fellow from Exeter called Baker. The magistrate has sent him the travelling money and he will be here in three days' time.

October 14th

Mr Trench, the official hangman, came up to Muckleberry Peverell on the coach. By the time he arrived, a collection had raised one pound four shillings and sixpence as a bonus for the hangman if he whipped Blomfield hard until he yelped.

Mr Youngblood of the Peackcock Inn started the fund with a ten shilling donation.

'I have nothing against the hapless Blomfield,' he told me, when I protested. 'This is simply business.'

Mr Youngblood is doubtless hoping that the prospect of a good whipping will bring in good crowds and promote a healthy thirst among those in attendance.

We had a very disappointing whipping through last year when Oliver Curtis was found guilty of stealing two Turnips from one of Herbert Norris's fields. No one in the village remembered to give the hangman a bonus before he did his work and the whipping was midway between half-hearted and disinterested. There was very little squealing or shouting and no crying or sobbing or begging for mercy and, therefore, not much in the way of entertainment. Mr Youngblood, the Publican, was fair furious. He had bought in four extra barrels of beer but sales were worse than middling as spectators drifted away from a very disappointing event.

Fortunately for Mr Youngblood, the whipping of Blomfield went very well.

The hangman had brought his own whip, an impressive eight feet of Blood hardened leather with knots every foot and scarring hooks at the end. Poor Blomfield squealed and yelled and when the whipping was over there was plenty of Blood dripping from the hangman's whip.

Afterwards, Blomfield was given a rousing ovation and as much free beer as he could drink. He was well pleased.

When I was called to the Inn I assumed that Blomfield needed treatment for his back. However, the star of the show was standing at the bar enjoying his free beer and signing an autograph for Osbert the pot boy. The stripes on his back were well clustered and the Blood on his back had clotted nicely.

'You'll have good scars,' I told him as I passed by.

'Do you think so?' he asked, proudly raising his tankard in salute. 'Thank you, Doctor!'

He would, I suspected, earn free beer and pies for the rest of his life by showing his scarred back to visitors. He is fortunate in that Ebenezer Williams, the only other local man to have good whip scars, died three months earlier. He'd lived well for twelve years on the consequences of stealing a chicken.

I'd been called not to see Blomfield but to see Trench, the hangman, who was sitting in a corner nursing a very sore arm and looking very sorry for himself.

He told me his painful elbow was a recurrent problem. I'd never before seen a case of whipper's elbow but I had read about the condition in a copy of *The Provincial Medical and Surgical Journal*.

Trench told me that the muscles of his forearm were sore and I found a very tender spot on the outside of his elbow. He yelped so loudly when I touched it that everyone in the bar turned round to look. When they saw that it was the hangman who was yelping, there was a considerable amount of good hearted jeering.

'Have you had this before?' I asked.

He nodded. 'It comes on every time I do a good whipping.'

'Have you considered retiring from the whipping business?' I asked.

He shook his head sadly. 'It's impossible to make a decent living out of hangings these days,' he complained. 'People being hanged used to give a decent tip to make a clean job of it but nowadays we have a much rougher class of clientele and they never tip.' He pursed his lips thoughtfully. 'Can't remember when I last had a decent tip,' he complained. 'Last fellow gave me a tanner and handed it over as though it were a golden guinea.'

'You've got whipper's elbow,' I told him.

'I know it,' he confessed. 'All the fellows in my line of business suffer from it. What can you do for me? A Poultice usually does the trick.'

I told him I would fetch him a medicated linseed Poultice with a tincture of woodlice. 'Would you like it on chamois leather, silk or sheepskin?'

'Whichever is the cheapest,' said the hangman miserably.

I went back to the surgery, found an old linseed soaked sheepskin Poultice and replenished it with a mixture of lead oxide, olive oil and water to which I added a pinch of ground orange peel and nutmeg, in addition to the tincture of woodlice. It's a good mixture, solid when cold but flexible at body temperature.

'How much do I owe you?' asked the hangman, when I'd finished tying the Poultice in place with a yard of linen bandage.

'A guinea,' I told him. 'But you can take the used Poultice off in a week's time and if you take it to a local Apothecary he'll give you two shillings for it.'

The hangman opened his purse and handed over a guinea.

I did not feel troubled by the knowledge that he had paid over most of the bonus he had been paid but I told Mr Youngblood to give him a pint of mead and to put the cost onto my account.

Immediately afterwards I regretted this act of generosity.

October 15th

This morning, Mistress Prout, the owner of a large cottage in Largepuddle Lane, sent her Maid to demand my immediate attendance at her residence. Mistress Pearl Prout treats everyone in Muckleberry Peverell as a serf and her rudeness is quite legendary.

'What is the matter with her?' I enquired of the Maid.

'A man has fallen off the roof,' replied the Maid, as though this were an everyday occurrence.

It turned out that the man who had fallen was Mr Phineas Larkin, a thatcher.

When I arrived at Mistress Prout's cottage, I found Mr Larkin, the poor sod, lying on the ground motionless.

Mr Larkin claims to be 93-years-old (though his mother is still alive and so this may be something of an exaggeration) and he is known as something of a character. He says he fought at the Battle of Waterloo where he lost two fingers and an assortment of toes to the gangrene. He once showed me a shrivelled object, now quite unrecognisable, which he swore had been a French officer's foot. He claimed, quite without regret or shame, that he had chopped off the foot and kept it as a souvenir after stealing the fellow's boots and greatcoat. 'He had no further need for the foot, the boots or the coat,' he explained.

'The thoughtless bastard is dead,' said Mistress Prout, who was fetched by the Maid when the two of us arrived at her cottage. 'Now I shall have to wait a month to find another thatcher to finish the job.'

We were discussing the difficulty of finding good thatchers, when Mr Larkin suddenly came to. He sat up, shook his head and, without a word, climbed up his ladder and resumed working on the cottage roof.

'That will be half a guinea,' I said to Mistress Prout.

'What for?'

'You sent for me and I am here,' I replied.

'You have done nothing!' retorted Mistress Prout. 'I have no intention of paying you a farthing.'

Just then, a fellow turned up carrying a large sack on his back. The poor fellow looked exhausted and dropped the sack to the ground with a great sigh.

'Ah, I bought a peck of potatoes and a bushel of peas from a farmer at Kenstone Market,' she said, turning away from me and towards the carrier. She opened the sack to check that the potatoes were in good order, and reached into a pocket in her skirt and took out a half-groat piece. She made a move as though to give the man the half-groat before pulling back her hand and returning the coin to her pocket.

'I'll give you this when you come back with the peas,' she promised, though I know her well and she is a woman who is far richer in promises than in deeds.

The man, paused as he watched the tuppence disappear, then turned and started to trudge back to whence he had come.

'I paid a shilling for the potatoes and the peas,' Mistress Prout explained. She seemed very pleased with herself. 'The fellow doesn't have a cart or a horse and uses that dullard as his donkey. He's had to carry that sack eight miles and now he's got to walk eight miles back and then do it all again.'

'The poor man looks exhausted,' I commented. 'You didn't even offer him a glass of water.'

Mistress Prout looked me up and down and sniffed. 'There is a stream along the side of the road.'

'You owe me half a guinea,' I said.

'I'm not paying you half a guinea! You have done nothing.'

'You sent for me to attend the thatcher!'

'You did nothing. He has recovered and is back at his work.' We both looked up at the roof where Mr Larkin was busy at his thatching. He seemed none the worse for his experience.

'Doesn't make a difference,' I said. 'You called me out and you must pay. If I'd had to provide any treatment it would have cost you more.'

'Why should I pay you anything? It wasn't me who fell off the roof.'

'Then the next time you send for me I shall not come,' I told her, and turned on my heel. 'Not even if you are dying,' I added.

'Wait!' cried Mistress Prout, alarmed by my threat. 'I'll pay you five shillings.'

We settled on seven shillings and sixpence which she took out of her pocket and counted out, mostly in sixpences.

As I walked back to the surgery, I passed the labourer trudging back home to fetch the other sack of peas. I stopped and gave him three groats and told him to buy a pint of ale and a pie at the Peacock Inn. The poor fellow was pitifully grateful.

Since I provided no treatment I do not think I shall tell Dr Challot about my visit to Mistress Prout. There will, therefore, be no need to mention the seven shillings and sixpence.

October 19th

Dr Mort deigned to come into the surgery this morning.

He was wearing a blue dress coat with a black velvet collar and matching cuffs. Underneath the coat he wore a silk patterned waistcoat with large blood stones as buttons and underneath that a lace frilled, embroidered shirt. Pinned to the lapel of the jacket was a small bouquet of miniature roses. He had a lace trimmed handkerchief half tucked into his sleeve and wore a beaver hat and a pair of black dancing pumps with white buck's skin breeches and white stockings.

I complimented him on his jacket and mischievously remarked that I had seen one or two similar garments on men travelling through Muckleberry Peverell. 'It must be a very fashionable style and colour in this area,' I commented.

Dr Mort went as white as a summer cloud. 'Fashionable here?' he said, clearly horrified. He looked as though he were about to cry.

'They looked to be wearing identical garments,' I told him. 'Indeed, their whole look was very similar. White breeches, patterned waistcoats and each had a bunch of roses as decoration. I think they were Drummers.'

'Fashion is out-of-date as soon as it is popular and recognisable,' said Dr Mort, full of dismay and fierce-some offended. He looked down at his jacket and fingered the lapels as though he had never properly examined them before. It occurred to me that it must be quite tiresome to live in a world where one was constantly searching for something to which one could take offence.

'There were two of them, you say, in jackets similar to mine? Here? In Muckleberry Peverell?'

'I would say they were identical rather than similar.'

Mort sat down and was so distressed by what I had told him that he did not even flick at the seat of the Chair with his handkerchief. He looked down at his coat and waistcoat as though he would have liked to tear them off and discard them.

'People in London would laugh if they knew,' said Mort softly. I have noticed that he worries a great deal about what people think of him and even more about what they say about him. The poor mutt seems to exist in a constant state of torment.

Since we had not seen Dr Mort for a week or so I asked him where he had been hiding.

'I have been attending to my work-life balance,' he said sternly. 'I had allowed the balance to drift too much in the direction of work. That is not healthy for the mind.'

I stared at him in astonishment.

'Work is an appalling nuisance,' he said. 'A friend of mine is training to be a barrister. The week before last he worked for two days in succession!' He said this as though it had been an imposition beyond a normal man's endurance. 'On Monday last, I came into a little money from an aunt. It was little more than a pittance but it needed to be spent.'

'Do you never save any money?' I asked him.

He looked at me as though I were mad. 'Money is the root of evil and causes much pain. It's essential for a healthy soul to get rid of it as quickly as possible. I see no virtue in saving but I do believe in spending,' he said. 'A fellow should always spend every penny he can lay his hands on. It is his duty. If men like me don't spend how are bootmakers, cabmen and coffee shop owners to make a living? The poor devils would starve, and their families with them. Besides, God put me here to enjoy myself and damnit that's what I intend to do. Strewth, to do otherwise would be a blasphemy and I'll not allow any man to accuse me of that particular sin.'

I was about to remonstrate with him and to point out that a career in medicine requires dedication and hard work when he announced that he did not expect to be a working man for much longer.

When I asked him what he meant, he told me that he was heavily taken with a young woman called Miss Imelda Whitestone whom he had seen at a wedding he had attended.

'I thought you were taken with that niece of the Duke of Wellington's?'

'I was,' he confessed. 'But her father threw me out of the house when he found out that I was a medical man. Apparently the Duke had an unfortunate experience with a Doctor who did something absurd to his ear and he has acquired a stern dislike of all medical practitioners. The father is terrified that if his daughter marries a medical man then the Duke will cast him off and have nothing more to do with him.'

'So you have now already replaced her with Miss Whitestone?'

'From what I recall of her, Miss Whitestone seems an agreeable person,' said Dr Mort with a nod. 'I did not see her from the frontal aspect but I recall that she has broad hips and would doubtless make a good Wife and Mother. I shall make a stroke in that direction.'

'Have you actually spoken to her?' I asked him.

'Hardly,' he replied with a dismissive wave of a hand. 'It was a wedding and the place was packed with bridesmaids – all with aching voids to be filled.' He laughed. 'There were more cavities to be filled than can be found in a dentist's waiting room.'

'But did you not express your intentions to Miss Whitestone?'

Dr Mort shrugged. 'She did not at first take my fancy for I hear she is not a comely creature and she is rather ancient for my tastes. However, she is so plain that I am persuaded that she is a virgin and clean throughout and I hear tell that she has a fortune of a clean £80,000 in Government bonds. The bonds are invested at 2 per cent which should give a nice, steady income of £1,600 a year.'

'But if you have not spoken to her how do you know she will agree to marry you?'

Dr Mort, plainly astonished, stared at me as if I were suffering from the hatters' disease. 'How could she resist me?' he demanded. 'I am the most handsome and best dressed man I know.'

'How old is this paragon?'

'Quite ancient I must admit; she must be 25 if she is a day,' he replied. 'In view of her age, her father is bound to be desperate. He is one of those baronets who live in the shires and make their money out of farming. The whole family is ludicrously rich. Miss Whitestone inherited her fortune from an aunt who was very taken with her. I should be able to squeeze a damned good dowry out of her father to supplement her fortune. I am told that he has two spare town houses which he never uses but rents out and an additional very pleasant, unused estate in Northamptonshire which I gather he inherited from a cousin. I would be happy with either of the town houses, the tenants could easily be evicted, together with the estate which comes complete with several hundred acres of excellent hunting country.'

I stared at him in astonishment.

Mort shrugged. 'There are two other Daughters coming up to her age and they cannot be married off until Imelda is married off and out of the house.' He paused, thinking. 'One of the sisters, a girl called Sophie, is a pretty little thing with charming ankles and a delicious neck. I would not in the slightest mind having her as a sister-in-law.' He put an unnecessary amount of emphasis on the word 'having' so that there was no doubt about what was in his mind.

'Why do you always assume that pretty women will fall at your feet?' I asked.

'Oh, they are the least trouble to seduce,' he replied with a smirk. 'No one ever talks to them because the ugly ones are considered easier sport, like birds with broken wings are easier to shoot. It's a nonsense, of course. I have no doubt that Miss Whitestone is a virgin still.'

Much to his annoyance, I set Mort to work pounding foxglove leaves with a stone mortar. 'Turn them into a good, fine powder,' I instructed him. 'There is no better cure for the dropsy than the foxglove.'

'What a quaint business medicine is!' said Mort with a snort and a giggle. 'Who'd have thought a Doctor would treat fat ankles with a foxglove posy!'

On balance, it seems to me to be no exaggeration to say that Mort is as thick as a brick but nowhere near as useful. I would think he probably needs someone to hold his hand if he wants to cross a road. I've had pig's bladders which made more sense.

As each year goes by I realise that I know and understand less and less – even though, paradoxically, I suppose I must know more. The more I learn the more I realise I don't know anything. I suspect that young folk like Mort are brimmed with cockiness because they have no idea how much they don't know.

November 20th

I was busy mixing up the ingredients for my suppositories when Nellie came into the room with a basket of wood for the fire.

'What are you making?' she asked.

I explained.

'How do they work?' asked Nellie with commendable curiosity. 'Is there a magic ingredient?'

I confessed that the suppositories had no active ingredients and were, therefore, entirely harmless as well as entirely useless.

'So why do men buy them?'

'The suppositories banish their fears,' I explained. She had heard about the Reverend Callwallader and instantly understood the logic of my endeavour.

'How much do you charge?'

'At least one guinea,' I replied.

'A whole guinea?' said Nellie, clearly astonished. She picked up one of the suppositories I had already prepared. 'For one of these?'

'I believe that if I charge too little the suppositories will be less effective,' I told her.

'So, maybe they would work better if you charged five guineas each.'

I thought about this. 'With some customers, maybe this is true.'

Nellie, who had clearly been joshing, looked as if she were about to keel over. 'Do you need some help in the work of making them?' she asked.

I thought for a moment. I did find the making of the suppositories a tedious business. Another pair of hands would doubtless speed things up.

We agreed that I would pay her half a groat an hour to assist in the making of more suppositories. And after a couple of hours work I realised that I would be able to leave the production of the suppositories entirely to Nellie who was competent, hard-working and, as I already knew from experience, impressively nimble fingered.

November 22nd

We have been exceptionally busy this week. On Monday morning I saw 12 patients. I then had to visit six patients in their homes. And in the evening there were another nine patients to be seen.

Unlike large towns and cities, we in Muckleberry Peverell are not yet quite overrun with wise women, bone-setters, urine healers, phrenologists and hucksters selling patent medicines. The consequence is that Dr Challot and myself are pretty much the only providers of medical services. (I discount Dr Mort for he is hardly ever to be found and when he is available he is only prepared to offer succour and comfort to healthy young women who are, I suspect, as eager for the games of 'Doctor and patient' that he plays as he is himself.)

At first I thought this busy time was simply an anomaly. But Tuesday was just as busy and when I arrived at the surgery on the Wednesday morning, I found that the practice was even busier, with a crowd of patients gathered outside the door. I made time to go upstairs and confront Dr Challot who was, as usual, still in Bed, comfortably snuggled between two seemingly naked trollops – neither of them tretis nor toothsome. The trio were sitting up and Dr Challot had a dish of tea in his hand.

'I bought a practice from the Widow Blackburnt,' he told me carelessly when I asked if he knew why we had so many patients to deal with. 'Her late husband was an Apothecary in the village of Maidenstoke, no more than an hour and a half away by foot. He had a good practice. I paid her 50 Sovereigns to redirect his patients to me.'

'You didn't ask me. Or even tell me!' I said, feeling mortally aggrieved.

'Why should I ask you?' retorted Dr Challot, sipping at his tea and idly and rather absent-mindedly fondling an errant jug belonging to the raven haired trollop on his left.

'I'm a partner and I have to do most of the work!' I retorted.

'Junior partner!' snapped Dr Challot. 'And you have young Mort to help you.'

'Mort is never here,' I protested.

Dr Challot, a picture of indifference, merely shrugged. 'You should get back to the patients,' he told me. 'When I have completed my examinations of these two patients I will be down directly to take charge.' He reached under the blankets and one of the trollops yelped, though whether it was with surprise or delight it was impossible to tell.

Consumed with anger and feeling myself redden with what seemed to me to be well-founded fury, I left and hurried back down the stairs. But, as I stood in the doorway, I turned back to ask a final question. 'Have you already paid the widow the 50 Sovereigns?'

Dr Challot laughed. 'Of course not! I told her I will pay her the 50 Sovereigns in a year's time when she has redirected enough of her husband's patients in our direction.'

I nodded, closed the door and hurried down the stairs. There was no chance of the hapless Widow Blackburnt receiving a penny from Dr Challot. He would simply insist that he had not seen any of her husband's patients and so did not owe her a penny.

Downstairs I set to work dealing with the patients who were waiting – most of whom were patients who had been sent to us by the Widow Blackburnt.

A man in his 40s, sporting a huge, bulbous heliotrope nose, complained of a weak leg. He told me that in the absence of Dr Blackburnt, he had seen his village wise woman who had instructed him to collect as many snails as he could find, put them into a muslin bag, crush them and rub the slime from the snails onto his weak leg.

'Has this helped relieve the weakness?'

'Not in the slightest,' the fellow retorted with rare honesty. 'But we will have a better crop of vegetables this year for there are no snails in our garden.'

'Where does your local wise woman live?' I asked, smiling to myself at the gullibility of the old man and the way that the ignorance of simple folk enables these silly old unscientific superstitions to live on.

'She has the cottage next door to mine,' said the man. 'She is a good woman. She has kindly allowed me to collect snails from her garden.'

'Does she have a vegetable patch?'

'Oh yes.'

I did not say anything but found myself feeling admiration for the wise woman who had so easily cleared the neighbourhood of snails.

She rather reminded me of the farmer who had his fields ploughed and was paid for the privilege.

'Can you recommend anything other than snails?' asked the poor dupe.

I prescribed a treacle and brimstone Poultice which will, I have no doubt, do him far more good than the crushed snails!

The next patient, a woman with complexion like watered milk complained that she was suffering from melancholy. I told her to eat plenty of cabbage and to take it with salt and honey added. I find that this remedy, which was used by the Egyptians, the Greeks and the Romans, never fails. Cabbage, honey and salt also make an exceedingly good remedy for all varieties of the colic.

It is pity that the local wise woman does not forget her snails and learn a little more about real, modern, scientific medicine. Still, I suppose that on balance it is a good thing that she does not know these things for if she did she would treat all our patients, and our practice would be a very sorry one.

November 24th

A young mother in her early 20s came in to see me carrying a baby of around 12 months. Two small toddlers followed in her wake. The woman introduced herself as Mistress Uffcomb.

'I produce too much milk and I need treatment to reduce the pressure on my glands,' she explained, after I had admired the baby and asked her what I could do for her. She unfastened her blouse and proudly pulled out a pair of hugely swollen breasts.

'Is your baby feeding well?' I asked.

'Oh yes, sir. He feeds very well. But he cannot cope with the quantities of milk I am making. I had the same problem with my other two children. It has always been both a curse and a blessing.'

'Have you tried offering yourself as a wet nurse?'

She shook her head. 'There are no requirements at the moment,' she said and paused. 'And besides,' she added, 'my husband does not like the idea of my feeding another man's babies. He is very easily aroused by jealousy.'

I nodded, though this did not make a good deal of sense.

'He is the Blacksmith in our village of Brassington-under-Wold,' added the woman. 'He is a very large man and rather short tempered.'

I nodded again, thinking that the woman was probably wise to give some considerable weight to her husband's wishes. I remembered having heard of the fellow. He had won prizes in a number of wrestling and boxing contests.

'Dr Blackburnt always used to get rid of the excess for me,' said Mistress Uffcomb. She leant forwards and lowered her voice. 'He never charged me for the treatment,' she said. 'He used to treat me once a week all the year around. He said it would keep my dumplings healthy and in good shape.' She paused and lifted up one of her breasts, fondling it as though she were at the market and it were a large, white, blue veined, exotic fruit which she was thinking of purchasing and turning into a luscious pudding. 'Dr Blackburnt said I produce most excellent milk which has a fine soft, creamy taste.'

'How exactly did Dr Blackburnt help remove the excess milk,' I asked, hardly recognising my own voice. I feared I already knew the answer to my question.

'Oh he suckled it out of me,' said Mistress Uffcomb. 'He said it was the only natural way to do it and the way least likely to do harm to the pap or the nipple.'

'He sucked the milk out of your breast?'

'Oh yes. But he was very kind. He didn't charge me a penny for the treatments. I shall miss him so very much.'

'And he did this once a week?'

'At least once a week throughout the year, sometimes more often. If they were swollen he would see me whenever it was necessary. He was fearful obliging and called my milk his ambrosia.'

I found myself trying to remember how Dr Blackburnt had expired. It seemed likely that he might well have found himself beaten to Death by a Blacksmith wielding a large Hammer. Indeed, if the Blacksmith were truly as large as Mistress Uffcomb suggested, he could have probably beaten the Apothecary to a pulp with no weapons other than his fists. I went quite cold at the thought.

'He gave you the treatments even when you did not have a child to nurse?'

'Oh yes. He said that it would be a good thing to keep the milk flowing.'

'And how long did the treatment take?'

'It usually took about half an hour or so, sometimes a little longer. I found it a very relaxing and pleasant treatment; not at all unpleasant. If she was at home, Mistress Blackburnt would bring me a dish of fresh posset to sip during the treatment. She always put a clove or two into it because she knew I liked my posset a little spicy.' She smiled at me, as though about to share a private piece of knowledge. 'Dr Blackburnt said he could always taste the cloves and spices in my milk.'

'Splendid!' I said, rather weakly, for I could not think of anything else to say.

'Shall you start my treatment now, Doctor?' asked Mistress Uffcomb. She stood up, made as though to move towards the couch and hesitated. 'Sometimes I would sit on Dr Blackburnt's lap, sometimes he knelt before me and sometimes he would lie with me on his couch. He said that was the most comfortable position for us both. I am happy with whichever you prefer.'

'Oh no, no,' I protested quickly, holding up a hand. 'I fear I cannot treat you in the way favoured by Dr Blackburnt.'

'You cannot treat me?' she cried.

'You can easily express the surplus with your fingers,' I suggested. I mimed a suitable action with my fingers.

'Oh no, that would not be at all suitable,' said Mistress Uffcomb, quite shocked. 'I would much prefer the treatment as prescribed by Dr Blackburnt.' She held out the Breast she was holding, as though it were a delicacy she was encouraging me to try. It occurred to me that the Breast appeared to be roughly the same size as the dome on St Paul's.

'It isn't possible,' I said. 'I have an indisposition to milk.'

'An indisposition to milk?' she cried, clearly disappointed.

'I fear so. Milk brings me out in a terrible rash and gives me arthritis of the knees. I shall be crippled if I drink your milk.'

'Oh.'

'I would have been deeply honoured to help you in such a way,' I said, in an attempt to soothe the woman's clear distress. 'It would have been a privilege and no burden other than for my indisposition.'

'But surely if your indisposition is to cow's milk you will not be indisposed by a mother's pure milk?'

'Any sort of milk,' I lied firmly. 'I am indisposed if I drink cow's milk, goat's milk, sheep's milk or mother's milk. Perhaps someone else here might be able to help you? Dr Challot or Dr Mort?'

Mistress Uffcomb shook her head. 'I fear not,' she said. 'I made enquiries before I came. Dr Challot is not a clean living man and Dr Mort is far too young. I should be concerned to have Dr Challot take my milk and embarrassed to allow Dr Mort to suckle me. My husband would not be happy for either of them to treat me.' She picked up her baby, called together the two infants who had sat quietly on the floor, and headed for the door.

I paused, thinking of what she had just said.

'Does your husband know how Dr Blackburnt treated you?'

'Oh yes, of course.'

'And he knew that you were coming to see me?'

'It was he who suggested I see you. He said you were neither particularly young nor good looking. He will be mortally disappointed that you cannot oblige. Indeed, he will, I know, be sorely disappointed – grievously so.'

'Maybe your husband might be able to help remove the excess milk?' I suggested, rather desperately. I was not overwhelmed with delight to know that I was considered neither young nor good looking.

Mistress Uffcomb looked quite shocked at my suggestion. 'Good heavens no, Doctor!' she said. 'He has no medical training whatsoever. He would be most incapable and I would not dream of suggesting it to him.' She paused. 'He will be very disappointed that you cannot oblige.' She paused and looked me in the eye. 'Grievously disappointed,' she repeated.

'You think he may be upset?' I asked, surprised. It seemed strange that the fellow would object to a strange baby suckling on his Wife but allow an Apothecary to do the same thing.

'Most upset,' said Mistress Uffcomb. 'He is easily distressed and he loves me very much. He knows that I suffer terribly if I am not properly treated and he hates to see me in discomfort.'

I sighed. I really did not want to incur the wrath of a champion boxer, the largest and most fierce-some Blacksmith in the region. 'Maybe I could try a small taste,' I suggested. 'Just to see how severe my indisposition might become if we persevered with the treatment.'

'That would be an excellent notion,' said Mistress Uffcomb with a smile of satisfaction. She put the baby back down on the floor.

'Perhaps, if we were to lie on the couch for the first treatment?' I suggested with a sigh.

'I think that would be an excellent place to start,' she agreed moving over to the couch and lying down. 'Would you prefer to begin with the right or the left dumpling? Dr Blackburnt always preferred the right one though he was always careful to be sure to offer each dumpling the same amount of attention.'

'I shall endeavour to do likewise,' I said as I lay down on the couch beside her.

'And there won't be a charge?' she said.

'No, no charge,' I mumbled, as one of her bloated nipples slipped easily into my mouth.

As a river of milk began to stream down my throat it occurred to me that I might not be earning any money but I would at least be saving the cost of a midday meal. Mistress Uffcomb put an arm around me and I both heard and felt her purring with satisfaction.

Suddenly, I heard a screech of laughter.

I sat up with a jolt. Mistress Swain, Dr Challot's housekeeper, was standing in the doorway.

'You should have let me know your little fancy, Doctor!' she said, pulling a droopy, flabby Breast out of her blouse and pointing it in my direction. It looked like a partially deflated balloon.

Mistress Uffcomb grabbed at me and tried to pull me back into the position I had so recently vacated.

'I am helping to relieve this young woman's engorgement,' I announced, realising as I spoke that I probably sounded rather pompous. I wiped a trickle of milk from my chin.

'I have no doubt you will next persuade her to relieve you of your own engorgement!' replied Mistress Swain, with another fiercesome cackle.

I leapt to my feet.

'Thank you, Doctor,' said Mistress Uffcomb, attempting to stuff her breasts back into her blouse and to button them away out of sight. It was clearly a monumental task. 'I feel a little relieved,' she said, as she struggled. 'But since today's treatment has been interrupted, I shall return at 11.00 a.m. tomorrow so that you can continue.' And with that she was gone, her two infants following her like lambs.

'Anytime you're feeling peckish, just let me know!' repeated Mistress Swain, stuffing her own paltry offering back into the dark of her grubby blouse.

I shuddered.

I shall arrange to be away attending to an emergency tomorrow at 11.00 a.m.

November 27th

Last Tuesday I was called to the local court-house to confirm that a man who had been hung for stealing half a sheep was dead and in a fit state to be buried. (His colleague in crime, who had apparently taken the other half of the sheep, was still at large.)

'We can't bury the fellow without a piece of paper signed by a medical person such as yourself,' said the hangman, a cockalorum who was clearly more than slightly peeved by what he clearly considered a slur on his own determinational abilities. He was a short, stout fellow with generous dewlaps and wattles and the ruddy nose and cheeks of a man who is partial to a more than occasional glass of port. 'When I hang ''em they die,' he frequently proclaimed, with all the obvious pride of a man who takes pride in his work. I hadn't seen him before assumed he had taken over from the last hangman – the one with whipper's elbow.

Since the unfortunate Hangee still had the noose around his neck, it wasn't difficult to confirm that he was indeed as dead as a Lychgate nail. His eyes were bulging and his tongue was sticking out of his purple lips.

'You can bury him,' I told the hangman.

I scribbled a note on a piece of paper I had brought with me and handed it to him.

'That's it?' he asked, examining the note.

'That's it,' I agreed.

'You're not going to examine him?'

'I just did. He's dead. You can bury him.'

'And you get five shillings for that?'

'I charge five shillings for having the status that entitles me to sign that piece of paper,' I told him, rather stiffly. 'I don't charge anything to confirm that he's dead. Any fool can see he's dead.' I paused. 'Even you can probably see that he's dead,' I added, more than slightly annoyed by his manner. 'Are you going to take the rope from around his neck?'

'I leave 'em with the noose,' he said. 'I never use a rope more than once. Only courteous to the client, in my honourable opinion.'

'Well, you can bury him and his rope,' I said, and left to collect my five shillings from the courtroom clerk.

That was last Tuesday, three days ago.

Today, a boy came round to the surgery to ask me to call in at the court-house again.

Anticipating another very welcome five shillings fee I hurried round before I had my luncheon.

'Have you hung another one?' I asked the clerk, a mousy little fellow who has pimples and, I happen to know, a curiously swollen right bollock. 'I thought the hangman would have gone somewhere else by now? Where's the corpse?'

The clerk, took me down a long corridor, unlocked a heavy, wooden door and showed me into a cell wherein lay the fellow I had certified dead earlier in the week.

'Isn't this the one I have already certified?' I asked him.

'It is,' said the clerk.

'Well he's still dead,' I told him. 'Why do you bother locking the door?'

'If we don't keep the corpses locked up they get stolen,' said the clerk. 'Body snatchers take them and sell them to you sort of people.'

'What do you mean?' I demanded. 'My sort of people?'

'You Doctors,' said the clerk. 'You're always wanting dead bodies to play with.'

'Well, I don't want any dead bodies!' I retorted. 'And why do you want me to certify him dead again? Are you planning to pay another five shillings? If you pay another five shillings I'll certify him dead as often as you like.' I thought for a moment. 'You can have five certificates for a guinea,' I said, thinking this quite a sound idea.

'I need him uncertifying,' said the clerk.

'What the devil for?'

'It seems we hanged the wrong man,' said the clerk. 'Another fellow confessed to stealing the other half of that sheep.'

'I can't uncertify him,' I protested. 'He's dead and dead is dead whatever you say. I can't bring him back to life. He's dead and he stinks and you need to bury him before he's eaten by maggots.'

'Well, it's very embarrassing,' complained the clerk. 'We can't hang the real criminal for the crime if we've already hung someone else for it.'

'Why not?'

'It'll look terrible if it gets out. People will know we made a mistake.'

'You could let the second fellow go free?'

The clerk was clearly appalled by this.

'Or hang him for something else?'

'What?'

'I don't know. Something. He must have done something bad in his life. Hang him for it.'

'That's it! Brilliant!' said the clerk, rubbing his hands. 'We'll say it was a conspiracy. They were a gang of three. We've hung one, one to hang and one still to catch. Come back this afternoon and you can certify the second one. I don't suppose you could hang him for us as well, could you? You were right about the hangman. He buggered off to Winchester and we don't have a hangman here.'

I indignantly told him that I didn't do hangings.

'Well, give him a shave and a haircut then,' said the clerk. 'He looks too disreputable to hang.'

'That'll be four pence for the shave and ten pence for the haircut,' I told him, that being the usual rate for shaving and trimming dead bodies.

I hate shaving and hair cutting but another 14 pence is another 14 pence.

November 28th

I spent the evening trying to repair the battered body of Ebenezer Tallyrand.

Mr Tayllrand is a furniture maker who was born in Sweden. Owing to his land of origin he is clearly of foreign origin and therefore not widely trusted in the district.

I was called to attend by his wife.

Dr Mort, who happened to be with me when I was called, accompanied me though as usual I found him to be rather more trouble than he is worth.

'He's in here, Doctor,' said Mistress Tallyrand, leading me into the parlour. 'I tried to get him upstairs but he couldn't make it on his own and he's far too heavy for me.'

'What seems to be the matter?' I asked, and regretted the words as soon as they had spilt from my lips. The unfortunate devil, sprawled on an old horse-hair sofa, looked as though he had been run over by a hard ridden gig. His face was bloodied and bruised and judging by the way his left arm and leg were arranged, a number of essential bones had been broken.

'He can't talk,' said Mistress Tallyrand. 'Two fellows brought him home from the market and told me that he'd been beaten up by an angry crowd.'

'What on earth provoked a crowd to beat him up?' I enquired, surprised. Although Mr Tallyrand is foreign and therefore not English, he is a not entirely unreasonable fellow. He specialises in making Chairs and Tables and if I ever have enough money to buy my own furniture I will certainly consider taking my custom to him.

Mr Tallyrand struggled to speak but only succeeded in spewing some Blood and a couple of teeth down his chin. I couldn't understand a word he said though I admit he does have a thick foreign accent and I have always had difficulty in understanding him.

'He was trying to sell a new type of Chair,' explained Mistress Tallyrand. 'It was the first time he'd taken it along to the market.'

'And he was beaten up because of a Chair?'

Mistress Tallyrand nodded.

'What the devil sort of Chair was it to occasion such a response?' enquired, astonished and quite genuinely puzzled. I had never hought of furniture as something likely to arouse strong emotions. Vho, even after six pints of strong mead, is likely to be aroused to iolence by a Chair?

'It was a new invention and he was very proud of it,' said Mistress Tallyrand with a sigh. 'He called the Chair the first of a new range of 'horizontally packaged chattels' and he thought they would be a huge success. He packed the pieces for the Chair in a sack so that they could be carried home without any inconvenience. He said he believed his new invention would make our fortune.'

'What the devil is a horizontally packaged chattel?' I asked.

'Here's one,' explained Mistress Tallyrand, crossing the room and picking up a few pieces of wood. 'This is his first Chair.' There were pieces which looked as though they might be Chair legs, a flat piece that looked as if it would serve as a seat and another piece which would make the back for a Chair.

'But it's in bits!' I exclaimed. 'Has it fallen apart? It can't have been very well made if it's fallen apart.'

'Oh no,' said Mistress Tallyrand. 'It's supposed to look like this.'

Her unfortunate husband made another attempt to speak. Once again his attempt was in vain and once again Blood and teeth were all that came out of his mouth.

'The idea is that people buy all the pieces for a new Chair or Table and take them home where they connect the pieces together with little bits of prepared wood. All you need is a Hammer.'

'Why on earth would people buy a Chair that they have to finish making themselves?' I demanded.

'It makes it easier to transport the Chair,' explained Mistress Tallyrand.

'But the customer who has bought the Chair has to finish making it when he gets back home?'

'It's very easy to do. And we provide a Sheet of instructions for those who can read and a little Wooden Mallet for those who do not have a Hammer of their own.'

'I take it the idea didn't go down too well?'

Mistress Tallyrand shook her head and I could see that there were tears in her eyes. 'The crowd became very agitated and angry when Mr Tallyrand explained what had to be done.'

'And the crowd attacked your husband?'

'It was unprovoked.'

'But I'm not surprised they attacked him!' exclaimed Dr Mort. 'What would you think if you were ill, called me in, as ye have done and I gave you a potful of Leeches and told you to apply them yourself?'

Mr Tallyrand sighed, tried to get up but collapsed back onto the sofa. He was a terrible colour and appeared to have lost a great deal of Blood. I realised that it was too late to apply Leeches. There wouldn't be enough Blood left to give the poor creatures a snack let alone a decent meal.

'What would you think, eh?' Dr Mort repeated. 'You'd be shocked wouldn't ye? And what if the butcher brought round a pig and told you to make yourself a couple of sausages. Or the hansom cab driver brought round his cab and buggered off home, leaving you to drive the cab wherever it was that you wanted to go.'

Mistress Tallyrand looked at me and seemed quite shocked. It was clear that neither she nor her husband had thought through their plan.

'So they set up on him?' I said.

'They used the legs of his Chair to attack him, then burnt all his furniture,' admitted Mistress Tallyrand. 'This Chair here is the only one remaining.'

'I am not surprised,' I said.

I looked closely at Mr Tallyrand and as I did so he gave out a great sigh, dribbled a few more teeth across his chin and subsided back onto the horsehair sofa. He must have started the day with pretty much a full complement of natural teeth. I bent forward and peered at him. His eyes were glassy and there was no sign of him breathing. 'He's gone now,' I said. 'I'm afraid he paid the ultimate price for a really daft idea.'

'They were nicely turned Chair legs though,' said Mistress Tallyrand, with no little pride. 'I must say that he always turned a lovely leg.'

She picked up a piece of wood and I could see it was, indeed, nicely turned.

'Everyone always praised his legs,' she added.

I noticed that there was Blood, hair and something that looked like bits of brain clinging to the end of the wooden leg.

'Wipe it clean, chop it in two and it'll make a decent piece of kindling,' I said.

She looked at the leg as though seeing it for the first time. 'Oh yes, thank you Doctor,' she said. 'And what about my husband? Is there nothing else you can do for him?'

'Oh, he's gone,' I said, without looking at him any further. 'Dead as a nail I'm afraid. Call the undertaker and ask him to take Mr Tallyrand away.'

'Thank you, Doctor,' said Mistress Tallyrand, attempting a small curtsey which was, I suspect, in deference to Dr Mort more than myself.

'And tell him you don't want a coffin you have to finish making yourself!' said Dr Mort. He repeated the remark, clearly thinking it quite a good jest.

'I may be a lazy good for nothing and the very worst sort of raindrop but I a good source of a fine jest, am I not?' he said, turning to me.

I ignored him.

November 29th

I am increasingly concerned about Dr Mort for he appears to have an unusual and rather personal approach to the practice of medicine. One concern which I have shared with Dr Challot is, of course, the fact that when he deigns to favour us with his attendance, Dr Mort is willing only to attend to young, female and comely patients. Moreover, he has a tendency to expect them all to undress completely – always managing to find some excuse to instruct them to disrobe even if their complaint does not seem to merit such an approach.

The other day, I wandered into the consulting room, thinking it to be empty, and found Dr Mort and the young Wife of a local farmer. The Wife was quite naked and sitting on Dr Mort's lap. When I enquired about the nature of the young woman's complaint he told me that she had come to the surgery complaining of a painful tooth.

'He even manages to convince most of them that rogering is the best cure for whatever ails them,' complained Dr Challot, more concerned I think that Dr Mort was being more successful in this regard than he had ever been, than for any professional or moral reason.

On one occasion recently we were asked by a groom's father to check that a bride to be was a virgin. Dr Mort spent two hours examining the young woman and only at the end of that time did he provide her with the certificate she required.

'Was she a virgin?' I asked him later.

'She may well have been when she entered the consulting room,' replied Dr Mort. 'But she was most certainly not when she left.'

'But how could you provide her with the certificate she required?'

'She said she was a virgin when she arrived,' said Dr Mort. 'I decided that the only way to be certain of the situation was to give her a most thorough examination myself. But since she had clearly been a virgin when she arrived I was happy to give her the note she required.'

On another occasion we visited Sir Everett Baxter's home to attend to Sir Everett himself, who was constrained by a devilish imposition from the gout. Before we left we heard music coming from the drawing room and found his two Daughters making music. One, a sixteen year old, was playing the violin and the other, a year younger, the piano.

I listened with astonishment as Dr Mort suggested to their mother that he examine them to confirm that they were both healthy. Moreover, he offered to provide them with pre-nuptial certificates, valid for ten years, confirming their good health and purity.

Although I then left the property I understand that the examinations took the rest of the afternoon and most of the evening.

I took young Dr Mort with me to visit Mistress Burpalot, the young widow of Mr Silus Burpalot who had suffered a fit of some kind. (It still irks me to have to refer to Mort as Dr Mort. I had to serve a long and painful Apprenticeship before being given that privilege.)

Since my own steed, Bess, was at the blacksmith's for attention, I was riding a donkey that day, the only conveyance available for hire, while Dr Mort was riding a huge black stallion which was, apparently, a gift from his father. The donkey was a particularly seedy looking example which walked so slowly that several times I felt that I could move more speedily were I to dismount, abandon the ancient beast and revert to Shanks's pony. I fear that we must have looked rather too much like Don Quixote and his squire Sancho

Panza – with me in the unfortunate and not to be admired role of Sancho Panza.

'You take charge,' I told the Apprentice, naively, as we rode up to the front door. 'I will stay silent and observe how you deal with the situation.'

A young Maid with about twelve summers behind her, showed us into the drawing room and pointed in the direction of Mistress Burpalot who was reclining upon a chaise longue. The maid seemed rather simple minded and stood for a moment gawping; only leaving when her mistress dismissed her.

'What appears to be the trouble?' enquired Mort. This seemed a fair beginning and mentally I gave him full marks.

'I fear I may have had some sort of fit or seizure,' replied the woman, putting the back of her hand against her forehead in what appeared to be a rather staged version of a swoon.

'Then, madam, I must remove your clothing!' said Dr Mort firmly.

Mistress Burpalot sat up. 'Good gracious,' she said. 'Is that entirely necessary?'

'Do you feel that there is any chance that you might have a relapse?' he asked.

'Oh do you know I feel there may be such a risk. I cannot deny the possibility. I feel very faint.'

'Then off must come your clothing.'

'All of it?'

'All of it!' cried Dr Mort, leaping forward to assist in the disrobing process. He was never keen when it came to applying Leeches but always eager when it came to helping a young woman to disrobe. 'I would be failing in my professional duty if I did not insist upon it.'

'Only my tailleur du corps balleine' is allowed to see me within my chemise!' protested the woman, though I confess I thought the protest a weak one.

'I do not wish to see ye within your chemise!' said Dr Mort firmly. 'I wish to see ye without your chemise.'

'Loosening the clothing is usually considered a perfectly adequate response in these circumstances,' I whispered rather anxiously. I could feel myself reddening at Dr Mort's recklessness.

Dr Mort, however, ignoring me completely, had already succeeded in unfastening a dozen of the buttons which ran down the back of the lady's dress. I had never before seen such nimble fingerwork. It was, I thought, something of a pity that Dr Mort did not prove to have such nimble fingers when assisting on the operating Table. He did not have to do all the work for Mistress Burpalot was of considerable assistance. She stood and her fingers worked as feverishly as did his.

I estimate that took the two of them less than three minutes to unbutton, remove and discard all the clothing which Mistress Burpalot had been wearing. The dress came first, followed by a crinoline cage and a hooped petticoat decorated around the edge with small forget-me-nots, a pair of pantalettes, together with a curious waistband which supported them, the like of which I had never seen before, a camisole bodice, a corset cover, a thin corset with stays (designed to support and project the bosom of the wearer) and a final chemise.

Eventually Mistress Burpalot wore nothing but a pair of white silk stockings, held up with pale blue garters, and a pair of delicate pale blue silk house slippers.

'Ye may keep the stockings and the slippers,' said Dr Mort, with unexpected generosity.

'Sir, I am grateful for I would not like you to see me quite naked. Nevertheless, you now see me at a grave disadvantage,' said Mistress Burpalot, fluttering her eyes at her saviour. She attempted to cover her most intimate womanly parts with her two hands but the hands moved about like butterflies on summer flowers and were of little consequence.

'Do ye feel better now ye are free of those encumbrances?' asked Dr Mort.

'Oh indeed I do feel very much better, Doctor,' replied Mistress Burpalot. 'Though I fear my heart is pounding. Would you be kind enough to examine me to see if I need a letting or a Leeching or some other treatment?' She sat down on the couch, lifted her legs onto the couch as she did so, and lay before him. 'I am yours to do with as you may think necessary,' she added.

'I think we can safely leave you now,' I said to Mistress Burpalot. 'You seem nicely recovered. It is possible that your accoutrements were too tightly fastened. We have several other calls to make within the neighbourhood.'

Dr Mort turned to me. 'Ye look after the other calls,' he said, sitting on the edge of the chaise longue.

He spoke as though he were the teacher and I the pupil. 'I think I must stay here and make certain there is no relapse,' he told me, speaking most sternly, as though there were a risk that Mistress Burpalot might die in moments if he were to leave her.

Mistress Burpalot laid a hand upon his leg, rather more above the knee than seemed entirely seemly. 'Oh I would be most grateful if you would stay,' she said to Dr Mort. 'It will make me feel so much better to know that I am in your most assuredly capable hands.'

She looked up at me, as though aware of my presence for the first time. 'Would you be kind enough to close the door on your way out while your master attends to my needs?'

I left but reasserted my crumbled authority by riding away on Dr Mort's magnificent stallion, leaving him to go home on my donkey.

Sadly, the damned stallion was a little lively for my taste and the animal threw me a mile from home. I sustained no serious injuries but was more than adequately muddied. I have no idea what happened to the damned horse.

November 30th

Dr Mort is proving to be something of a liability as far as our patients are concerned, though much appreciated by the undertakers in the area. Dr Challot, who is doubtless concerned that if he terminates Dr Mort's Apprenticeship he may be expected to return the payment he received (and which he has, I suspect, already spent on beer and strumpets) will do nothing to protect our reputations.

Yesterday, Dr Mort bled a man whose pulse was regular but weak due to losing a large quantity of Blood in a farm accident. Mort used 14 Leeches and cut the man's veins to lower his Blood pressure.

Predictably, the poor fellow died. His corpse was so white it could have been made of marble.

And this afternoon I discovered that we had run out of arsenic.

When I asked Dr Mort if he knew why the arsenic jar was empty, he admitted that he had given Mistress Bertha Ottilie a large dose of the stuff on the basis that if a small dose does a Patient good then a large dose must be infinitely more efficacious.

I now understand why Mistress Ottilie died so unexpectedly.

December 1st

Dr Mort turned up at the surgery decidedly the worse for wear this morning. Actually, it was only just morning when he arrived for within three minutes the noon clock had struck.

'We had a good time in the Strand yesterday evening,' he boasted. 'I attended a cock fight in Madam Venables' bordello and then some chums and I visited the inns and hostelries between Fleet Street and Trafalgar Square. At Charing Cross we broke every window in the Blue Boar, smashed all the furniture and put two portermen, an Ostler and two constables in the way of needing medical attention.'

He roared with laughter at these exploits, for which he clearly expected to be congratulated.

'Good heavens, sir!' cried Dr Challot, who was out of Bed before mid-afternoon for the first time in months. 'Have you no respect for your reputation and your position as a medical man. Were you arrested? Do you have to go to court?'

'To court? Yes, begad. And it was a damned good jape. I had to attend the court this morning but only as a witness. The magistrate fined the innkeeper three guineas for allowing a disturbance on his premises. The fellow could not stand straight and had both arms in bandages. He had also lost half a dozen teeth and the magistrate fined him an extra ten shillings for failing to speak clearly.'

'You and your companions were not fined for causing the disturbance?' I remarked, both aghast and envious.

'Oh no, not at all,' laughed Dr Mort as though this were an impossible eventuality even to contemplate. 'The magistrate is the uncle of Sir Oliver Lentil, one of my drinking companions.'

I am beginning to wonder if Mort's mother hired a wet nurse with dubious morals. It is well known that a wet nurse has to be chosen carefully since the baby she feeds will likely absorb her moral qualities. Hire a drunkard or fool or Whore and the resultant child will grow up with terrible habits. I suspect that Mort must have taken milk from the bosom of a truly disreputable woman.

December 2nd

Dr Challot, Dr Mort and I performed an amputation on a farm worker. Mort, who wore riding gloves throughout the operation, claiming that he did not like discovering bits of flesh under his fingernails, was very drunk and cascaded in the middle of the operation.

One of the new-fangled Post Boxes has been installed in the street not far from Dr Challot's consulting rooms. I cannot see how these devices can possibly be of any value but Dr Challot surprised me by purchasing a Sheet of the new One Penny Stamps which were issued some years ago but which we have never yet had occasion to use. The Stamps, which are black, contain a picture of Her Majesty. The idea is that having written a missive, a Stamp is affixed to the letter and the letter placed in the box to be collected and delivered. I still think it unlikely that this will ever work. Indeed, I doubt if Dr Challot will not be the only citizen to find humour in having to lick the back side of good Queen Victoria.

December 3rd

It snowed heavily and it was far too cold to go outdoors this morning, especially since both my boots have holes in the soles. The snow drifts are four or five feet deep in places and snow-blossom was falling heavily. According to the newspaper which was delivered this morning, campaigners are still blaming the new Railways for the lamentable weather. The campaign against the Railways is being led by a nine-year-old child called Eviane who is reputed to be a resident of the Paupers' Lunatic Asylum in Tours in France. The child, doubtless illiterate, claims that she received a vision from an angel who told her that the Railways are the work of the devil and will lead to the world either freezing over or boiling. She does not seem clear which of these consequences she favours. Larrikins, kinching delinquents and lunatic asylum inmates everywhere believe her every word and there have apparently been demonstrations in London, Manchester and Birmingham. In London the police had to shoot eight of the protestors in order to disperse a crowd of nearly a thousand lunatics, most of whom were far too congealed to be considered for entry to any institution.

'Your trains are destroying our future!' cried one eleven-year-old who was dragged away by policemen after attempting to tie herself to a tree with a piece of string. (She had, in error, tied herself to one of the policemen who was bravely attempting to prevent her tying herself to the tree.)

Such scenes had never before been seen in England and an editorial writer in *The Times* suggested that never before had so many lunatics been gathered in one place.

'Shoot all the crazy bastards and save us all some money,' a Member of Parliament was quoted as suggesting.

Showing what I thought to be commendable devotion to duty, I left the Peacock Inn after luncheon (having stuffed old newspapers into my boots), braved the demonstrating children (there were five of them) and managed to make it as far as the consulting rooms at Dr Challot's home.

Once there, I made myself a glass of hot mead, removed my boots and attempted to dry my socks in front of the meagre fire which Mistress Swain had lit in the consulting room. The fire was so miserable that I had to sit with my feet on the dog irons before I could feel any warmth.

At ten thirty, the postman arrived with a letter from Mistress Luella Biddulph asking me to visit. The letter had been written that morning and Mistress Biddulph did not say if the problem was an urgent one. The Biddulph home is a half hour ride in good conditions and a two hour trudge on foot. Since my horse is still exhausted and lame and the donkey I had rented was still with Dr Mort, I faced a four hour trudge. I looked at my steaming socks and leaky boots and sighed. There are times when being a general practitioner can be distinctly unattractive.

And then a notion burst upon me.

I wrote back asking Mistress Biddulph to be more specific about her request for a visit. I gave the letter to Mistress Swain and told her to put it into the new Post Box which is, fortunately, situated no more than two hundred yards from Dr Challot's front door.

I must say that this new scheme is something of a wonder. You just put a letter inside the box – making sure that a small picture of the Queen has been stuck onto the envelope. The box is emptied regularly and the mail inside delivered to the addressee. I am told that housewives use the postal service to order deliveries from the grocer and the butcher. A shopping order can be posted in the morning and the required victuals delivered that same afternoon.

At two thirty that afternoon, I received a reply from Mistress Biddulph

'My husband has the Stomach ache and the Vomiting,' she wrote. 'He ate three dozen oysters and twelve pints of mead last evening. Do you think these might be the cause of his affliction?'

I made up a bottle of slibber-sauce medicine (nauseating enough to be guaranteed to work), wrapped it in brown paper, addressed the packet, enclosed my determination, the instructions on how to best use the treatment and my bill for half a guinea and tied everything into a packet small enough to pass through the aperture into the Post Box. I sent Mistress Swain out to place the treatment in the box.

At six thirty in the evening, the postman brought a small packet which contained my half guinea payment and a note of thanks from Mistress Biddulph.

I am very much in favour of these new Post Boxes for the system has saved me considerable discomfort. Indeed, I can see that the new system may soon make it unnecessary for anyone to leave the house except to journey to the nearest Post Box.

I have written a note to the Postmaster asking that the Post Boxes have more capacious mouths to accommodate larger bottles of medicine. I added a postscript suggesting that a Post Box be placed outside every house in England.

December 4th

Dr Mort came to me and asked me to be his second. I had no idea what he was talking about.

'Your second what?' I asked him.

'I eventually managed to discern that our half-witted Apprentice had been challenged to a duel and instead of offering a grovelling apology (surely the sensible course of action for an overweight buffoon with no discernible physical skills) the fool has accepted the challenge.

'Who the devil has challenged you to a duel? It's 1853 for heaven's sake.'

'Baron Whipton of Walsall. He is always challenging people to duels. He is known for it.'

'Why the devil did he challenge you to a duel?'

'I was in a Leaping House rogering a wench called Fanny Bottom, a prostitute he fancied. He tapped me on the shoulder with his glove and challenged me. He quite put me off my stroke.'

'He didn't wait until you'd finished your work?'

'No, he did not. I thought it damnably rude of him.'

'What sort of weapons will be used?' I asked.

Dr Mort stared at me, clearly puzzled.

'Pistols, swords or fists?' I asked.

'Pistols, swords or fists?' he repeated as though these were words he had never heard before.

'Or do you intend to battle with snowballs?'

'I hadn't thought about weapons being involved,' said Dr Mort, his voice rather softer and less confident and his visage now considerably paler.

'What did you think was going to happen?' I asked. 'Were you expecting that the pair of you would stand toe to toe and simply hurl abuse at each other?'

'I confess I hadn't really thought about there being weapons involved,' Mort repeated. 'How do we find out?'

'You'd better ask the Baron for the name of his second. I will then speak to him and see what is proposed. What sort of weapon does the Baron normally prefer?'

'Oh, pistols, I suspect,' replied Dr Mort, the light dawning. 'Come to think of it he is renowned as a crack shot.'

'Can you shoot?' I asked Dr Mort.

'Never touched a pistol in my life,' said Mort, with a discernible shiver. 'Horrid, noisy things.'

'Well, either we must persuade the Baron to accept another type of weapon or you must take lessons.'

December 5th

I met Sir Enoch Drinkwater who is the Baron Whipton of Walsall's chosen second for the duel with Dr Mort.

Sir Enoch is very short, hardly an inch above five feet in height, and quite the roundest man I have ever met. The circumference of his waist must match or possibly exceed the length of him from heel to crown. It would be a damned jolly jape to roll him down a long hill.

'What sort of weapon did the Baron have in mind?' I asked.

'Pistols,' replied Sir Enoch. 'The Baron always favours the pistol. He has a pair of very fine duelling pistols and your fellow Mort can take his pick of the pair. We find that pistols bring the occasion to a rapid conclusion. Four of the last men with whom the Baron duelled died within the hour. Sword play can drag on for hours and interfere with much of the day – causing havoc with appointments and suchlike.' Sir Enoch had a curiously squeaky voice which made it difficult for me to take him entirely seriously.

'The thing is,' I said, 'that Dr Mort is not an accomplished shot. Indeed, he has never touched a pistol in his life.'

Sir Enoch shrugged and pulled a face. There was the hint of a smirk. 'We'll meet at dawn tomorrow in Regents Park. No point in dragging these things out. You can arrange for an undertaker to be present if you like. It makes sense to have the body moved away quite quickly. It is our experience that it can sometimes be difficult to obtain a hearse if you don't have one immediately available.'

'Wait a minute!' I cried. 'Wait a minute. Aren't we supposed to discuss these things? You can't just decide the weapon, the place and the time!'

'Why the devil not?' demanded Sir Enoch.

'Because it isn't seemly!' I replied.

'Are you accusing me of unseemly conduct?' demanded Sir Enoch.

'I think I am, sir!' I replied, perhaps rather incautiously.

A moment later something landed on my chest and fell to the floor at my feet. I looked down. It was a glove. I looked across at Sir Enoch. He was wearing a glove on his right hand but his left hand was naked.

'Name your second, sir!' squeaked Sir Enoch. 'We will fight our duel immediately after the Baron shoots your fellow. Pistols. I'll bring my own pair.'

I stared at him for a moment. 'Are you challenging me to a duel?'

'I just did.'

'Well, I don't accept your challenge,' I said firmly, though it occurred to me fleetingly that with a fellow so obscenely fat, and wider than a large barn door, it would not much matter that I too had never touched a pistol for a bullet fired by a blind man would unerringly hit the target.

'What do you mean?' said Sir Enoch, incredulously. 'You can't decide whether or not to accept a duel!'

'I took the Hippocratic Oath,' I pointed out. 'I am not allowed to shoot people in public parks.'

'That's arrant skimble-skamble. I have fought duels with three Doctors.'

'What happened to them?'

'They all died, though one took a week because I shot a little low and off-centre and caught his liver.'

'I have very bad eyesight,' I lied quickly. 'I am damned near blind.'

'That has no bearing on the issue at hand.'

'Of course it does. You cannot challenge a blind man to a duel. It would be unseemly.'

'That is twice you have accused me of being unseemly!' cried Sir Enoch. 'I challenge you to another duel.'

I stared at him.

'I will shoot you and we will fight another duel and I will shoot you again,' he cried. His anger taking his squeaky voice up into an area usually reserved for those lady opera singers who can smash expensive wine glasses with a single note.

I looked at him and thought for a moment.

'I am a very experienced shot,' I lied, changing tack. 'I have won medals for my shooting. It would be unfair of me to allow you to challenge me to a duel.'

'Pshaw!' said Sir Enoch. 'I am a Drinkwater. I know no fear.'

'And what are you going to do if I don't turn up?'

He stared at me and frowned. 'What do you mean?'

'What do you plan to do if I refuse to fight a duel?'

The fat, little fellow stared at me open mouthed and you could almost hear his brain trying to start up. 'What do you mean: If you refuse to fight?'

'I'm not fighting a duel,' I told him. 'It's a stupid idea.'

'I shall tell the world. You will be dishonoured!'

'Pshaw to you in spades! I cannot think of anyone I know who will think any the worse of me for refusing to stand still in Regents Park while a small, fat man shoots holes in my liver. On the contrary, everyone I know would think me mad to risk my life for such a pathetic reason.'

'I shall tell the world you refuse to fight!' cried the fat fellow, as though this would frighten me into accepting his pathetic challenge.

'Please do so,' I said. 'I shall also tell everyone that you challenged me to a duel and that I refused to meet you because you are a small, fat buffoon with the mind of a slug and the morals of a rodent. It will be impossible for you to creep up behind me and shoot me in the back because everyone would know that you were the murderer. You would be arrested, disgraced and hung as a common criminal.'

I walked away from him.

'What about your man Mort?' shouted the fat fellow.

'He can do whatever the devil he likes,' I said. 'If he has any sense, which I doubt, he too will refuse to fight a silly duel with the Baron Whatshisname of Wherever.'

December 6th

'What has been decided?' asked Dr Mort, when I saw him this morning. He seemed desperately concerned, as well he might have been.

'It's off if you don't want to fight,' I told him.

'What do you mean?' he asked. He was trying hard not to look delighted but failing in that endeavour.

I told him that I too had been challenged to a duel and that I had refused. 'If I were you I'd do the same,' I told him.

'But they will tell everyone I refused to fight!' exclaimed Dr Mort.

'Who cares?' I said, with a shrug. 'If you fight the duel you will die. If you refuse to fight the duel you may be momentarily embarrassed.' I paused. 'Actually, I don't think the Baron of Whatsit will tell anyone you turned him down. He will be too embarrassed.'

Mort thought about this for a while. 'Do you know,' he said, looking rather pleased. 'I think you are right.'

And so neither of us fought our duels.

And to our delight and our surprise we never heard anything more from Baron Whipton of Walsall or Sir Enoch.

December 7th

Dr Challot was due to appear in court to defend himself against an accusation that he had deliberately caused the demise of a certain Gilbert Blossom by giving him an overdose of arsenic. The action was brought not by the authorities but by the widow of Mr Blossom who was claiming £150 in damages.

The case has been taking up much of Challot's time for the last few weeks.

Two months ago, a solicitor acting for Widow Blossom presented Dr Challot with a sheaf of affadavits from citizens all claiming that Mr Blossom had been a good living man who had been healthy until he had started to receive treatment from Dr Challot.

'This looks bad,' I said to Dr Challot, as I leafed through the affadavits.

There were six affadavits and at first eyewink they looked terribly convincing. However, on close examination I noticed that the citizens who had signed the affadavits had all signed with an X. Moreover, their statements were identical and four of the men who had signed were brothers who had given their address as the Lamb Inn.

We sat in silence for a few minutes.

'Where the devil did the lawyer find all those people to sign affadavits?' asked Dr Challot.

'At the Lamb Inn, by the looks of it,' I suggested. 'Most of these people can be found there every evening.'

We sat in silence again.

'You mean to say the lawyer simply went into the Lamb Inn and persuaded all these people to sign affadavits?'

'These fellows would sign anything for a pint of porter.'

We went back to sitting in silence.

'Damnit! I'll buy some affadavits of my own,' said Dr Challot, at last.

By ten o'clock that evening he had visited The Peacock Inn, The Plough, The King's Head and The Red Lion and had acquired 23 affadavits from citizens claiming that Mr Blossom had been at Death's door when he had first sought treatment from Dr Challot. 'Death,' they all wrote, 'was a release, and Dr Challot did everything possible to save the unfortunate Mr Blossom.' Of Dr Challot's collection of affadavits, 19 were signed with an X.

The total cost? Twelve shillings and nine pence.

After Dr Challot had presented his sheaf of affadavits to the court, the case brought by Widow Blossom was abandoned.

December 8th

I worked 17 hours today. I saw a grand total of 43 patients, travelled 10 leagues on horseback and performed three operations. At least, it seemed like 10 leagues. I suppose it might have been a mile or two less.

Now that we have more patients to look after, it seems that Dr Challot and Dr Mort are doing less work than ever.

Even though we have far more patients to look after, Dr Challot does not rise from his Bed before noon at the earliest and is drunk for most of the rest of the day. Unfortunately, he somehow manages to remain alert enough to keep a record of the number of patients I see and, therefore, the number of guineas the practice has earned. (I strongly suspect that Mistress Swain provides him with this information.) I am making him a rich man and exhausting myself in the process.

Dr Mort, whose only two qualities appear to be ignorance and arrogance, turns up once or twice a week at most and has taken to bringing with him friends from London who attend as spectators. Dr Mort tells our patients that the men who attend him are medical students or young Doctors who have come to watch his expertise and learn from him. The patients, fooled by his charm, seem enormously impressed by this nonsense even though the spectators, putative medical men, stand around and snigger and make ribald remarks as patients (nearly all nubile and slightly naïve young women) are persuaded to undress. Twice Dr Mort has operated on patients while showing off to his companions. Once he removed an aching tooth and left the Patient with a fractured jaw and on the other occasion he dealt with a troublesome bunion by removing the entire foot. The second of these patients died within an hour, of shock and exsanguination. The first will, I fear, die of starvation within a fortnight. On both occasions Dr Mort had turned up at the surgery in a severely cappernoited condition. These disasters do not trouble Dr Mort who dismisses them as the 'slightly regrettable but inevitable consequences' of performing sophisticated medical procedures. I fail to see how removing a rotten tooth or soothing an irritable bunion can be regarded as 'sophisticated' medical procedures.

When I mentioned to Dr Challot that I was worried about Dr Mort's approach to the practise of medicine, Dr Challot was quick to defend his new student.

'Dr Mort has brought new standards to this practice!' he cried. 'He has brought social status and I have heard that he is extremely popular with our younger female patients.'

'There are one or two who favour his unusual approach to medical matters,' I agreed. 'But there are many more who are disturbed by his insistence that all female patients should undress completely whatever is wrong with them. The fellow now has more notches on his pizzle than a bowsaw.'

'Such diligence and application should be commended!' answered Dr Challot.

'But he steadfastly refuses to see male patients of any age or females over 30,' I pointed out.

'Specialism is an inevitable part of modern medical practice,' said Dr Challot, whose loyalty to Dr Mort, purchased in gold, was clearly unswerving.

'He's nothing but another one of those damned raindrops!' I protested.

Dr Challot frowned. 'A raindrop?'

I explained that the word is used to describe young people who are rather wet and entirely self-interested and whose interests are ephemeral. 'It is a word of disparagement used to describe young persons who are extremely wet and who evaporate whenever the heat is turned up.'

The result of Dr Challot's refusal to drag his raddled form out of bed, and of his uncritical support for Dr Mort's unusual approach to the practise of medicine, is that my work load has become quite unbearable. I am desperate to leave the practice but I have to find 30 guineas to buy my freedom. I spoke about this to Nellie and she pointed out that if we promote my orgasm remedy a little more enthusiastically, I could have that sum saved up within a month. The problem, of course, is that I am working so hard at the practice that there is very little time for selling the orgasm remedy.

December 10th

We managed to find time to attend two race meetings where Nellie and I succeeded in finding several customers for the orgasm remedy.

Nellie pointed out that if we attended two or three more meetings I would have enough money to buy myself out of Dr Challot's practice.

I really don't know how I would manage without her determination and incessant optimism. Nellie has resigned from her position as a Chambermaid at the Peacock Inn. She proudly tells anyone and everyone that she is my mistress. She regards this as a clear promotion.

December 12th

Dr Challot called me into his bedroom to announce that in future he would be cutting my percentage of the practice earnings in half.

When I protested, he retorted that I would still be able to earn the same amount of money because he had increased the size of the practice.

'I had to pay out good money to buy Dr Blackburnt's patients,' he said. 'You'll be able to see twice as many patients as before. This is all valuable experience for a young Doctor such as yourself.'

'But dealing with all those extra patients will require more time than there are hours in the day!' I protested.

'You have Dr Mort to share the burden.'

'Dr Mort is hardly ever here!' I replied indignantly. 'And on those rare occasions when he does deign to turn up, his only interest is in examining young Maidens. He now steadfastly refuses to see female patients unless they are exceptionally good looking and particularly free and easy with their favours. Yesterday he refused to see either of the Miss Davendishes, neither of whom has yet seen 20, because he said they were not comely enough for his eyes.'

'I heard from Mistress Swain that you yourself have not been averse to taking advantage of the patients,' sneered Dr Challot.

'If you mean Mistress Uffcomb,' I replied, feeling my cheeks adopting the hue of a beetroot, 'then I can assure you that I was merely treating a Patient with a painful condition. The remedy was one she had requested herself and one which had been regularly prescribed by Dr Blackburnt.'

Dr Challot responded to this with more sneering and a rather unprofessional wink of conspiracy.

'Call it what you will,' he agreed. 'I'm not a man to criticise another practitioner's chosen form of treatment.' He grabbed the two naked harlots of the day and squeezed their breasts with unfettered enthusiasm. The two harlots squealed and half-heartedly pretended to try to escape from him. This, of course, they could have easily done had they been genuinely so minded.

'If you cut my earnings in half I will hardly be able to live!' I protested. 'I already have a massive, unpaid bill at the Inn. My boots are leaky and worn and my newest clothes were all purchased second hand from Dr Blackburnt's widow.'

'He always had impeccable taste.'

'But he was a good six inches shorter than me and a good deal rounder in the girth. The trouser legs barely reach my shins and I cannot button my only jacket.'

'Ah, balderdash,' muttered Dr Challot. 'Stop whingeing and go out and treat some patients.'

'I will take no more of this!' I cried, suddenly emboldened with anger. 'Pay me what you owe until today. I will go and find work elsewhere. I wish you good luck with your practice and I hope that

Dr Mort proves to be a more responsible fellow than he appears to be at the moment.'

With that announcement, I stormed out of Dr Challot's bedroom, tripped over an empty wine flagon and fell through the open door and down half a flight of stairs.

'Mind you don't try poaching any of my patients!' I heard Dr Challot shout. 'Though you can have the large breasted one – I gather from Mistress Swain that she pays you in milk rather than coin and I have plenty of the former available to me.'

There was much laughter from the two Whores in his bed.

'And don't forget that you cannot leave the practice without paying me 30 guineas!' cried Dr Challot as an addendum.

It was only when I got outside that I realised that I had no idea what I was going to do next. It did occur to me that I might have been wiser to have found myself another position before giving notice to Dr Challot.

And I still had no idea where I was going to find the 30 guineas required to buy myself out of our agreement.

December 13th

For once in my life, fortune smiled in my direction, for the very next morning Mistress Youngblood banged on my bedroom door with such urgency that she must surely have awakened most people in the building, including any who had died in the night.

'What on earth is the matter?' I asked, bleary eyed. 'Is the building on fire? Has Her Majesty commanded my presence at court?'

'Not quite, but here's a footman from the Duke of Somerset downstairs,' said Mistress Youngblood. She spoke with unusual respect. 'He has come to fetch you. The Duke requires your presence.'

I stared at her and frowned. 'What the devil does the Duke want from me?'

Mistress Youngblood leant forward and lowered her voice. 'Mr Somerset would only say it's a confidential medical matter. There is a carriage outside our front door. It has the Duke's coat of arms on the doors.'

'Is the Duke of Somerset's footman really called Somerset? That's an amazing coincidence.'

'Servants in the Duke of Somerset's employment take their name from their employer,' explained Mistress Youngblood. 'I believe that in the servants' hall, the Duke's valet enjoys the title, 'Duke of Somerset'.'

'How far away does the Duke live?' I asked.

'Three or four hours' drive,' answered Mistress Youngblood.

'Then I'll have my breakfast first,' I told her, clambering out of Bed and shivering the moment I did so. I couldn't help wondering why the devil the Duke had called for me. As a humble Apothecary I am not allowed to charge a fee for a consultation – only for a treatment. I am allowed to dispense medicaments and to charge for them and I am, of course, allowed to perform surgery. Fellows of the Royal College of Physicians do not dirty their professional fingers by supplying medicaments or performing operations.

Mistress Youngblood seemed rather shocked at my request but she wasn't the one reluctant to undertake a five or six journeys with an empty stomach. 'Are you sure? Mr Somerset is waiting in our hallway.'

'Then tell him to have a bite of breakfast too,' I told her. 'And send up someone to light my fire before I freeze to Death.'

'Can't Nellie do that?' asked Mistress Youngblood, nodding in the direction of my Bed companion who had awakened and was rubbing the sleep out of her eyes. 'Surely she hasn't forgotten how to light a fire!'

'Nellie has other responsibilities now,' I replied rather pompously. 'Please send up a Chambermaid with a bucket of wood.'

'I'll send up Blossom,' said Mistress Youngblood. 'Would it be convenient if she also brought your bill? I understand it is mounting steadily.'

An hour later, clothed, fed and warmed, I was seated in the back of the Duke of Somerset's carriage with two eggs, four rashers of bacon and a pint of coffee swilling around inside me. The coach had come with four servants: a coachman, an assistant coachman and two footmen who were hanging onto the back of the coach and no doubt grateful for the fact that it was neither raining nor snowing.

To be honest, I would have rather ridden to the Duke's estate by donkey. I hate carriage travel. The damned things sway and shake and cause in me a great feeling of sickness. However, Nellie who accompanied me, would have committed murder if I had not agreed to ride in the carriage. I took with me my medical satchel, together with a pot of Leeches and my set of scarifying equipment.

'Have you got a supply of your orgasm remedies?' asked Nellie as I packed my medical satchel.

'A Duke won't want one of those!' I protested.

'Put a few in your bag,' insisted Nellie. 'I bet you that's what he wants.'

And so, since she is proving far better at business than I am, I did as she suggested.

The journey took us seven hours, though this included several stoppages. There was one unscheduled halt so that I could go behind a tree and empty my bladder and one scheduled stop to feed and water the horses and thaw out the servants who had been suffering somewhat out in the open.

The Duke of Somerset lives on a massive estate.

Half an hour after we had turned into the driveway, we still had not reached the castle. I learned later that the estate was like a small town with its own chapel (complete with a Vicar and a curate), forge (complete with Blacksmith) painters' shop (complete with painters), carpenters workshop (complete with carpenters), greenhouses, walled garden, farms, sawmill, hothouse and schoolroom.

When we finally arrived at our destination, the coachman drove around to what was clearly the back of the castle. There was no moat, which I found rather a let-down, and therefore no drawbridge. I have always thought that castles aren't really castles if they don't have moats and drawbridges.

'Why have we stopped here?' Nellie asked me, clearly rather disappointed that our journey had ended in such a way.

The footman who had opened the carriage door looked a trifle nonplussed. 'This is the servants and tradesmen's entrance,' he replied.

'Do servants and tradesmen arrive by carriage?' I asked.

He admitted that they did not.

'When the Duke sees his Physician, does the Physician enter by the back door?'

'No, sir,' admitted Mr Somerset.

'Then drive us to the front door where we can enter properly,' I instructed him.

And thus it was done.

Despite the absence of a moat and drawbridge, the castle itself was most imposing and had clearly been equipped with no account to cost. The reception hall was furnished with solid regency furniture decorated, quite curiously, with girls' heads and bronze animal claws. In a corner stood a candelabrum which must have weighed five hundredweight but which bore but a single candle.

'His Grace will see you in the smoking room,' said a fellow who I assumed to be the butler. 'The winter smoking room,' he added helpfully. Even more helpfully the Butler led the way through a maze of absurdly well-furnished corridors and eventually into a room the size of a large Church or a medium sized Cathedral. An elderly man in a purple coat was sitting in a Chair in front of a blazing fire. He was attempting to play a set of Bagpipes but the task was proving rather too much for him. A woman in a nightgown was sitting at a spinet. The two musicians appeared to be playing entirely different pieces of music but neither seemed to mind.

'Is that the Duke?' I whispered to the Butler as we entered the room. We were so far from the fireplace that there was no chance that we could have been overheard even if we had both shouted.

'It is,' replied the butler. 'You should address him as Your Grace.'

'And the woman playing the spinet is the Duchess?'

'Good heavens no, sir. That is Mademoiselle Floella,' replied the butler. 'She is the Duke's senior mistress. When the Duke married the present Duchess, it was Mademoiselle Floella who gave the Duchess private instructions on the Duke's preferences, and on bedroom matters in general, just before the honeymoon. She and the Duke and Duchess are very close. Indeed, Mademoiselle Floella travelled with the couple to Italy in case her services were required during the honeymoon.'

I glanced at Nellie. She appeared to be having some little difficulty stifling a giggle.

'Dr Bullock,' said the butler, introducing me.

The Duke stopped pumping air into the bagpipes and looked up. He was wearing the worst wig I have ever seen and it occurred to m that his position almost certainly meant that no one ever dared say anything to him about it.

'Is this your remedy?' he demanded, pointing at Nellie. 'I like 'em with a bit more meat on 'em.'

'No, no, this is my assistant,' I said.

Just then a young woman came into the room as though she were an actress making an entrance on stage at a key moment in Act Three. She was wearing a low-necked, blue silk gown and around her neck lay at least six rows of pearls. The fingers of both hands were well decorated with rings, with the prize being a huge diamond settled on the wedding finger of her left hand. It was so big that I couldn't help thinking that if she wore it constantly she must have had an ache in her arm at the end of each day.

'My wife, the Duchess,' said the Duke, introducing her. He didn't bother to introduce us to her.

The mistress stood up from the spinet, smoothed down her negligee and stared for a moment at her well positioned rival. 'I've finished with him for now,' she said. 'You can have what's left.'

The Duchess ignoring this remark, sat down on the arm of the Duke's Chair and put her arm around his neck in a most proprietorial manner. It occurred to me that the relationships within this unusual ménage a trois might not be as entirely comfortable as the Butler had intimated.

'What appears to be the problem, your Grace?' I asked. 'Would you like me to examine you?'

'I hear you're the fellow who's got some sort of remedy for orgasms,' said the Duke.

'That's correct, your Grace.'

'I want one.'

'Certainly, sir.' I glanced at Nellie. She smiled at me. It was an 'I told you so' smile. I opened my bag and took out one of my orgasm remedies.

'Is that it?'

'It is.'

'What do I do with it? Chew it? Swallow it? Rub it on me rogering tool?'

'No, your Grace,' I said. 'It has to go into the back passage.'

'Up me Arse?'

'Precisely, your Grace.'

'Good God! How long will it last?'

'One remedy will provide you with an additional 100 orgasms,' I told him. 'Would you like me to insert it for you?'

'Give it to my wife. She can put it in later.' He laughed. 'It'll be a nice change for her to put something in my arse.'

The Duchess blushed.

'Better leave two more or I'll need to have you fetched again next week,' said the Duke.

I took another two remedies from my bag and placed them on a huge Chippendale sideboard.

'You can go now,' said the Duke, turning back to the fire. 'The Butler will settle your account.'

'How much do we owe you?' asked the butler, when we had left the room.

'Thirty guineas,' said Nellie, before I could say a word.

'Is that for all three items or for each one?'

'For each one,' answered Nellie, without a moment's hesitation. I glanced at her, horrified. I felt certain that we were going to be thrown out or arrested for gouging.

'Ninety guineas then,' said the butler. By now we had reached the reception hall. 'If you would be kind enough to wait here, please.'

Three or four minutes later he was back with a small bag of money. He poured the contents onto a Table and counted out ninety guineas. I nearly fainted when I saw all that gold.

'Can you arrange for the Duke's carriage to take us back home?' I asked.

'Certainly, sir,' replied the butler.

And less than ten minutes later we were once again sitting in the Duke's carriage, but this time we were heading home. And to our mutual delight we were ninety guineas better off than we had been at the start of the day.

Life was definitely looking up.

December 14th

It was with great delight that I took a bag containing 30 Sovereigns to Dr Challot's bedroom. Actually, to be honest, there was a frisson of fear mixed in with the delight. I was walking away from my first job and into a very uncertain future. The Duke of Somerset had single-handedly transformed my finances but it didn't seem likely that we would come across many customers prepared to pay 30 guineas for each of the remedies. (I was well aware that if it had not been for Nellie's quick thinking I would have left the Duke of Somerset's castle with considerably fewer Sovereigns in my possession.)

'What's this?' demanded my employer, peering into the bag before pouring the contents into his hand. One of his ever present Whores was fast asleep and lying half in the Bed. The other was laid out on the floor and appeared to be drunk. The one on the floor was naked. The one in Bed was also naked as far as I could tell.

'I'm buying myself out of your employment,' I told him. I held out a receipt which I had prepared, and handed it to him. 'You just have to sign here,' I told him.

'Sign? What for?'

'To confirm that I have paid what I owe and that I am now free to work elsewhere.'

'I'm not signing anything,' said Dr Challot, holding out the paper but keeping hold of the Sovereigns, which he had now poured back into the small, leather bag in which I had brought them.

'Then I'll take these back,' I told him, grabbing the bag of Sovereigns.

I refused to hand back the Sovereigns until we had found a pen and ink, he had signed the receipt and I had it tucked safely in an inside pocket.

'Why the devil would you want to leave?' asked Challot, in the wheedling voice he usually reserved for his dealings with tradesmen who had plucked up the courage to ask to be paid. As long as I had known him, Dr Challot had never enjoyed paying bills to anyone – most especially tradesmen. He once told me that he thought they ought to be grateful to be allowed to supply him with whatever it was they sold. Not surprisingly this was not a view which was widely reciprocated. 'I have been so good to you,' he said. 'I trained you, I taught you everything I know. I gave you a start in life. Without me you would have been nothing.'

'I am doing all the work and receiving very little of the reward,' I pointed out, without exaggeration. I did not mention the fact that he had taught me remarkably little nor that he had taken me in as a student only because my father had paid him well for my Apprenticeship.

'But what about me?' demanded Dr Challot. 'What am I to do if you go?' He added a soupcon of guilt to leaven the self-pity. 'And if you leave who will look after the patients?'

'You have Dr Mort,' I pointed out.

'Mort is bloody useless!' cried Challot. 'He is like all these youngsters. There was an article about them in the *Morning Post*. I think there's something wrong with this new generation of Young Victorians. They constantly need praise for getting up in the morning. They're self-centred, intolerant, demanding, petulant, hypocritical, narcissistic and damnably lazy.'

'A few days ago you were praising him to the skies!' I pointed out.

'He hasn't been in since then. Not seen hide nor hair of the drunken sot,' said Dr Challot irritably. He sighed, stuck a hand under the bedclothes and scratched himself noisily. 'It's probably just as well. I gather from Mistress Swain that four irate fathers have been turning up at odd times waiting for the worthless bastard to turn up. She said one fellow with a pistol threatened to shoot him, one carrying a huge cudgel threatened to beat his head to a pulp, a third threatened to make him eat himself and the fourth said he intended to tear him into tiny pieces, add mint and sage and turn him into a stew.'

'Then you will have to take a greater interest in the practice yourself,' I told him. 'Since you bought Dr Blackburnt's practice, the workload has risen enormously.'

'I daren't go out of the house lest they mistake me for Mort!' complained Dr Challot. Suddenly, he flew into a rage. 'You're an ungrateful bastard!' he said, suddenly changing tack. 'I'm too damned kind, that's my trouble. Kindness has always been my weakness.'

Dr Challot made as though to throw the Sovereigns at me, but changed his mind when the horror of the action hit home. He then leant out of Bed. When I realised that he was reaching around under the Bed for his night-soil pail (which I know is emptied no more than twice a week even though it may be damnably close to primful) I departed as quickly as I was able. The thud and crash of the night-soil pail hitting the door behind me confirmed that I had been well minded to do so. The stink which followed me down the stairs was abominable.

'You bastard!' I heard Dr Challot cry. 'Come back and clean up this foul mess.'

I hurried down the stairs and left without more ado.

I hesitated for a moment about whether to say 'goodbye' to Mistress Swain, eventually deciding that that a speedy exit from the premises was the wisest course of action.

December 15th

'So, what do I do now?' I asked Nellie.

Having left Dr Challot's employment, I was now without a job or an income. To be honest, I felt rather depressed and more than a little frightened.

'Can you find another position at a different practice?' asked Nellie. 'Or can you start your own practice?' It was eleven in the morning but we were still in Bed. I had nowhere I had to be and so had little incentive to clamber out into the world. She put her head on my chest.

'There are no other practices around here and I don't know of any vacancies in practices further afield,' I confessed. 'And to start my own practice I would need money.'

We lay together for a few moments and neither of us spoke. I pulled the blanket a little higher. It seemed to be a very cold morning.

'Besides,' I added, 'I'm not sure I want to do either of those things.'

The truth was that I was tired of what sometimes seemed a glum, pointless grind. I was tired too of the corruption which seemed endemic within the profession, with prescribing habits being influenced by generous luncheons and free gifts.

I had begun my medical career believing that I would be able to help people who were sick but I was no longer convinced that I was making much of a difference. It sometimes seemed as though we one of us knew as much as we led people to believe. Most of the me, I didn't really know why my patients were ill, and the remedies offered were as much of a mystery as the ailments themselves.

Moreover, I had lost all faith in the profession's leaders who were, it sometimes seemed to me, devoted mainly to enriching themselves by forming close arrangements with one or more of the many companies offering healing products for sale. The medical journals were packed with advertising for new remedies which were often untried and frequently turned out to be lethal.

I had reluctantly come to the conclusion that there is very little integrity in medicine, and I found myself wondering how long this state of affairs has existed. Did Hippocrates, the Father of Medicine, accept free meals from the makers of successful and fashionable herbal potions?

The odd thing was that the only time I felt I was doing something useful was when I was selling my orgasm extension remedy.

My patients always came in to see me looking anxious and concerned, and they always left looking relieved and optimistic. There were no risks, no dangers and no downside. None of my patients was ever harmed by my remedy because it contained nothing that could do any harm. A Doctor can't ask for much more than that.

'Perhaps, we should explore ways to sell the suppository,' said Nellie.

I noticed, in passing, that she had turned the first person singular into the first person plural. 'I' had become 'we'. I had no objection to this for I recognised that she was far better able than I to deal with the business side of affairs. Besides, I was beginning to think of us as being in a partnership in all senses of the word.

And, moreover, I found, rather to my surprise, that my feelings towards her were also acquiring a tenderness which I had not previously experienced.

'The first thing we must do is to give the remedy a memorable name,' she insisted.

I pointed out that Hercules Tomkins, the bone saw Drummer, had suggested that I call the medicament 'Dr Bollock's Stiffness Enhancing Remedy'.

Nellie was not enamoured of this suggestion which she rightly thought might be misleading.

December 16th

I am planning to keep body and soul within calling distance of each other (without spending the remains of the fee paid by the Duke of Somerset) by hiring myself out to act as a medical officer at a variety of sporting events in the region.

Dr Challot used to attend some of these events but he is, I hear, now very much occupied with attempting to deal with all his patients by himself. Dr Mort, not unpredictably, has disappeared.

It is surprising how often the contestants in even the most peaceful sounding activities can be quite severely and unexpectedly injured. The usual fee for attendance now seems to be half a guinea, though for this I am expected to provide whatever Plaisters and other medicaments may be required. At Nellie's insistence, I always packed in my medical satchel around half a dozen packets containing my orgasm remedy. 'You never know when the opportunity might arise to make a sale,' she pointed out.

The first event I was hired to attend was the forthcoming annual Hat Fair in Uncumber-by-Water.

I invited Nellie to accompany me as my assistant. Her main task was to carry my medical satchel and a bag containing a few dozen orgasm remedies. I hoped she might prove to be a successful saleswoman.

Mistress Youngblood, suspecting that my motives were not entirely honour bound, wanted to charge me a shilling for Nellie's time and told me that I could keep her until the following morning for an additional one shilling and six pence. I had to remind her that Nellie no longer worked for the Peacock Inn. I fear Mistress Youngblood is poorly informed for that particular train left the station some time ago.

In preparation for the Hat Fair, I handed Nellie two shillings and sixpence to purchase a new frock and a hat suitable for the occasion. She had only one rather threadbare shift and although it was undoubtedly clean (she washed it every month) it looked what it was: a hand-me-down shift.

Three hours later, she returned carrying a very large, brown paper parcel under her arm and, with some difficulty, also carrying a large, wooden Chair. The parcel was well tied with string. Nellie was still wearing the shift she had been wearing when she'd left but upon her head rested a magnificent creation which was generously decorated with a number of real birds' feathers and two bunches of artificial cherries.

'Whose Chair is that?' I enquired, fearing that she may have appropriated it without the knowledge of the owner.

'It's mine,' she answered immediately. 'It's a very good Chair and I bought it for nine pence.' She put the Chair down and ran the fingers of her spare hand over the back of it admiringly.

And, indeed, it was a very good Chair; well-made, with nicely turned legs and what looked like a very comfortably shaped back.

'Why did you buy a Chair?' I asked.

'It's for my house,' she replied. 'When I have my own house I'm going to fill it with nice things and I'll need a Chair won't I?'

I agreed that a house without at least one Chair would be a very empty place indeed.

'Did you also manage to buy a frock?' I asked. I indicated the parcel she was carrying. 'Is that it?'

She nodded.

'You bought the frock, the hat and the Chair for two shillings and sixpence?'

'I've got four pence halfpenny change,' she said, reaching into a pocket which had been cleverly sewn into a seam of her shift and pulling out the coins. She offered them to me.

'You can keep the change,' I told her, marvelling at the fact that she had bought so much for so little.

'Do you like my hat?' she asked.

'I like it very much. It's a splendid hat.'

'It belonged to a lady,' Nellie told me proudly. 'Lady Farley-Wallop died and left all her clothes and hats to her Maid.'

'And the Maid sold you the hat?'

'And she also sold me the dress which 'aint a frock by the way because it's a dress. It's a very fine dress. It's got pearl buttons made out of real pearl and lace made of real lace.'

'Are you going to unwrap the parcel and let me look at it?'

When Nellie finally succeeded in removing the string from around her parcel (there was a good deal of it) I could see that she was right: it was a very fine dress made of silk in a very fetching watchen blue.

'Will it fit you?' I asked.

'I have to take it in a bit,' replied Nellie. 'But Lady Farley-Wallop's Maid showed me how and gave me a needle and cotton.' She plunged a hand into her pocket again and pulled out a reel of cotton and a needle. 'And she gave me a corset with stays, three pairs of white cotton stockings, a garter and three petticoats fitted with broderie anglaise.'

'But, despite the glory of the dress, it was the Chair of which Nellie was most proud.

December 17th

Resplendent in her new dress and hat, Nellie looked like a duchess when we left the Peacock Inn this morning. I looked down at my faded coat, stained trousers and battered, leaky boots and resolved that I had to do something about improving my appearance.

The Hat Fair in the village of Uncumber-by-Water is an extraordinary event.

Several thousand people come to watch such events as hat trimming and hat hurling and there is also a competition for Best Hat, with a prize of £5 for the winner.

Apart from drinking, skulduggery and horizontal exercises, these events are a honeypot for knaves, blockheads, prating gablers, mangie rascals, slabberdegullions, ninnie lobcocks, doddipol oltheads, grouthead gnatsnappers and noddiespeak simpletons. But events of this nature are the only source of entertainment in the area.

It was the hat hurling event which proved most contentious and left me more than ever convinced that the majority of professional hatters are as mad as March Hares. Maybe there is something in the work they do which contributes to their lunacy. I have heard it said that the Mercury used in their work might contribute to their mental instability but the Royal Physicians, encouraged no doubt by a close and profitable relationship with the Mercury vendors, have confirmed that Mercury is one of the safest and most effective substances available. To reassure the public that the stuff is perfectly safe, one eminent Royal Physician ate four ounces of Mercury in public – and forced his children to each eat a two ounce portion.

As always happens with these events, the Hat Fair was well attended by the usual variety of pie-men, pudding men and gingerbread sellers and a vast gallimaufry of hornswogglers and ghemobole specialists. A number of showmen had also turned up and their colourful wooden caravans and carts were interspersed with a variety of large tents and small marquees. Some of the shows and entertainments offered by these travellers are quite extraordinary.

The sign outside one tent advertised 'The Pig Faced Lady: The Ugliest Woman in the whole of the South of England'.

Intrigued, I paid my tuppence and entered a poorly lit, evil smelling, fowsty tent in which the strangest creature I have ever seen sat at a wooden Table, the front of which was covered with a red velvet drape so that her legs could not be seen. Her face was badly deformed and she wore a rather moth eaten red wig which did nothing much for her overall appearance. The showman, wearing a black frock coat and a black top hat, both of which had seen much better days, stood to one side and kept up a constant patter, explaining that he had rescued the unfortunate female from a husband who had beaten her, chained her, forced her to work in the fields for 18 hours a day and kept her on a diet of stale bread and old Turnips. From time to time, the showman asked the woman a question about her history. On each occasion the woman grunted something incomprehensible in reply. On the first occasion that this happened, the showman explained that the woman had a malformed jaw which prevented her speaking clearly. He then assured us that he had spent many hours learning to understand her manner of speech. She was, he said, a most intelligent woman who loved nothing more than sitting by the fireside reading an instalment of Mr Dickens' latest story.

'I buy her every instalment as it comes out,' he promised us. 'I spare no expense to keep this woman content and comfortable.'

'How extraordinary life can be,' I thought.

It was not until later that I discovered the full extent of the strangeness of the world populated by fairground people.

The trouble started when Mr Piebellow, an impressively muscular hatter who had thought himself to be the likely winner of the hat hurling contest (with an impressive hurl of three chains and seven yards) accused another competitor, Ezekial Lumpstone, of adding weights to the brim of a hat which had travelled three chains and nine yards, and of thereby taking the two guinea prize by deceit.

Mr Piebellow claimed that he had heard a rumour that Mr Lumpstone had won hat hurling contests all over England by using his especially adapted headgear.

'That hat has been adulterated!' cried Mr Piebellow to the judges. 'It is not a usual hat. It is not a hat which a man could buy in a hat shop. It is not a hat which a man would wear.'

The accusation appeared to be an accurate one, and, indeed, the owner of the adultered hat did not dispute the accuracy.

'There are no rules outlawing this hat,' said Mr Lumpstone, holding aloft the winning item of headgear and adding that as far as he knew there were no rules at all in hat hurling events, other than the rule that the prize would be awarded to the owner of the hat which travelled furthest.

However, there had been much betting on the outcome of the competition, and several gentlemen who had been attracted from a cock fight in a nearby hostelry had been passing around large bundles of £5 notes. Many gin soaked oaths were uttered when the word was spread that the contest may have been fixed.

'Well if there are no rules I could mount my horse with my hat on my head, ride a mile and drop the hat on the ground,' argued Mr Piebellow. He stuck his hands on his hips and threw out his chest.

'Oh no you couldn't!' objected Mr Lumpstone, wagging a fat finger at the complainant. 'The competition is a hat hurling event. It is not a 'carrying a hat on a horse event'.'

By this time, the judges were alarmed by the way things were going and, in an attempt to deflect attention from themselves, asked the organiser of the event (a local brewer) to adjudicate.

The adjudicator, a reluctant umpire, said that he thought that a heavy hat would be more difficult to throw and that, therefore, it seemed to him that Mr Lumpstone had been handicapping himself by adding lead weights to the brim. As a corollary, he added that if Mr Lumpstone had, despite this handicap, managed to hurl his hat further than anyone else, then his hat was the winning hat and he was entitled to the first prize.

Mr Piebellow responded by arguing that the brewer didn't know what he was talking about and pointed out that a modest increase in the weight of a hat improved the distance it could be thrown.

However, before any reply could be made, Mr Piebellow made a fist and hit the organiser of the event, the adjudicator, firmly on the nose, causing a considerable amount of Bleeding.

Looking back, I think it was this point that marked the moment when things got rather out of hand.

Certainly the two Deaths which occurred followed directly after the punch was thrown.

When I had accepted the commission to act as medical officer for the Hat Fair, I had expected to earn my fee by merely treating a few spectators for injuries sustained as a result of being hit by mis-thrown headgear.

Instead, I found myself dealing with three broken noses, two cracked skulls, three dislocations and four fractured bones; and certifying two Deaths. I think it is proper to point out that the two hat makers who died had nothing to do with the hat hurling event but were both involved in fashionable hat trimming. I regret to say that there was much enthusiastic use of cudgels.

A local undertaker paid me twelve shillings to help him load the two cadavers onto his cart (which he had brought with him more, I suspect, in honest hope than in real expectation) and to provide him with written confirmations of Death. He was in a hurry to take the bodies away, and I was later told by Nellie that she suspected he intended to sell the corpses to those patent medicine manufacturers who use human liver, lung, brain and hair in the preparation of their medicaments.

However, our attendance at the meeting was not unsuccessful.

In addition to the modest fee I was paid for my attendance at the meeting (and which I consider I earned several times over) and the twelve shillings from the undertaker (for certifying and loading) I succeeded in selling seven of my suppositories.

Or maybe that should be 'we succeeded in selling seven of our suppositories' for Nellie proved to be an excellent saleswoman, identifying and charming potential buyers with uncanny skill.

At her suggestion, we gave away free condoms (linen or tortoiseshell, according to the purchaser's choice) with every one of my suppositories. Bought in bulk from one of the local Leech suppliers these lagniappes are an excellent advertisement. Although second-hand, the condoms look to be in fine condition and unless you examine them closely it is difficult to tell that they have been 'previously enjoyed', as I think the phrase is.

If things continue to go well, I am thinking of ordering a supply of promotional condoms with my name, or the name of my remedy (when Nellie and I have thought of something suitable) printed along the length of the item.

When I first entered the medical profession, I had no idea that I would one day reach such heights. My father would, I know, burst with pride at the idea of his son's name being engraved on the side of a tortoiseshell condom.

Indeed, if I had to choose between being awarded a knighthood and having my name engraved along the side of tortoiseshell condoms, the decision would be a fine run thing.

December 18th

Nellie and I travelled an hour and a half by horseback to attend a Dollymop Footrace held in the village of Piddleham. I was delighted that Nellie accompanied me for she has proved herself quite indispensable in many ways. On this occasion, we managed to rent two decent horses from the Ostler at the Peacock Inn. I did not enquire too closely where he had found the horses or to whom they belonged.

The race, organised by the Earl of Leamington Spa, involved twelve dollymops or Whores running around a quarter of a mile track laid out in the parkland of the Earl's estate.

The Whores were dressed only in short shifts, and were expected to run until there was only one of them left standing.

These races have become extraordinarily popular in recent months and are clear evidence of the popularity of athletic events in general and of the rising popularity of women's sport in particular. It is not uncommon for several of the competitors to push themselves so hard that they collapse into unconsciousness. My job was to do my best to keep the Whores running. Each Whore was allowed to pause for two minutes every hour for medical treatment, to take on food or fluid or for publicly consummated calls of nature.

These short breaks are monitored most severely by the seconds appointed by the Earl who takes a close interest in the proceedings.

The prize for the winning Whore was £50 – a huge sum for a dollymop. But the big money was in the betting. The Earl of Leamington Spa had wagered £10,000 on the event (most of it with the Duke of Nettleworth and Baron Bloxwich) and had brought in suitably racy Whores from distant parts of the country. One of the Whores had, it was rumoured, been imported from Paris where she had won a number of similar races, including one which had lasted for the better part of two days.

A huge audience had collected around the perimeter of the course and there was a good deal of gambling done with the bookmakers, some of whom had travelled for half a day to set up their booths. The usual tents and marquees had been set up by travelling showmen, and I noticed that the showman promoting The Ugliest Woman in the Whole South of England (who had been at the Hat Fair) was present.

The event was, in truth, something of a bore for when you have watched a dozen Whores run around a field once, there is little incentive to watch them run around a field a second time. The only difference is that on the second and subsequent laps there was much more huffing and puffing and the pace was noticeably slower.

And by the time they are on their tenth lap, the enthusiasm of the spectator is hard to sustain, even when the exhausted Whores are running half naked and there is a good deal of bouncing and jiggling going on.

After twenty laps, the least fit and the most amply proportioned of the Whores were beginning to weaken and their huffing and puffing had become painfully audible even when they were making their way around the opposite side of the track. They were however, all reluctant to admit defeat since the prize was so great that it would afford the winner an opportunity to retire from personal, physical endeavours and set up her own establishment in a not entirely unfashionable area.

The first dollymop collapsed at the end of the 24th lap and not even a whipping from one of the Duke's whipper inners could encourage her to continue. With her naked posterior well striped she crawled away semi-conscious.

It took nine hours to wear away the other Whores and the winner was not, as had been expected, one of the 13-year-olds who had been entered, and whose slight build was thought to give them an advantage, but a sturdy woman of considerable experience who had been entered by the Duke of Nettleworth and who was fuelled by determination and ambition. (One wag remarked that it was by no means the first time she had been entered by the Duke.)

It was considered a great pity when she collapsed and died just two minutes after winning the event. The prize of £50 was awarded to the runner up, a patently pox ridden red-headed Whore from Shoreditch, though the Duke insisted on claiming the £10,000 wager since there could be no argument that it had been one of his favoured Whores who had won the race.

The day was a great success for Nellie and myself.

Other than insisting that the competing Whores were well supplied with water and roused with salts when they collapsed, I had very little medical work to do. This meant, therefore, that Nellie and I had plenty of time in which to sell our still as yet unnamed remedy.

At the end of half an hour, we had sold all the remedies we had taken with us and I had 24 gold Sovereigns in my pocket.

Hearing that I was a medical man, I had also provided advice and some treatment to a woman with swollen ankles, a man with deafness caused by wax in his ears and three women requiring a remedy for fatness of the whole body. My fees for dealing with these patients amounted to a modest five groats. It was all they could raise. It seems clear to me where the future must now lie.

What a mixture were the folk at this event! The men were a fine aggregation of palliards, priggers, jarkmen and vagabonds and the women were slaistered wantons, slammerkins, dells, bawdy-baskets and doxies.

Finally, a dwarf appeared wanting a remedy for his baldness.

The aroma surrounding the urling reminded me of the smell of the Ugliest Woman in the Whole of the South of England.

'What do you do?' I asked him.

'I'm a stick man,' he replied, as though this ought to be self-explanatory.

Never having heard of this occupation before I asked him to explain what it entailed.

'Have you heard of the Ugliest Woman in the Whole of the South of England?'

I said I had not only heard of her but that I had seen her too.

The dwarf explained that he was actually the owner of the Stall and the Ugliest Woman in the Whole of the South of England, and that the man in the top hat was hired by him for his huckster skills. Prior to working with the bear the huckster had, explained the dwarf, been a professional army recruit who had joined the militia no less than 15 times, receiving ten shillings for signing on before disappearing to another part of the country.

'Why don't you bill her as the Ugliest Woman in the World?' I asked. 'She would surely qualify.'

'Oh the public is very funny about these things,' said the dwarf. 'If I billed her as the Ugliest Woman in the World they would be inclined to disbelieve, to suspect that I was over egging the pudding if you understand my meaning. And they would pass on by. But they will be ready to believe that she must be the Ugliest Woman in the Whole of the South of England, and when they see and they look at her they will say to themselves, 'this woman is surely the ugliest woman in the whole world' and they will be impressed and they will tell their friends to come and see her.'

'Where did you find such a woman?' I asked, impressed at the dwarf's commercial acumen.

'Oh, t'aint a woman at all!' laughed the dwarf. 'She's a brown bear I bought from a traveller in Malmesbury. The traveller used to make her dance but she slowed down too much to dance well enough to draw in the customers. Too old I daresay. The joints seemed a little too sore and creaky.'

He explained, without embarrassment, that he had shaved the bear's face, neck and arms, the only parts of her which were visible, and that he had fitted her with white gloves to disguise her paws which might have given the game away. He said that he sat the bear at a Table draped with a long cloth while he sat underneath the Table with a stick. (Hence he described himself as a 'stick man'.) Whenever the showman asked a question, he poked the bear with the stick. The bear grunted in response to being poked and the showman, the fellow with the top hat, having explained that the 'woman' had malformed jaws which prevented her speaking clearly, 'translated' and made up some suitable remarks.

'How do you keep the bear sitting still?' asked Nellie.

'Gin, ma'am. Half a bucket of gin a day keeps her well satisfied and perfectly still. But she's chained to the Table, a good piece of

English oak, just in case she of a sudden takes it into her head to roam.'

'So she doesn't really read Mr Dickens' work?' I said.

The dwarf laughed.

It was a very unpleasant sort of laugh.

Nellie and I agreed that we felt sorry for the unfortunate bear.

I prescribed a honey and dung poultice for the dwarf's baldness and charged him a guinea and a half which he can well afford.

December 19th

Nellie and I decided that if our remedy is to become truly successful we must go to London. It is, after all, in the world's capital city that all business ventures must be tested if they are to thrive. We decided that we would travel by Railway.

When we arrived at the Railway station, I was shocked to see a crowd of gangrels, mostly children, standing outside holding up banners and shouting slogans. 'Shut the Railways!' was the only one I could identify. Two police constables were standing at the back of the crowd looking rather nonplussed. They wore smart blue uniforms with brass buttons.

'What the devil is going on?' I asked one of the constables.

'They're demonstrating against the Railway,' said the taller of the two. He had a very impressive handlebar moustache which must have taken him years to grow and to groom.

'Why don't they like the Railway?' asked Nellie.

'They say the Railway is changing the weather,' replied the officer. 'They're worried about all that grey smoke that comes out of the chimney on the engine. They say it goes up into the sky and forms big, grey clouds.'

I looked up at the sky. There were several big grey clouds visible. t looked like rain. There was no immediate way of knowing whether r not the clouds had been caused by smoke from train engines. Since I could neither see nor hear any trains, it was difficult to say ne way or the other.

'Are you going to arrest them?' I asked the policeman, for I was ot aware that we were living in a paedarchical society.

He shrugged. 'We've been told they are mostly oddlings, obdurate and easily over-mirthed, and that we must leave them well alone,' he replied, though he could not say why.

One of the ringleaders, a girl of about ten or eleven, had climbed up onto a dog cart which had been left outside the station. She was making a speech. She wore a grubby frock which looked as though it had once been pink in colour, and both she and the garment looked as though they needed a damned good wash. Judging from her speech, she had no doubts that the trains were causing the clouds though she did not waste time providing scientific justification for her opinion.

'We has Sunday afternoons to ourselves,' said the girl with a sniff, 'and when it rained last Sunday it spoilt our fun. We was going to have Maypole dance training with the curate but it was raining and the Vicar's Wife came out and stopped it. She said the grass was too wet. She said it was dangerous 'cus we might slip and fall down. It was the trains what done it because they made the clouds which made the rain. They're ruining my life and I am only ten.' She wiped her nose on her sleeve and burst into tears and, sobbing loudly, had to be helped down out of the dogcart. Through the layer of mud and grime it was possible to see that her face was quite red. She looked very bitter.

'She should be at work,' said Nellie.

It seemed to me that demonstrators are getting younger, increasingly self-centred and more stupid than ever. The grithserjeant agreed with me when I mentioned this to him.

'Oh yes, sir. There's so many of them here that I gather Sir Egbert's factory has had to shut down for the day. Sir Egbert has threatened to sack this lot and to bring in workers from the Continent. French ones I gather.'

The policeman pronounced the words 'Continent' and 'French' with great contempt.

'I cannot see the local population greeting an influx of Froggy workers with much enthusiasm,' he added.

'Shouldn't you do something? Move the demonstrators on? Send them back to work?'

'In due course, sir. In due course.'

'Are the trains still running?' I asked.

'Oh yes, sir. There was some trouble earlier. A couple of the urchins lay down on the track. I think it was their intention to stop the train. But that's all over now.'

'Good heavens. What happened?'

'The train ran straight over them, sir. Cut both of them into three parts. The train driver said he hadn't seen them and if he had seen them he doubts if he'd have been able to stop and if he had been able to stop, he doubts if he would have done. You can't blame him, can you? People who lie down on the tracks must expect to be chopped into three. We can't have people interfering with other folks' lives – especially when the people doing the interfering are children who ought to be at work. There was a short delay while we cleared away the bits and washed the Blood off the rails. The station master said he thought Blood on the rails might make the wheels slip, so my colleague and I washed it off with buckets of water. Things should be running normally now.'

Just then, a small group of men and women arrived. They were, it was soon clear, the parents of the demonstrating, proudworthy children. And two or three minutes later, the entire demonstration was over as children were led, largely by the ears, back to work.

'I find these things tend to sort themselves out in time,' said the policeman with the handlebar moustache. 'Best not to rush in before giving events a chance to unfold of their own accord.'

And as the pseudomaniacs were dragged away, it would have been unreasonable not to agree with him.

Ten minutes later, our train chugged into the station and, having purchased our tickets to the metropolis, we climbed aboard.

December 20th

When we arrived in London, Nellie and I had no idea what to do or where to go.

We found a small boarding house near Paddington Station and rented a squalid little skyparlour about the size of a wardrobe for two shillings a night. The mattress was spunkstained and soggier than marshland and there were neither sheets nor blankets, merely a oralium as thin as paper. The landlady, a woman who looked like a ferret, and a constipated one at that, said we could have breakfast and dinner for another one shilling a day each but Nellie, who had caught sight of the kitchen, thanked her and said we would thribble for ourselves. Nellie is a sharp one for making do and muddling through.

'It would perhaps have saved time to have two meals a day provided for us,' I protested.

'There were two dead dogs in the kitchen,' whispered Nellie, though there was no one around to hear. 'They had been half skinned and were clearly intended to be used in a pie or stew of some kind. Moreover, I saw two large rats sitting on the Table where the cook was preparing food. They were tucking into a loaf of bread and seemed quite at home.'

Leaving our bags in our room (both bags were largely filled with supplies of the orgasm remedy, for Nellie and I had worked solidly for two days to prepare a large supply, more in hope than expectation, of good sales) we went out into the street to explore London, a city neither of us had ever visited before.

The sights before us were a startling revelation. It was difficult to believe that we were still in the same country or, indeed, on the same planet. Everything around us seemed to be brighter, noisier and faster paced. Even the smells seemed that much more pungent and quite impossible to escape.

Within a quarter of a mile of our boarding house, we came across an open space where a group of enterprising travellers had set up a fair ground and the place was more than seemly thrung with knavish titivils, swingebucklers and tittuping girls. Nellie and I gazed about us in astonishment for this was far more dramatic than anything we had ever seen before. It seemed likely that we were the only straight-fingered folk within a mile. There was a fire-eater, a pair of Siamese twins, a man advertised as weighing 55 stone and being 'the fattest man in the world', a fanfaronade which I was quite prepared to believe, and a woman covered in hair who was promoted as 'the baboon lady' and who reminded me of St Uncumber, the bearded woman and benefactress of wives who, according to Sir Thomas More, would, for a peck of oats provide any unfortunate wife with a horse upon which an evil husband could be persuaded to ride to the devil. There was an oyster shell on a Table which smoked a churchwarden Pipe and a tank full of goldfish were taking part in a most convincing naval engagement; towing small boats from which puffs of smoke and small explosions appeared at intervals as tiny fireworks were set off by long fuses.

I spent some minutes puzzling over the oyster but eventually decided that a small boy or a dwarf was doubtless cramped under the Table where the oyster was displayed, puffing away on the Pipe with the aid of a piece of rubber tubing. The flimflam men are nothing if not full of imagination.

A tiny fellow, little more than two and a half feet tall and dressed in red breeches and a red velvet coat, was advertised as the English Tom Thumb, and a placard outside a red and white striped tent promised that inside we would find a three-headed woman. We were assured that every head would reply if spoken to. We watched a man walk behind a wire screen while wearing a top hat. The top hat was visible and a barker was inviting people to throw wooden balls. 'Three balls for a penny. Knock off the top hat and win a guinea.' Lots of people threw balls, a few even hit the hat but no one won the guinea. 'Do you think the hat is glued onto his head?' asked Nellie.

We did not stay long at the fair but noticed a music hall theatre, next to the open space, which had advertisements outside for coming artistes, including a bunch of rough riders from Texas in the United States due to re-enact a battle with a troupe of wild Red Indians. My cynicism led me to wonder where the rough riders and the Red Indians really came from. I suspected that when they went home for Christmas and Mothering Sunday, they probably headed back to Macclesfield or Cirencester.

Everything in London was so much bigger, so much more dramatic and so much more urgent. There were posters everywhere advertising a prize fight and an open air pig roast.

But beneath the colour and the noise there was a clear air of desperation everywhere; as though it were important to everyone that their business, whatever it might be, should be concluded immediately if not much sooner.

In the street, the barkers outside each shop and stall were fired by their own enthusiasms as they shouted louder and louder; each one vainly trying to out-shout the others. It seemed to me that London offered enormous promise. But it also seemed strangely alarming; frightening even. I felt certain that if I could think of a way to promote our remedy it would be possible to sell far more than it had been possible to sell at home or at the country fairs nearby.

'How do we start?' I asked Nellie.

When there was no reply I turned round and saw that she was deep in conversation with a short, squat, balding fellow in a grubby suit who was smoking a huge cigar. I started towards her but halted and waited a moment. The two of them were deep in conversation and I suspected that Nellie was already much closer to finding an answer to my question than I was ever likely to be.

After a couple of minutes, Nellie turned towards me, smiled and beckoned for me to join them.

'This is the man I told you about,' said Nellie, introducing me to the short fellow.

Close up his suit was even grubbier than it had been from a distance. The lapels were well decorated with egg yolk, fat stains and cigar ash. He smelt strongly of Alcohol but did not appear to be unduly under the influence.

It is my experience that some people are easy to like, others are easy to dislike and some, a very few, are easy to loathe. I realise that with some individuals these categories may vary from observer to observer. And they may also vary from time to time. Someone you meet and dislike on Wednesday might have been easy to like if you'd met them on Friday under entirely different circumstances. But there are some individuals who are likeable or unlikeable for everyone, and under virtually any circumstances.

And the short fellow seemed to me to be one of the eternally likeable souls. It occurred to me that if he had wanted to make a living as a confidence trickster he would have undoubtedly been enormously successful.

'This is Mr Binky Beaminster,' said Nellie. 'He is the manager of the theatre.'

'Which theatre?' I asked.

'This one,' said Nellie, turning slightly and pointing to the theatre a yard or two away from us.

'Oh,' I said, feeling about as embarrassed as anyone would feel under the circumstances.

'I have explained our predicament to Mr Beaminster,' said Nellie. 'And he thinks he may be able to help us.'

I listened attentively, and in awe, as she explained that Mr Beaminster's theatre was unexpectedly empty for two days and two evenings and that he was prepared to allow us to have the use of the theatre for the unoccupied dates.

'Mr Beaminster will provide the theatre free of charge if we undertake to give him one half of our gross proceeds,' Nellie explained, as I was about to explain that we did not have enough money to pay to hire the theatre. 'And he will put up posters and use his crier to tour the area promoting the event.'

'You're lucky, there will be a good many people in London,' said Mr Beaminster. 'There is a public execution to be held in Tilbury. They're expecting a quarter of a million spectators, coming in from all over the South of England. It'll be a fine day out for them and a finer day for the pick pockets and Whores.'

'Who is being hung?'

'Elsie Oliphant and her lover Roger Teesdale. They murdered her husband, buried him under the floorboards and moved away when the stench became too much. The landlord found him the same day they moved out and they were arrested living a quarter of a mile away.'

'Not the brightest of God's creatures then?'

Mr Beaminster told us that the crowds love a double hanging.

'The hangman is using a short drop so both of them will be strangled slowly,' he said. 'There'll be big bets laid on which of them stops kicking first. He's a good half a foot taller than her so the big money will be on Elsie.'

It seemed extraordinary to me that people would travel long distances for such barbaric 'entertainment'.

'You'll do well,' said Mr Beaminster. 'Those people who come into London will be looking for some cheap entertainment in the evening. And a good many of them will come to listen to you.'

This all seemed too wonderful to be true until I realised that I had no idea what I was going to say to an audience, or how I could possibly entertain a theatre full of patrons.

'We won't charge anything for admittance,' said Mr Beaminster. 'That'll fill the place up nicely. And I'll get a couple of journalists I know to do a write up for their papers beforehand. That won't be difficult if we get a few celebrities to attend.'

'But we don't know any celebrities!' I pointed out.

'Oh, don't worry about that. I know scores of celebrities who would go to the unveiling of a horse trough if they thought it might mean their getting a mention in one of the newspapers. I know two troubadours, one called Bozo and the other called something else, and a couple of travelling poets, pantywaists the pair of them, who are very effective media influencers.' He smiled knowingly. 'The celebrities will come if I tell them that there will be journalists there and the journalists will turn up if they know there are going to be celebrities present. These journalists and celebrities are a band of scofflaws, screelpokes and scobberlotchers but they can all be bought for a modest price. I know a couple of artists who'll come along, hang around outside the entrance and sketch famous people as they go in.' He suddenly stopped as a thought occurred to him. 'And I'll invite a couple of clergymen. They'll happily turn up for a chance to promote themselves.'

I did not quite see how we were going to be helped by self-promoting clergymen but the theatre manager was so enthusiastic that I did not like to say anything sceptical. Besides, I now had the added problem of thinking of something to say to the journalists. No one else seemed in the slightest bit concerned by my uncertainties.

'We'll clean up!' Mr Beaminster assured us. 'The Reverend Cedric Callwallader's limited orgasm theory has been the talk of London for weeks. He and his Wife Henrietta have been filling lecture halls all over the city. Of the two of them, Mistress Henrietta Callwallader has been particularly active. What a harridan she is! Men everywhere are counting their orgasms and limiting their encounters to preserve their sexual longevity. Mistresses and Whores are complaining bitterly that business has never been slower. The punters will turn up in their droves. And the Whores will buy the stuff themselves to present to their best clients.'

'When is the theatre going to be free?' I asked, hesitantly.

'Tomorrow!' said Nellie brightly. 'Isn't that wonderful? If things go as well as Mr Beaminster expects he will fix us up with other odd nights in theatres and pubs in and around London.'

'How the devil am I going to entertain a whole theatre audience?' I asked.

'Not a problem,' Mr Beaminster assured me, with far greater confidence than I felt. 'We are going to create an extravaganza. I know half a dozen actors and actresses who are resting at the moment.'

Puzzled, I looked at him.

'How it works is very simple,' said Mr Beaminster. 'They sit in the audience and you call them on stage one at a time to tell you how your product has changed their lives. What's your product called?'

'We haven't got a name for it, yet,' I said, feeling rather foolish.

'Oh you must have a name,' said Mr Beaminster. 'And a good name!'

'"Dr Bullock's Remedy for Active Gentlemen",' replied Nellie instantly. She looked at me for approval.

I smiled. 'Perfect!'

'Splendid!' said Mr Beaminister. 'Dr Bollock's Remedy for Active Gentlemen'.'

'Bullock,' I said, correcting him.

He looked at me. 'Oh, I think not!' he said. 'Dr Bollock's Remedy for Active Gentlemen' sounds considerably more convincing and memorable.'

And I suspect he is right.

On the way back to our boarding house we bought a haggis from a street vendor. This is, it appears, a dish popular with the natives of Scotland, and the vendor explained that it consists of Blood pudding rolled in lard and baked in a sheep's stomach. We also bought two pickled rams' testicles. We washed down this challenging feast with two large glasses of potato and caraway schnapps.

We both enjoyed the schnapps but found both the haggis and the pickled rams' testicles to be something of an acquired taste. I would have preferred a chunk of good cheese and a loaf of bread.

December 22nd

To my astonishment, our first day in the theatre proved to be a sensational success. It was, indeed, so successful that we sold out of our stocks of Dr Bollock's Remedy for Active Gentlemen. The following morning Nellie and I had to rush around pharmacies buying up the ingredients we needed to make another batch. At Nellie's suggestion we bought the ingredients we needed at half a dozen establishments to prevent anyone working out the composition of the Remedy.

The four actors and three actresses we hired were so utterly convincing that we hired them for a month to tour London with us.

One of the actors actually cried on stage when he had finished explaining how the Remedy had changed his life for the better. Since, at the time, he hadn't even seen an example of the Remedy this was impressive. The actresses were marvellous too. One, a diminutive redhead who was, we were told, well-known to have formerly been occupied as the mistress of a prominent politician, managed a combination of coquettishness and gratefulness which seemed to me to be most convincing.

As promised, the event was attended by a vast number of well-dressed gentlemen and a good number of elegantly attired women who didn't look as if they spent their evenings serving mead in a tavern or looking after squabbling infants in a back street hovel.

My delight at the success we seemed to be enjoying was tempered only by the newspaper coverage.

The Daily Telegraph and Courier ran a large story on its front page in which an anonymous writer sneered at the Remedy and quoted extensively one of the media influencers who had been introduced to us by the theatre manager.

'Dr Bollock's Remedy for Active Gentlemen' will put at risk the purity of London womanhood!' warned a Reverend Adcock who seemed keen to share the limelight with the Reverend Cadwallader. 'This product will release the previously contained urges and unnaturally overzealous desires of thousands of men. London will henceforth be a dangerous and exhausting place for wives and mistresses as men unleash their desires and unburden themselves of their insatiability.'

And on and on it went.

The appropriately named Reverend Adcock had not felt at all constrained and he had let himself go on at some considerable length about the danger the remedy posed to the people of London and England. For some reason he did not seem unduly concerned about the welfare of the men and women of Wales or Scotland.

Nellie and I were quite upset when we read the Reverend Adcock's diatribe, but we were even more horrified when we read the editorial in *The Times* newspaper. *The Times* had carried a fairly straightforward description of the Remedy on its news pages, quoting at length the contributions made by the hired actors and actresses and the three clergymen who had been invited to attend. They had even quoted at some length from my own description of the Remedy's effectiveness. One Doctor had been reported to have dismissed my Remedy as 'yet another patent medicine which will be crowding the shelves of low pharmacies throughout the land' and another, taking entirely the opposite view, had welcomed a responsibly prepared medicament to counter the anxieties caused by the threatening nonsense talked by the Reverend Cedric Cadwallader. But the editorial writer seemed content to concentrate on the warnings of the doryphores and their hysterical threats outlining the hazards our simple remedy posed to the community.

'This is awful!' I said to the theatre manager.

'We'll go back to the country and you can find work as an assistant,' said Nellie, in an attempt to cheer me up. 'There must be loads of apothecaries who need assistants,' she added optimistically.

The theatre manager looked at us both as if we were stark raving mad. 'What the devil are you on about?' he demanded. 'This is the best publicity you could have hoped for.' He rubbed his hands and told us that he had it on good authority that both I and Dr Bollock's Remedy for Active Gentlemen were due to be praised to the skies or damned to the depths in a variety of other publications including *The Strand, The News of the World, The Examiner, John Bull Magazine* and the *Illustrated London News.*

'Do you mean it doesn't matter what they say as long as they say something?' asked Nellie.

'Your Wife has hit the nail squarely on the head!' said Mr Beaminster with a big grin, as he hurried off to attend to something unspecified.

What the theatre manager said was important, of course, but it was only the second word of the sentence that either of us heard.

'I never said anything that might have encouraged him to think that we were…' began Nellie.

'I liked the way it sounded,' I said, interrupting.

We looked at each for a moment. We hugged and kissed. And three hours later I gave a crisp five pound note to a Clergyman.

We were married in the Church of St Dympna where the 83-year-old Sexton, deaf as a post and as speedy as an arthritic three-legged tortoise, was my Best Man and his 81-year-old Wife was Nellie's Bridesmaid, although for some reason the old lady seemed to think that Nellie was a young Queen Victoria and the ceremony was the young Queen's Coronation.

After the ceremony, we gave the Best Man and the Bridesmaid a guinea each. We bought Charlie, our King Charles Spaniel, a large bone from a nearby butcher. All three seemed well delighted. But none was as delighted as Nellie and me.

December 25th

Since it was Christmas Day I ate and drank too much and my wife had to put a toads' tongue poultice on my head to ease the symptoms. I had much wind and blew out many candles in error. I gave Nellie a new hat for Christmas and she gave me a pair of new boots.

December 28th

The theatre manager's optimism proved to be well founded.

Dr Bollock's Remedy for Active Gentlemen became the talk of London, and Nellie and I were kept busy ten hours a day making up batches of the suppository. We were selling as many Remedies as we could make and, at Nellie's suggestion, we raised the price to ten guineas and abandoned the idea of giving away linen or tortoiseshell condoms.

When our brief engagement at the Music Hall Theatre had finished, we moved to another lecture hall for another two days. The manager of the Music Hall Theatre confessed that he had made more money out of our arrangement than he could have hoped to make from a full house of the music hall. I had not realised just how popular evening lectures had become – particularly free ones.

After two nights, Nellie and I moved out of the boarding house we had found when we'd first arrived in London and moved into a spacious but absurdly expensive suite at Brown's Hotel. I convinced myself that the expense was necessary because we needed the space to prepare the suppositories. We arranged for the manager to place two additional Tables in our living room and tipped him generously.

We became almost accustomed to seeing real celebrities in the audience.

At one event, Nellie spotted Mr Charles Dickens listening avidly. Afterwards, Mr Dickens came backstage and offered me valuable advice on presentation. It was he who suggested that I use a lectern as a prop. He is a lovely man and he happily gave Nellie his autograph. She says she thinks it may one day be valuable and I suspect she is right.

A surprising number of eminent medical men came to see me at the events we organised. I remember vividly meeting a Dr Roget, who told me that he had for some time been working on a special dictionary which he plans to call his 'Thesaurus'. I confess I did not understand what it was about but he is convinced that when it is finished it will prove to be every bit as popular as *Dr Johnson's Dictionary*. He bought two copies of 'Dr Bollock's Remedy for Active Gentlemen' and promised to send me a copy of his 'Thesaurus' when it is finished.

I was told that the Duke of Wellington, the diminutive Iron Duke himself, had sent an assistant to one of our events to purchase a supply of 'Dr Bollock's Remedy for Active Gentlemen'. And it was no surprise to anyone that Mr Gladstone and Lord Palmerston had purchased supplies. Nellie approached both gentlemen for endorsements but although Lord Palmerston's aide said the good Lord had given the suggestion serious thought, nothing came of the idea.

Much of the press coverage was negative but to our surprise we discovered that the worse the attacks were the more suppositories we sold. Articles praising Dr Bollock's Remedy for Active Gentlemen did relatively little for sales but whenever a Clergyman or moral crusader attacked the Remedy our sales rose, in some cases quite dramatically.

A number of magazines asked me to contribute articles or to provide lists of my favourite recipes, music hall acts and other things. I was on two occasions asked to provide my advice for 'Healthy living' and I hired a journalist with *The Times* to write these articles and to put my name on them. I did not see the point in taking part in these things but Nellie insisted that I should do so, always as Dr Bollock. She argued that the publicity would help promote the Remedy, and the evidence proved her right.

After the success of London, we decided that a tour of the provinces might be successful. After some consideration, we decided that the entire tour should be done by Railway, and so we planned to visit only those towns and cities which had Railway stopping points. We announced that we would talk about the Remedy in Birmingham and Manchester and travel to all the spa towns such as Bath Spa and Leamington Spa. It seemed likely that the hypochondriacs attracted to those bathing places might prove to be good customers. We planned to rent lecture halls and theatres rather than giving the owners a share of the profits. Nellie thought that this would be much more profitable.

Nellie and I hired the actors and actresses who had been so successful on our first nights in London and arranged for them to travel with us, together with two troubadours and the two poets who acted as our liaison officers with the local newspapers. One of the poets, whose name was Theophilis Theophrastus, called himself our Publicity Relationship Officer. Nellie, who had become the de facto manager of the entire enterprise, and had proved adept at every aspect of the business, also hired a well-known journalist to write a dozen unsolicited testimonials which could be used for marketing.

But, immediately after our Grand Tour was announced and promoted in the national Press, we received a substantial offer for the rights to Dr Bollock's Remedy for Active Gentlemen. Excited by the publicity we were getting, a large and successful Patent Medicine Company offered the huge sum of £15,000 for the right to sell the product exclusively.

Naturally, the company wanted details of the recipe.

The pessary I had originally prepared as a contraceptive contained a number of ingredients. The base ingredients were glycerine and cocoa butter with nutmeg. Tobacco and ground orange peel were added to this. On a whim I had added a little senna, some soap shavings and a good portion of gentian root. I had also added a good portion of duck fat and ear wax to help give the pessary a better shape and form.

'We need additional ingredients,' I said to Nellie. 'If the company realises that the recipe consists only of the ingredients we currently use they will see very little value in the product.'

'So maybe we need two or three more ingredients,' she suggested wisely. 'That will convince them that the product must be effective.'

And so, after some thought, we decided to add ginger, peppermint, cranberry, chaste tree berry, ginseng and garlic to the mixture and to add a little more wax to the jelly of the suppository.

We are confident that the change will in no way damage the efficacy of the product.

We have cancelled our tour which now seems unnecessary.

December 30th

Another company has now offered to purchase Dr Bollock's Remedy for Active Gentlemen, and Nellie and I are allowing the two competing companies to push up the price.

December 31st

We have now sold 'Dr Bollock's Remedy for Active Gentlemen' for the splendid sum of £25,000 plus a royalty on every single Remedy sold. The company which bought the Remedy is arranging its own nation-wide tour and has hired the performers we had selected for our own proposed tour.

Epilogue

With a relatively small portion of the money we were paid for 'Dr Bollock's Remedy for Active Gentlemen', Nellie and I have purchased a Manor House in the West Country. The House comes with several cottages and half a square mile of moorland, woodland and pastureland. We have also purchased a trap, a gig, a brougham and seven horses and Nellie is in the process of appointing indoor and outdoor staff. Nellie pointed out with some delight that we now have somewhere to put her Chair. There is plenty of space within which Charlie, the King Charles Spaniel, can take the exercise he so much enjoys and my old Bess, now retired from her equine labours, has a field and a stable to herself.

On Nellie's recommendation, we have invested the remainder of our money in Government bonds which will pay an income quite sufficient for us to live very comfortably.

To our surprise, several patent medicine companies have asked us to prepare new products. One has requested that we prepare a Dr Bollock's pessary to help older women look and feel younger.

We have, however, turned down all these suggestions for we intend to enjoy a quiet and contented early retirement. I intend to become a gentleman farmer and shall, therefore hire men to do the farming and a bailiff to ensure that they do whatever it is they need to do. Since we also own a large stretch of a river, and two lakes, I also intend to take up fishing. I have hired a water bailiff to ensure there are fish available but I will do the fishing myself.

Nellie is expecting our first child. If it is a boy we intend to call him Binky after Binky Beaminster, the theatre manager who was so helpful to us.

Dr Challot is still working as an apothecary in Muckleberry Peverell. Dr Mort, whose father lost all his money after unsuccessful investments in the railway companies, is now working full time as Dr Challot's apprentice. Unable to afford to rent my old room at the Peacock Inn, Dr Mort lives in the attic at Dr Challot's residence and survives on a diet of Mistress Swain's Turnip soup.

If you enjoyed this book we would be enormously grateful if you would write a short review.

Vernon Coleman is the author of 100 books. For a list of books available please see either www.vernoncoleman.com or Vernon Coleman's author page on Amazon.

Printed in Great Britain
by Amazon